THE CROSSING

CHRISTINA JAMES was born in Spalding and sets her novels in the evocative Fenland countryside of South Lincolnshire. She works as a bookseller, researcher and teacher. She has a lifelong fascination with crime fiction and its history. She is also a well-established non-fiction writer, under a separate name.

Also by Christina James

In the Family (2012)
Almost Love (2013)
Sausage Hall (2014)

THE CROSSING

Christina James

CROMER

PUBLISHED BY SALT
12 Norwich Road, Cromer, Norfolk NR27 0AX United Kingdom

Printed in Great Britain by Clays Ltd, St Ives plc

Typeset in Sabon 10/13

ISBN 978 1 78463 041 6 paperback

1 3 5 7 9 8 6 4 2

For James and Annika, editorial partners in crime

Chapter One

SHORT AND VERY plump with a squashed-up face and tightly-permed greying hair, Ruby Grummett was not an attractive woman; nor was she particularly intelligent. However, she took her job as a crossing-keeper seriously and performed it with pride. She lived with her husband Bob, who also worked for the railway, in a one-storey tied house with a signal box in the isolated hamlet of Sutterton Dowdyke. There were not many trains daily there, and not much road traffic either, but it was a crossing quite regularly used by slow-moving agricultural vehicles, usually of both great size and length. In the earlier upgrading of the railway to a continental crossing system, the decision had been made to continue the presence of a crossing keeper to supervise the road users and manage the gates.

It was a cold January afternoon. Daylight had barely penetrated the treacherous yellow fog that had enveloped the countryside since dawn. Bob had completed an early shift at the rail depot and returned home briefly for lunch, before setting off on his bicycle to visit the pig that he kept at a friend's smallholding. The milk van and the post van were the only vehicles that Ruby had opened the crossing-gates for that day.

She had been expecting the Peterborough to Skegness train, always punctual, to come thundering past, but the line had remained deserted. The train was already much more than thirty minutes late and she decided it must have been cancelled. She thought it unlikely anyone else would come knocking for her to open the gates today: there had been severe fog warnings and the advice on the radio was for inhabitants of the region to stay at home unless their journey was absolutely unavoidable.

Ruby decided to take a bath before her daughters returned home. This had become her habit during the winter months, because the stove didn't yield enough hot water for everyone to wash in the mornings and Bob thought the immersion heater should be reserved for summer use. She had stripped to her all-in-one foundation garment when the doorbell rang, followed almost at once by a business-like rapping at the door.

She knew immediately who the caller was: this was the signature greeting of Fred Lister, the driver of the council's tanker lorry. She was surprised that he was out on such a day. She threw on her candlewick dressing-gown and knotted it tightly where her waist had once been.

The bell rang again. It was unlike Fred to be impatient. Ruby hunted briefly for her shoes before thrusting her feet into Bob's checked carpet slippers.

"All right, I'm coming!" she called.

She hastened to the door and opened it.

"Hello, Fred. I thought it was you. Surprised you had to work today, though."

"Couple of emergencies: cesspits that needed cleaning out in a hurry. We're late now. I'd the afternoon off but the fog's held us up so we've only just finished. I need to get off home now."

"I'll be quick," said Ruby. "On your own, are you?"

"No, Gilly's there, waiting in the cab. He wants to get back, too."

Fred turned and walked down the short path that led from the house to the road, stopping to wait for her at the signal

box steps. As she climbed them, Ruby paused to examine her watch, holding it up close to her face so that she could see it properly.

Fred called jovially up to her, "Make sure you know what you're doing! Trains'll all be up the creek today."

"I'll check!" she called back.

The system in the box told Ruby that no train was approaching and, though she thought briefly of calling the stationmaster at Peterborough to see if the Skegness train had left the station, she knew that Fred was in a hurry and she'd never known that train to run three quarters of an hour late. It must have been cancelled.

Fred had left the engine running. She put the gates into action and, as they rose, saw Fred walk round to the driver's side after a quick word with Gilly, who waved up at her. The lorry moved slowly forwards. Then, suddenly, the system leapt into life. The Skegness train! Her heart lurched painfully. She whirled to the window to try to alert Fred and met his eye – he'd paused mid-crossing as he always did to lean out of his cab to wave and blow her a kiss and saw his saucy grin switch to a yell of disbelief as he heard the unmistakeable sound of a fast-approaching train and then flicked his head round to see a great black shape come hurtling out of the fog. The impact filled Ruby's vision and ears with a roaring intensity and shattered the glass of the box and deafened her. Just before she fainted, she saw the lorry tossed high into the air. She did not witness its descent as it hit the roof of her house, nor see the building turn one hundred and eighty degrees, as if pirouetting on a turntable.

Chapter Two

DETECTIVE INSPECTOR TIM Yates was bathing his baby daughter. He came home for bath-time as often as he could. At first it had been to take the pressure off Katrin, still weak and wobbly from Sophia's birth, but he had quickly become addicted to the experience. It was like a daily rite of passage, the event that firmly closed down all the travails of his working day and replaced them with family life. He looked into his daughter's opaline eyes and smiled as he lowered her into the bath. She was kicking vigorously, putting her absolute trust in him as he supported her head and protected her face from the water. Gently, he allowed the mildly soapy water to lap over her. After a while, he lifted her out and enveloped her in a fluffy towel. Bliss, he thought. Why had it not been possible for him and Katrin to create this kind of evening calm, this shutting-out of the rest of the world, when they'd been on their own?

He carried Sophia to her bedroom. Katrin was there, sorting tiny clothes into piles. She smiled at him.

"Do you want me to dress her? Dinner's nearly ready. Just another five minutes."

"No, I'll do it. Do us a favour and turn on the TV. It's nearly time for the six o'clock news. I don't want to watch all of it, but today there'll be something about the government's proposed reforms to the police force and I'd like to know what idiocies they're intending to push at us now."

"OK."

He noted that Katrin sounded weary. He looked up at her. Apart from a slight sort of ripple around her waistline, she'd got her figure back quickly – she was probably, he thought, slimmer than she'd been before. But the glow that had transformed her complexion in the later stages of pregnancy had completely disappeared, replaced by a pale translucency that made her seem fragile. Her face was gaunt, her high cheekbones accentuated now that there was little flesh to obscure them. Tim's heart went out to her. He wished he could speed up the healing process, take over all of Sophia's care until Katrin became her usual robust self again.

"You look tired. Why don't you go and sit down? I'll serve the dinner. I'll clear up afterwards, too."

She smiled again, more broadly this time, and a flash of her former mischievousness flitted across her face.

"All right, I will. And I'll hold you to that promise!" She gave him a quick kiss on her way past. "I *am* tired, but I'm angry with myself for giving in to it. I've got absolutely nothing to feel feeble about. We're so lucky to have Sophia – and your coming home earlier most days is a real bonus."

Tim laid his daughter on her changing mat and expertly fixed her nappy. He eased her into a clean babygro and wrapped her in a shawl. The whole process took only a couple of minutes; he congratulated himself that he was getting to be a dab hand at it already. He looked at his watch: five to six. There was time for a song if he was quick. Tim had surprised Katrin, and himself even more, by singing to his daughter every evening. What should it be tonight? Deciding quickly, he sang a few verses of Maddy Prior's 'The Fox'.

Sophia was asleep before he laid her in her cot in her snug winter sleeping bag. The signature tune of the news was rum-

bling away in the distance. He closed Sophia's door soundlessly and hastened downstairs.

The Home Secretary was being interviewed. She was in combative mood. Her hair was greying but had once been a fiery auburn, like his own. Tim had a soft spot for redheads, even bad 'uns. During the course of his career, he'd met shoplifters, forgers and even a murderer who had had red hair and they'd always seemed to him a slight cut above, whatever they'd done. He'd rarely met a 'ginner' who was stupid.

He reflected on this as he watched. What the woman was saying seemed to him to be the usual crass monologue – mainly admonishments tinged with a little faint praise – which was disheartening. The country was coming out of the longest recession on record, she said, but funds were still scarce. Everyone had to tighten their belts, and the police were no exception. She had no wish to interfere with the running of individual police forces – Tim snorted at this – but the public had a right to expect results. From now on, resources would be allocated to those forces who proved most effective at . . . Tim groaned. He could guess at what was coming next: some kind of plan to place police forces in competition with each other. He didn't need to wonder what effect such an announcement would have on Superintendent Thornton. He'd be in overdrive immediately. He'd probably call Tim at home this evening. Tim looked at the Home Secretary again as she concluded with a homily about how much the public owed to the police and how important it was for the high standards that had been achieved over the past three years to be maintained. Once again, his hypothesis about redheads had proved correct. This woman wasn't stupid, but she was dangerous. He thought of the song that he'd been singing a few minutes before. She was like a fox – a cunning, duplicitous, grizzled old vixen. He sighed and reached across for the TV remote.

"Just a minute," said Katrin. "This looks important."

Tim sank back into the sofa. The picture on the screen was hard to make sense of at first. It seemed to be a shot of some heavy lifting gear removing something from a low building. The building itself had been uprooted as if it were a tree. It had come to rest at a drunken angle, one of its walls caved in.

The female newscaster had begun to speak.

"All the emergency services were called to a remote crossing near the hamlet of Sutterton Dowdyke in South Lincolnshire this afternoon after a train was derailed when it hit a council lorry standing on the crossing. We understand there were no casualties among the passengers and staff on the train, but the lorry driver was severely injured and his passenger died at the scene. Police have not yet released their names. The crossing-keeper, Mrs Ruby Grummett, had just opened the gates to let the lorry across. There was thick fog obscuring the track. However, Mrs Grummett is understood to have observed the usual safety precautions. Quentin Havers has more."

The picture closed in on a short well-built reporter who was standing next to the wrecked house, buttoned up in a duffle coat with a fancily-knotted scarf at his throat. His comb-over had blown across his face and he was shouting to make himself heard above the din of the machinery.

"I doubt if he'll say anything worth hearing," said Tim, turning to Katrin. "Should I turn it off now? Christ, though, what an awful accident! I'm glad that I'm not one of the Boston uniforms this evening. Shall we eat?"

Katrin nodded to both of his questions.

"Let's hope no-one calls you about the accident. I'm not convinced they'll confine the investigation to uniforms."

"If no-one's to blame it won't be a CID matter," said Tim, confidently. "I'll lay the table. Fancy a glass of wine with your dinner?"

Katrin was about to answer when the telephone rang. Tim looked at it askance.

"I'll get it, shall I?" she said.

"Thanks."

"Ah, Katrin." Superintendent Thornton's voice came booming out of the phone. "How are you, my dear? Looking forward to coming back to work?"

Katrin's lips twitched as she struggled to formulate a suitable reply. She found the Superintendent's transparent betrayal of self-interest more endearing than irritating, though she knew that Tim would have said the opposite. Thornton spared her the trouble of having to think of a reply by ploughing on.

"Is Yates there? If he is, I suppose he's seen the news?"

"Yes," said Katrin. "I'll get him, shall I?" She raised her head to see Tim standing in the doorway, gesticulating urgently. Then he dropped his arms and shrugged. Wiping his hands on a tea-towel, he walked slowly across the room to take the phone from her. "I told you so," she mouthed.

"Good evening, sir."

"Yates? You've seen the news?"

"Yes, sir. I thought you might call about that. But the Home Secretary's proposals haven't been . . ."

"I'm not talking about the Home Secretary. I mean the accident at Sutterton Dowdyke. Did you see the story about that?"

"Yes, but . . ."

"But what? It's on our patch, isn't it?"

"Yes, but the news item indicated that no-one was at fault. I didn't think we'd have to get involved, therefore. It's a job for the uniforms, isn't it?"

Superintendent Thornton sighed and began to enunciate slowly, as if talking to a child.

"They have to say that on the news. Did you really think that someone has died and no-one will be expected to carry

the can? The railway company will be under investigation for using faulty equipment; and of course they'll try to blame it on the crossing-keeper. They'll say she was negligent, not them. I want you to get over there, Yates. Preserve as much of it as you can as a crime scene. Don't let anyone tamper with the warning equipment, in particular."

"But . . ."

"But *what*, Yates?"

"I was just about to eat my supper, sir."

"Supper?" said Superintendent Thornton, as if Tim had just confessed to trafficking in pornography. "Well, a policeman's lot, and all that. I don't suppose it will be the first time you've missed your supper in the line of duty."

"No, sir."

"And I'm certain it won't be the last!" The Superintendent chuckled grimly as he put down the phone.

"Don't worry," said Katrin as Tim gave her a sheepish look. "I can eat on my own. I'll save some food for you – it should re-heat OK."

"Thank you," said Tim, kissing the top of her head. "You're an angel." He was already lifting his jacket from the back of the chair on which he'd draped it.

"Just one thing," said Katrin. Tim raised an eyebrow.

"You said that you'd do the clearing up. I'm still going to hold you to that when you come back!"

Chapter Three

LESS THAN HALF an hour later, Tim arrived at the scene of the accident. The Boston police had already closed Dowdyke Road. Two uniforms Tim didn't know were stationed at the top of the road, where it joined the A16. They'd placed a couple of hurdles across the junction. Tim showed one of the policemen his ID.

"DI Yates, South Lincs CID. Sorry, I don't think I know you?"

"PC Walton, sir."

"Have you had many people trying to get through?"

"Some press and the BBC, sir. We were instructed to let them proceed. One local inhabitant – Mr Cushing, who lives in the bungalow further down the lane. And Councillor Start."

"Councillor Start? Is he a relative?"

"I don't know, sir. He said he knew Mrs Grummett through chapel and wanted to see that she was OK."

"But Mrs Grummett's been taken to hospital, hasn't she?"

"Yes. I told him that. But he still wanted to drive on. He said he wanted to check that her daughters were coping."

"Really? So you let him past?"

"Yes." When Tim made no comment, the policeman looked uncomfortable. "I hope that was the right thing to do? He's a well-known local man, after all."

"I'm sure it was fine," said Tim. "Isn't someone going to set

up a diversion? Then you won't have to stand here all night!"

"I believe they're working on it, sir," said PC Walton, as he dragged the hurdles to the side of the road to allow Tim through.

During the short interchange with PC Walton, Tim noticed it was growing even colder. The icy fog that had been swirling over the Fens all day was getting thicker by the minute. He wasn't familiar with Dowdyke Road, so he drove very slowly, barely touching twenty miles an hour as he edged round the sharp bends. He was well aware of the depth of the Fenland ditches that lined the road on either side.

The fog began to glow a lurid yellow. He rounded a final bend and came up sharp against the heavy lifting gear that he'd seen on the news. Two workmen dressed in fluorescent overalls were operating the machinery. One of them gestured towards him. A policeman appeared from the other side of the contraption. Tim got out of his car.

"Giash!" he said. "I'm glad to see you here. But surprised: this is a long way from your usual beat, isn't it?"

"Good evening, sir. I was in Boston this afternoon, on a training course. Superintendent Thornton called before I'd left and asked me to come straight here."

Tim grinned, though he was annoyed that Thornton hadn't mentioned this.

"So you didn't get any supper either?"

Giash looked blank.

"Never mind – just a joke! Who's here, exactly?"

"Just myself and Verity Tandy from the force. We're waiting for a crash forensics team from Peterborough. And there are two Boston coppers stationed at either end of this road – I expect you've seen the ones at the junction you came in on."

Tim nodded.

"Where did all this gear come from?"

"The fire brigade brought it. I think it belongs to Boston Council."

Tim indicated a small group of people huddled on the grass verge.

"Who are they?"

"One of the daughters of the crossing-keeper and her uncle and aunt, who showed up before she did. She's not been here long – came home from work as usual. She's the short stout one. The bloke standing next to her is a local reporter."

"Are the BBC still here?"

"They left after the news broadcast."

"Who's the old guy standing next to the reporter? Is he the uncle?"

"No, that's Councillor Start. He's been here a while. He claims to be a friend, but the daughter doesn't seem to know him that well."

"The large lady standing next to the daughter is the aunt?"

"Yes. Elsie, her name is. Elsie Grummett."

"So where's the uncle, then?"

"I'm not sure. I'd better take a look – we've already had to warn him about trying to get into the building. It's not safe. It's been ripped completely off its foundations."

"I'll come with you. We need to get some tape put round the building immediately."

PC Chakrabati regarded Tim with respectful amusement.

"I'm sure you're right, sir. Perhaps you could advise me on how to do it. I'm not quite sure how to keep it in place, while all this work is going on."

Tim had the grace to look abashed. Wryly he told himself that he'd just made an unthinking bureaucracy-obsessed gaffe worthy of Superintendent Thornton himself. He was also aware that Thornton had originated the idea.

"You're right, we'll leave it until they take the machinery away. Could you introduce me to the daughter?"

As they stepped across the road, the short stout woman detached herself from the group and walked towards them. Tim held out his hand.

"DI Tim Yates, South Lincs police," he said. "I'm very sorry this has happened. Have you heard how your mother is?"

The woman didn't take Tim's hand. She stood and stared at him for several minutes, her large white face bobbing up and down so that the row of tight curls on her forehead bounced. Behind her heavy-framed spectacles, the brown eyes that regarded him were either perplexed or suspicious, he couldn't tell which. She was very short indeed, barely reaching his elbow. Her several double chins sank into each other and eventually into a thick short neck that disappeared rapidly into her shoulders. She didn't answer his question, but countered it with one of her own. Her voice was grating and squeaky at the same time.

"Can I go in for a look round?" she said. "I want me pyjama case. It's important."

"I'm sorry, Ms Grummett, we can't allow anyone nearer to the building than this. It's not safe."

"Kayleigh," she said.

"I'm sorry?"

"Kayleigh, me name's Kayleigh. I don't know about not going in. Me Uncle Ivan's . . ."

"Now, Kayleigh!" The large lady gave the young woman a dig with her elbow. She turned to Tim apologetically. She had a flat face wrinkled in whorls, like a Chelsea bun. Her expression was more guileful than perplexed. "She isn't herself," she said. "And no wonder, poor lass."

Tim signalled to Giash to nip round the side of the house. He knew that the policeman had immediately picked up his

meaning. If Uncle Ivan was rooting about in the wreckage, he needed to be brought out, sharpish, and reprimanded. Tim turned back to the large woman.

"I understand you're Mrs Elsie Grummett?"

"That's right."

"Where's your other niece?"

It was the large woman's turn to look blank.

"Come again?"

"Kayleigh has a sister, I believe. Where is she at the moment?"

"Oh, you mean Philippa!"

"I suppose I do." He turned to Kayleigh. "Is your sister's name Philippa?" The young woman continued to regard him with silent, bovine stupidity. To Tim's surprise, the man whom Giash had identified as Councillor Start, who'd been hovering on the periphery since Tim had introduced himself, now butted in.

"Philippa's at Peter Cushing's house, just up the road. She's having tea with his daughter. There seemed no reason to alter the arrangement, under the circumstances."

"I see," said Tim. "Thank you, Councillor Start. It's very good of you to take so much trouble to support the family here. I'm sure they appreciate it. I'm intrigued to know how you know where Philippa is, though."

The Councillor, a tall, untidily built man with very thin greasy grey hair and a pendulous lower lip, laughed noisily.

"Oh, no mystery. Peter came along to see if he could help about the time that I arrived. He told us that Philippa was quite safe. She can stay the night there if she likes."

"She didn't come with him to see what had happened?"

"No, he left her at his house when he walked down. No point in upsetting her, was there?"

"Perhaps not. How old is Philippa?"

"Fifteen or sixteen, I think."

"Sixteen," squeaked Kayleigh.

"Thank you," said Tim. He supposed that Philippa must be as slow and incurious as her sister. Extraordinary even so that a teenage girl would not want to see what had happened to her home after it had been hit by a train.

Giash returned, accompanied by a very dishevelled man carrying a poodle-dog pyjama case. He held it out to Kayleigh.

"Don't touch that!" yelled Elsie. "It's all covered in shit!"

Her husband glowered at her. He had an unprepossessing face, not improved by a decided squint, and short grey hair that stood up like a brush at the back of his head.

"What do you expect?" he demanded. "Bloody yo-yo lorry, wasn't it? Do you think I enjoyed crawling through all that muck? Look at me trousers."

"Never mind, I'll take it," said Kayleigh. "Thanks." She grabbed the pyjama case.

"I must ask you to leave that with me," Tim said. "The house is being impounded as a crime scene, at least until we get to the bottom of what happened. I can't allow you to remove things from it at the moment. That object is a health hazard, too. It has to be bagged up."

"No!" said Kayleigh. "It's mine. You can't have it."

She sounded like a spoilt five-year-old. She was holding the pyjama case behind her back now, evidently trying to evade his reach.

"Kayleigh, love," said Elsie wheedlingly, "I think you've got to do what the policeman says."

"Shut up." Tim was startled to hear Ivan Grummett hiss this command at his wife, sotto voce. It sounded vicious.

"Where's PC Tandy?" Tim said to Giash. "Could you ask her to come and help here?" He turned to Ivan Grummett.

"And I'd like a few words with you, sir. I understand you were asked not to run the risk of going into the building?"

"I told Bob I'd do it," said Ivan Grummett truculently. "He had to go to the hospital with Ruby."

Tim's concentration was broken for a moment when an Audi emerged from behind the machinery and glided past. Councillor Start was sitting at the wheel. Tim hadn't noticed the councillor melt away while he was talking to Kayleigh. He considered asking him to stop before reflecting that the man was neither a witness of the accident nor a member of the Grummett family. Strictly speaking, he shouldn't have been admitted to the scene in the first place. Probably best for everyone if he left now.

Verity Tandy appeared at his side.

"PC Chakrabati said you wanted to see me, sir."

Tim looked at her appraisingly. She'd lost quite a lot of weight since joining the Spalding team. She was more attractive now and he'd become more impressed with her competence. Not that the two issues were linked in his mind, he swiftly added to himself, hearing a reprimand from Katrin as clearly as if she'd been standing at his elbow. He took Verity to one side.

"I'd like you to get that pyjama case from the Grummett girl without causing a scene, if you can," he said. "Her name's Kayleigh. Be careful, it's covered in ordure."

Verity grinned. "Shit, you mean, sir."

"Quite," said Tim primly.

Chapter Four

THERE CAN BE no-one who measures time as minutely as I do. I count the seconds, the minutes, the hours, the days, the weeks, the months, the years, the decades. My life is parcelled out in units of time. You may shrug and say that so is everyone's, but my time's passing is different from yours. It *is* me; it consumes me.

While I was still a girl, I was singled out. Most girls – most boys, too, I imagine – believe they're special. It gives them their goals, the energy they need to leap all those early hurdles before adulthood can be negotiated. They know that if only they can find the strength to push on, they'll become footballers, rock stars, millionaires, beauty queens. But my own special thing was dark, not light and full of hope. It disgusted me. It was to be feared, to be dreaded when it came. It consumed my innocence and hovered over my future. It always came with the dark. I hate the dark.

It's never dark here if I have the choice. But it's never naturally light, either. My rooms are artificially lit: I burn electricity twenty-four hours a day. Lurking just behind the yellow glare of my low-watt lights, the bottomless darkness remains. It bides its time, always prepared to pounce.

Submission doesn't come easily to me. This helps me to survive but causes so much of my pain. I've been held here by the Lover. He can be kind; he can be cruel. He has demons to

fight. Sometimes he is absent for long periods of time, which I count and parcel up exactly. It makes me afraid when he's away for too long; afraid because I'm still here, trapped here. Alone with Ariadne. If the lights go out, it will be dark and I'll be afraid. If he doesn't return after three weeks, I shall know that he will never come again. And we'll be trapped. We'll die.

Always he has returned. Then he's often unhappy with me. Sometimes he rages at a small fault, something I've missed or not understood; sometimes I've deliberately disobeyed or tried to refuse his demands. I've done this even though I know that he'll chastise me, that he'll lash out at me and kick and bite, and I'll be bruised and hurt for many days. Then there might be day upon day of visits when he hits me again, because he can't bear to see the bruises that are already there. Or I flinch when I see his hand descending. He can't bear cowardice, as he frequently tells me. Ariadne watches.

Then it will stop. He'll be sorry; he'll be tender. Usually it's after he's been absent again for a few days, given me a chance to heal. He won't ask my forgiveness; it wouldn't occur to him. But he'll say that if I'm kind and nice and better behaved, perhaps we can lead a more normal life. Perhaps, just perhaps, we can emerge from the dark together. I believe in his love for me. And then there is Ariadne.

Chapter Five

DC JULIET ARMSTRONG smoothed back dark unruly curls and secured them in a pony-tail at the nape of her neck. She flicked a sideways glance at her three-quarters reflection. This evening, she was properly off-duty – not even on call – and she'd dressed carefully in casually conservative clothes. Jeans would probably be too informal, so she'd decided upon neat black trousers, a pale blue short-sleeved shirt and a chunky, navy-blue, cable-knit cardigan – a 'boyfriend cardigan', the shop assistant had called it (which had almost lost her the sale).

Juliet was still smarting from a conversation she'd had with her boss, DI Tim Yates, earlier in the day, when he'd asked her what she was planning to do with her evening and she'd told him rather shyly that she'd joined Fenland Folklore, a small society devoted to exploring old Lincolnshire customs and folk tales. Tim himself belonged to the much more prestigious South Lincolnshire Local History Society. It met quarterly at the premises of the Archaeological Society and because of its connections with that venerated institution had even managed to attract some lottery funding. Juliet had expected Tim to be vaguely amused that she'd opted for the humbler organisation, but had been quite unprepared for his scathing comments.

"I'm surprised you want to waste your time with them. Bunch of old biddies dressed in curtains, in all probability,

digging up bogus magic and pretending that the lullabies sung by Victorian shepherds' wives were inscrutable ancient charms against the Devil. Why don't you apply to join the Local History Society? I'll put in a good word for you."

Juliet had felt her cheeks burning with anger.

"I'm not interested in the Local History Society, thank you. It's the old Fenland folk tales and what's been captured from a half-lost oral tradition that fascinates me. I'm not sure that Fenland Folklore is dominated by the sort of ladies you describe, but if it is, they can't be any worse than some of the pompous, self-regarding people I met at the Archaeological Society during the Claudia McRae enquiry."

"Hey, steady on," said Tim, holding up both hands palms-first in a gesture of submission. "I was only ribbing you. I'm sure you'll have a great time."

"Thank you, sir," Juliet had said, her voice crisp and metallic. "I hope that you have a nice evening, too."

Juliet frequently beat herself up after she'd let Tim get under her skin like this. She'd now allowed their conversation to cast a shadow over an evening that she'd been looking forward to. She gave herself a mental shake, determined to exorcise Tim's slights. It was a mystery to her why she cared so much for his good opinion. She knew that Katrin would have laughed at him, told him that he was being absurdly pompous.

Katrin often acted as her ally. The last time Juliet had seen her she'd expressed an interest in Fenland Folklore herself and said that she'd give one of the meetings a try, if she could find a babysitter. Juliet hadn't mentioned this to Tim. She'd let him find out for himself, if it happened.

Fenland Folklore held its meetings at Moose Hall in Love Lane, Spalding. Juliet was fascinated by both names. Had there ever been moose in South Lincolnshire? And was Love Lane an abbreviation for 'Lovers' Lane', or had it gained its

appellation from some long-dead philanthropist's outpouring of endearment to all who passed that way? Love Lane started at the church, which may have been significant. Perhaps the proffered love was of a spiritual kind.

It was a murky evening, cold with the swirling fog. Juliet had debated riding to the meeting on her bicycle, but doubted whether in such poor visibility she would be safe from the lorries that were bound to come thundering down the High Street. It was a little too far to walk, so she'd had to make the effort to retrieve her elderly Fiat from its lock-up garage. This took a bit longer than she'd expected, with the result that she arrived at the meeting shortly after it had started.

She was ushered into a room furnished with a semi-circle of metal and canvas chairs by a woman with bushy grey hair who was indeed wearing a 'curtain', Tim's name for a full-length floral skirt, usually of the home-made variety. Juliet sighed inwardly. Perhaps Tim had been right. She took a seat at the edge of the semi-circle, moving as silently as she could, and focused her attention on the two men seated on a small raised dais at the top of the room. She divined that one of them was Richard Lennard, the President of Fenland Folklore, and that he was introducing the evening's guest speaker in somewhat fulsome terms.

". . .Francis Abbott, who will talk to us about his researches into the East Anglian oral folk tradition and how some of the tales became associated with Christian moral teachings, especially after they were written down. We're very fortunate to have Francis with us this evening, because he is the foremost authority on . . ." Juliet barely listened to the rest of this encomium. She was focusing on Richard Lennard himself. She knew that he was the headteacher at the local girls' High School. He was tall with aquiline features and an abundance of wavy black hair. Self-consciously debonair and charismatic,

he seemed an unlikely person to be associated with a modest, amateurish organisation like Fenland Folklore. She caught his eye once and he stared right through her.

Francis Abbott rose to his feet and walked the few steps to the lectern that had been placed to one side of the podium. He was a tubby little man dressed in lovat green tweed who cleared his throat anxiously several times before he began to speak. Juliet's heart sank further. Quirky amateurishness she could stand, but not an evening of boredom made the more excruciating by the inept delivery of a nervous speaker.

She needn't have worried. Once Francis Abbott had warmed up, he spoke with eloquence and grace. Juliet quickly became absorbed in his narration of some of the folk tales that he'd gathered that were particularly associated with Spalding and its hinterland. The last of these was especially compelling.

"There was once a shy and simple fair-haired boy who fell in love with one of the girls in his village. She had magnificent thick, long, dark tresses that were threaded through with just a glint of gold. The girl took no notice of the boy, who was pining away because of her indifference to him.

"In desperation, his mother suggested he visited a strange old woman who lived in a hovel at the end of the village to ask for her help. Some of the villagers thought the old woman was as wise as she was ancient, but more were afraid of her and her mutterings and avoided her as a witch. The boy's mother had no way of telling the truth, but she did know that her son would die if he couldn't be rescued from the wasting disease triggered by his distress.

"The dame was gentle and kind to the lad. She gave him a box of sweetmeats to present to the girl, but said that there was one condition: he must not arrange to meet her after she had eaten them. Instead, he must return to the old woman, who would herself tell him how his gift had been received.

"The boy had intended to give the sweetmeats to the girl on the following morning, but it took him most of the day to find her. It was therefore dusk when he finally returned to the old woman's house. She invited him in, offered him a seat at her hearth. When he became uneasy and said that he should return to his mother, the old woman told him to calm himself. She said the girl had not yet had time to eat the sweetmeats, but when she'd finished them the crone would know and give him the information he craved immediately. He would have to stay where he was until then: otherwise, he might meet the girl again accidentally and then the spell would be broken.

"At nightfall, the boy's mother went to knock on the old woman's door to ask when her son would be returning. The old woman didn't reply, but the boy shouted through the door that he was quite safe and would come back to her as soon as his business was done. Reluctantly, the mother trudged home.

"Towards midnight, the villagers heard terrible sounds emerging from the hovel, but were too afraid to investigate until the following morning. Led by the boy's mother, a small deputation then demanded entry. The old woman welcomed them with smiles and let them in. Inside, the tumbledown cottage was neat and tidy. Everything was in its place, except for a single blood-stained rag which had been thrown into one corner. The old woman explained it by saying that it had been used to wrap meat. The boy's mother thought that she recognised it as a fragment of her son's shirt, and stepped forward for a closer look, but the old woman barred her way. The villagers were overcome by a terrible chilliness combined with a foul stench in the air, and left.

"The boy did not return home. The villagers were certain that the old woman had harmed or killed him, but dared not return to the hovel to accuse her. From time to time, they

heard moans and banging noises coming from the dwelling, but ignored them.

"After many years, when the boy's mother is herself old and bent, a large animal is seen loping through the village. It has yellow fur and fierce black eyes. The villagers see the door to the old woman's cottage has been left swinging open. They gather up the courage to go inside. There they find the emaciated body of a middle-aged man. It is still warm; he has only just died."

Juliet found this story haunting. It was the last of the tales to be told by Francis Abbott that evening. After a prolonged round of applause orchestrated by himself, Richard Lennard courteously gestured to the speaker to resume his seat while he led the debate about what meaning this folk-tale might have had for its early narrators and listeners. Juliet could see that Frances Abbott was only half-engaged with this part of the proceedings: she guessed he belonged to the school of thought that said that folk tales should be allowed to exist in their own right, not as primitive romans à clefs – a sentiment that on balance she shared. But Richard Lennard ploughed on, clearly in his element. Having offered his own views, which Juliet found hard to follow but seemed to be based on elaborate sociological theories that struck no chord with her, he invited the members of the audience to share theirs.

"Yes?" he said. "Veronica?"

"I'd say it was a warning not to get too carried away by infatuation," she said. "Whatever it is you love, the sacrifice can never be worth it. You just end up getting trapped and horribly damaged."

The woman spoke softly, but there was an edge to her voice. She was sitting almost at the centre of the semi-circle. Juliet leant forward so that she could see her more clearly. The woman was in her late thirties, slightly-built and very pale.

"Thank you, Veronica," said Richard Lennard, somewhat patronisingly, Juliet thought. He moved on swiftly, clearly not encouraging debate on the point the woman had made. "Anyone else have anything to say?"

"Well, if you insist on reading summat into it, I'd say it was a champion attempt to warn men not to let women get out of hand. Female dominance leads to male emasculation. End of story."

Everyone laughed. The speaker was a powerfully-built man in his seventies who sported a patriarch's long white beard. Richard Lennard beamed at him.

"Ever true to your principles, aren't you, George?" he chaffed. "Well, if none of us has anything to add, I'm going to ask Francis Abbott to wind up this session by giving us his own views about this tale. Francis, it's a very powerful story, is it not?"

"Yes, indeed."

"What do you yourself read into it? Tell us your own view, now that you've heard some of our thoughts." Richard Lennard preened himself a little as he spoke. Juliet saw that he considered the explanation he had offered to have most merit. It was certainly the most sophisticated.

Francis Abbott, who until this point had been meek and compliant to the point of self-effacement, suddenly skewered him with a look.

"There's no point in trying to read anything into tales of this kind," he said, quite fiercely. "They grew up over long periods of time and were subject to the memories and the imaginations of those who told them. The version I've given you is itself an amalgam of the three most authentic versions of this story I could find. To attribute to it a 'meaning', as if it were a deliberate parable, would be both to give it a didactic weight that it can't sustain and to detract from its beauty as an

evolving piece of literature originally passed down as part of the oral tradition."

Richard Lennard possessed the type of near-flawless olive skin which did not blush easily. Nevetherless, Juliet thought she saw his complexion darken. He almost stammered his reply.

"Quite so," he said. "And now it remains for us once again to thank Francis Abbott in the usual way, before we adjourn for refreshments."

There was another enthusiastic round of applause.

'Refreshments' consisted of coffee or wine. Juliet debated whether to stay and decided that on this occasion she wouldn't. She didn't know anyone else in the room and thought it would be too daunting to try to insinuate herself into one of the little gatherings that were now beginning to form near the trestle table on which coffee pots and a few bottles of wine were standing. Much better to arrive before the start of the next meeting and get to know one or two people then.

The folk tale had made a deep impression on her. Mulling it over on her way home, she thought that, although she agreed with Francis Abbott's strictures, it probably did contain a moral for those who looked for it, but not about the battle of the sexes. She believed its message was that you should find the strength to question happenings that seem strange or sinister and to challenge acts you have witnessed that cannot be accounted for in a 'good' way.

Chapter Six

WHILE JULIET WAS attempting to bring an extra dimension into her life by absorbing local culture, DC Andy Carstairs was sitting in the Pied Calf pub with his older sister, Shelagh, who had recently been berating him for showing interest in nothing but his job. As a result of this nagging, he'd been talked into meeting Shelagh's friend Jocelyn for a 'casual drink'. It was not so much a blind date as a managed date, with Shelagh in attendance as the mistress of ceremonies. He felt restless and awkward.

Shelagh was more direct than Andy, who prided himself on his subtlety. Where the interests of her little brother were concerned she always declared herself to be totally onside, which in Andy's book meant bossy. Periodically, Shelagh took Andy in hand by devising some kind of project to enhance the quality of his life: hence, over the years, his wardrobe had had a makeover, his hair had been stylishly 'feathered' and, for some months now, Shelagh had assumed the role of presiding genius of a punishing gym regime that had resulted in no significant improvement to his shape. This mystified Shelagh, who despite her sharpness seemed to have no suspicion that after a session at the gym Andy habitually recharged his batteries by calling in at his local for a pint or two, an enterprise aided by the fact that both the gym Shelagh had selected and the hostelry were within handy walking distance of his flat.

Why Shelagh had decided that Andy's existence had become unbearable without a *petite amie* was not easily comprehensible, as she herself was now in her mid-thirties and had been 'between boyfriends' for some time. Yet it was clearly preying on her mind that, after a short disastrous relationship with a girl called Ruth four years previously, Andy hadn't had a single date. She'd pointed out that he was pushing thirty and had neither the good looks nor stellar career that would guarantee plenty of choice. Andy was too much of a gentleman to retaliate that Shelagh had herself passed that milestone half a decade ago and too lazy to resist when she suggested she should introduce him to Jocelyn, one of her more recent friends.

Agreeing with Shelagh had seemed like the only option at the time, but now that he was awaiting the arrival of a woman whose sole recommendation was an endorsement from his sister, he felt trapped. Jocelyn was bound either to look like the back of a bus or to be an air-head. At the same time, he was irritated and embarrassed by the fact that she was now twenty minutes late. It was one thing to feel lukewarm about a proposed encounter, quite another to have to face the humiliation of being stood up.

"Another drink?" Shelagh asked brightly. "Jocelyn must have been delayed. When I've got the drinks in I'll give her a call."

"Lime and lemonade, please," said Andy morosely.

"Is that all? Don't you think a drop of something stronger might help you to relax? Tell you what, why don't I buy a bottle of wine? I'll ask for three glasses. It'll break the ice when Jocelyn arrives."

"Sorry, Shelagh, I've already told you: I'm on call tonight and I can't drink alcohol in case I'm needed somewhere."

"How likely is that?"

"On a weekday evening, not very, but . . ." As if on cue,

Andy's mobile started ringing.

"Hello? DI Yates. Good evening, sir. Yes. Yes, no bother. I'm on my way."

He looked up slowly, flinching from his sister's furious glare, yet relieved.

"I'm sorry, Shelagh, it's just one of those things. Can't be helped. Please explain to Jocelyn – if she turns up."

Shelagh's face and neck had turned brick red, a sure sign that she was angry.

"She'll turn up. You're not the only one who has a demanding job."

Despite her anger, she looked vulnerable sitting there, her plans for the evening in tatters, both of her match-making targets behaving in a refractory way. Andy's resistance melted. He stood up and embraced her.

"I know you think you're doing your best by me, and I'm grateful, honestly I am. Do explain to Jocelyn. We'll fix a date another time, if she's still game."

Andy straightened to his full height, circumnavigated the closely-packed tables and pushed his way through the crowd standing at the bar. When he'd almost reached the door, he turned back to give Shelagh a wave. She responded with a tiny flick of her wrist, then, to his surprise, suddenly leapt to her feet, her face transformed by an ear-to-ear grin.

"Jocelyn!" she called.

Facing forward again, Andy saw a tall, willowy woman framed in the doorway. She had long, straight dark hair cut in a fringe at the front. She was wearing a cherry-red duffle coat and jeans. She smiled back, her eyes twinkling, to expose even white teeth. Andy was impressed enough to pluck up the courage to introduce himself. He took the few steps necessary to reach her and tapped her gently on the arm.

"Jocelyn?" he said. "I'm Andy Carstairs. I'm sorry, there's

been an emergency and I've been called in to work. I do apologise. Perhaps we can rearrange some other time?"

She pouted a mock reprimand.

"Shame!" she said. "I'd been looking forward to meeting you. Still, I suppose that we *have* now met, at least, and Shelagh and I can have a drink together and a good gossip if you can't stay. Some other time, you say? Yes, certainly. Suggest some dates to Shelagh and I'll find one that fits. Make it quite soon – otherwise I may forget about you."

She laughed lightly. Andy nodded and carried on through the door into the street. He looked over his shoulder as the pub door swung to behind him.

"Fuck!" he said.

Chapter Seven

KAYLEIGH GRUMMETT WAS still resisting Verity Tandy's attempt to prise the dog pyjama case from her when suddenly the fat young woman looked up and beamed.

"Hello, Mr Cushing!" she chirruped in her squeaky voice. Tim, who was standing nearby, recognised the name at once: Cushing was the neighbour from down the road who had taken responsibility for looking after Philippa Grummett. He was standing in a shaft of light thrown by one of the big lamps that had been set up by the firemen, so Tim could see him clearly. He was a gnome-like little man with a large bald head.

"I thought you might like a cup of tea," said the small man. He had an incongruously deep and confident voice. "I can bring it down for you if you like, or you can come up to the house."

Verity Tandy looked at Tim for guidance. He could see she thought he'd likely refuse. He knew Verity would welcome a cup of tea – she'd been standing there in the freezing fog for at least two hours. He was curious to meet the other daughter and he also thought they might get more sense out of Kayleigh if they accepted. For all he knew, the girl was suffering from the shock of witnessing the damage that had been done to her home and needed a warm drink. Perhaps she was less stupid under normal circumstances. He turned to Peter Cushing.

"I'm DI Yates, South Lincolnshire Police," he said. "That's

a very kind offer, sir." He saw the Chelsea-bun-faced aunt hovering in the background. "How many of us can you cope with?"

"As many folk as would like to come," said Cushing expansively. He was relishing his temporary importance.

While they were talking, Kayleigh absent-mindedly let go of the pyjama case. She appeared not to notice what she'd done, so absorbed was she in what Cushing was saying. Verity, who'd been holding one corner of it, passed it discreetly to Giash Chakrabati, who bagged it and took it away.

Tim and Kayleigh, Verity and the Grummett uncle and aunt formed a straggling procession and walked up the lane in the wake of Peter Cushing. He led them to the side entrance of a foursquare yellow brick bungalow dating from the early 1960s.

"We're here, Mother!" he called, as he opened the door and stepped inside, gesturing the others to follow. They all crowded into a small kitchen, which was warm and damp and poorly-lit. A large pan of something was bubbling on the stove. A thin woman wearing an apron bustled in from the room beyond.

"Goodness, don't stay in here!" she said. "Come through into the living room." She gave Kayleigh's cheek a solicitous tweak, causing her chins to wobble. "You all right, duckie? Terrible thing to have happened." She looked around at the others for confirmation. Kayleigh's lip trembled and her sluggish eyes filled with tears. "Now then, sweetheart. Come and have some tea."

Kayleigh blew her nose loudly and allowed Mrs Cushing to lead her into a larger room where two sofas and several chairs had been arranged around the gas fire. Two teenage girls were sitting together on one of the sofas. One was tiny and dark, very much in the physical mould of her parents. The other was a tall, rangy blonde with hair so pale that it was almost silver.

Tim was surprised. Surely this couldn't be Philippa Grummett?

"Move up and let your sister sit with you," said Mrs Cushing, chivvying the girl in jovial fashion. "She's feeling a bit upset, aren't you, Kayleigh, my lovely?"

The blonde girl took in all the visitors, meeting Tim's eye fleetingly. He thought she looked intelligent but watchful, the antithesis of Kayleigh. The Cushing girl made a genuine attempt to squeeze herself up against the arm of the sofa. Philippa Grummett moved very slightly. Kayleigh sat down next to her as gingerly as possible for someone of her bulk.

"What's the matter with you?" Philippa said to Kayleigh. She spoke with a slight Lincolnshire accent, but in a voice that was both cultured and articulate. "You're not hurt, are you?"

Kayleigh allowed the tears to course down her cheeks, dabbing at them occasionally with a tissue from the pocket of the overall she was still wearing.

"Now, don't get at her, Philly," said Mrs Cushing. "I know you two don't get on, but there's a time and a place. Do sit down," she continued. Awkwardly, Tim, Verity and the other Grummetts did as they were told while she busied herself handing round cups of tea.

"Is there any news of Ruby?" she asked Tim. "Poor woman!"

"As far as I understand, she's not physically hurt, but she's very shocked. I'm going to the hospital shortly. I don't know if I'll be allowed to see her tonight, but if there *is* any news I'll ask PC Tandy to telephone her daughters." It dawned on Tim as he spoke that neither Kayleigh nor Philippa had exhibited the slightest interest in their mother's well-being. Presumably they knew their father was at the hospital with her, but neither had mentioned him, either. They had expressed no wish to see either parent.

"Will you both be staying here tonight?" asked Verity. Kay-

leigh stopped wiping her eyes. She looked bewildered, as if her fate was completely outside her control.

"It's already settled that Philly will stay, and Kayleigh's very welcome, too," said Mrs Cushing quickly. "There's a double bed in Alice's room and I can make up a mattress on the floor."

Philippa and Alice exchanged glances. Tim guessed that both were determined not to share a bed with Kayleigh.

"That's very nice of you," said the Grummett aunt. "I think Ivan and I had better be going now, but we'll call in again tomorrow."

"PC Tandy and I are leaving as well," said Tim. "We're going to the hospital. If either of you wants to come with us to see your mother, we can take you with us. We'll get a patrol car to bring you back."

There was a silence.

"I don't think I'll come tonight," said Philippa at length. "I'll see her when she's feeling more herself."

Kayleigh was rooting in the large handbag that she carried on one arm.

"'Ere," she said to Mrs Cushing, slinging at her a cellophane package which skidded across the little coffee table. "A packet of tomatoes. I bought them for Mam. You 'ave them, Mrs Cushing."

Chapter Eight

TIM THANKED MRS Cushing and extricated himself and Verity from her claustrophobic living room. Peter Cushing followed.

"Are you all right getting back to your car? The fog's mighty dense out there."

"I'm sure we'll be OK, Mr Cushing," he said. "We can see the glow of the searchlights at the accident site and no unauthorised vehicles will be coming down this road."

Tim slackened his pace to walk alongside Verity.

"What did you make of that?" he asked.

"I'm not sure, sir. Funny situation. The neighbour's being super-helpful, though I suppose that's not really unusual in the circumstances. But the Grummett sisters obviously can't stand each other. They don't seem all that worried about their parents, either."

"What beggars belief is that they're sisters at all. They're totally unlike each other, not just in looks, but in behaviour, the way they talk, everything."

"Intelligence, too."

"Especially intelligence. I suppose Kayleigh may have some kind of learning disability and when we meet the parents we'll find they're more like Philippa, but I doubt it, somehow. Their names are mismatched, too: I'd never have expected the same woman to call one daughter Kayleigh and the other Philippa.

They just don't go together."

"Philippa and Alice Cushing were both wearing the Boston Grammar School uniform."

"I thought that was a boys' school?"

"Girls are allowed into the sixth form. What I meant was, it's unlikely that Kayleigh . . ."

Tim stopped suddenly.

"Is someone following us?"

Verity paused, too. The flat-faced Grummett aunt came lumbering out of the gloom. She was breathless, as if she'd been trying to catch them up.

"Sorry to trouble you, mister," she shouted to Tim, unnecessarily loudly now that she was only a few steps away. "Me and Ivan was wondering if we could follow you to the hospital? Only we'd like to make sure Ruby's all right." She fixed Verity's eye and simpered incongruously as she finished speaking. Her husband came puffing along behind her and stood alongside, silent and eyeing them warily. Tim noted that, like his niece Kayleigh, he had a 'lazy' eye. Tim had developed a dislike for this couple. He doubted they were any more concerned about Ruby Grummett than the woman's daughters appeared to be. He suspected them of sensationalism, of glorying vicariously in a catastrophe because it involved members of their family.

"My advice to you would be to go home and come back again tomorrow, especially if you're not familiar with the roads. This fog is dangerous, and it would be doubly dangerous to try to follow us. If you give me your phone number I'll make sure someone calls you from the hospital."

Verity took out her notebook.

"Let me have the number . . ."

"Don't bother, Else," her husband growled. "If he don't want to help us, we'll find our own way. We've every right. Come on."

He quickened his pace, passing Verity and Tim and striding on as fast as his wheezing chest would allow. Elsie also scurried past them, heaving her considerable bulk along the road as nimbly as she could. Again Tim noticed she left a curious smell in her wake. He hadn't managed to place it the first time – in fact, he'd thought then that the stench might be coming from the mangled tanker lorry – but now its cause was unmistakeable: body odour with a vengeance, the reek of skin and clothes that had not been washed for many days. The Grummett family appeared to exist in a time-bubble: they were as peasant-like as it was possible to be in the twenty-first century. How did Philippa Grummett, sixth form pupil at Boston Grammar School, manage to tolerate her relations?

"Slow down a bit, Verity," he said. "I want to have a word with Giash when we get back to the car. I'd prefer it if Ivan and Elsie Grummett weren't hanging around."

They slackened their pace. It wasn't long before orange headlights showed fuzzily through the fog, advancing at some speed.

"Slow down, you idiot," Tim muttered, as Ivan's pick-up truck roared past them.

"Should I call PC Walton and ask him to caution them?" said Verity.

"Don't bother," said Tim. "Ivan Grummett strikes me as the type who might complain to the Press that he was badly treated by the police during a family crisis. With a bit of luck, he'll think better of going to the hospital, but if not, we don't want to have to waste time dealing with his carping."

Giash was talking to the firemen and Andy Carstairs, who had arrived while they'd been at the Cushings'.

"Hello, Andy, thanks for coming." Tim turned to Giash. "How's it going?"

"Not bad," said Giash. "There's little risk of fire or a gas

leak, now. We're going to secure the site and there'll be a police guard here all night. More journalists may come tomorrow and no doubt there'll be casual sightseers as well. The accident crew have managed to get the engine standing upright. The house is obviously unsafe: we need to make sure that no-one tries to get into it, for whatever reason. Fire Chief Towson's offered to leave a couple of his men here, as well. What do you think, sir? Do we need them?"

"If the building collapses further, they could be useful. But, hell, the visibility here is terrible and it's probably dangerous for them to work under strength rather than as a team. Why don't we suggest they go home now and come back at 7 a.m. tomorrow?"

Giash nodded.

"Do you want me and PC Tandy to stay, sir?"

"No. I'd like PC Tandy to come to the hospital with me to try to interview Ruby Grummett, but I don't want to leave you here without a partner. The Boston cops are in pairs, aren't they?"

"Yes."

"Leave it to them, then. You get off home, now. You too, Andy. I'm sorry if it's been a bit of a wild goose chase for you. You probably had better things to do."

There was irony in Andy's smile.

"Well, as a matter of fact I did, but there is one other important thing that Giash has picked up. You need to know about it."

"Can it wait?"

"I think you'll want to know now. The pyjama case that Giash says Kayleigh Grummett was trying to hang on to and then forgot about is stuffed full of £50 notes."

"How much money altogether?"

"I haven't counted it. Some of it is . . . contaminated."

"You mean, covered in shit?"

Verity Tandy and Giash Chakrabati both laughed.

"Yes, sir. It needs examining properly, in a lab. But my guess is that there's ten grand at least, probably more."

"Take it away and get it analysed, will you? Find out if any of the notes were stolen if you can."

Chapter Nine

As Tim and Verity arrived at the Pilgrim Hospital, the fog seemed to be getting denser. Inside, the hospital was suffocatingly warm. People in wet coats sitting in the corridors and waiting areas contributed to the humidity.

When Tim announced himself, the male receptionist turned away to a cubby-hole of a back office and made a call. He emerged looking cheerful.

"Mrs Grummett's awake and able to see you, though she's been sedated. There'll be a nurse with you when you talk to her. She may not remember much at the moment. The doctor stresses that she mustn't be upset. Some of her family are with her. She's on the third floor. Staff Nurse Shaw will meet you at the lift and escort you."

"Is it my imagination, or was he treating us like disruptives?" Tim asked as they walked away. "And 'escort', indeed! Where did he get that from?"

Verity shrugged.

"Most people behave unnaturally when they're talking to a police officer."

"I suppose you're right. I can't say I've noticed."

Staff Nurse Shaw was a tall, broad-shouldered man with a loping gait. Apparently he had no phobias about policemen.

"If you'd just wait right here," he said, gesturing to a small waiting room containing some chairs and a television screen,

"I'll check that Ruby's ready for you."

He was back in a couple of minutes.

"She's got family with her but they say they're leaving. Her husband would like to stay. That OK with you?" He flashed Verity a broad smile.

"Yes, that's fine," said Tim. He was watching Ivan and Elsie Grummett through the glass screen of the little waiting room. They were heading for the stairs, he with his hands in his pockets, she close behind him. They seemed to be in some hurry.

"Ah, there they go," said Staff Nurse Shaw. "You follow me, now."

Ruby Grummett was sitting up in bed. She'd removed her dress but wasn't wearing a hospital gown. Her short, plump body was encased in a fearsomely unyielding all-in-one foundation garment. Its broad white straps cut deep into her shoulders, the flesh bulging around them. Sitting on a chair beside the bed was a stocky man, also short, whose baldness was relieved by a few tufts of grey hair sticking up above his ears. He had curiously fat and blubbery lips.

"The police are here, Ruby love," he said.

Ruby Grummett lay back on the pillows and passed a hand rather theatrically across her black button eyes. She started muttering, but in a voice so low that Tim couldn't catch what she was saying. He picked up that she had a very strong regional accent, stronger than either her husband's or Kayleigh's. The skin around her mouth was pursed and cross-hatched with wrinkles. She looked older than her husband.

Bob Grummett leaned across and awkwardly grasped her other hand.

"There's nothing to worry about, duckie. They just want to ask you a few questions. If you get tired, just tell them and they'll go away." He turned to Tim. "That's right, isn't it?"

"We don't want to put Mrs Grummett under further strain," said Tim, "but the sooner we can collect witness statements after an accident, the better." He addressed Ruby directly. "If you can just manage to talk to us for ten minutes or so, Mrs Grummett, we'd be grateful."

She nodded and rolled her eyes, clinging on to her husband's hand. It struck Tim she was overdoing it, though this might have been uncharitable of him. When she spoke again, the words were more distinct.

"How's Fred?"

Tim looked blank.

"Fred Lister, the lorry driver," Verity said quietly to Tim. "I think he's survived." She looked at Staff Nurse Shaw for confirmation.

"He is alive," he whispered. "But only just. His mate died instantly, though they brought him here. I don't think you should tell her that."

Tim took a step closer to the bed.

"Fred's alive," he said, "but poorly."

She nodded, her face creasing.

"Mrs Grummett, can you tell us exactly what happened at the crossing, just as you remember it? If there are parts of the accident that you don't remember, tell us that, too."

She looked at him blankly.

"Let's start at the beginning," said Verity soothingly. "It's been a very foggy day, hasn't it? I doubt if many people came to use the crossing, did they?"

Ruby shook her head.

"No. Just the postman and the milkman. I didn't think Fred would be out today, but he said he'd had a rush job on."

"Did he come to the door to ask you to open the gates?"

"Yes. I was going to have a bath. I came out in my dressing-gown. I was wearing Bob's slippers. I knew the Skegness train

hadn't gone by, but I thought they'd cancelled it. The system said the line was clear. It did! I checked! It said it was clear." The words had come tumbling faster and faster. She began to rock backwards and forwards in the bed.

"DI Yates, I'm sorry, but I think I'm going to have to say that's it for today. She's still too distressed to have a calm conversation with you. Dr Butler asked me to make sure that she didn't get agitated. She'll still be here tomorrow. She'll probably make more sense then."

Tim nodded. He felt thwarted, especially as he suspected that although the woman was undoubtedly upset, she was hamming up the trauma.

"Of course," he said aloud. "Mr Grummett, could I have a word with you before we leave?"

Bob Grummett met his eye. He saw the same half-shifty, half-insolent expression that he'd noted when he'd spoken to Ivan Grummett. Unlike Ivan, Bob also appeared to be afraid of something. He looked away quickly, brought himself creakingly to his feet and followed Tim out into the foyer.

"First of all, I'm very sorry that you're all having to suffer like this. It must be terrible for you, losing your home and having all the worry of looking after your wife."

The man relaxed visibly.

"We've cordoned off your house as a possible crime scene at the moment." Bob Grummett's head jerked back in an involuntary gesture of panic.

"They can't prosecute her, can they? They can't make out it was her fault?"

"It's possible that Mrs Grummett will be prosecuted, but I wouldn't dwell on it too much at the moment. In all probability, the coroner will decide it was an accident. But there'll have to be an inquest. It's also possible the railway company will be found negligent. I wouldn't worry your wife with any of this

until she's recovered. But I must ask you not to attempt to go back into the house to retrieve anything at the moment. The building is dangerously damaged. We've put a police guard on it, so you needn't be afraid of anyone else getting in. Do you have somewhere to stay tonight?"

Bob Grummett's ruddy face paled noticeably. It was as if the enormity of what had happened had just hit him.

"I suppose I can go to Ivan's. Or to my other brother – David's. He lives in Boston."

"He might be a better bet, as we'll want to talk to Mrs Grummett again tomorrow and I assume you'd like to be here again?"

He nodded.

"Thank you. We'll come at 11.00 a.m., if that suits you? I understand the doctor wants to see her first."

He nodded again. Tim wasn't sure that he was really taking in what was being said to him. Nevertheless, he decided to plough on.

"There's just one other thing, Mr Grummett."

Immediately a shutter came down on Bob Grummett's face. His expression was transformed from that of a sad and helpless man in late middle age to something a lot more shifty and unpleasant.

"Oh?" he said.

"Your daughter Kayleigh was worried about a pyjama case and insisted that your brother Ivan retrieved it from the house – against specific police instructions not to go in, I might add. We wanted to bag it because it was contaminated, but your daughter wouldn't give it up until her attention was distracted by someone else. Subsequently, one of my officers opened it up and found that it contained a very large sum of money. Can you tell me how it got there, or perhaps I should say, where it came from?"

Bob Grummett's mental agility barely exceeded his daughter's. His eyes flickered as he struggled to make up a plausible excuse. Finally he shrugged.

"That's Kayleigh for you. Always been a bit of a hoarder. I suppose she just saved it up out of her wages. We've no time for banks in our family."

"I see," said Tim. "Thank you. Both your daughters are all right, by the way. They're staying with your neighbour."

Again Bob Grummett looked blank. Eventually he tried an uncertain smile.

"That was good of Peter," he said.

Chapter Ten

TIM WAS LATE getting into work the following morning: an unheard-of circumstance before Sophia was born, but now he quite often forgot the time when he was playing with her. As he dashed up the stairs to his office, he felt philosophical about this minor delinquency – after all, he'd been at work in Boston until almost midnight the night before – but he'd barely reached his desk when Andy Carstairs came across to tell him quietly that Superintendent Thornton was looking for him. Andy's demeanour indicated that the Superintendent was not in a good mood.

"There's someone with him," he said to Tim. "I think he wanted to introduce you to her."

Tim sighed. He made his way to the Superintendent's office without benefit of the cup of coffee he'd promised himself and tried to peer discreetly through the small, square glass window in the door. He could see the back of a woman with long yellow hair seated opposite Thornton at his desk.

"Ah, Yates, come in!" Thornton made an exaggeratedly sweeping gesture with his right arm. "We were wondering where you'd got to."

Feeling at a distinct disadvantage, Tim opened the door and walked as smartly as possible into the office. He debated whether to offer an excuse and decided against it. It would be outrageous if Thornton had been discussing his timekeeping with this woman.

She turned to look at him. She had turquoise-blue eyes set in a rosy round face and her buttercup-coloured hair was crimped in light waves. She was dressed in turquoise, too. She looks like a mermaid, Tim thought.

"Sit down, Yates. Ms Trotter has to go in a minute: she hasn't got all day. I understand you haven't met?"

"It would be surprising if we had," she said. She had a lilting voice. Welsh? Wondered Tim. "I've only been in post for a couple of weeks."

"Ms Trotter works for the Crown Prosecution Service, Yates," said Thornton. He smirked at her. "As I said, DI Yates was at the scene last night. We've not had a chance to catch up yet." The last sentence was delivered in a darker tone of voice, with a thunderous look at Tim.

Tim stretched out his hand.

"Melanie Trotter," she said.

"I'm pleased to meet you. I think I can guess why you're here."

"No need to guess, Yates, we can tell you. Ms Trotter has come to find out if there's a case for prosecuting someone for the Dowdyke disaster. What's your preliminary assessment of the matter?"

"I think we should wait for the coroner's report, sir. There are some things that have yet to be investigated."

"Such as?"

"Such as whether the warning system was faulty. If it was, the railway company might be liable. But we also need to know that Ruby Grummett followed all the correct safety procedures."

"Ruby Grummett being the crossing-keeper?"

"Yes, sir."

"You've seen her? What does she say?"

"She was pretty shocked last night. I'm returning to interview her later this morning."

"Good, good. So your initial view is that there is probably not a case to prosecute?"

"I wouldn't say that, sir. As I mentioned, I think we should wait for the coroner's report." Tim considered mentioning the pyjama case of money and the side investigation that he'd asked Andy Carstairs to carry out, but decided not to. He'd tell Thornton about it, of course, but not while Melanie Trotter was there. He knew the CPS of old. They were terriers, often pursuing cases that the police themselves believed to be too flimsy, then getting the force a bad name when the judge threw them out. The turquoise mermaid didn't look like a terrier, however.

"I think that's a perfectly sensible suggestion," she said, turning on him the full force of her smile. "Just keep me in the loop, if you would."

"Certainly," said Tim.

She stood up, smoothing down her pencil skirt as she did so, and leant across the desk to shake hands with Thornton.

"Thank you, Superintendent, it's been a pleasure to meet you. And you as well, DI Yates," she added, as Tim opened the door for her.

"Not your run-of-the-mill CPS person," said the Superintendent when it had barely closed on her. He appeared to have found something intensely satisfying about the encounter. He stared into space for a couple of seconds.

"Will that be all, sir?"

"Eh? No, Yates, that isn't all. You'll keep her in the loop, as she asks, of course, but I wanted to see you about something else as well. I'm being pestered to look at cold cases again. Do you have anyone to spare who can do some preliminary work on this. What's Armstrong up to at the moment? I suppose she's helping you with the Grummett woman."

"No, actually, it was Juliet's – DC Armstrong's – night off

last night, sir, so I asked PC Tandy to help me interview Mrs Grummett. I've asked her to meet me at the Pilgrim Hospital again today."

"Oh. Shaping up, is she? I must confess I didn't think too much of her when Boston cajoled me into accepting her transfer." He lowered his voice. "I don't like fat girls."

It was on the tip of Tim's tongue to say he didn't like fat girls either, but that Verity Tandy had slimmed down a bit over the past few months. He stopped himself just in time, realising with shame how Katrin, or Juliet, for that matter, would react if they knew.

"She was very helpful in the de Vries case, sir. I think she has the makings of an excellent officer."

"Yes. Good. Well, in that case ask Armstrong to look at some of these, do a bit of preliminary work on them – not too much – and preferably find some good reasons why we can't open them again. Or just get her to take a token look at one of them. Then I – or she – can write a report and we'll be off the hook for another year or two." He handed Tim a thick folder with a dusty buff cardboard cover. Outsize papers and photographs were poking out untidily from it.

"Don't you like cold cases, sir?"

"It's not a question of liking or disliking them. The fact is, they're harder to solve. Diminishing returns, Yates. They don't do anything for our statistics."

Tim tried not to grin. He was convinced that if a section could be cut into the Superintendent's brain a set of Excel spreadsheets would be revealed, filed neatly inside it, all the formulae correctly calculated.

"And, Yates, don't tell that Trotter woman anything without running it past me first."

Evidently Melanie Trotter's spell had dissolved within a very short time after her departure.

Chapter Eleven

IT WAS ALMOST ten-thirty. Tim had taken Juliet the folder and given her Thornton's instructions and was heading to his car when his mobile rang.

"DI Yates?"

"Yes." He said. "PC Tandy? Are you on your way to the hospital?"

"There's been a complication, sir."

"Oh? What sort of complication?"

"I was on an early shift with PC Chakrabati this morning, sir – I started at 6 a.m. I told Sarge you'd be needing me at Boston and he said to work the first four hours and then he'd send someone else out to Giash. Just ordinary patrol work. But we were called to the girls' school about half an hour ago. Someone hanging round, apparently. Several of the girls saw him. It was reported by a mother dropping her daughter off. Sarge says there isn't another WPC to help Giash to interview the girls at the moment, and he can't very well do it on his own. Them being girls," she concluded, rather unnecessarily. There was a tremor in her voice. Surely she can't be scared of me? Tim thought.

He sighed, but his reply was friendly enough.

"Well, it can't be helped. Stay where you are. Let me know how you get on. We'd barely started on the interview with Mrs Grummett, anyway. I'll ask DC Armstrong to come with

me. Mrs Grummett being a woman," he couldn't resist adding. Actually, he was pleased. Verity Tandy had held her own the previous evening, but Juliet was always his preferred partner in tricky situations.

"Thank you, sir." She sounded as if she'd been forgiven for some misdemeanour. Perhaps she *is* scared of me, thought Tim. I can't imagine why.

"Keep me posted," he said again. "Good luck!"

Chapter Twelve

THE STIFF SCHOOL secretary escorted Verity and Giash to the headteacher's office and asked them to wait. She offered tea in such an abrupt way they felt obliged to decline.

Richard Lennard entered the room a good quarter of an hour later. He pointed his nose at the ceiling and walked in rather an affected way, without looking at the ground. Verity put him down as vain immediately. She didn't like vain men.

"PC Tandy?" he said, stretching out his hand. "Thank you for helping with this business. I'm sure it's all a fuss about nothing, but obviously we can't be too careful." He ignored Giash.

Verity blinked, half flustered and half annoyed. She regretted that she hadn't stood up when he'd entered the room. Having him towering over her made her feel at a disadvantage; and she resented the slight to her partner.

"Good morning, Mr Lennard. This is PC Chakrabati. I'm sorry, I don't understand. Surely there can be few things more serious than having a prowler lurking near a girls' school?"

Richard Lennard directed a perfunctory nod at Giash and let out a forced bark of a laugh.

"I'd agree with you, if there is such a person. The parent who reported seeing him, Mrs Painter, is quite a fanciful lady, as is her daughter. And, as you know, when girls get togeth-

er they're likely to become somewhat hysterical. To be quite frank, I think that between them they've imagined the whole thing. Quite unintentionally, of course."

"I see," said Verity. "We'd like to interview Mrs Painter and the girls anyway. We'll make up our own minds about how much truth there is in what they say."

"I'm afraid Mrs Painter couldn't stay. She has a job somewhere or other. Of course you may meet the students. Do you want to see them individually or as a group?"

"As a group is fine. And we'd like Mrs Painter's contact details."

"I'll ask my PA to write them down for you. I'll also ask her to fetch the girls."

Richard Lennard moved over to his desk and pushed the button on his intercom.

"Kathleen? Bring in the three students now, if you would."

Verity stood up.

"Just one thing, Mr Lennard. We'd like to see them on their own, if you don't mind."

A frown of annoyance crossed the headteacher's face, but he was a smooth enough operator to banish it in a second. He continued the conversation without missing a beat.

"Really?" he said. "I'm not sure that's advisable. It's my duty to look after their welfare, in the absence of their parents. I'm not suggesting you would do anything improper, but they might get upset. Someone from the school should be here to terminate the interview if we feel it appropriate."

"You're absolutely correct," Verity said, as if conceding a point. "And, to follow the rules strictly, that person should be a woman. One of the female staff, perhaps?"

"They're all teaching at the moment. I really think . . ."

"Your secretary, then? Perhaps you could spare her for a few minutes?" Secretly Verity thought if there was one person

before whom the girls were unlikely to give way to tears, it would be that sharp-faced woman.

"We can ask her."

There was a businesslike rap at the door. The secretary entered, the three girls following in single file in her wake. Verity watched them keenly. The first was tall and willowy, with long dark hair, very long legs and a shorter skirt than Verity would have thought school rules permitted. The second was dumpy, with frizzy hair and full red cheeks. She, too, wore a short skirt, though it did nothing to complement her saddlebag thighs and unsculpted legs. Verity felt a wave of sympathy. Turn back the clock a dozen years and she wouldn't have looked unlike this girl. The third girl was also slender, taller even than the first, but more conservatively dressed. Although she didn't lack grace, she gave the impression of being very robust: there was a strength and solidity about her. Her hair was so fair it gleamed silver in the artificial light. Verity recognised her immediately.

"Philippa!" she said. "I thought you'd be taking the day off school today. And I thought you went to Boston High."

The girl shot her a look of blank amazement. She turned to the headteacher as if asking him to explain. He seemed embarrassed.

"You're speaking to Cassandra Knipes," he said. "She's our head girl. Perhaps you've confused her with someone else?" There was a strained edge to his voice that Verity noted, even as she burned with embarrassment herself.

"I'm sorry," she said, addressing Cassandra. "You remind me exactly of a young woman whom I met yesterday evening. You both have very distinctive hair. In fact, you could be her twin. But, as Mr Lennard says, I must be mistaken."

The interview had got off to a poor start. Giash threw her a sympathetic look: he'd decided to remain in the background

after Richard Lennard's snub. Verity could see the wisdom of this, though she'd have welcomed some help to dig herself out of the hole.

"Would you mind staying with us?" Verity said to the secretary. "In the role of responsible adult." The short, fat girl stifled a giggle. Like Cassandra Knipes, the secretary turned automatically to Richard Lennard for advice.

"I've said it's OK by me if you have time, Mrs Hargreaves," he said smoothly, his urbanity swiftly reasserting itself. Mrs Hargreaves clucked her tongue disapprovingly.

"If you say so, Mr Lennard."

"Thank you. I'll fetch more chairs," he said, darting with a sudden burst of energy to a pile of wood and steel chairs stacked behind the door. He returned with four and fanned them out in a semi-circle next to the chair Verity occupied. Giash remained standing against the wall.

"I'll stand," said Mrs Hargreaves.

Lennard gestured to the three girls to be seated and took the last chair himself. Still humbled by her faux pas, Verity didn't pluck up the courage to remind him that he'd agreed to leave them to it. The interview consequently began in very stilted fashion, constrained both by Kathleen Hargreaves' cold stare and Richard Lennard's slippery smile.

"I'm PC Tandy," Verity said. "Let's start with your names. I know Cassandra's now." She smiled at Cassandra, who looked down at her feet.

"I'm Leonora Painter," piped the short, fat girl.

"Isobel Baxter."

"Now tell me about this morning. Were you walking to school together?"

"No," said Isobel. "Cassie and I were walking together – I usually call for her on my way. Leo's mother brought her in the car. When we came round the corner, there was a man hover-

ing near the school gate. Leo's mother had parked on the other side of the road. She flashed her headlights at us so we went over to speak to her. She told us to get in the car with Leo. She said the man was behaving strangely and we shouldn't try to get past him."

"How was he behaving strangely?"

"He was walking up and down by the entrance to the drive, muttering to himself," said Leonora. "And he was wearing a long, dirty mac."

"A dirty old man in a mac," said Isobel. "That's what Mrs Painter thought."

"Did he do anything else?"

"You mean . . . expose himself, or something?" said Cassandra tentatively. Mrs Hargreaves's face darkened with disapproval. It said plainly that Cassandra should know nothing of such things.

"Yes, that, or anything else at all that any of you found worrying," Verity continued.

"Not really," said Isobel.

"No," said Cassandra.

"Mum and I just got a feeling about him," said Leonora defensively.

"Did he speak to any of you?"

All three girls shook their heads.

"Had you ever seen him before?"

"No," said Leonora and Isobel, almost in unison.

"Cassandra?"

"I'm not sure. There was something familiar about him – but from the past, if you know what I mean. From a long time ago. Almost as if I dreamt it."

Verity nodded.

"Well," said Richard Lennard briskly, "PC Tandy isn't here to listen to your dreams." He turned to Verity. "The bell's just

rung for the next lesson. If they hurry, they'll get to it in time. I don't think there's anything else you need to ask them, do you?"

"Not now," said Verity. "But we always take reports of this nature seriously. Mrs Painter was right to bring it to your attention." She smiled at the girls. "I'm going to give you each one of my cards. My mobile number is printed on them. I want you to call me if you see this man hanging around again. Is that OK?"

The girls nodded, took the cards, and rose to their feet.

"Thank you," said Cassandra, taking the lead.

"Yes, thank you," said the other two in unison.

As soon as they'd gone, Kathleen Hargreaves gave Verity a tight nod. "I'll be getting on, then." She marched out of the door and closed it behind her.

"What did I tell you?" said Richard Lennard, but in a friendly way. He was being magnanimous now his point had been proved. "They have vivid imaginations, bless them. And Mrs Painter should know better."

"We'll still arrange to talk to her, even so," said Verity. "The experience was obviously unsettling and I don't think it should be ignored."

"Unsettling mostly for Leonora Painter and her mother. I got the impression that Isobel and Cassandra were baffled by their behaviour."

"You may be right about Isobel. I'm not so sure about Cassandra. Does she have relatives at the school, by the way? Sisters or cousins?"

"I don't think so. She's an only child. Her parents are quite elderly – relatively speaking, of course."

"Curious," said Verity, almost to herself. "I saw a girl last night who would have passed for her double."

Richard Lennard smiled benignly.

"Yes, well, that happens to me quite frequently. When you see as many adolescent girls as I do, you realise there are only so many physical types. Sometimes I catch myself out calling a student by the name of someone I knew years ago."

"I'm sure that's true. But you must agree that Cassandra's looks are unusual. Not many girls are as fair as she is, especially in this area. The girl I saw last night had a similar physique, too: slender but tall and strong-looking, and with similar delicate features."

Instead of replying, Richard Lennard glanced at his watch. Verity took the hint.

"We mustn't keep you any longer. Here's my card. Please report it at once if the loiterer comes back. You should make sure you have staff patrolling the school grounds and the area outside the gate when the students are arriving and leaving, at least for a week or two."

"Certainly. There should have been staff on duty this morning." He frowned. "I shall check to see where they were."

"We'll arrange for a patrol car to drop by at intervals to carry out spot-check surveillance."

"Well, what did you make of that? I've never seen a colleague so badly treated. I'm sorry. I didn't quite know how to handle it," said Verity, as she and Giash were walking away from the school.

"Don't worry. It's happened to me before, though not often."

"Racial prejudice?" Verity was uncomfortable saying the words, but she thought to ignore the issue would be ridiculous.

"Perhaps. But it may not be as straightforward as that. My cousin's family removed their daughter from that school. Mr Lennard may recognise the name."

"He didn't thank me for offering to patrol the area around the school."

"No. My overall impression was that he didn't want us to have anything whatever to do with the school. His attitude to the safety of the girls was hard to understand."

Verity found it troubling. Besides the headmaster's strange behaviour there was the uncanny similarity between Philippa Grummett and Cassandra Knipes.

She looked at her watch. There was no prospect now of her reaching the Pilgrim Hospital in time to help DI Yates interview Ruby Grummett. She called Tim's mobile.

"DI Yates? It's PC Tandy. I'm afraid that dealing with the incident at school took longer than I thought . . ."

"Don't worry about it. I've asked DC Armstrong to accompany me."

"Damn!" said Verity aloud, as she ended the call. She'd become intrigued by the Grummett case. Now she'd probably not be asked to help with it again.

"Bad luck!" said Giash sympathetically. "But don't take it too much to heart. You're on his radar now. You've made a good impression on him lately."

Chapter Thirteen

JULIET ARMSTRONG HADN'T been near the Pilgrim Hospital since she'd been obliged to spend more than a week there the year before, recovering from Weil's disease. Her stay had given her plenty to think about, especially after she'd formed an unsettling friendship with a doctor called Louise Butler which had been brought to an abrupt end by a misunderstanding. She took a deep breath as she and Tim went in.

Having already been primed by Katrin that Juliet might find returning to the hospital difficult (Katrin had reminded him only of how ill Juliet had been when first admitted, though she had an inkling of the Butler dimension), Tim picked up on her nervousness.

"I don't suppose this place has good memories for you," he said, squeezing her elbow briefly and giving her a sympathetic smile. "I'm sorry I had to ask you to come."

"It's my job," said Juliet. "Besides, I'm certain I'll find this more interesting than ploughing through Superintendent Thornton's cold-case file."

They both laughed.

"I'm not so sure about that," said Tim, after he'd thought about it. "Some of our most interesting cases have started out as cold cases: Kathryn Sheppard's murder, for example, and the skeletons at Kevan de Vries's house in Sutterton."

"I don't think Superintendent Thornton counts those skel-

etons," said Juliet. "They didn't do anything for his statistics because the crime was too old to get a conviction, even if wasting time on them *was* mitigated by getting Harry Briggs put away for murder."

"Yes. That's Thornton's problem with cold cases: they often don't make much of an impression on the stats. And even though we caught Harry Briggs, Tony Sentance eluded us completely. I'm sure Thornton blames me for that: he thought I was preoccupied with the skeletons so diluted my efforts elsewhere. Perhaps that's why he's so against making more than a cursory effort with the current round of cold cases."

"What's his take on the railway accident? Does he want to see Ruby Grummett prosecuted?"

"My guess is he'd prefer to see the railway company charged with negligence. He does have some social conscience. Besides, it would be a bigger case. I think he'd like a prosecution. He's taken a shine to the new woman working at the prosecutor's office, Melanie Trotter."

Juliet laughed.

"I can't imagine him taking a shine to anyone, not in the romantic sense, anyway."

"I didn't mean that, exactly," said Tim. "But you never know. I don't think his marriage is all plain sailing."

"Have you met Mrs Thornton?"

"No. As you know, she doesn't deign to come to police socials. But I've heard him speaking to her on the phone. I think he's paid quite dearly for sticking with his little-woman-in-the-home ideals. Mrs Thornton may enjoy not being part of the workforce, but she sounds as if she's anything but a meek wife. He may have got the worst of both worlds: no second income, and no say in what goes on at home, either."

"You're making me feel sorry for him!"

"Don't bother . . ."

"Excuse me! DI Yates?"

"Staff Nurse Shaw! Good morning."

"Good morning, DI Yates." The nurse eyed Juliet curiously and gave her a grin. "Is PC Tandy coming today?"

"No, she's on another case. This is my colleague, DC Armstrong."

The nurse gave her a nod.

"I'm sorry; I'm afraid you may have had a wasted journey," he said. "Mrs Grummett is no better today; in fact, she's considerably worse."

"How is she injured?" asked Juliet.

"She has no physical injuries, but her mind has been deeply afflicted by the accident. She's under heavy sedation now. I think it unlikely that Dr Butler will let you see her today."

"Dr Butler?" Juliet felt her face flush. She hoped neither Tim nor the nurse had noticed.

"Yes. Mrs Grummett is her patient. Do you know Dr Butler?" His benevolent brown eyes shone with curiosity.

"She treated me when I was a patient last year," said Juliet quietly.

"Well, I'm sure she'll be pleased to see you again. She's talking to Mr Grummett now, but she's asked to meet DI Yates. That's why I'm here.

"Bob Grummett is here, too, you say?" said Tim.

"Yes. He went home yesterday evening, but was back here just after breakfast. He's very worried about his wife."

"He's bound to be," said Tim. "I'd like to speak to him after Dr Butler has finished with him. Could you provide a room where we can talk in private?"

"There's the little waiting room at the top of the ward. No one's using it at the moment and since it isn't visiting time you're unlikely to be disturbed."

"Thank you," said Tim. "Juliet, I'd like you to talk to Dr

Butler while I see Bob Grummett. Find out how long she proposes to sedate Ruby and ask her to let us know when we'll be able to interview her."

Juliet couldn't decide whether Tim was trying to be helpful or mischievous.

"Yes, sir," she said. She turned to the staff nurse.

"Where should I wait?"

"You may as well wait with DI Yates. You'll see Dr Butler when she comes past the window. I'll let her know you'd like to see her. I don't think she'll be long."

Juliet didn't have to wait at all. As Staff Nurse Shaw opened the swing doors to the ward and stood to one side to let her and Tim in, she saw Louise Butler approaching. She looked tired. Her hair was fastened back in a severe chignon and she was wearing dark-rimmed spectacles which Juliet thought too heavy for her face. She was momentarily taken aback when she saw Juliet.

"DC Armstrong! I didn't expect you." She turned to Tim. "Good morning, DI Yates. I did know that you were investigating the level crossing accident. Staff Nurse Shaw told me. And I do want a word. But I had the impression that you'd be accompanied by a policewoman today – a WPC, I mean."

"He's right – I'd intended to bring PC Tandy with me. She was here last night, shortly after Mrs Grummett was admitted. But she's been called to another case today, so I asked DC Armstrong instead."

Louise Butler gave Juliet an appraising look.

"It's good to see you again," she said, although without much warmth. "I hope you're quite well?"

"Yes, thank you," said Juliet. She felt and sounded awkward.

"Well, I'm afraid you may both be disappointed," Louise

Butler continued briskly. "We've had to keep Mrs Grummett under sedation. She isn't coping well with the trauma. You won't be able to see her today."

"We half-expected that," said Tim genially. "Thank you for updating us. May I see Mr Grummett, if he's here?"

"He's by his wife's bedside at the moment. I suppose it's all right for you to talk to him here, as long as you keep it brief. Staff Nurse Shaw, would you mind asking Mr Grummett to come in? I'm not sure that his wife is entirely asleep and I don't want her to be alarmed. Well, if you'll excuse me . . ." she continued.

Tim spoke quickly. "I wonder if you could spare DC Armstrong a little of your time? We'd like some more details about Mrs Grummett's condition. How long she's likely to take to recover, when we can talk to her, that sort of thing."

"I'm not sure I can answer those questions, but if you come with me, I'll see what I can do," said the doctor, meeting Juliet's eye.

"Thank you," Juliet said humbly. "I'd appreciate it."

Bob Grummett came shambling up to Tim, who noticed for the first time that he walked with a sideways roll, like a music hall sailor. What remained of his hair was dishevelled and sticking up in greasy tufts on his head. He was wearing the same shirt as the day before. In the broad light of day he looked crumpled and creased, dirtier than someone who had merely missed one morning's ablutions. He glanced sideways at Tim from beneath droopy eyelids.

"Now then, cock," he said. "What can I do you for?"

He laughed loudly, obviously thinking this mode of expression – or perhaps his gratuitous insolence – was amusing.

"Could you keep your voice down?" a passing nurse hissed testily.

"Mr Grummett, hello. Should we go into the waiting room? Then we won't be disturbing anyone else."

Bob Grummett shrugged.

"It's all right by me, as long as Rube doesn't wake up. I want to be with her when she does."

"How is she?"

"She's in quite a bad way. It was all one hell of a shock to her. I doubt she'll ever be the same again," he replied, with more than a hint of melodrama. They'd entered the small ante-room and Tim had shut the door firmly. Bob Grummett seemed to be incapable of speaking quietly.

"It's understandable that she's ill after such a horrific accident. I'm certain she'll recover, though. You'd be surprised at how resilient people are."

Bob Grummett stared at him blankly. Tim realised he hadn't understood the meaning of the adjective.

"Any way," Tim continued, "I wish her well. We'll be checking in every so often, monitoring her progress."

"Why's that? So that you can charge her when she's better?" The railwayman had turned sullen and mistrustful.

"I'm not in a position to be able to say whether there'll be any charges to face," said Tim. "There'll have to be an enquiry into how the accident happened and there'll certainly be an inquest for the man who died. If Mrs Grummett is charged, it's likely she won't be expected to bear the blame alone. Her employers will come under scrutiny as well."

"Come again?" Once more, the puzzled look. Tim struggled to put his observation more simply.

"The railway company. Your bosses. It may be that some or all of the blame lies with them."

"Aye, I shouldn't wonder. That won't help Rube, though."

"The main thing is that Mrs Grummett gets better. All the rest of it will take months to sort out. We can't speculate –

there's no point in trying to guess what will happen."

"What're you here for, then? Rube can't talk to you now, anyway."

"No, I know that, though I did hope to see her. But I mainly came to have a word with you."

Bob Grummett's face shut.

"Oh?"

"Yes. I wanted to pick up where we left off yesterday," said Tim firmly. "You know what I'm talking about: the money in the pyjama case. Where did it come from?"

"I told you, it's Kayleigh's. You'll have to ask her."

"You have no objection if I do that?"

"She's a grown woman."

"She is, but a very young one. I understand she's eighteen?"

"Yes."

"I get the impression that she's quite . . . naïve."

"Come again?" Bob Grummett repeated. This time Tim was irritated. He couldn't believe the man was as dense as he was making out.

"If we question her, would you like to be present, Mr Grummett?"

"I suppose so. If you think it will do any good. And if she likes the idea."

"Is she still staying with the Cushings?"

"As far as I know. I haven't spoken to her since the accident."

"Have you spoken to either of your daughters today?"

Bob Grummett looked perplexed. Tim hoped that he wasn't going to say 'Come again?' a third time. If he did, Tim thought he might hit him. There was a long pause.

"Oh, you mean Philippa," he said, almost to himself. "No, I haven't spoken to her or Kayleigh. Why do you ask?"

"I just thought they might have been worried about their

mother, want to know how she was," said Tim, his voice heavy with an irony that was completely lost on its target.

"No," said Bob Grummett in a neutral tone, "but I'd better be getting back to her myself."

"Would you like some tea or coffee?" asked Louise Butler, gesturing to Juliet to take one of two chairs placed opposite each other at the small table in her office.

"Thank you. Tea, please."

"I'm glad you said that. I'd have had to go to the canteen for coffee, but I can make tea myself." She filled a small kettle at her sink and plugged it in. "You really are quite well now?"

"Yes," said Juliet. "It took a few months to get my energy back, but I'm as good as new. Thanks mostly to you," she added shyly.

Louise gave her a sharp look.

"I seem to remember you were quite run down when you were admitted here," she said, "to use the popular term for being over- stressed and anxious. I hope you're making sure you get some time to yourself. I know your job makes unreasonable demands at all hours of the day or night, but being able to switch off is the key."

Juliet laughed.

"I doubt you get much opportunity to practise what you preach," she said. "As it happens, I have been trying to take more time for myself recently. I've joined Fenland Folklore. It's a society that meets to discuss old Lincolnshire legends and customs."

"Excellent! I suppose you were influenced by DI Yates? He's interested in history, isn't he?"

"Yes, but he's a bit of a purist. He thinks Fenland Folklore is for amateurs and therefore beneath his contempt."

"Well, I know you have more sense than to take notice of

that. Tell me more about it. I'm interested in old Lincolnshire myself."

"Really?" said Juliet.

"Yes, although I have to confess that it's the medical and sociological aspects of folklore that I find intriguing. Old folk tales are so often based on some kind of fact, even though it's been disguised or distorted. There was a lot of inbreeding in South Lincolnshire, right up to the end of the twentieth century in some of the more out-of-the-way places, and I'd love to have the opportunity to investigate it further. When I first qualified, I worked as a registrar at Peterborough District Hospital and I was living in pretty grim digs in Peterborough. When I had a bit of time to myself, I'd go out for drives and one day I came across the village of Twenty, near Bourne. Almost all of the children who lived there had pronounced squints and several of them were 'educationally challenged', if that's the correct term. I went back a few times and made friends with the vicar, who showed me the parish records. I discovered there'd been so much intermarrying in the village that almost all the children had the same great-grandfather. Of course we've long understood that too much inbreeding produces defects – Charles Darwin was aware of this and probably others long before him. But there's a great deal of work still to be done on the specifics. I'm sure this knowledge is responsible for taboos in many different societies. It's a subject that's always fascinated me."

"And you say it's captured in folklore?"

"In stories of all kinds. Many old tales are much more obscure in their meaning than the Oedipus story. Probably because they've been changed as they were handed down, but sometimes because the underlying facts had to be conveyed indirectly, for safety reasons. In mediaeval times, incest might be condoned, turned a blind eye to, or punished very severely, for

example. The shift in attitudes from one society or period to another is striking. Since we have no genetic profile for people from earlier times, history and folklore are all we have to help us piece together what happened and its effects. I'd love to have done research into genetics. Unfortunately, I couldn't afford to become a researcher."

"That's a pity," said Juliet. "But if you're interested in folklore, why don't you come to the next meeting of Fenland Folklore? You have to apply to the chairman to join, but that's just a detail. He won't turn you down. I'll write down his e-mail address for you."

"Thank you. I'll give it a try. When's the next meeting?"

"We meet on Mondays, once a fortnight. So the next full meeting will be a week on Monday. But there's also an extra meeting on Thursday, because there's quite a well-known folklorist visiting the area and the Society has persuaded her to give us a talk."

"I'll try to come, if I manage to get accepted in time. You met yesterday, then?"

"Yes. It was rather a strange meeting, actually. We were asked to interpret quite a savage old tale about a witch who kept a man incarcerated for many years before finally killing him. One of the men in the group was showing off with his knowledge of psychology. He spoilt it for the rest of us – or for me, at any rate."

"Typical!" said Louise. She was smiling. "Shall we..?"

Juliet's phone made a sound akin to a tiny bell tolling.

"That's Tim – DI Yates – wondering if I'm ready to leave. And I haven't asked you about Mrs Grummett yet! I'm sorry for sidetracking you."

"It was my fault as much as yours. But I don't think you'll need to keep DI Yates waiting very long. Ruby Grummett is traumatised, I'm certain of that, but she's probably not as ill as

she'd have us believe: she's not a very good actress. But obviously she's sustained a bad shock and for a woman of her age, especially one who's not particularly fit, that could be serious, potentially fatal. We're therefore keeping her under sedation for thirty-six hours. We'll start to lower the dose tomorrow. You should be able to interview her on Thursday, if she's still here."

"I see," said Juliet. "Thank you. Why do you think she's pretending to be worse than she is?"

"It's not unusual in cases where patients feel guilty or think they might be held to account – for negligence or breaking the law, for example. They could be trying to get sympathy, buy time to think about how to defend themselves, perhaps even persuade a doctor that they're unfit to testify or to be tried."

"That makes sense. And we can't guarantee that Mrs Grummett won't have to stand trial. It'll depend on the coroner's report. Is there any news of the lorry driver?"

"He's still in a coma. I'd say his chances of surviving are no more than 50 – 50. As for his leading a normal life again, I think it's unlikely."

"That and the mate's death is a terrible thing for her to have on her conscience."

"You're right. But I think there's something else going on as well."

"What do you mean?"

"That husband of hers. I'm sure he's devoted to her, but it seems to me he has another reason for haunting the ward all the time. He doesn't want to let her out of his sight, which is absurd, because at the moment she's not going anywhere."

"What do you make of that?"

"I'm not sure. If I could hazard a guess, I'd say it's because he's afraid she'll say something that he doesn't want anyone else to hear. He may have put her up to faking how bad she is.

On the other hand, she may be faking so that she doesn't have to listen to him."

The tiny bell in Juliet's phone tolled again.

"Thank you," she said. "I must go. I'll come back on Thursday, and I'll send you those details. Hopefully you'll know by then if you can come to hear the folklorist. Will you let me know if you decide to discharge Mrs Grummett early?"

"Certainly." Louise Butler held out her hand. Juliet took it and shook it warmly.

Chapter Fourteen

DURING THE DRIVE back to Spalding, Tim didn't quiz Juliet about her meeting with Louise Butler. She told him that Dr Butler had said they wouldn't be able to return until Thursday to interview Ruby Grummett, which he found exasperating until she mentioned that the doctor had also said she suspected Ruby of malingering. He sensed they had an ally in the doctor and should be patient. He didn't ask Juliet why it had taken her so long to find out such a small amount of information. The meeting had certainly improved her mood; he reminded himself to tell Katrin.

Verity Tandy was waiting to see him. She'd gained in self-confidence since joining the Spalding team, but she was still a bit frightened of Tim himself. She was seated at one of the hot desks outside his office and stood to meet him when she saw him.

"Do you have a moment, sir?"

"Of course," he replied. Juliet smiled briefly at Verity and disappeared. He gestured at the door to his office. "Come in."

Verity sat down self-consciously at the small table in the room. Tim took the other seat.

"Is it about your visit to the school?"

"Yes. There was something that worried me about it."

"People who hang around school kids for no good reason are always worrying," said Tim. "What does the headmaster

think – it *is* a man, isn't it? I think I met him a couple of years ago."

"He's the main problem," said Verity. "He just doesn't seem to be taking the incident seriously. I've interviewed the three girls and I think they genuinely found this man creepy, though they were too inhibited by the head's presence to say so. Once they'd gone, he was quite scathing about the mother who'd been with them when they saw the man. More or less told me she was a trouble-maker who was likely to embroider the facts."

"He may have a point about that. How did the woman herself strike you?"

"I haven't met her yet. She'd left by the time I arrived. He's given me her address."

"Well, make sure you do see her. It may just be a clash of personalities; or you may think he's right once you've met her. I must say that when I met Alex Cooper he seemed 100 per cent committed to the welfare of the pupils."

"Who did you say, sir?"

"Alex Cooper. That's the name of the head, isn't it?"

"No, sir. His name's Richard Lennard."

"Really? I must be out of date, then. I wonder what happened to Alex Cooper. He was very go-ahead."

"In that case, he's probably moved on to something more ambitious."

"I suppose you're right. Anyway, ignore what I just said. I don't know Richard Lennard, so follow your own hunch."

"Thank you, sir. How's Mrs Grummett?"

"Heavily sedated but swinging the lead, on good authority. No, I take that back – and please don't repeat it. It's confidential. The doctor who's looking after her thinks she may be putting it on a bit, either to gain sympathy or stall for time. There's something about that whole case that doesn't stack up.

If the accident itself was straightforward, the Grummett family certainly isn't. And yet – you must forgive me for sounding prejudiced – they're hardly bright enough to carry off any kind of scam. Except for the daughter – the younger one, that is. Heaven only knows how they managed to have a child like her."

"That reminds me. One of the girls I interviewed at Spalding High School looked just like her."

"Really? Astonishing, considering how distinctive she is. But perhaps it was a relative."

"I don't think so. At any rate, this girl – her name is Cassandra Knipes – just looked blank when I called her Philippa. If she's related to a Philippa, she'd surely have told me."

"Both unusual names, aren't they? I suppose they could have common ancestors without knowing. That's probably true of a lot of people round here."

"I suppose so," said Verity doubtfully.

"Anyway," said Tim, standing up, "make an appointment to see the mother – what's her name, incidentally?"

"Mrs Painter. Her daughter's name's Leonora."

"Another fancy name! Was she a blonde bombshell, too?"

Verity was visibly taken aback for a moment.

"I'm sorry, that sounded sexist. I didn't mean it to."

She smiled.

"Since you ask, sir, Leonora was the ugly duckling of the three. Overweight, and with rather a nervous, fussy manner."

"The mother's probably awful, then."

"I sympathise with the girl," said Verity sternly. "She reminds me of myself at her age."

Damn, thought Tim. I let myself in for that one.

"Yes, well, arrange to see the mother as soon as you can, and keep me informed."

Chapter Fifteen

FIVE YEARS AGO, the Lover gave me a television. I was grateful. I'd been shut away from the world for so long, I feared I might no longer understand it. Ariadne must understand, too. We both watch it avidly, especially when he's away. He forbids us the news or current affairs programmes. I don't know why. If anyone noticed when he took me, they gave up the search long ago: it will have been assumed that I'd simply gone home. I'd never have gone home in a thousand years, but how were they to know?

The Lover's been jumpy for the past few days. It's partly because Ariadne's still ill. He only hits her rarely, but always when she's sick; it infuriates him when either of us is sick. I had to grab hold of his arm when he lashed out again. He let it fall, but he made it quite clear that she needs to pull herself together, and quickly. She seems a little better today. Perhaps she's making an effort.

She doesn't speak well, but I understand her. I know that she wants to watch the television. I look at my watch. It's nearly 6 p.m. Time for the news. I consider carefully. He's been here once already: it would be unlike him to visit again. If he catches us watching the news we'll be punished. I look at Ariadne. She's ill and struggling bravely to fight it. I turn on the television. I keep the sound right down.

The national news is never very interesting – stories about

Europe are what I like best. But I love the local news. I put up with all the dull stuff about the budget, the banks, redundancies and the NHS until eventually the picture sequence that announces Look East flashes by. I resist the temptation to turn up the volume. If I hear him coming I shall switch off quickly.

There's been a railway accident. There are pictures of a derailed train and a half-demolished house. Firemen and policemen are being interviewed. I don't think it happened today: the people being interviewed are too calm. The commentator stands and speaks alone for a few seconds before offering the microphone to a short young woman standing beside him. She has a fat pasty face and curly hair. She says a few words before the picture widens to take in another young woman, someone who's still a girl. The camera focuses on her face and I gasp. I scrabble for the remote control, desperate to turn up the sound, but I'm so upset I'm fumbling and before I can hear her voice she's gone. I know that girl. She is mine.

Ariadne makes a noise. Her eyes are wide with alarm. I realise that tears are streaming down my face. I may have cried out. She puts her hands over her ears. She's very agitated. I must prevent her from having an attack. I must help her to get better quickly, before he comes back. I kill the news. I take my daughter in my arms.

Chapter Sixteen

DRESSED IN SKINNY jeans and a shocking pink shirt tied at the waist to reveal her midriff, Mrs Painter lit a cigarette from the one she already held in her hand as she opened the door to Verity. Stringy orange hair with black roots fell to her shoulders. Her face was a mask of foundation and thick blue eye make-up, accentuated by a mass of harsh black eyeliner and mascara. Beneath the maquillage, her cheeks were hollow, her eye sockets ringed with bruise-like shadows that the cosmetics couldn't quite conceal. Candelabra earrings hung from her ears. At first glance, she might have been mistaken for a woman in her mid-30s, but Verity thought she was probably much older. She was as skinny as her daughter was plump.

She'd agreed to see Verity that afternoon and said she would prefer it if the interview could take place before Leonora came home from school. She lived in a cottage on the Cowbit road. It was of a type quite common locally: clad in rough grey rendering, with windows in the eaves and a small porch at the front. It probably dated from the mid-nineteenth century. When Verity stepped inside she found herself in a narrow corridor that ran the length of the house.

"In here," said Mrs Painter, leading the way to a kitchen that might once have been pleasantly bucolic but was now in need of some loving care, not to mention a good scrub. It was poky and dark and smelt of past cooking. Mrs Painter

sat down at the table and continued her manoeuvres with the cigarettes while gesturing at a second chair. Lifting it out, Verity discovered it was piled high with an assorted jumble of mail.

"Just chuck that lot on the floor," said Mrs Painter, her new smoke now clamped between her lips. She shifted her own position nervily. Verity caught a flash of glitter. Mrs Painter's navel had been pierced and adorned with a crystal hanging from a silver ring.

"Thank you for seeing me at such short notice, Mrs Painter," said Verity. "Mr Lennard told me you have a job. I hope you haven't taken time off specially."

"My name's Cindy," the woman said, meeting her eye briefly before allowing her gaze to wander off towards the wall cabinets. "Makes me feel a hundred years old if you call me that." She flicked ash into a tea-cup. "I work at Barker's the Florists in Crowland, making up wreaths and commercial flower arrangements. It's flexible: we don't have much on at the moment. I can work longer hours when we're busy."

"Do you always take Leonora to school?"

"Not usually. She can get the bus. She missed it this morning."

"So you don't do the school run every day?"

"I've just said, haven't I? I'm beginning to wonder if I should, though. If there's strange men hanging about."

"I'd like you to tell me about the incident this morning, in as much detail as you can remember. I've seen the three girls. They were quite vague about why you thought the man might be dangerous."

Cindy Painter exhaled.

"Are you surprised? They don't have the sense they was born with when they get to that age. Think everything's funny and forget all the stuff we taught them when they was nippers.

Especially when they get together." She tapped the fingers of her left hand rhythmically on the top of the table.

Verity smiled encouragingly.

"So, you drove Leonora in your car down Stonegate and parked outside the school. Was it right outside the school, or some way up the road?"

"It was right outside, but on the opposite side of the street. Her name's Leo, by the way. No-one uses Leonora."

Verity didn't want to introduce a complication by contradicting her. As it was, getting a coherent statement from the woman was like extracting hen's teeth.

"And she was still in the car when you saw the man?"

"Yes. She was about to get out. Messing about collecting her stuff, she was. I told her to get a move on as she'd already made me late."

"But even though you were having a conversation with her, you still saw the man?"

"Yes."

"What was he doing?"

"Nothing. Just looking over the school wall, watching the kids as they got off the buses and that."

"That's all?"

"No. Leo's two friends came walking down the road and he turned round then and started staring at them."

"Did he speak to them?"

"I don't think so, no. But he was giving me the creeps and they didn't look very happy, either. So I opened the car door and told them to get in for a few minutes."

"That was nice of you, when you were already late."

"Yes, well, anyone'd do what they could with a pervert about, wouldn't they?" Cindy Painter fidgeted in her chair again, but Verity could tell the compliment had pleased her. "You want a cup of tea or something?"

"No, thanks. It's kind of you to ask. Were the girls frightened when they got into the car?"

"Not that frightened. They didn't like the look of him, though."

"Did you see his face?"

"Not clearly. They may have done. They was closer than we was."

"Could you describe his build?"

"He was very small, almost girlish. He was wearing a mac, so it was hard to see much else. And a cap."

"Can you remember any more about his clothes?"

"The mac was grubby. Beige, but grubby. I don't know about the cap. It was certainly darker than the mac."

"And you didn't know him?"

Cindy Painter rolled her eyes.

"I'd hardly have reported him if I had, would I?"

"I see. Well, I've written down what you've told me, Mrs . . . Cindy. I'd be grateful if you could read through the statement and sign it if you agree that it's accurate."

She took the sheet of paper from Verity and worked through it slowly, pointing at each word and repeating it to herself under her breath. Verity had the impression that she found reading difficult. After some time, she signed it and lit another cigarette.

"That's all correct."

"Thank you," said Verity. "We're going to make sure a police car regularly patrols the area around the school. Let me know if you see the man again. Here's my card."

"There's one other thing," said Cindy Painter, drawing fiercely on the cigarette.

"Yes?"

"That Mr Lennard. He didn't believe me. He thought I'd just invented the whole thing."

"I don't think he thought you'd invented it, Cindy. He perhaps thought you'd attached more significance to the man's being there than he would have done. But he wasn't there."

"No, he wasn't," she agreed vigorously. "So he shouldn't cast aspersions." She narrowed her eyes. "Do you think he's up to the job?"

"I don't have an opinion on that," said Verity. "I'm sure he must be well-respected in the teaching profession. Otherwise he wouldn't have the job."

"Yes, well, I'll show you out, then," Cindy said, unconvinced.

Chapter Seventeen

STILL IN A good mood after her meeting with Louise Butler, Juliet had started work on the cold case folder. The files contained details of more than a dozen unsolved cases, some of which were relatively recent, some almost as old as herself. One related to a burglary at a jeweller's shop which had happened when Juliet was a very young trainee. She remembered it well, though she'd been too junior to be assigned to the case. The owner's wife had been hit with a crowbar and left blind and mentally impaired. Another contained details of the murder of a market stallholder who'd been attacked very early one morning almost twenty years before while loading her van from a lock-up shed. At first, her death had been assumed the result of a botched robbery, but various circumstances – the fact that the woman had been alone when she was usually accompanied and the lack of defensive wounds – had caused the police to suspect her sister, who was also her business partner. The sister had produced an alibi, however, and there was no proof that she'd been present. Juliet lifted out the notes to see if the police had kept evidence that might be re-tested for DNA. She saw that the victim's clothes and the hammer that she'd been hit with were preserved at the police warehouse. They'd last been tested for DNA five years ago and yielded nothing that could be used. Juliet didn't think that the testing techniques had become significantly more sensitive in the in-

tervening period, but she removed the documents from the file and put them to one side. She'd check this was correct before she dismissed the idea.

More than half the files covered missing persons cases. Most were assumed to have left home because they wanted to, possibly deliberately changing identity to get away from relatives or start a completely new life. Not much resource was devoted to investigating 'mispers' unless they were minors or suspicious circumstances suggested they'd come to harm. Juliet always hated having to tell worried parents or desolate partners that the police had no reason to believe their loved one had not left home of their own volition and therefore his or her disappearance would not be investigated further. Even so, she knew that this was the correct way of handling it: most would either turn up again eventually or successfully build the new life for themselves they wanted. Sometimes they were located but refused to get in touch with those they'd left. It wasn't just that the police didn't have the bandwidth to deal with all of them: it was also a question of the individual's right not to be pestered. Juliet sighed.

She worked methodically through the folder, lifting out the mispers files as she went and spreading them in a semi-circle round her desk, each with the first page open so she could see their photographs. There were eight altogether. Several belonged to women who'd been victims of domestic abuse. There was a chance they'd finally summoned up the courage to leave their partners and make a new start, but Juliet knew this was unlikely. Without exception, their expressions looked squashed and totally defeated, as if they were no longer able to think for themselves. Their files had been kept because the police thought it more probable they'd been murdered than escaped. Two of the more recent files were of local villains – not known to each other as far as she could see – who'd

absconded from an open prison that had gained some notoriety in the Press because of its higher-than-average number of runaways. Juliet was just lifting out the last mispers file when Tim appeared and looked over her shoulder.

"Not mispers," he said. "Don't bother to pursue any of those: you'll be on a hiding to nothing. Unless you can help to re-arrest those two," he added, indicating the two cons.

"I often wish we had more time to give mispers," said Juliet. "Probably more of them need our help than we think."

"I'm sure you're right, but we could spend all our time on them and, for every two we find, at least one won't thank us for it. Obviously if we think they may have been murdered, that's a different matter."

"Several of these were battered wives."

"Well," Tim frowned, "read the files carefully and see if there are any leads that have been missed, or real possibilities that more advanced forensics can throw up something new. Otherwise, if you must focus on mispers, I'd stick with the cons. We'll get a few brownie points if we can catch them. Surely all the cases in that file aren't mispers?"

"They aren't," said Juliet. "There's the Bourne jewellery burglary . . ."

"Oh, for God's sake don't dig that up again. It's been re-opened at least three times. Dreadful that the victim was so badly hurt, but we'll never solve it. I'm convinced it was a professional contract job. Thieves from London or Birmingham, probably. None of the jewellery ever showed up with any of the local fences. Complete waste of time even trying to work out where it went."

Juliet snorted.

"You sound more like Superintendent Thornton every day," she said. "Do you really want me to work on any of these?"

"If I'm entirely honest, no," said Tim. "But Thornton's re-

quested it and you know his hands are tied. He's got to be seen to be doing something. He'd prefer you just to focus on one, if you can. Have a look at the cons. We know some of their cronies and we can . . . PC Tandy, did you manage to meet the schoolgirl's mother?"

"Yes, sir," said Verity, drawing closer.

"Get anything useful?"

"Not really. Mr Lennard may be right about her. She wasn't a very impressive witness."

"Ah," said Tim. "That doesn't surprise me. I thought as much." Juliet threw Verity a quick smile.

"I still think that his attitude was strange," said Verity defensively. "It didn't seem right for someone who's in charge of several hundred girls. It was almost like listening to one of those men who think that women who get raped deserve it."

"No-one's been raped, have they?"

"No, but . . ."

"I know what you mean," said Juliet. "You get a feeling sometimes. If I were you, I'd hold on to your first impression. It's an odd kind of attitude for someone in his position." She was opening the final mispers file as she spoke.

"Well, I'll leave you to it," said Tim airily. "Once Juliet gets started on intuition, I begin to feel lost."

Verity wasn't listening.

"Who's that?" she said.

"What? Oh, it's a misper. I haven't checked it out yet. Let's see. Helena Nurmi. An au pair from Finland who disappeared in 1993."

Tim stopped in his tracks.

"It doesn't sound promising," he said. "You can bet that she ran off with her boyfriend. Something like that, anyway. Don't bother with that one. Why are you so interested in her,

anyway?" he said, turning to Verity. He found the look on her face disconcerting. "Are you all right?"

"Yes," she said. "It's just that . . . she's the image of Philippa Grummett. And Cassandra Knipes."

"I'm beginning to think you've got this doppelganger idea on the brain. Let me have a look."

Juliet passed him the file. Tim scrutinised the photograph for a long moment.

"It's a poor photo," he said. "But you may have got something. Not many women have such very fair hair, do they? Not round here, anyway. Maybe it's not just an au pair's normal vanishing act."

Juliet took back the file.

"Helena Nurmi," she read. "Twenty years old. Disappeared in the summer of 1993, a few weeks before she was due to return home. The main suspect was Matthew Start, the son of her employer."

"Matthew Start! Any relation to Councillor Start?"

"I don't know, sir. It just says ' son of her employer'."

"Look into it, Juliet, will you? I don't like coincidences, as you know. And we've got at least two here. There's the Grummett daughter, Philippa, who apparently has a double and also looks like a woman who disappeared twenty years ago; and there's Councillor Start, at whose house that woman was possibly employed, who turned up at the Grummett house immediately after the accident yesterday. Check out the missing details, will you?"

"Yes, sir."

"What about the school prowler, sir?" said Verity. Juliet sensed she had spoken at least in part because she wanted Tim to acknowledge her quick-wittedness.

"What about him? You've just told me he was a figment of the parent's imagination."

"I didn't quite say that," said Verity carefully. "I think Mrs Painter may have over-reacted. But obviously there *was* someone hanging round the school."

"You promised to send a patrol car every so often, didn't you? We'll do it for a week, see if anything else happens. If not, we'll consider it an isolated incident."

Chapter Eighteen

MY LIFE RUNS within narrow limits because I am a prisoner, but I am sane. The Lover is not sane. Our daughter lives with me and I protect her. The Lover and I wage a perpetual bargain. These are the facts of my existence.

He brought me here when the sun was shining brightly. I could feel it on my neck as I stepped inside. He had given me flowers from the garden ("Impractical," he'd smiled, "but I want you to have them."); he'd paid for my ticket. The ticket was tucked in my purse, in the cheerful red handbag swinging from my shoulder. He'd given in, understood that I must move on. My suitcase was in his car; he was ready to take me to the station. He just wanted me to see his new office, then we would leave. I crossed the threshold. He kissed me quickly as he closed the door behind us, heaving it shut with a clang. There were thick blinds at the windows, all of them tight shut.

I was afraid. I didn't want him to close the door. I caught a glimpse of his face as he blotted out the sunlight. It was set, determined. No longer smiling. Then we were in total blackness.

"Put on the light," I said. I was terrified. He knows I can't bear the dark.

"In a minute," he said soothingly, but I heard the metallic edginess of control in his voice. He stroked my cheek. I shied away.

"Put on the light!" I shouted.

"Later," he said. His voice was harder now. Truculent, not wheedling. He pinched my arm. I shook him off, flung myself at the wall, scrabbling for a light switch. He grabbed me from behind, turned me round, hit my face with his open hand. His accuracy was uncanny. It was as if he could see me, even in the pitch black of this place. I covered my face with my hands.

"You stupid bitch! What do you think you're doing?"

I tried to shout out. The noise that came from my mouth was a strangled croak.

"Shut up!" he said grimly. He put his hand over my mouth. "If you don't shut your mouth, I'll shut it for you. Are you going to stop now?"

I nodded.

"Are you going to stop?" I could hear the rage.

"Yes," I said.

"Good. Give me your hands."

I stretched out my hands to where I thought he was standing. One was sticky with blood. The blow had made my nose bleed. He tied them tight, fastened them to something above my head. He grabbed my neck roughly so that I was facing him: I could feel his breath on my cheek, smell the mint that he'd been sucking. He was squeezing my neck. I thought he was going to throttle me. I jerked my head away.

"Hold still if you don't want me to hurt you. Then I'll put on the light."

I obeyed. I could cope if I could see.

He fastened something round my neck. It was made of rough leather. I heard a click, then a louder one. I could hear him cutting at something. My hands fell to my sides. He taped them behind my back. I heard him step away.

"I'm going now," he said. "I'm going to leave you to think about what you've done. You haven't been nice to me. You haven't been good. Be nice and good and I will love you."

"Put on the light!" I shrieked. "You promised me you'd put on the light!"

"All in good time." He wasn't trying to soothe me now. "Light is a privilege. It must be earned. You have to be good. Good and nice. Then I'll love you."

I heard him walk the few steps to the door. A narrow strip of sunlight glowed on my prison momentarily before it was extinguished. I was facing the wall. A smooth grey wall. It was featureless, except for a bracket that had been fastened to it at more or less the height of my neck. A chain was attached to the bracket and its other end to the halter around my neck.

Just before the door slammed shut I looked down at my feet and caught a glimpse of the scattered flowers and my red handbag lying beside them.

I don't know how long I remained standing there. I remember flushing with shame when I could stop myself from peeing no longer, feeling the urine trickle down my legs.

I could not banish my fear of darkness, but I alleviated the panic by closing my eyes and thinking of daylight. The chain restricted me too much to allow me to sit down, but I could lean my head against the wall. I think I even slept in short bursts, like a horse standing in its stall.

He kept me there for a very long time. I don't know how long, but it must have been for days. My terror at being in the darkness was eclipsed by the fierce certainty that I'd die of thirst. My lips swelled and my throat inside the halter felt like sandpaper. The halter chafed the skin on my neck until it was raw.

He came back when I could barely stand. I'd been thinking that if I fainted I would break my neck.

This time he turned on the light. As if I did not know who he was and he needed to protect his identity, he was wearing a balaclava and black leather gloves. I could see his eyes gleam-

ing through the slits of the helmet. He pulled back my head by the hair so that my face was upturned and thrust a baby's bottle between my lips. I sucked on the teat, drawing the water thirstily into my mouth. When I'd gulped a few mouthfuls he took it away again, pushing my head down so that the halter jarred my neck as he did so.

"Please!" I whispered, my voice hoarse and broken. "Please, more water!"

"Please, more water!" he mimicked in a little-girl voice. "Not yet. You're not being nice to me. And you stink!"

He removed the teat from the bottle, poured the rest of the water on the ground, and replaced the teat, reversing it and wedging it into the neck of the bottle as tenderly as if he were a young mother meticulously obeying the rules of hygiene she'd been taught. He turned to leave.

"Please, don't go!"

He shrugged and walked away, snapping off the light again as he went.

I had not cried until this point: I didn't want to jeopardise my sanity by giving way to the fear and the hopelessness. But now I screamed and howled like a wild animal in the darkness. After I'd sobbed myself into a frenzy, I gradually managed to calm down. The sobs died in judders. It was at that moment that I took a grip on myself and vowed that this man would not win. I'd be patient and canny and I would escape, or he would have to let me go. People would come looking for me. He would not dare to keep me here for long. First I must assert myself.

Only a few hours later he came again, this time with soup, which he tried to feed to me from the baby's bottle. I dashed it from his hand. He was still wearing the balaclava, but I saw his eyes register shock, even fear, before the anger eclipsed it. Without a word he abandoned me once more to the darkness.

I felt triumphant that I'd made him retreat, but it didn't last. I was hungry, cold, thirsty and filthy. He was trying to break me. I would have to find more intelligent ways of defying him if I wanted to survive.

More days yawned before he came back. He picked up the bottle from the floor, where it had lain many hours in the dirt and urine, and offered it to me. Obediently, I drank it. It was cold and fetid and made me vomit immediately. He told me that I disgusted him, abandoned me to the darkness again.

He returned sooner than I expected, switching on the light immediately. He was panicking about something. I knew the symptoms too well, could tell from his mannerisms, from his frenetic tone. What came next was a shock.

He undid the halter, shoving my head free. The raw skin on my neck bled as he drew the leather across it, but I barely noticed. I was jubilant. I was certain he was going to release me.

"I won't tell anyone," I said. "If you let me go, I promise never to say a word."

He wasn't wearing the balaclava. He cocked his head to one side, his eyes bright and amoral as a bird's.

"Let you go?" he said. "But I love you. You are mine. This is where you belong. I have to keep you safe."

He hadn't unbound my hands. He left them tied behind my back, shoving me to one side while he fiddled with something on the wall. A panel in the wall slid open, allowing me to see the thickness of the masonry. The rough edge of stone at the opening must have been fifteen inches wide.

He pushed me through it and followed, fiddling with the wall on the other side. The panel slid back, ponderous but unstoppable. There was a dim light set up high, almost touching the ceiling. Shadowily, it revealed a steep staircase that seemed to descend into the ground forever.

"Walk down the stairs."

I was dehydrated and weak from lack of food and sleep. It was hard to keep my balance with my hands tied behind my back.

"Move!"

I stumbled down the stairs as fast as I could. I tripped when I'd nearly reached the bottom and fell headlong, hitting my head on the ground.

"Get up!"

Dazed, I raised myself and pushed up on to my feet from a kneeling position. There was a door set in the wall next to the staircase. The Lover brushed past me and tapped on a metal panel.

Another huge door swung open. Light came pouring from the room beyond. He turned to me. He was smiling. His eyes were moist with some sentiment I couldn't read. I expected him to grab me again, hurl me into the room with a force made unnecessary by the fact that I could barely stand. Instead, he cut the ties and softly reached for one of my hands, which he held as he led me into the room like a husband introducing a bride to her new home.

The space beyond the door was large and sparsely but adequately furnished as a sitting room. There was a two-seater sofa and two wood-framed easy chairs, with a coffee table wedged between them. At the far end it narrowed into a passage, from which I could see other doors leading off. To the right of where I stood there was a small kitchenette, separated from the main room by a sort of breakfast bar. The place resembled a conventional flat, except for certain details: the ceiling was so low that I could barely stand upright and there were no windows. It was a prison.

Its significance burst upon me within seconds. I turned to him in panic. He was still clutching my hand. I tried to snatch

it away, but he tightened his grip. I couldn't stop my face twisting with fear.

"Let me go!" I said. "Please let me go! I'll do whatever you ask. Please don't leave me here."

His anger was immediate. He hit me across the face again.

"Don't you like it?" he said. "Ungrateful bitch! Do you know how long it's taken me to build this for you? How much money I've spent to make it nice for you?"

"It's . . . lovely. But I can't stay here. Please, I can't stay here. I need to be above ground. I need fresh air." I could hear myself gibbering.

He was gentle again.

"You just need to get used to it. You haven't seen it properly yet. Come with me and I'll show you."

He was nervous in those early days; his own fear made him volatile. I could smell it on him when he came. I thought they might be looking for me – or they might not. Either way, it was hopeless. No-one would find me here and I knew he'd kill me if I tried to escape and he caught me. They'd give up the search quite soon, too. I was an alien, a foreign national, in the country legally, but still part of the moving flotsam and jetsam of temporary workers. No roots. No friends. No privilege. No proper status.

What I most wanted, what above all I needed to keep my sanity, was not to be incarcerated in darkness. He'd tethered me like a beast again and the third time he returned he lifted my skirt and mounted me from behind as if I was an animal. I tried to resist him but he yanked the halter. I thought he'd abandon me to the darkness again or break my neck. He was yanking hard as he fucked me. I tried to think of the times when we'd been real lovers, when he'd been tender and I'd wanted him, had loved him. Even then, he'd sometimes fright-

ened me. The sex had been gentle and violent by turns. He'd seemed sometimes to love me, to love our love, and sometimes to be disgusted by it.

Now I was disgusted by the Lover and his sweaty probing body, but even more by the dirtiness that he made me suffer. He subjected me to every kind of squalor. When finally he unloosed the halter, I'd been tethered for a month, unable to wash, unable to cleanse myself of the detritus from his couplings, unable to eat or drink without his help, rough and sparse as it was, obliged to urinate and defecate where I stood. I had been trapped like a beast in a stall.

He had humiliated me to the point of non-endurance: or so I persuaded him. There was still left in me a spark, a small glimmer of humanity, a small vestige of the same defiance that I'd summoned to stand up to my stepfather. The Lover feared that more shame would kill me. He thought he'd broken me in and so he let me go. Not to return to the world outside, no. I knew that could never happen now. I might plead and cajole and promise: in fact, I did none of these things, knowing that he would never believe that I would keep silent.

And so the bargaining began. When he allowed me the freedom of my prison his foresight astonished me. He'd thought of everything. There was a shower and a toilet, a bed and a sitting area, a stove and cooking utensils. There was a store-cupboard containing dry goods and a small fridge, which was empty when first he showed it to me (he'd fed me on bread while I was tethered). He promised to fill it for me 'if you are good'. There was a suitcase containing my clothes and the other few possessions I'd brought to England. I almost laughed at his frugality. I suppose he had to get rid of this stuff somehow; and if he hadn't brought it here, it would have gone to waste, and he'd have had to buy me new things. Yet even though I knew he had no plans to release me, the thought that

he'd worked out a way of keeping me alive here day after day, month after month, year after year until the years turned into decades, still shocked me to the core. It was terrible to know that I might live out my life in this place until it ended.

Being good, being nice. That was what he continually exhorted, encouraged, pleaded for, demanded, shouted for, lashed out at me for, hurt me and left me in the dark for days for. Only he knew the rules for being good and nice. It was my duty to guess them – my duty to guess them, his right to have me guess. And so I bargained.

His headaches were bad. I'd massage his head. Someone had insulted him. I'd listen to the rigmarole, agree with him. This was risky: in the course of his narrative, he might see his own fault, take the other's side, smack me with the flat of his hand for being slow to see it myself. But of course I could not criticise. He wanted sex, I'd provide it. I'd try to make it reciprocal, encourage him to love me as well as using me. Sometimes it worked, sometimes it didn't. Sometimes I was his angel and his darling. Sometimes I was a fucking whore, to be used and punished as he pleased. The sex was violent then. And there was violence with no sex, visits when he just wanted to hurt me. He'd strike me across the face until it was swollen with bruises, make me lie on the floor so that he could stamp on my hands or knee me in the back. Worse were the times when he tried to destroy me by spitting his words of contempt, his handsome face hideously twisted, to make me despise myself, make me hate everything about me. He'd leave me then, often for several days. He hoped that I was writhing in the misery of self-loathing. His ultimate punishment was always the darkness.

Then he'd come back, perhaps with fresh food or books and, finally, the television. Then he'd be calmer, say that I wouldn't be imprisoned forever, that it was just a halfway

house until he could trust me to be with him, rely on me not to run away, consent to be his wife.

The wife business was a mirage right from the start. I'd refused to be his wife when I was free and he'd said this had insulted him so deeply he wouldn't ask again. Not only did he not ask, but after some years I realised he'd probably married since he'd incarcerated me. I first suspected when his visits began to follow a more regular pattern. Then after the television came I knew the time and I saw that his visits were mostly during the day and rarely coincided with conventional mealtimes. And once I caught a glimpse of a wedding ring, before he followed my gaze and hid his hand. He left precipitately.

I've said that my life is run as a bargain. It doesn't sound as if the deal works well for me, I know. But within my limits, I succeed. He hasn't withheld food for many months. He hasn't left us in darkness for even longer. He rarely beats Ariadne. When he beats me, at my own request he takes me into the bedroom so that although she can hear, she can't see what he is doing. We never have sex in front of her: I have insisted on that. And Ariadne and I are both still alive.

They may sound like small victories. Viewed by a free person, I suppose they are. But we are the ultimate captives. And our gaoler is a madman.

Chapter Nineteen

TIM WAS STANDING in his office with his back to the door, gazing abstractedly out of the window as he tried to talk on the telephone to Bob Grummett without losing his temper.

"I know you can't speak for Kayleigh, Mr Grummett," he said in a tensely patient voice, "but what I'm asking is when is it *likely* that I can see you both together? I'm going to visit your wife this morning. Dr Butler has okayed it. And I'd like to talk to you and your daughter before I return to Spalding, if possible. I'm also going to visit the site of the accident. Is Kayleigh still staying with Mr and Mrs Cushing?"

He waited in silence for what seemed like several minutes while Bob Grummett spun a long and convoluted story about the two girls not getting on. Exasperatingly, the story meandered to no conclusion, nor in the process of listening to it did Tim receive an answer to his question.

"Mr Grummett, could you tell me quite simply in words of one syllable at what time Kayleigh will be leaving work today, where she is going afterwards and whether you will yourself be available when she gets there? If I can't see you both then, my only alternative is to interview her while she's at work and ask you to accompany me."

"She won't like that!" The words leapt out of the phone so loud that Tim had to hold it away from his ear.

"What she likes is rather beside the point!" He shouted back, before remembering that if he didn't treat Kayleigh with kid gloves she or her father might try to claim that the police had not behaved with appropriate compassion.

Juliet entered the room at that moment and grimaced at Tim. He acknowledged her wry reproach.

"All right," he mouthed. "I'll try to be nice to him." He put the phone on 'speak'.

"What was that clicking noise?" Bob Grummett's disembodied voice was suspicious.

"DC Armstrong has just come into the room. She'll be accompanying me when I come to see you, so it's best that she hears what we're talking about now. Otherwise I'll only have to repeat it to her later."

"Is she the girl who came to the hospital with you last time?"

"I'm not sure that DC Armstrong would describe herself as a 'girl'."

"She seemed all right to me," said Bob Grummett reflectively. "She coming with you when you see Rube?"

"That is my intention," said Tim, realising too late that he sounded pompous. Juliet was looking amused – whether the cause was Bob Grummett or Tim himself, it was hard to tell.

"Rube'll probably get on better with her. Kayleigh, too. Not too keen on uniforms, you see. That female copper was a bit rough on her."

"If you mean . . ."

Juliet put her hand on Tim's arm. He let the sentence hang in mid-air for a few seconds and started again.

"Speaking of Kayleigh," he said, bracing himself once more, "can we try to establish a time at which to speak to you together today?"

"Won't it do when we're at the hospital?"

"It would 'do' fine, but Kayleigh'll be at work, won't she?"

"Not today, no. She'll be with her Mam. Got herself signed off sick with worry," said Bob Grummett proudly.

Tim passed his hand across his eyes, a 'heaven give me strength' look etched into his face.

Juliet moved further towards the phone.

"That's perfect, Mr Grummett," she said. "Thank you very much indeed. I'm sure the hospital will arrange somewhere quiet for us to talk with you and Kayleigh once we've seen Mrs Grummett – or we can find a space in the cafeteria. Shall we meet there in about an hour? Will Kayleigh be there then?"

"She's there now, I shouldn't wonder. Should I bring Mr Dixon with me?"

"Who's Mr Dixon?"

"My sollicingtor. Mr Yates said I should get one."

Tim groaned.

"That's up to you, Mr Grummett," said Juliet briskly. "We only want to ask you a few questions, but if you would feel more comfortable with Mr Dixon there, by all means ask him to attend. I'd advise that he only comes to the meeting with you and Kayleigh, though, and not to the ward. Otherwise, Mrs Grummett might be alarmed."

"You're right." Bob Grummett pondered for a long minute. "Perhaps best leave him out of it for now," he concluded. "He can always come along later."

"We'll see you at 11.30, then," said Juliet. "At the hospital."

"Aye." There came the sound of a receiver being noisily set down.

"Heaven give me strength!" Tim and Juliet chorused together, her voice a descant of mimicry. She burst out laughing. Tim was cross.

"It's all right for you," he said. "I'd been trying to get sense

out of him for at least a quarter of an hour before you came in."

"And probably still would be doing, if I hadn't."

"That's true. How did you manage to cut through all his crap?"

"I didn't," said Juliet. "I just let him know that I was on his side."

"Okay, I admit it. He's an old fool and I haven't got the patience to deal with it. Is he, though?"

"Is he what?"

"Is he an old fool, or is he actually being quite devious?"

"Are the two things mutually exclusive?"

"I'd have thought so, usually."

"Usually, perhaps, but I'd suggest not in his case. I think he's trying to be cagey and probably congratulates himself that he's keeping you guessing. But, as you've pointed out, he wasn't exactly at the front of the queue when the brains were being handed out. The question isn't whether he's trying to deceive you, though, it's why. Unless he's what local folk call 'ornery' – in which case he's just winding you up for the hell of it – he can have no good reason for being so obstructive all the time. Which suggests that he's hiding something."

"Agreed," said Tim. "Ask him what it is, will you, since you're such a lovely 'girl'? It'll save us a lot of time."

This time they were both laughing.

"Come on," said Tim. "Time for a coffee before we brave the Grummetts."

Juliet set off for the small office kitchen with Tim in her wake. She seemed to be enjoying life more than at any point since he'd known her, certainly since she'd recovered from the previous year's illness. He wondered if there was a reason for it.

Chapter Twenty

RUBY GRUMMETT WAS sitting up in bed, looking sallow and fractious. Her black boot-button eyes stared at the wall opposite, suffused with a kind of vacant hostility. She was wearing a high-necked nightdress with a lace yoke and long sleeves, made from a faded yellow fleecy material which had seen better days and did not flatter her complexion. No bare skin was visible except her face, about one inch of neck below her double chin and her hands, which lay inert on top of the sheets. Her fingers were swollen like sausages; her wedding ring was cutting cruelly into the flesh.

When Tim and Juliet entered the ward, her entire family was gathered round her bed. Bob sat nearest her, having wedged his chair between her locker and the top end of the bed, his face filled with concern. Kayleigh occupied a chair next to him. She was examining the contents of her handbag. Philippa was seated on the opposite side of the bed, her face invisible to the two police officers.

Ruby was not as agitated as she had been on the occasion of their previous visit, but she was obviously preoccupied with something. Her muttered words, though not inaudible, were incomprehensible. Kayleigh raised her head to take a long look at her mother and giggled inconsequentially. Philippa threw her sister a glance of utter contempt before bowing her head to scrutinise her fingernails. Bob stretched out his hand to take

one of Ruby's. She didn't push him away, but she seemed not to relish the gesture, either. They both raised their heads as they became aware of Tim and Juliet, their hands fixed in an awkward clasp above the bedclothes.

"Mrs Grummett," said Tim, giving her a smile that he intended to be reassuring, "it's good to see you sitting up. How are you feeling?"

"How do you think?" she countered. "I aren't well. It's the shock."

"Of course," said Tim, as sympathetically as he could, "but Dr Butler tells me that you're a strong woman. She has every hope you'll make a full recovery."

"What does *she* know? She's only a slip of a lass."

Tim felt Juliet bridle. He smiled inwardly. For once, he sensed he had the upper hand in the dealing-with-awkward-witnesses stakes.

"Dr Butler's more experienced than she may appear," said Tim firmly, "and she's been taking good care of you. She hasn't let me disturb you until today."

"What do you want?" The black eyes snapped suspiciously. Even Bob Grummett could see that his wife wasn't handling the situation well.

"Now, Rube," he admonished. "They're only doing their job. You're going to have to talk to them sooner or later. Might as well be now."

She fixed her stare on the wall opposite. Only one of the beds on that side of the ward was occupied, by an old woman in the last stages of dementia. Most of the time she lay prone against her pillows, but at intervals she called out in a harsh, guttural voice, thrashing her arms and legs about under the bedclothes.

"Nurse! Nurse! Bring me a rag. I need to wipe my nose. Bring me a rag. I fancy some bread and milk, Ma."

"The Lord help me if I end up like her," said Ruby Grummett, with more feeling than Tim had seen her show so far. He was about to reassure her when Juliet cut in, her voice smooth and cool. Silently Tim prayed that he alone would be able to detect her underlying anger; Juliet had disguised it, but none too well. Its intensity surprised him.

"There's no reason why you should, Mrs Grummett," said Juliet. "As DI Yates says, you're a strong woman. You'll recover. And you have nothing to fear from us. We just need you to answer a few questions – the sort of questions we'd ask anyone who'd been witness to an accident."

"I was more than a witness," Ruby Grummett muttered, almost to herself.

"A little more than a witness, I agree," said Juliet in the same even no-nonsense voice. "But that doesn't mean we're pre-judging you in any way."

"No, but you might. Accidents cost a lot. The bosses will be wanting their scapegoat."

"Allow me to reassure you that we have no interest in the railway company 'bosses', except to help the Crown Prosecution Service to gauge how far they are culpable." Juliet and Tim glanced across simultaneously at Bob Grummett, who had his head cocked on one side, a puzzled expression on his face. "I mean," Juliet added, "that if anyone is to blame for the accident – and it is far from clear that anyone is – the actions of all those who could possibly be held to blame will be examined without prejudice. That is, without any kind of bias or favouritism," she concluded, seeing Bob look blank again. She realised that Tim was right about the man. He probably possessed the intelligence of the average eight-year-old, but she saw little evidence of the native cunning that Tim also claimed to detect.

"They'll pin it on me, you can be sure of that," said Ruby grimly.

"Now, Mam," said Kayleigh, "Don't jump to conclusions. It'll be all right, you'll see. Did I tell you when I saw Mrs Cushing this morning that she asked to be remembered to you?"

"Much good that will do me," said Ruby, muttering once again.

"She's been very good to us since the accident. We owe her a lot." It was Philippa, speaking for the first time.

"Who asked you what you thought?" said Kayleigh, evidently emboldened by her proximity to Bob. "No-one cares what you think."

Philippa did not retaliate. Instead she resumed her inspection of her hands. Tim decided that he and Juliet had listened long enough to this unpleasant family interchange.

"Mrs Grummett, we really do need to make some progress now. I'm happy to interview you here with your family present, or to ask them to give us a few minutes on our own with you. Which would you prefer?"

The round black eyes searched his face.

"Bob can stay," Ruby said at length. "Send the girls away. This is nothing to do with them."

"But . . ."

"Shut UP, Kayleigh, and just go, will you? Take your sister for a cup of tea or something." From the awkward position in which he was sitting, Bob craned his neck urgently towards Tim, evidently seeking approval for this instruction. Tim nodded briefly.

"There's a café on the second floor," he said. "If you'd wait there, DC Armstrong and I would like to meet you briefly to ask you a few questions before we leave."

"Both of us?" enquired Philippa.

"No, just your sister," said Tim, observing with interest her almost imperceptible flinching from the term. "But it would be nice if you'd keep her company until we come."

"I don't need *her* company," said Kayleigh rudely.

Philippa managed a weak smile of embarrassment.

"I'll come anyway."

"May we sit down?" said Tim to Ruby Grummett, after her daughters had gone.

"I can't stop you, can I? Besides, you make me that nervy, standing up," she added in a more reasonable tone, evidently responding to some pressure from Bob's hand. Turning back to face Ruby again, Juliet noticed her snatch angrily away from his grasp.

Tim took the chair that had been vacated by Kayleigh, moving it further from Bob and nearer to the end of the bed. Juliet sat in Philippa's chair. Seated, they had to look up at Ruby, propped high as she was by her nest of pillows and the elaborate back rest contraption. This change in their relative positions seemed to give her some confidence.

"What do you want me to do now?"

"We want to make this as easy as possible for you, Mrs Grummett. Just describe the events leading up to the accident, and what you can remember of the accident itself, as simply and clearly as possible."

"Starting from when? When Fred came knocking at the door?"

"That would be helpf . . ." Tim began.

"A little bit before that," Juliet cut in. "I think you should start at the point that you realised the Skegness train was late and tell us what you decided to do about it."

Ruby's little black eyes widened briefly in alarm.

"Do about it? What could I do about it? It was delayed by the fog. Besides, I don't do the timetables."

"I know that. But you have to check on the timetables, don't you?"

"What do you mean?"

"I mean it's your job to make sure the people who use the crossing and the passengers on the trains are kept safe. So you have to know when the trains are scheduled to come and also if they're going to be late."

"Yes."

"So my question is," Juliet said, making her voice as soft and friendly as possible, "when did you start to think about the Skegness train? Was it before Fred knocked on the door, or at that moment? Did you in fact think about the Skegness train at all?"

"Of course I did!" Ruby's indignation sounded genuine. "The fog was that bad I was surprised any trains were running that day. The Skegnesser hadn't passed by and I thought it must've been cancelled, so I was going for my bath. I was getting undressed when Fred came. I didn't expect to see him, either. He said he'd been working on an emergency."

"So you put on your dressing gown and went out to open the gates for him?"

"Yes."

"Did you take any precautions at that point?"

"What do you mean?"

"Did you take steps to check that the line was clear?"

"I checked the system in the box. It wasn't registering anything."

"Do you always rely on the system?"

Ruby didn't answer. She passed the back of her hand across her forehead.

"Don't pick on her!" said Bob Grummett threateningly. Juliet ignored him, continuing to speak directly to his wife.

"Mrs Grummett, I assure you I'm not trying to bully you, or distress you more than I can help. But we do need to find out the exact circumstances of the accident. Has any maintenance work ever been carried out on the system?"

Ruby paused for a long minute. Juliet could almost see the woman calculating her get-out story.

"No, I don't think so. Do you, Bob?"

He shrugged, slower on the uptake than she.

"I'm away from the house more than you are. The folk from HQ usually come to see you, not me."

"We can check to see if there are maintenance records," said Juliet quickly.

"Has there always been a telephone at the crossing since you became the crossing keeper?"

"Yes," said Bob, "they've been standard for a long time."

"Thank you," said Juliet. "Could you let Mrs Grummett answer for herself, please? Mrs Grummett, what was the telephone used for?"

"Instructions from HQ, mostly. For emergencies or delays: anything unusual, really. Owt they couldn't deal with through the mail."

"Would severe fog, causing major delays and some trains being cancelled, be regarded as an emergency?"

"Of course it would."

"Did you receive a call from HQ advising you that the Skegness train had been delayed?"

"No." The reply came quickly, full of relief and indignation.

"You're quite sure?"

"Of course I'm sure!"

"But you yourself were aware of how dense the fog was and the likelihood it would cause delays?"

"Yes, but I've told you: I assumed the train had been cancelled."

"Did you try to contact HQ yourself, to find out if this was the case?"

"I . . . No. I don't, normally. I wait for them to contact me."

"But as the fog was so bad, wouldn't it have made sense to call HQ on this occasion? Did the idea not even cross your mind?"

"Yes. It did. But Fred was in a hurry. He had to get back home."

"He hasn't got there yet, has he?" It was Tim's intervention that broke the spell of calm concentration that Juliet had managed to weave around Ruby Grummett. The woman's face crumpled. Juliet shot Tim a look of exasperation.

"I think we'd better leave it there for now," she said.

"Yes," said Bob Grummett truculently. "I think you better had."

"I'm sorry Mrs Grummett is upset," said Tim, "Perhaps we can come back after we've talked to Kayleigh. Are you coming with us?"

"I'll catch you up later," said Bob gruffly.

"OK if we start without you?"

"Yes, you carry on – the sooner we get all this over the better." Bob's voice was filled with fatigue.

He seemed to have forgotten his insistence that he should be present when they spoke to his daughter.

They found Kayleigh and Philippa sitting in the café, which was otherwise almost deserted. The only other occupants were an old man who was hunched, dozing, on one of a row of chairs ranged along the back of the room and a young woman nursing a baby near the door. She looked up expectantly when Juliet and Tim entered, her bright smile turning to a frown of disappointment. Neither she nor the old man, assuming he was conscious, was within earshot of the two girls.

Kayleigh was in the act of polishing off a cream-filled doughnut. Licking her fingers, she sucked enthusiastically at the straw of the tall plastic cup in front of her, plumbing the

depths of the drink. An untouched cup of tea stood before Philippa. When she saw the two detectives approaching, she picked up a spoon and began to stir it nervously.

"Hi," Tim grinned. "Can we join you? Anyone want a top-up?"

Kayleigh held out the plastic cup.

"I'll have another one of those."

"Sure. What was it?"

"A frappuccino."

"I'd like a cup of tea," said Juliet. She turned to Philippa. "Would you like us to get you one? Yours looks as if it's gone cold."

Philippa shook her head.

"I didn't really want it."

Tim went to buy the drinks. Kayleigh took a mobile phone from her handbag and started playing with it.

"How is Mam?" said Philippa. "Did she manage to answer your questions?"

"Some of them," Juliet replied. "We're taking it gently with her. We'll go back and finish the interview later."

Philippa nodded.

"She's bound to feel guilty about the accident. That doesn't mean it was her fault, does it?"

"No," said Juliet. "Her feelings have nothing to do with who's to blame. But I shouldn't really be talking to you about it."

Tim returned with three cups of tea, a frappuccino and two small packets of biscuits, which he opened and tipped out on to a plate. He offered it around. Juliet and Kayleigh each took one.

"I understand you've got the day off work," he said to Kayleigh conversationally.

"Yeah, I'm off sick. It's all been a bit much." She didn't take

her eyes off her mobile. She was playing a game of some kind.

"I understand," said Tim. Juliet noted approvingly that there wasn't even a trace of irony in his voice. "What about you, Philippa? Did your Dad decide to keep you off school today?"

"No," she said. "We've all got the day off. It's a teachers' training day. I could've stayed with Alice, but Mrs Cushing thought I ought to come and see Mam."

"Didn't you want to see her?"

Philippa gave a small shrug.

"I didn't know whether she'd want to see me."

"Probably didn't, you're such a misery," said Kayleigh, suddenly looking up from her game. Tim turned to her.

"I'm sorry you're feeling the strain of all this," he said to her. "It's not surprising. But I do need to ask you a few questions, too."

Kayleigh's fat face closed tight. She screwed up her eyes so much that they almost disappeared. Philippa, meanwhile, was looking at Kayleigh with some curiosity.

"What's Kayleigh done?" she said. "She was at work at the time of the accident, wasn't she?"

"I haven't done anything," said Kayleigh plaintively. She sounded like a guilty child protesting her innocence in a playground dispute. "I only asked Uncle Ivan to get me pyjama case for me, that's all."

"You mean that pink dog thing?"

"Just because you don't like it . . ."

"Why the pyjama case, Kayleigh?" Juliet asked. "Of all the things that you might have asked your uncle to save from the house, why that? Did it mean something special?"

Kayleigh's face was a blank.

"She always made a great fuss if I tried to go near it," said Philippa. "I don't know why. It's an ugly thing."

"It was a present from Auntie Elsie."

"Kayleigh," said Juliet. "What was in the pyjama case? Do you remember?"

"Yes." The answer came reluctantly. The voice was sullen.

"Go on. Tell me what was in it."

"Some money."

"How much money?"

"I don't know."

"You don't expect them to believe . . ." Philippa began.

"Please, Philippa, I'm talking to Kayleigh." Kayleigh flashed her sister a look of triumph.

"Yes, you shut up, Miss Goody-Two-Shoes."

"Kayleigh, concentrate, please. It was a lot of money, wasn't it?"

Kayleigh nodded.

"Do you have any idea how much?"

She shook her head. Her lip was wobbling.

"I don't want to get into trouble for it. I was only asked to look after it. They promised me an iPad this time . . ." The tears were coursing down her cheeks now.

"Haven't you done enough today without upsetting her as well?"

Bob Grummett was standing over them, his pink scalp shining under the café striplights, the grey tufts of hair sticking up around his ears.

"Mr Grummett! Can I get you some tea?" said Tim.

"I don't want your tea and neither do they. Have you finished with Kayleigh now?"

"Not quite," said Tim firmly. "Kayleigh, who asked you to look after the money? Was it your Dad? Your Uncle Ivan?"

Kayleigh squinted at her father fearfully through a camouflage of tears.

"I don't know," she said, reverting to her primary school act.

"OK," said Juliet. "It's all right, Kayleigh." She turned suddenly to Bob Grummett.

"Mr Grummett, did you give Kayleigh the money to look after?"

"I don't know what you're talking about," he blustered. "I want to see Mr Dixon! I want to see my sollicingtor!"

The woman behind the cafeteria counter was frowning at the commotion.

"All right, Mr Grummett," said Tim. "As you wish. We'll set up a formal interview for you and Kayleigh with your solicitor present. Perhaps you could give DC Armstrong his details. And we would still like to see Mrs Grummett again before we leave, if you think she's calmer again now."

Bob Grummett rolled puzzled eyes at Tim, angry like a cornered bull.

"You can't see her without Mr Dixon," he said. "Or any of my family. We don't trust you."

Taking her cue from her father's tone, Kayleigh stopped snivelling and thrust her nose in the air. She stood up, her bulk bumping against the table, slopping tea into saucers.

"Come on, Dad," she said, taking his arm. "Let's get out of here."

Her father got to his feet more slowly, as if dazed by his own behaviour.

"Here's my card," said Juliet. "I'd be grateful if you'd call me today to tell me how to contact your solicitor."

He scraped the card clumsily from the surface of the table.

"We'll be going then," he said lamely. "Philippa, you come too."

He and Kayleigh turned to leave. Philippa hung back.

"Was there really a lot of money in the pyjama case?" she asked Juliet.

"Yes, there was."

"How much?"

"I can't tell you that. But a lot."

"But we're always so hard up," said Philippa in wonder. "Always. We've never got two pennies to rub together. Where could the money have come from?"

"That's one of the things we need to know," said Juliet. "If you find out any more about it, will you tell us?"

"Come *on*, Philippa!" Bob called.

Chapter Twenty-One

TIM WAS IN a bad mood as he drove away from the Pilgrim Hospital with Juliet silent at his side. Well-acquainted with all the shades of his character, Juliet knew when it was worth trying to jog him out of his rare periods of low spirits and when, as now, it was best to let him surface from the depths on his own.

Juliet could understand his anger. Tim had been bested by both Bob Grummett and his daughter Kayleigh, undoubtedly two of the most gormless characters she'd ever encountered, and he'd failed to get a full statement from Ruby Grummett, although three days had now passed since the railway accident. It would be practically impossible to obtain a complete and candid account from Ruby now: her already imperfect recollection of events was likely genuinely to grow hazier, not to mention the spin that she'd have had time to add to it. And if Bob's lawyer was to be present at future interviews he would no doubt abet Ruby in further airbrushing.

She glanced across at the speedometer. Tim was driving at almost 50 mph in a built-up area, his mind obviously elsewhere. She was about to warn him when he suddenly slowed and took an unfamiliar turning.

"Where are you going?" she asked.

"I thought I'd told you," he said ungraciously. "I want to stop off at the Grummetts' lodge."

"Is the safety work still going on?"

"That's my understanding. The Boston police photographed the scene as soon as they could. They've taken witness statements from the train driver and the people travelling in the first carriages. The fire brigade's tidied up and a local firm's been hired to make the building stable. It'll have to be demolished, of course, but not until the coroner's reached his verdict. If the conclusions he draws cause the CPS to launch a prosecution, the lodge will have to be left as it is until after the trial. You know what judges are like: always game for going walkabout with juries. You can just see them turning up there in a bus, can't you, all wearing safety boots and hard hats and pretending to be serious when actually they're having a jolly good time?" Tim chuckled bitterly.

"Do you think there *will* be a trial?"

Tim took one hand off the wheel to make an awkward 'How should I know?' gesture.

"Difficult to tell. I'd say there's more than a fifty-fifty chance that the CPS thinks it can make a charge of criminal negligence stick. Possibly even manslaughter. I'm far from sure that Ruby Grummett will be the defendant, though; or, if she is, she won't be in the dock on her own. From what she's told us so far, the railway company is at least equally to blame."

"I'm sure they'll put forward a different view, most likely backed up by better solicitors than this Mr Dixon."

"You're right, but unless they can prove that someone called her to tell her that train had been delayed, she's got a strong defence. And that warning system sounds as if it was faulty. Whether it was regularly maintained or not is something else they'll have to prove.

"You think she'll get off, then?"

"I wouldn't put it as high as that. I think she'll probably escape a custodial sentence, but not be allowed to go back

to her job. The railway company will likely come to an arrangement with her, pay her some kind of 'without prejudice' compensation in return for taking early retirement. There may be a genuine need for it, if her mind's been affected. All they'd require is a doctor's opinion that she's no longer mentally competent." He looked across at Juliet. Her expression was uncharacteristically stern, her features set in a look of distaste or disapproval. "You don't seem to wish Ruby Grummett well," he added. "Do you have a reason, other than that the whole family seems quite unpleasant?"

"Well, there's that, of course, although you almost pity them for not knowing any better. They're like throwbacks from the past: they're how you imagine totally uneducated peasants behaved in the nineteenth century. All except Philippa. She's one of the reasons why I've taken a dislike to Ruby, although it's putting it a bit strongly to say that I 'don't wish her well'. They slight that girl and I'm not sure why. I also think that Ruby knows she's guilty, at least partly, and she's determined not to admit it. And I agree that Bob has something else to hide as well, almost certainly connected with the money. He's probably committed a relatively trivial offence that he doesn't want us to find out about. It beggars belief that he's an accomplished criminal. The whole Grummett charade makes me feel uneasy."

"I know what you mean. There's something shifty about them and the way they act. The uncle and aunt are as bad; the uncle seems to be in on the money scam, whatever it is. We're just approaching Dowdyke Road now," he added. "Surely that poor copper hasn't been standing here for the whole of the past three days." He lowered his window. "PC Walton, good morning."

"Good afternoon, sir." Tim looked at his watch. It was almost 1.30 p.m.

"Good *afternoon*, I should have said. It's been a busy morning. This is DC Armstrong. I was just saying to her that I hope you haven't been standing here ever since I last saw you?"

"No, sir. There'll be lorries up and down to remove some of the stuff from the wrecked house today. I've been sent to make sure they get through all right, and to discourage sightseers."

"It's a bit cold for sightseers, isn't it?"

"You'd be surprised. The Press came back again yesterday. And another gentleman. I let him through, as he said he was a family friend."

"What was his name?"

"I didn't ask him, sir. I think it might have been Councillor Start again, but I didn't get a good look at him the other night." The constable was immediately on his guard, afraid that he'd not asked enough questions. Tim was momentarily irritated, but realised that Walton was not party to the information that he and Juliet had just been discussing.

"Never mind. If I carry on, am I going to get stuck, or in the way of one of these lorries you've been telling us about?"

"I don't think so, not at the moment. There's a salvage truck there now. It's taking out what it can for the family and the builders are helping. My guess is they'll be busy until dark."

"Thank you," said Tim. He raised the window. The policeman stood back and gave him a half-salute.

"Damn! Damn! Damn!" said Tim, as they drove away.

"What's the matter?"

"I wanted to see the house more or less as it was at the time of the accident. There's no chance of that now. I should have come here yesterday. I was just trying to save time by fitting it in with a visit to the hospital."

"But you said they'll have to leave it until the coroner's seen it."

"Yes. But it's not the building I'm interested in: it's the Grummetts' stuff. I wanted to know if there was anything else there that might suggest some kind of criminal activity."

"If the salvage lorry's still there, you could look through the things it's collected before it goes."

"That's true. Technically, I need a warrant to do that, but who's going to know?"

As they rounded the final bend before the railway crossing, they saw a small knot of figures standing by the side of the road. Two of them, clad in donkey jackets, were obviously workmen. One of the others, although he had his back to them, was immediately recognisable as the diminutive Peter Cushing. He raised his head as he heard their car approach and gesticulated excitedly at his nearest companion, who turned to look in their direction.

"Jesus!" muttered Tim. "Ivan Grummett's here. That's all I need."

"I haven't met him yet," said Juliet. "Which one is he?"

"The scruffy one standing next to the little guy. He's got a pronounced squint. The little guy's Cushing, the neighbour who took in Philippa and Kayleigh Grummett on the night of the accident. Presumably the other two are salvage men."

The heavy lifting machinery was still in place. As Tim parked his car opposite the group of men the arm of a mobile crane was whirring over their heads. It nosed down gently to the ruined building and delivered its cargo of an upright steel joist to a man who was waiting to receive it. Juliet watched, fascinated.

"It's amazing how delicately they can handle those huge machines," she said.

"What?" asked Tim, snapping free from his seat belt. "Oh, yes, I see what you mean. Perhaps you could help me by handling this lot delicately. I'm afraid I might not manage it."

He stepped out of the car rapidly and strode over to the men, all of whom were now watching him.

"Mr Grummett!" he said, holding out his hand. "This is DC Juliet Armstrong." Juliet also offered her hand. Ivan Grummett took it, ignoring Tim's.

"I hadn't expected to see you here today," continued Tim brightly.

"I could say the same about you," Ivan replied, regarding him balefully. "My brother asked me to come, to make sure his things aren't damaged any further. And that we get out as much as we can," he added meaningfully. The two workmen bristled. Like Tim, they probably assumed that he was doubting their honesty.

"Most of it's too damaged to be of much use again," said one of them with a sort of offhand glee. "What hasn't been broken or crushed is as like as not covered in shit."

"Quite," said Tim.

"Mr Grummett," said Juliet in a low, confidential tone, "Would you mind if we took a look at your brother's things, before they're taken away? We'd like to see if they can give us any further clues about the accident. I assume they're being put into storage?"

"Supposed to be," said the same workman. "But I don't think the boss will agree to store some of this, unless the crates are sealed and wrapped in plastic. It's contaminated, see. As I've just been saying." He flicked a triumphant grin at Ivan.

"Bob thought this might happen," said Ivan, looking with loathing at the workman.

"Perhaps we can help," said Juliet. "We could have the items collected and taken to a police warehouse until Mr Grummett is ready to sift through them to see what he wants to keep. How many crates are there?"

"We haven't finished yet," said the workman, "but we've

filled six crates already. My guess is there'll be another couple. We can't lift out the large pieces of furniture. They're proper wedged in, for one thing, and if we try to free them, we might cause a further collapse, for another."

Slowly and deliberately, Ivan Grummett took out a pipe and lit it. He drew on it equally slowly, regarding them all malevolently with his good eye. The other eye was screwed shut against the smoke. There was an uncomfortable silence which he made no attempt to break.

"What do you think, Mr Grummett?" said Juliet finally.

"I don't have Bob's permission for you to take owt away. I ought to ask him first."

"By all means. But he's busy with your sister-in-law at the moment. She's still not well. If you can't get hold of him today, the crates might be left out in the open overnight. And there won't be a police guard on the road after the work's stopped for the day. Wouldn't it be better to let us take the crates away now? We can give you a receipt for them."

"Yes," said Tim. "And we'll promise not to open them until we get your brother's permission."

Ivan drew on his pipe again, probably mulling over any pitfalls to this proposition. He was smarter than Bob, thought Tim, but not by much.

"I suppose it's the best option. Best of a bad bunch, that is," he conceded. "All right, you take them, then, but this goes with me." He pointed at the ground in front of him. A square black tin box, fastened with a padlock, had been placed there. Tim and Juliet hadn't noticed it before.

"What's that?" asked Tim.

"It's a box," said Ivan.

"DI Yates means to ask what's in it," said Juliet, anticipating Tim's sigh of frustration.

"Papers. That's all. No interest to you."

"What sort of papers, Mr Grummett?"

"Marriage lines, employment contracts, birth certificates, that sort of thing," said Ivan. "Family papers. As I've said, of no interest outside the family."

"We'd like . . ."

"We'll have to ask you to sign a receipt for those," said Juliet quickly, anticipating that Tim was about to refuse to let Ivan take the box.

"All right."

"Well, if you'll excuse us, we've got to get back to work," said the other workman, speaking for the first time. He and his mate wandered off.

"If you'll come with me, Mr Grummett, we can sort out the receipt in the comfort of the car," said Juliet. Tim was left standing with Peter Cushing.

"It's good of you and your wife to look after Philippa and Kayleigh."

"Oh, it's nothing, really," the small man's deep voice boomed out. "We're neighbours. And it's only Philippa now: Kayleigh's going to stay with her uncle and aunt from tonight. Besides, we're chapel, and since Fred Start's made it his business to help, we thought we ought to, too. Bob and Ruby are chapel as well – a bit lapsed, maybe."

Tim wasn't listening to the final sentence.

"Do you mean Councillor Start?" he asked. "Has he been here again?"

"Yesterday," replied Peter Cushing. "Why? Does it matter?"

"No, not at all," said Tim. "Did he want anything specific?"

"He came up here to check on the work that's going on and then dropped by to see the girls. Philippa's always been a bit of a favourite with him."

"Really? Does she like him, too?"

"I've no idea."

"Thank you, Mr Cushing. You've been very helpful."

"Would you like to come back for some tea?"

"Not today. But this won't be our last visit; we'll take up your kind offer another time."

"Of course. Any time. Just knock on the door."

Tim became aware of Juliet standing at his elbow and at the same moment heard the sound of an engine revving. He watched Ivan Grummett drive away, the exhaust of his battered old pick-up filling the atmosphere with fumes.

"Well done," Tim said with heavy sarcasm. "There goes the only evidence we're likely to find to help us understand what's going on here. In the meantime, you've managed to saddle the force with approximately eight large crates of, and I quote, 'contaminated' household goods."

Juliet looked crestfallen, but only for a minute.

"It was worth a try," she said defiantly. "We might just have swung it."

"Yes, we might," Tim agreed, already repentant. "Besides," he added, grinning impishly for the first time that day, "there's a little job coming up for Andy Carstairs now. I'm sure a practically-minded person like him won't mind sifting his way through several crates of shit."

Chapter Twenty-Two

ANDY CARSTAIRS WAS just going off duty. He'd arranged to meet Jocelyn Greaves for a drink again, this time unchaperoned by his sister Shelagh. He was returning to his flat for a hot bath and a shave, with the intention of arriving at the pub just a couple of minutes late, to demonstrate he wasn't too keen.

Andy sometimes had a kind of foreboding about Tim: it was haunting him now, making him uneasy as he left the police station. Tim had an uncanny habit of calling Andy with an emergency at times when it was least convenient: Andy's disastrous first date with Jocelyn was only the latest of many instances. He walked briskly away from the station, as if putting distance between himself and his place of work could act as a talisman against Tim's catching up with him. He promised himself that once he was in the bathroom he would ignore any messages from his boss. After all, he wasn't supposed to be on call this evening. He hadn't made that mistake again.

Home for Andy was a spacious two-bedroomed flat situated over a ladies' dress agency in New Road. He reached it in a little less than ten minutes. He was just inserting his key into the lock when his mobile started to ring. Cursing, Andy let go of the key and removed the device from his pocket. Tim's number was flashing on the screen. Andy dithered for a

moment at the top of the short flight of steps to his flat, trying to summon the resolution not to answer.

"Carstairs," he said gruffly, in what he hoped was an off-putting tone.

"Is that you, Andy?" said Tim.

"Of course it's me."

"Doesn't sound like you. Are you going down with a cold?"

"I don't think so, no."

"Good. Because I've got a little job for you."

Andy groaned.

"There's no need to sound like that. Although I must admit that it isn't a very pleasant job."

"I don't care what sort of job it is. When do you want me to do it?"

"Not until tomorrow. You'll need to be able to see properly."

"Oh, that's all right then. Fine. What is it?"

"I've just been at the Grummetts' house. Their possessions are being removed. I'd like someone to sift through them, see if there's anything there that would explain why they were keeping such a large sum of money in the house."

"Fine. But don't you need a warrant? And where's all this stuff being kept?"

"Juliet persuaded Bob Grummett's brother to let us take it to the police warehouse. Technically speaking, we do need a warrant; we'll get one if necessary. The important thing is that Ivan Grummett's accepted a receipt for it, so we've got it for a while before Bob can object. But I want it searched as quickly as possible, because Bob's appointed a solicitor and no doubt the guy'll raise all sorts of objections as soon as he gets involved."

"OK," said Andy. "I'll do it tomorrow."

"Great. You'll need protective clothing. And a face mask."

"Why? Oh, shit, don't tell me. I can guess."

"Shit's about right," said Tim, laughing. "Make sure you get kitted out properly. I don't want you going down with typhoid or something."

"Don't worry, I will. Who's the solicitor, by the way?"

"Someone called Dixon. Do you know of a solicitor by that name?"

"Doesn't ring any bells. Which law firm does he work for?"

"I don't know. But if Bob Grummett appointed him, I can't imagine he'll be a hot shot. Talking about hot, why were you so annoyed when you first answered the phone? Not got a hot date lined up, have you?"

"As a matter of fact . . ."

Andy stopped trying to speak. Tim was too busy laughing to listen to him.

"Good guess, wasn't it," he said at length.

"I don't see what's so funny about it. Presumably you went on a few dates yourself before you met Katrin – and before she married you, come to that. For your information, you fucked up my first date with this girl by calling me out to Sutterton Dowdyke the other day when I was supposed to be meeting her for a drink."

"I'm sorry about that. Who is she, anyway?"

Tim's question was studiedly offhand, but Andy could hear the curiosity crackling through his boss's words.

"No-one you know. She's a journalist."

"Well, I've met a few of those. Try me."

"Jocelyn Greaves."

"No, can't say I've heard of her. Well, enjoy your evening. And thanks for going to look through the Grummetts' crates tomorrow. I know you won't enjoy it, but it's got to be done."

"Goodnight, sir," said Andy. "Since when was enjoyment an objective of this job?" he muttered to himself, as he stuffed

the phone back in his pocket. He looked at his watch. He still had plenty of time.

Andy had suggested that he and Jocelyn should meet at The Punch Bowl at seven p.m. for a quick drink before going on to the Chinese restaurant in The Crescent. True to his plan, he walked into the pub when the minute hand on his watch was precisely halfway between 7 p.m. and 7.05 p.m. Looking around, he was gratified to see that Jocelyn had already arrived. She was seated at a small table near the door, casually but carefully dressed in a black sweater and black jeans, which were tucked into knee-length black boots. Her only jewellery was a rather spectacular pair of dangly silver earrings which shone against her dark hair. She'd hung her red duffle coat on the back of the chair. Andy noted that she'd already bought herself a glass of red wine.

She smiled as soon as she caught his eye.

"Let me buy you a drink," she said, standing up as she spoke.

"No need. I can get it. Would you like another?"

"I asked first. And I've barely touched this one. Not trying to get me drunk, are you?" She grinned.

Belatedly Andy realised he should try to be a little more gracious. He grinned back.

"Sorry. I'm a bit out of practice. A pint of real ale would hit the spot nicely, thanks. Any kind they've got."

She nodded and gestured at the chair opposite hers at the table before heading for the bar.

When she returned with his drink, they chatted for a few minutes about general topics before she asked the inevitable question.

"Tell me a bit more about your job. What exactly is it that you're doing – that you're working on at the moment, I mean?

Detective work has always intrigued me."

"I'm sure you know that I'm not allowed to give you much detail about what I'm doing. You must have met detectives before, in your own line of work. "

"Some. Mainly private ones, actually."

"Really? I've never met one, to my recollection."

"Generally they're quite seedy. Not like the real thing."

"I'll take that as a compliment. But how did you manage to meet them? I'd be astonished if they were thick on the ground in South Lincolnshire."

Jocelyn laughed, throwing back her head. Her silver earrings shimmered with the movement.

"Oh, you'd be surprised. But perhaps you didn't know that I was a *freelance* journalist."

"I think I did know that. Shelagh probably told me. What does that have to do with it?"

"It means I get to choose what I write about. Oh, I cover the bread and butter stuff as well, to pay the bills. But investigative journalism is what really interests me."

"You mean you pay people to tell you stuff?"

"Certainly not! You're confusing it with chequebook journalism."

"What is it, then?"

"It's about producing a dossier of evidence, a series of articles or a documentary, on a topic that it's in the public interest to expose."

Andy looked sceptical.

"'In the public interest': that's a much over-used phrase. It's the sort of thing that politicians' wives say when they spill the beans after they've been covering up for their husbands for years and suddenly get ditched for a newer model."

"Well, I admit that's an example of the type of witness I might want to interview. But I usually have a more serious

purpose than helping vindictive women wreak revenge."

"Kill me with it, then. What are *you* working on at the moment?"

"Like you, I can't give too much away. But I will tell you it involves the High School."

"You'd better be careful about what you're saying. If you know about anything that puts the students or the teachers at the school at risk, you have a legal obligation to tell the police."

Jocelyn's face paled. Andy realised that he'd sounded sterner than he intended.

"Sorry. I put that badly. And I'm sure you wouldn't jeopardise the safety of anyone at the school."

"You're right, I wouldn't. But I can see I'm going to have to tell you about it now. It concerns how the school premises are sometimes being used in the evenings and at weekends. I've found out that a sort of Masonic lodge is holding meetings there."

"The Masons aren't my cup of tea, but as far as I know there's nothing illegal about their activities, even though they are a bit too secretive for my liking. Pillars of society, some of them."

"I didn't say they were Masons. It's a group or club that models itself on the Masons, probably to give themselves bogus respectability."

Andy's curiosity was whetted in spite of himself.

"What's the name of this group?"

"I'm not sure. I've heard they call themselves 'The Bricklayers' and also 'The Doll-makers'. The first might suggest an analogy to 'Masons'. I hate to think what the second could imply."

"It all sounds very tenuous," said Andy. "Who told you they were holding meetings at the school?"

"No-one did. I overheard one of them inviting someone. He said they were meeting at the school one Saturday morning. You don't believe me, do you? You think this all sounds too far-fetched." She looked unhappy. Andy saw that she'd folded her hands together. Now she was clasping and unclasping her fingers nervously.

"I don't disbelieve you, but I can see nothing sinister about that. Lots of schools hire out their facilities. Some of them have to, as a return for money given by the government for refurbishment schemes."

"I know that. But this other person asked how they could be sure they wouldn't be disturbed and Councillor Start told them that the head-teacher had spelt out to all the students in no uncertain terms that they must stay away on that day. Those were the words he used – 'in no uncertain terms'."

"Councillor Start!"

"Yes. He's big in the group. In fact, I think he might be their leader. Do you know him? I realise he's quite a local bigwig. That's partly why I'd like to expose him, if he *is* engaged in something shady."

"I only met him very recently. But the circumstances were . . . unusual."

"Can you tell me about it, or is it confidential?"

She looked up at him earnestly. Andy thought she seemed sincere rather than fanatical. He kept reminding himself that he didn't know this woman, but he didn't think she was a nutter or trying to fabricate something out of nothing. He fervently wanted to believe she was genuine. He hesitated only for a few seconds.

"It was on Tuesday. I was called to the scene of the railway accident at Sutterton Dowdyke. You must have heard about it."

She nodded.

"I arrived several hours after the accident. My boss and several other members of the force were there, as well as the fire brigade. And Councillor Start. A policeman had been posted at the end of the road and told not to let anyone through, but somehow he'd blagged his way in. He disappeared suddenly once we became aware of him – just melted away."

"What was he doing there?"

"I've no idea. He didn't explain himself. As far as I could see, it was something to do with looking after the daughters of the crossing-keeper, who'd been taken to hospital. Or one of them, anyway, the younger of the two. The lodge house was completely destroyed in the accident, so I suppose that was fair enough. He professed to be a family friend. On the other hand, a neighbour had already taken the girl under his wing."

"What was the neighbour's name?"

"Cushing. Peter Cushing, I think. Funny little man with a deep voice."

Jocelyn stared at him without replying. Now she did look manic, he thought. He resolved to change the subject.

"Anyway," he said, "we've talked enough shop for one evening and probably both said more than we should have into the bargain. Let's talk about something else."

"All right," said Jocelyn abstractedly. "I'm sorry for keeping on about it. But there's just one other thing."

"Go on, then. After that, I insist that you tell me how many brothers and sisters you have, what your favourite colour is and which football team you support. And whether you come here often."

She managed a wan smile.

"Peter Cushing's another one of the group I mentioned," she said.

Chapter Twenty-Three

ARIADNE IS SICK. She's been unable to eat for days. She can drink only droplets of water from a spoon. She lies on her bed all day, sweating and shivering. I'm spending all my energy on caring for her, but when the oxygen levels drop I have to lie down myself until the faintness passes.

The poor air distresses Ariadne. Her breathing is shallow; each gasp she takes rasps her chest and throat. She has a pain in her back. She points to it often, her face twisted in agony. I think there's something wrong with her kidneys. When she's hot, her heart races; when she's cold, the heartbeat is faint. When she opens her eyes, they don't focus. There's a morbidity about her skin, a green clamminess that terrifies me.

The Lover has not visited for a week. Ariadne's illness will make him angry when he comes. She can no longer pretend that she's well. He'll scream she's faking it to annoy him and he'll hit her, or hit me. But we need him because there's almost no food left. She's not eating, but I have to, so that I can care for her. The food he brings is shoddy: the packets of dried goods are frequently split, the perishable items glutinous with decay. Still, it is food. Today there is only flour, which I mix with water and try to fry.

I smooth back the sweat-streak hair from Ariadne's brow. She is heartbreakingly fair. Damp curls corkscrew on her forehead. Are the others still as blonde, or have the Lincolnshire

winters darkened their tresses and coarsened their skin, so fine and unblemished when they were taken away?

Ariadne stirs, sighs, seems to sink deeper into her torpor. It's not like sleep: she's not unconscious. I sense she is creeping towards the end. I can't let her die.

There was too much death in my old life. I mean 'murder', but shy from the word. I am a murderer. Can murder ever be justified? It's a thought I still wrestle with every day. The Lover is a monster, but I've taken a life. He takes only liberty, dignity and joy.

Ariadne is lying in an unnatural position. The terrible rattling in her chest and throat begins again.

I say, "You'll be better soon."

It's a lie. All of this is a lie. I've always known I would find the strength and courage to break free from it one day. Now that Ariadne is sick, she's shown me the way. Feverishly elated, I know what I must do.

Chapter Twenty-Four

JULIET WAS SEARCHING for information on Councillor Start. She could find no criminal records for Start himself. His son, Matthew Start, had been convicted of speeding a few years previously, but the endorsement on his licence had almost expired. He hadn't been banned from driving. There were no other convictions. The cold case file said he'd been charged with rape, but there was no trace of this in the records. Destroyed after a time lapse, she guessed, if he'd been found not guilty.

A Google search brought up the website of Start Construction. Her trawl through it revealed a host of glossy pictures of newly-built houses and some aerial views of whole estates. There were internal shots of rooms in show houses, some pitifully small despite the benefit of a wide-angled lens. The company's strap-line was *Let Start's Kick-Start Your Dreams*. The Starts specialised in capitalising on the aspirations of young couples who could just about manage to raise the deposit for a mortgage.

She clicked a link on a sidebar marked 'Renovations and Improvements'. These photographs depicted quite a different order of building project. The illustrations were of substantial conservatories added to old farmhouses, tasteful extensions that segued almost seamlessly into the matched brick of period homes and, displayed as the jewel in the crown, several shots

of the cellar of a Victorian terrace house in Pinchbeck Road that had been converted into a leisure complex.

Other links provided advice on payment plans, insurance and how to obtain a quotation. The last page gave details, including mugshots, of the directors and key employees. Councillor Frederick Start was CEO of the company, Matthew Start its Managing Director. None of the other names or photos meant anything to Juliet except one: she noted with some curiosity that the Company Secretary was Mrs Veronica Start. Staring out at her was the pale and somewhat mournful face of someone whom she recognised but at first could not place. It came to her quite quickly: she'd seen the woman at the Fenland Folklore meeting she'd attended. She clicked on the biographical note against Mrs Start's name and read that 'Mrs Veronica Start teaches modern languages at Spalding High School and acts as part-time Company Secretary at Start Construction. She has been with Start's for seventeen years.'

This was interesting but revealed nothing exceptional. Juliet would hazard a guess that most of the local businesses big enough to boast a board of directors provided as many sinecures as they could to family members. But perhaps Matthew Start's wife really fulfilled the function of Company Secretary and was not the holder of a nominal role yielding a handsome salary. Veronica Start didn't look like a sponger.

Disappointed with what she could glean from the website, Juliet paged back to the Google listings. Scrolling through them with her practised eye, she skipped one about Councillor Start's support for the construction of a new wing at Oatfields, the council-run old people's home (he *would* support that, wouldn't he?) and another that praised him for being a generous sponsor of some of the runners in a half marathon designed to raise funds for the home. It was the fourth entry that caught her attention. It was a list of the governors of Spalding

High School. Clicking on the link led directly to the school's website and showed that Frederick Start was the chairman of the governors. He had occupied the role for so long that he must have first accepted it when Matthew was a schoolboy. Perhaps he also had a daughter – Juliet would check.

She'd like to know what Councillor Start got out of being a governor. Local kudos? He had that already, in spades. Respectability? A possible motive: there could be few more laudable pursuits than giving up your time to help the next generation. Nevertheless, she'd be on the look-out for any more tangible benefits the Councillor might be obtaining: feeding an unhealthy interest in young girls, for example.

None of the other first-page Google entries looked interesting. Most related to charities or local events supported by the Starts; one or two were legal notices posted by them about new building work they proposed to undertake. The second page contained more legal notices, most of them now several years old, and fewer reports of charity events.

Juliet enjoyed carrying out this kind of background search and she was extremely thorough. She looked at her watch. She had time to trawl through a few more pages. She'd worked almost to the bottom of the third page when her perseverance was rewarded. 'Councillor Start to lead The Bricklayers', she read. She clicked on the entry. It was a very short piece – little more than a caption – that had appeared in The Spalding Guardian about three years previously.

> Councillor Frederick Start, the well-known local builder, has assumed the role of Master of The Bricklayers. Councillor Start is a founding member of The Bricklayers, a charitable organisation.

The article was accompanied by a small grainy photograph that could have been of almost anyone.

She hadn't heard of The Bricklayers. A further Google search revealed nothing about them. Whoever they were, The Bricklayers certainly didn't court publicity. Yet more intriguing was that, although a 'charitable organisation', they weren't registered as a charity. She wondered if they acted as some kind of obscure trade association, but she was pretty sure that would make them eligible for charitable status. They seemed to model themselves on the Freemasons, but she knew Masons always registered their Lodges as charities. If The Bricklayers engaged in similar activities, you'd expect them to want to claim similar benefits; if they didn't, the most likely reason would be a desire for secrecy. Charities had to publish their constitutions or Trust Deeds and also their accounts. Perhaps The Bricklayers didn't need to eke out their funds and thought that refusing charitable status was a price worth paying for lack of transparency. From Juliet's point of view, such secrecy suggested they sailed close to the law, if they weren't actually breaking it. And since they were so secretive, why the casual little piece in the local press? Had this been an accident, or placed there for a specific reason?

Juliet was keen to investigate further, but knew she'd have to ask Tim to let her spend the time on it. As far as she could tell, The Bricklayers had nothing to do with Councillor Start's interest in Philippa Grummett. Nothing would irritate Tim more than if she let herself get sidetracked, despite the lip-service he always paid to her hunches. The Starts' connection with Spalding High School was possibly relevant, though still tenuous, given that Philippa didn't attend the school. Juliet wondered if Verity Tandy's conviction that Philippa had a double who was a pupil at the school could be significant, before swiftly berating herself for chasing hares. Still, the report that an un-

desirable had been seen hanging around the school had to be taken seriously and Verity's account of the headmaster's casual attitude to the sighting was unsettling. She herself hadn't much liked Richard Lennard when she'd heard him speak at Fenland Folklore.

"Ah, Armstrong, I was hoping you'd be back," said a familiar voice at her shoulder. "Can you give me a report on your progress with the cold case file? I need to feed something back pretty swiftly. As in 'today'," he added, gimlet-eyed, as Juliet turned to answer him.

Juliet swallowed uncomfortably.

"I've only been able to spend limited time on it so far, sir," she replied. "I've been helping DI Yates with the Sutterton Dowdyke case."

The Superintendent's brow darkened.

"Indeed. I thought I'd made it clear . . ."

"But I've been through the file and selected the case I think I should work on," she added quickly.

"Good, good. Write me a couple of paragraphs on it, will you?"

"It's the one about the . . ."

"I don't mind which one it is. Just write me a few sentences about why you think it should be reopened, including some estimate of our chances of solving it, and get it to me, will you? In, shall we say, half an hour?"

Chapter Twenty-Five

TIM ARRIVED HOME well before Sophia's bath time that evening. His frustration at not being able to interview either Ruby or Kayleigh Grummett until he had fixed an interview with the enigmatic Mr Dixon had its compensations. He'd get on to Dixon tomorrow, or perhaps ask Juliet to do it for him. If the solicitor turned out to be a clever bastard, Juliet would schmooze him better than Tim could.

"Hello! You're early," said Katrin, coming into the hall to meet him with Sophia in her arms. She lifted her face for a kiss.

"You sound disappointed," said Tim. "I thought I'd get back for bath time."

"It's always great when you do. It means I can cook properly and we get more evening to ourselves afterwards. As long as your bête noir doesn't pester you, that is."

"My what? Oh, you mean Thornton. It's not likely he'll ring tonight. I've reached stalemate in the Grummett case until I can involve their solicitor and as far as I know there's nothing else that Thornton wants me for at the moment, besides some cold cases that Juliet's working on. We haven't got very far with those, either."

"I want to believe you," said Katrin, "despite all my previous experiences!" She laughed. Tim stood back and regarded her appreciatively. She seemed to be regaining some of her old bounce and sparkle. He hoped it would last.

"Talking of Juliet, how is she? Did she cope with going back to the hospital the other day? I thought it might be a bit traumatic for her: she was so ill when she was admitted there last year."

"She's fine. I listened to what you said about the hospital and asked her if she was okay about it. It didn't seem to worry her at all. She was a bit tentative with the doctor who treated her, a woman called Louise Butler who by chance has also been looking after Ruby Grummett, but after they'd gone off for a meeting Juliet seemed happy about that as well."

"Oh, yes?" said Katrin archly. "Tell me more. I'm curious."

"I can't think why. It was a fairly routine meeting. I tried to get some sense out of Bob Grummett while she went off to talk to Dr Butler about how serious Ruby's illness was and, more to the point, when we'd get to interview Ruby about the accident. Dr Butler said today and we've now managed to get a few details from her. Also Bob Grummett has decided to involve a solicitor. Do you know him, by the way? His name's Dixon. I can't say I've ever come across him, which is odd. I thought I knew most of the lawyers working in this area."

"I don't know a solicitor called Dixon. I once met a barrister of that name. But surely someone like Bob Grummett wouldn't hire a barrister? It would be taking a sledgehammer to crack a nut. And it would cost an arm and a leg."

"You're full of old wise-woman sayings tonight!" Tim laughed. "But you're right. It's highly unlikely that this guy's a barrister. Bob wouldn't want to spend the money on him, even though he could afford it, if that money in the pyjama case belongs to him. Why were you so intrigued when I mentioned Louise Butler? You don't know *her*, do you?"

"No, but I've met her. She went to the funeral that was held for the skeletons found in the de Vries cellar last year. It wasn't all that long after Juliet came out of hospital. I went

to the funeral partly to support her, partly because I did some work on that case myself. I could have sworn there was more between Dr Butler and Juliet than just a professional relationship. They seemed to be having some kind of tiff, as well. Juliet was quite upset."

Tim's eyes widened in amazement.

"Are you saying that Juliet's gay? No, surely not. I don't believe it. She's never struck me as being in the least like a dyke. Besides, I thought she was sweet on the bloke next door. Nick something. I think he was a Greek."

Katrin exploded into a fit of giggles.

"Really, Tim, you're an utter disgrace! There's no shame in it if Juliet is gay. And what do you mean, that she 'isn't like a dyke'? What exactly do you think dykes are like? I'd say they probably come in all shapes and guises. And even you can't really believe that her neighbour is called Nick and that he's a Greek. I think his name is Nick, but I'm pretty certain he's Polish, or of Polish origins. Actually, he's probably British."

"Whatever," said Tim huffily. "I wasn't implying anything. You know how much I respect Juliet. I just don't think she's gay, that's all. Or Louise Butler, either. Let's change the subject. How did you come to meet this Dixon the barrister? What was he working on?"

"It was before I came to Lincolnshire. I was working in London – it was my first job as a police researcher – and I was trying to find out more about a cache of photographs that had been discovered."

"What sort of photographs?"

"Soft porn. They weren't illegal, but the Met thought the people distributing them were probably engaged in flogging the hard stuff, as well. Charlie Dixon was one of the people who was interviewed. He was representing a client, not there on his own account. I was just observing – I can't remember

why. Oh, yes, it was because the client was a woman. Dixon wanted another woman present in the room if his client was going to be interviewed by a man. We must have been short of WPCs at the time, because my boss – it was Terry – asked me to stand in."

"Was Dixon helpful?"

"Not in the slightest. He was the worst kind of lawyer from the police point of view – charm itself, but Teflon-coated when it came to protecting his client. She was a bit of a scrubber, to be honest, but she must have had some money behind her, because I understood Dixon was very expensive. I seem to recall that he got her off."

"God, I hope it isn't him, then," said Tim. "The background of the case you mention sounds interesting, though, especially the bit about the client coming from a rough background. They don't come much rougher than Bob Grummett and his family – all except the younger daughter that I told you about."

While they were talking, Sophia had fallen asleep in Katrin's arms. She suddenly startled and woke up in alarm. She began to yell.

"Give her to me," said Tim. "A bath will settle her. Then we can have a nice evening together. What's for supper?"

Chapter Twenty-Six

JULIET WAS PREPARING for her second Fenland Folklore meeting in four days. For the first meeting, she'd dressed carefully to look smart but inconspicuous. Tonight, she decided to wear something more flamboyant. Knowing it would be cold at Moose Hall, she chose a cashmere sweater with broad horizontal stripes in pastel colours and teamed it with black jeans.

The bell of Juliet's flat rang punctually at 6.15 p.m. She felt like a schoolgirl on her first date. When she opened the door, Louise was standing there laughing and holding out a bottle of wine. Her hair, normally tucked into a smooth chignon for work, flowed onto her shoulders.

"Friendship present," she said. "I thought you might like a glass later, when I bring you home. I'll only be able to have a small one myself, of course. I won't be breaking any laws!"

"Thank you," said Juliet, smiling. She'd never seen Louise like this before – giggly and light-hearted. At the hospital her demeanour was serious and dignified, almost austere. "Come in for a moment?"

"Better not," said Louise, glancing at her watch as Juliet took the wine. "We ought to go if we're to get there in time. You're looking very nice. I love that jumper."

Juliet felt her face flush. "I'll just grab my coat."

Seated in the semi-circle of hard chairs arranged round the

small dais at Moose Hall were mostly the same people Juliet had met previously. She couldn't see Richard Lennard. Perhaps he'd been held up, or maybe he was meeting the speaker somewhere before the meeting started.

The slight, very pale woman who'd been given a bit of a put-down by Richard Lennard on the last occasion left her seat and came across to talk to them.

"Hello," she said. "I'm Veronica Start. I was going to introduce myself to you on Monday, but you disappeared too quickly. You're Juliet Armstrong, aren't you? And I'm guessing this must be Dr Butler."

"Yes," said Juliet. "But how do you know?" She'd had no inkling that this woman was Councillor Start's daughter-in-law. She seemed not to be the kind of person who would agree to accept a sinecure. Perhaps she really did work for the company.

"No mystery. I'm the membership secretary. Yours are the only two applications we've had this month."

"Pleased to meet you," said Louise, holding out her hand. Juliet noted that she'd resumed her usual reserved manner.

"You're a teacher, I believe?" said Juliet. "At the High School?"

"Yes. I teach modern languages. Now it's my turn to ask you how you know!"

"There are some biographical details in the Fenland Folklore literature. So Richard Lennard is one of your colleagues?"

"Rather more than that! He's my boss." She pulled a self-deprecating face. "Talking of Richard, I can't think where he's got to. I knew he was taking Miss Ferguson for tea before the meeting, but they both should have arrived by now. Richard's usually a stickler for punctuality. Should we sit together?"

She led them to the far side of the horseshoe of chairs.

"I need to be able to get out," she explained. "Richard or Miss Ferguson might need my help."

The statement seemed to make her nervous. As Juliet and Louise squeezed past her somewhat awkwardly, she tucked one leg behind the other in a convoluted movement and removed a pair of spectacles from her handbag. As she did so, she pushed back the sleeves of her jumper. For a moment Juliet was transfixed by the revelation of an ugly red mark on her arm. She looked away, but not before Veronica Start had noticed. Pulling the sleeve down to her wrist, she gave a false little laugh.

"I see you've noticed my scald. Stupid of me! I was draining a pan of potatoes and managed to pour boiling water right over me."

Louise leaned over and gently pushed back the sleeve again.

"You should really go to A & E with that, or at least visit your GP," she said. "It looks nasty to me."

Again the mirthless laugh. "It'll be fine. I did it a couple of days ago. It's getting better now, honestly."

"Still . . ."

"I'll just go and see if everything's ready for coffee afterwards," said Veronica.

"That's not a scald," Louise whispered to Juliet. "It looks as if she's been burned with an iron to me."

"Do you mean it wasn't an accident?"

"Could have been, though if the edge of the burn shows the mark of the tip of the iron, as I think, it's pretty unlikely. And why try to hide what kind of accident it was, anyway?"

Juliet looked grave. Evidence of domestic abuse both distressed and infuriated her.

The audience remained unentertained for a further ten minutes, gradually growing more and more restless. One or two of its members had already left, disgruntled, when a dumpy

little woman came bursting in, looking cross and dishevelled. She was wearing a checked coat in some shaggy fabric and had a trilby-style hat pulled low over her forehead. As far as her bulk and build would allow her, she strode to the front of the hall and negotiated the considerable step-up to the podium.

"Is anyone in charge here?" she demanded. She removed the hat, showing a scarlet-veined face under flattened grey curls.

Veronica Start appeared from somewhere, looking anxious and appeasing.

"Miss Ferguson?" she said. "Didn't you manage to find Richard?"

"As you can see, I did not 'manage to find him', as you put it, because he wasn't there. Spalding station's not exactly Clapham Junction, is it? I would've seen him if he'd turned up."

"There must have been some mistake – perhaps it's my fault. I apologise."

"Well, I'm here now. I took a taxi in the end. And I'd like a cup of tea. Then I'll get on with my talk." She turned to the audience and said in a gentler voice. "I'm very sorry to have kept all you good people waiting."

While Veronica hurried away, Miss Ferguson unloaded a large sheaf of papers from the capacious bag that she carried and arranged them on the lectern. She placed a pair of wire-framed glasses at the end of her nose and humorously observed the audience over the top of them.

"There's no need to look so worried. Bark's worse than my bite. Since there doesn't seem to be anyone here to introduce me, I'll just get on with it. I'd like to talk to you about local place names. You have some truly extraordinary ones round here. You can hear the magic in them, can't you? Pode Hole, Gedney Drove End, Sutterton Dowdyke . . ."

It was an engaging talk: Mary Ferguson had soon captured the audience's attention. They hung on her words as she discussed the etymological roots of local place names and what they could disclose about the remote history of the area. Ten minutes after she'd begun to speak, almost everyone had forgotten about the small contretemps that had heralded her arrival and lost sight of the fact that Richard Lennard was still not present.

After she'd delivered the speaker's tea, Veronica Start returned to her seat. Turning away from Juliet, she took out her mobile and rapidly tapped out a series of text messages. Juliet pretended to be entirely absorbed in the lecture, but flicked a glance or three sideways. She guessed at Veronica's purpose. She wondered if whatever it was Richard Lennard was doing had either made him too preoccupied to remember the Fenland Folklore event or, since no reply seemed to be coming through, if it had separated him from his phone.

Veronica was finding it hard to concentrate on what Mary Ferguson was saying. She scribbled a few notes. Juliet was also having difficulty in paying attention, even though the subject was fascinating. She glanced at Louise, who had seemed a bit fidgety at first, but now the speaker had moved from place names based on topography to ones based on the names of early inhabitants, she was entirely engrossed.

The lecture lasted about three quarters of an hour. Veronica Start rose to her feet and was about to deliver a vote of thanks when Mary Ferguson, having taken a large gulp from her glass of water, asked if there were any questions. Immediately four or five hands shot up. Veronica's reaction of anguish mixed with impatience was almost palpable. She sighed, slid her mobile out of its pouch and pressed a few keys quickly. Juliet decided she must be re-sending one of the messages she'd composed earlier. Once more, there seemed to be no reply.

When Mary Ferguson had finally satisfied her audience's curiosity, she beamed at Veronica, her earlier disgruntlement evidently forgotten. Veronica stepped forward with alacrity.

"Miss Ferguson, on behalf of all the members of Fenland Folklore, I'd like to thank you for a most stimulating and fascinating account."

There was enthusiastic applause.

"And now, may I get you a taxi?" Veronica continued, Juliet thought with as much haste as she could get away with.

"Should we leave?" said Louise to Juliet. "I have to start work at six tomorrow morning and it's quite a long drive home."

Juliet agreed with only a slight hesitation. Most unusually, she found herself torn between her personal and professional life, but a moment's thought told her that she had no right to question Veronica Start about Richard Lennard's non-appearance and no rational reason for believing that he was out breaking the law.

"Yes," she said. "Let's go. We'll stay for coffee another time. As you say, it's getting late now. I'm sorry you have to take me home – it's a bit out of your way."

"I'm more than happy to do that. We're going to have a glass of wine together, remember?"

But once both were seated in Louise's car they seemed to run out of things to talk about. There was an awkward silence before Louise suddenly said, "Do you think that you should report that burn on Mrs Start's arm?"

"I'm not sure. What do you think? Can you be sure that it's the result of abuse?"

"Not one hundred per cent, no. But it's more likely than not. Do you know anything about her husband?"

"No, only that he works for his father, who's quite well-known around here. Councillor Start – I don't know if you've

met him? He owns a property development business."

"As it happens, I have met him, but only recently. He came to the hospital to visit Ruby Grummett when I was doing my ward rounds. An oily individual, a bit full of his own importance."

"I didn't know he'd been visiting her. I wonder . . ."

By this time, Louise had parked the car and they were climbing the steps to Juliet's first floor flat. Louise placed a hand gently on Juliet's arm.

"No more shop talk!" she said. "We're as bad as each other, but no more tonight. We've only got half an hour or so before I'll have to go. Let's talk about something pleasant."

Juliet was rummaging in her bag for her key.

"What do you suggest?" she asked as she opened the door.

"Ourselves, perhaps," Louise replied. "I only know a very little about you. I'd like to know a lot more."

As Juliet shut the world behind them she felt light, carefree. Rarely could she remember having experienced this combined sense of peace and trusting friendship. She blotted out completely all worries relating to her job. She even managed to forget – albeit temporarily – the figure who almost always loomed largest in her thoughts, DI Tim Yates.

Chapter Twenty-Seven

TIM WAS LATER to reflect on how glad he was that he'd knocked off early to spend that evening with Katrin, because the following morning all hell broke loose.

He and Katrin had had a nice supper together and watched a film afterwards. They'd gone to bed relatively early and slept well. Sophia didn't disturb them until nearly 7 a.m., which was almost a record. Tim decided that he'd bolster this successful foray into family life by indulging in a family breakfast. He was just tucking into a plate of muesli (with no more than a fleeting regret for the bacon sandwich he could have bought in the police canteen) when his mobile rang. It was Superintendent Thornton's number that came up on the screen. This was unusual: the Superintendent had but a passing acquaintance with his smartphone. He rarely used it to make calls and never to send e-mails, regarding it as a capricious instrument invented by the Devil. Tim concluded that Thornton must be on his way to work.

"Good Morning, Superintendent Thornton."

"Eh? How did you know it was me? No matter. There's something urgent I want you to deal with. It's those construction workers at the Sutterton Dowdyke cottage. They've found what they think are the remains of a baby."

"In the ruins of the *house*, sir?" Tim was incredulous.

"No, not the house. Otherwise presumably someone would

have found them before this. In an outhouse. A pigsty, I believe. Concealed, not buried. Under a trapdoor in the floor."

"Good God. Are they sure?"

"Sure of what? That it's a baby? No, of course not, but all the signs are there. Clothing, etcetera. And a baby's skeleton's not like that of any other small mammals, not ones that live in this country, anyway, wouldn't you say, Yates?"

"Yes, but . . ." Tim started the sentence without knowing how he was going to finish it. His sense of decency made him want to protest, but on the other hand he'd believe the Grummett brothers capable of any act of violence or depravity that didn't require much wit. There was no evidence they suffered from the inconveniences of either imagination or conscience.

"But what? Be quick, Yates, this contraption seems to be on the blink."

"Is your battery running low?"

"I've no idea. Can you get over there, Yates, immediately? You'll need to call forensics, too. And have it sealed off. And don't let the Press anywhere near. And you'd better call in this B . . ."

Superintendent Thornton's voice had become progressively more fuzzy as he'd issued his chain of instructions. It died midsentence, before Tim could reply. Tim smiled sardonically at the thought that the Superintendent was probably still in full flow: it would take him a couple of minutes to realise that Tim could no longer hear what he was saying. But the moment of light-heartedness was short-lived. A dead baby! He glanced across at Sophia, who was lying in her cocoonababy, contentedly looking up at a dangling soft-toy hedgehog. The thought sickened him.

"You don't need to tell me who that was," said Katrin. "I could hear him. He seemed to be shouting at the top of his voice. Is he annoyed with you about something?"

"No, his mobile was running out of juice. Funny how people think they can counteract that by shouting. But it was something serious. I'm going to have to go."

Tim shovelled in another spoonful of muesli and washed it down with a few mouthfuls of tea. Standing up, he threw on his jacket and kissed Sophia on the top of her head before making his way round the table to where Katrin was sitting. He kissed her as well.

"Sorry," he said. "I'll see you this evening. I'll call you if I think I'm going to be late."

"Aren't you going to tell me what's happened?"

Tim shied away from the prospect. He knew that Katrin would be even more upset than he was that the body of a child had been discovered. He decided he'd wait until he could confirm the construction men weren't mistaken.

"We can talk about it this evening," he said. "I'll know more then."

Outside in his car, Tim called Andy Carstairs.

"Hello, Boss," said Andy, his voice dry with irony. "Checking up to see that I'm on the shit case and haven't done a runner?"

"No, but if you're heading for the police warehouse that's great, because it means you'll be nearer to Sutterton Dowdyke than I am."

"I'm not far away from there, as it happens. Is there a change of plan?"

"Not a complete change of plan – I still want you to look through the Grummetts' stuff. But I'd like you to meet me at the accident site first. You'll get there before I do. Can you make sure that the place is locked down? I'll ask Boston to put a copper at each end of the road again. Don't let the Press near and don't let any of the construction workers, or the salvage

men, if they're still there, leave the site before we've talked to them. Start taking statements from them if you like."

"Sure. But take statements about what, exactly?"

"Sorry, I should have explained better. They think they've found the remains of a child there. A baby. Thornton's just told me. They could be mistaken, but I think it's unlikely."

"Christ," said Andy flatly.

"Yes," said Tim. "Hardly bears thinking about, does it? I'm going to call in at the station to see Juliet. I need her to take a statement from Mrs Grummett now, with or without her solicitor, and we'll have to interview Bob Grummett and both daughters as well. I'll call Patti Gardner and ask her to do the forensics. Then I'll be with you as soon as I can."

Chapter Twenty-Eight

ANDY CARSTAIRS REACHED the ruined lodge house just as Patti Gardner was parking her white van. Andy was always a little uneasy with Patti. They were probably about the same age, but she seemed older. When he met her she was always engrossed in her job and he found making conversation difficult. He had noticed she and Tim had an awkward relationship. He doubted this was anything to do with work – in his experience, Patti was always a model of efficiency and co-operation – which led him to deduce there must have been 'something between them' at some point. Of course he wouldn't dream of raising the subject with Tim, and even less with Patti, but he was intrigued, nevertheless.

Andy parked his car immediately behind the van and went to meet her as she was opening the rear doors. She pushed back tousled hair and smiled at him.

"DC Carstairs, good morning. DI Yates didn't tell me you'd be here, but I've got plenty of clobber with me."

"Good morning, Ms Gardner. Clobber?" Andy was puzzled.

"Plastic suits. Hair caps. Foot covers. You weren't going to go in there without getting kitted out, were you?"

Andy considered lying and thought better of it.

"It had slipped my mind."

"Just as well I got here first, then," she said briskly. "Wait while I find something that fits."

As she was rummaging in the back of the van, a man appeared from behind the collapsed house. He was massive, tall and big-boned. Andy recognised one of the building contractors he'd met on his previous visit. The man's face was pale.

"I'm glad you've got here," he said. "We seem to have been waiting for ages. Give us the creeps, this has. Tom's been throwing up back there."

Andy uttered a silent prayer that 'Tom' had not vomited on the evidence. Patti was more forthright.

"I hope he managed to keep clear of the crime scene."

The man looked blank. Andy stretched out his hand.

"DC Carstairs. We met when I visited with DI Yates. I'm not sure I caught your name."

"It's Peat. Nick Peat. I won't shake hands. Mine are dirty. Do you want me to show you . . . it?"

"Thank you. Just give us a chance to put these suits on. Are you all right, sir?" Andy added. Nick Peat was wiping sweat from his forehead. His colour was ghastly.

"Just give us a minute," he said. "It's been a bit of a shock."

"Sit sideways in the passenger seat of my van, head between the knees," said Patti firmly. She opened the door for him. Meekly, he obeyed her, lowering his huge bulk and pushing down his head as far as it would go.

"There are some bottles of water next to that box," Patti said to Andy. "Could you pass me one? Mr Peat," she continued more gently, as Andy also did as he was told, "when the faint feeling passes, take some sips of water. It'll make you feel better."

By the time Andy had struggled into the white suit and covered his feet, Nick Peat appeared to have recovered. Patti donned her own suit with lightning speed.

"Does Mr Peat need to be togged out?" asked Andy,

doubting if even Patti's resourcefulness could produce a garment that would fit.

"No, he's already contaminated the site. We'll ask him to show us where it is and then keep him and his mate away from it."

Andy hoped that Nick Peat wouldn't be offended by her words, but he was walking slightly ahead of them and appeared not to hear. When Andy had first visited the lodge house, on the night of the accident, he'd noticed a small outhouse that had apparently been left intact. Squat and built of brick, it had a Dutch door and one tiny window, over which a grille had been fixed. The bottom half of the Dutch door was closed. Nick Peat's mate was leaning with his back against the wall beside it. He looked to be in a worse way than Nick was. His eyes were closed and there were traces of vomit on his overalls. Nick clapped a huge hand on his arm.

"You all right, mucker?"

Tom opened fishy eyes.

"This is DC Carstairs. He was here the other day, remember?"

Andy held out his hand.

"Best not," Tom muttered, closing his eyes again.

"Could you just show us the place," said Patti to Nick Peat. "You needn't stay with us. You can take your colleague to sit down somewhere while we take a preliminary look." He looked around him as if to ask where he might find somewhere congenial in this wilderness of wreckage and rubble.

"You can sit in the back of my car," Andy said quickly. "I'll let you in as soon as you've shown us. I'll need to take a statement, but after that I suggest you take the rest of the day off. Both of you."

"Boss won't like that," said Nick, shaking his head.

"Well, I'll speak to him. It's unlikely that you'll be allowed to do more work here today, in any case."

"I'm going to be sick again," said Tom, diving to one side of the building, where there was a small dyke.

"I'll show you," said Nick. "It's just through here."

He opened the half-gate. Andy and Patti followed. The outbuilding had a stone-flagged floor overlaid with duck-boards. These had rotted in places. In the middle of the floor a square had been cut in one of the duck-boards to create a sort of trapdoor, with a hinged lid. This was lying open. Nick Peat gestured towards it.

"It's in there," he said. "There's a hole in the stonework. The bones are in it."

"Thank you," said Andy.

"I'd best go and see to Tom," Nick Peat continued quickly.

"I'll come and find you in a minute."

"There's not room for both of us to look in there at once. Do you want me to go first?" said Patti.

"Wouldn't be a bad idea," said Andy. "You'll need to see it exactly as it was found."

"Not much hope of that. They're bound to have moved it. But I'll take some photos before we touch it. It's the best we can do." She withdrew a torch and a small camera from her pocket. "I don't suppose there's a light in here, is there?"

"There's a light fitting," said Andy, peering upwards, "but I'm pretty sure the electricity was switched off after the accident." He moved back to the door, found a switch and flicked it without result.

"I suppose that was inevitable. I'm going to have a job seeing this properly. It makes me wonder how *they* managed to see it. What were they doing in here, anyway?"

"I'll be asking them that, but my guess is they've been asked to clear this structure ready for demolition. They start early,

before it gets light. They've got some powerful lamps somewhere – I saw them the first time I was here. Do you want me to try to borrow one?"

"That would help."

Andy made for the door again. He was barely through it when he saw a diminutive figure approaching. He walked swiftly towards the man, to keep him as far away from the outbuilding as possible. As he came closer, he was startled to see the harrowed look on the unexpected visitor's face.

"Mr Cushing! Is something wrong?"

For a few seconds, Peter Cushing appeared unable to speak.

"Mr Cushing?"

"It's Philippa," he said, his face contorted as he fought back tears. "We've lost her. We can't find her anywhere. What am I going to say to Ruby and Bob?"

Chapter Twenty-Nine

TIM HAD JUST climbed into his car and was about to start the engine when his mobile started ringing again. Removing it from his pocket, he saw Superintendent Thornton's landline number flashing on the display screen.

"Superintendent Thornton! I'm on my way to Sutterton Dowdyke now. I've just been briefing DC Carstairs. He'll join me there – he'll probably arrive first, as he was already heading out that way. I've asked Patti Gardner to meet us, too. I should be with them in half an hour or so."

"I'm glad Carstairs is going to be there, Yates, because I have an emergency for you to deal with."

"But I thought this was the emergency. There can't be much that's more important than the discovery of a dead child."

"You're right there, Yates, but unfortunately I can think of at least one thing that *is* more important, and that's the disappearance of a living child. A girl called Cassandra Knipes was abducted on her way to school this morning. She's the head girl at Spalding High School."

"God help us! I hope this isn't anything to do with the prowler who was reported hanging round the school last week."

"Your guess is as good as mine, Yates, but I want you on this case straight away. As you know, if we're going to find her, we've got a window of about twenty-four hours, or forty-eight

at most, before the trail goes cold. And probably less than that if we want to find her alive," he concluded grimly.

"How do we know she was abducted?"

"Her mother saw it happen. The girl was waiting for a bus at the end of the road where she lives when a van drew up alongside her, a man got out and she was bundled into it."

"Why didn't the mother do anything?"

"She did. She called us straight away. Apparently she usually watches the girl set off from an upstairs window. The house is at the other end of the street from the bus stop, so too far away for her to have been able to take any kind of action, even if she was up to it. I get the impression she's rather elderly. Husband is wheelchair-bound."

"Did she get the number of the van?"

"No. She says she tried to see it, but couldn't make out any plates. They might have been covered over, or maybe she was just too far away. The van was plain black, with nothing to distinguish it – no painting or logos on the sides."

"Black's quite an unusual colour for a trade van."

"I daresay it is, Yates, but I don't think that's a very helpful observation at the moment. I've instructed road blocks to be set up on all the major trunk roads leading out of the county. I want you to get across to interview Mrs Knipes now. The address is Number 30, Woolram Wygate. I've sent PC Tandy already – she'll meet you there. I've asked her to search the area around the bus stop before she goes on to Mrs Knipes' house. It's a long shot, but the girl's assailant may have dropped something. I'm going to call the headmaster of Spalding High School now. After you've finished with Mrs Knipes, I'd like you to go and interview the girl's friends. Ask them if anyone's seen the prowler again. The head should have told us if they had, but you never know."

Tim was secretly impressed by the speed and thoroughness with which the Superintendent had acted.

"There's just one thing, Superintendent . . ."

"Yes, Yates, what is it? We need to get on with this *now*!"

"I know, sir, but I'm concerned about the headteacher – Richard Lennard. PC Tandy and PC Chakrabati went to see him about the prowler, and PC Tandy wasn't impressed. She thought he wasn't concerned enough – or that he was hiding something."

"There's no concrete reason to doubt him, is there? No evidence of a criminal record or anything in his previous history?"

"Not as far as I know, sir, but . . ."

"Then we have to work with what we have, Yates. The man holds a position of responsibility and one of his pupils has gone missing. We can't by-pass him on a whim of PC Tandy's, can we?"

"No, sir."

"And while you're at it, suggest to him that it won't be a good idea to talk to the Press. If the girl hasn't been found in the next couple of hours, naturally we'll hold a Press conference and involve the media in trying to find her. But we don't want all sorts of people talking to them and sending mixed messages. We all have to sing from the same hymn sheet."

"Yes, sir."

"But, Yates, keep an open mind about Lennard. See what you think when you meet him. If there is anything fishy about him, I'm sure you'll sniff it out."

"Yes, sir."

"Good, that's all. Get on with it."

The Superintendent rang off.

Despite the gravity of the situation, Tim couldn't help smiling. Mixed messages, indeed! The Superintendent had managed to introduce a few during the latter part of their

conversation. Hedging his bets, as usual. Still, he was at least prepared to consider Verity Tandy's assessment of Richard Lennard. Perhaps age was mellowing him.

Chapter Thirty

NUMBER 30, WOOLRAM Wygate was a large L-shaped dormer bungalow set in an extensive but unadorned lawn. The main door was at the side of the house, almost in the middle of the 'L', at right angles to the road. As Tim walked towards it he heard an explosion of yapping erupt from inside. His mood sank. He detested small fussy dogs more than any postman.

He was about to ring the bell when he heard footsteps behind him and turned to see PC Verity Tandy.

"Hello. Superintendent Thornton told me you'd be here."

"Good morning, sir. I've been to see Mrs Knipes already, to reassure her that you were on your way. I've had a look round the bus stop area, but I haven't found anything. My guess is the girl was snatched so fast that neither she nor her assailant left any trace, but you may feel it's worth doing a fingertip search."

"I think you're probably right. I'll take a look myself later. I don't want someone pouncing on me for not doing the job properly."

Verity Tandy grinned. Tim looked at her appraisingly. She'd repelled him when they first met, but he found her quite personable now.

"No prizes for guessing who 'someone' might be," she said.

"No, indeed," Tim replied rather primly. "I gather that

the Knipes keep a mutt," he added, to gloss over the short awkward silence that followed. "What kind is it?"

"I'm not very well up on dogs, but I think it's a shih tzu. It barks a lot, but it's a timid thing, really. Frustrated, probably. Doesn't get out much and thinks it's seeing a bit of the action now."

Tim laughed.

"I had no idea that you were a dog psychologist! I'll bear it in mind, in case I need advice in the future."

Verity smiled uncertainly. She didn't know how to take Tim.

"Shall I ring the bell, sir? Mr and Mrs Knipes told me to walk straight back in, but I don't like to. He's in a wheelchair," she added in a lower voice.

"Then I think we should do as they say," said Tim. "We'll knock first. After the row that dog's been making, they must know we're here already."

Verity knocked rather timidly and entered the house, Tim following.

"Hello? Mrs Knipes, it's PC Tandy. DI Yates is here now."

Tim was relieved to see no sign of the dog. He found himself standing in a spacious hall containing a large sofa and a desk. There was a staircase at one end.

He heard a tapping noise and the approach of slow footsteps. The door at the end of the hall opened and a gaunt, rather stooped woman with a thick, stylishly-cut grey bob advanced to meet him. She was leaning quite heavily on a gaily-patterned walking stick which more resembled a mountaineer's trekking pole than a conventional aid for the elderly. Her clothes were expensive. Tim recognised the type: Mrs Knipes was what his mother would have called 'county'. He reserved judgement. A residue of the working-class schoolboy he had once been mistrusted such people, even though he knew this made him guilty of stereotyping.

Mrs Knipes rested for a moment, pressing the heel of her foot hard against the floor as if relieving some deep-seated pain. Steadying herself against the door frame, she held out her hand.

"DI Yates, thank you for getting here so quickly. We appreciate it."

Her handshake was surprisingly firm. Moving closer to her, Tim saw she'd been crying. Her gaze met his briefly – her eyes were a watery pale blue – and dropped as quickly.

"You'll be wondering where my husband is. He's taken the dog into the study. He'll be back in a minute. He's just composing himself. He's finding this very hard. We both are."

"I understand how upset you are, Mrs Knipes, but whoever took your daughter doesn't have much of a head start. It was a stroke of luck you saw him. We'll start by asking you about it. Would you like to sit down somewhere?"

"What? Oh, yes, of course. I wasn't thinking. Come through to the drawing room. Would you like some tea?"

"Not for me, thank you," said Tim.

"Perhaps I could make some tea for you?" said Verity.

"That would be kind," said Mrs Knipes. "I do feel a bit shaky. There's a tray in the kitchen that I prepared for Arthur, and the tea caddy's next to it. You'll just need to take more cups from the cupboard."

Verity disappeared on her errand. Tim followed Mrs Knipes into a large, oblong room with French windows at either end. It contained two sofas set at right angles to each other, a number of matching chairs, some small tables and a piano. The walls were hung with water-colours of Lincolnshire scenes. Tim saw at a glance they were originals, not prints.

Mrs Knipes headed for one of the armchairs. The folded rug draped over its back and the clutter of books and knitting to one side of it announced that it was 'her' chair. She

propped her stick against it and settled herself, smoothing her skirt over her knees as she hoisted both legs on to a footstool. She took a silver-framed photograph from the table next to her and handed it to Tim.

"That's Cassandra. She's a lovely girl – really beautiful," she said dreamily, then added in a more businesslike voice, "Please, do be seated, DI Yates." She gestured in the direction of the sofas. Obeying, Tim perched on the end of the one nearest to him. He scrutinised the photograph while Mrs Knipes looked at him expectantly. Despite her professions of anguish, he thought her behaviour too serene for a woman whose only child had just been abducted.

"She's certainly very pretty – and striking. Such fair hair. It's quite unusual, isn't it? Almost silver. Did she have a boyfriend?"

"No," Mrs Knipes responded curtly. "I expect you'd like me to tell you what I saw."

"Yes, of course. But can we start a little further back? Did Cassandra appear quite as usual last night and this morning? Did she seem upset or preoccupied about anything?"

"No, I don't think so. My daughter has a very sunny disposition, Detective Inspector. She's not given to brooding. She's also practical: she knows not to do anything that could aggravate her father's condition."

"I see," said Tim, thinking that therefore if the girl was worried about something she'd have been likely to try to conceal the fact. "What is her father's 'condition', if you don't mind my asking?"

"Arthur had a combined stroke and heart attack two years ago. He's confined to a wheelchair now and can't move his legs. Someone comes in to wash him every day. Such an affliction is not unusual for his age, but that doesn't make it less distressing."

"I'm sorry." Tim was trying to work out roughly how old they were. Mrs Knipes' words indicated that her husband was her senior – and she must have been nearing seventy. How did they manage to have a daughter who was still in her teens? Biologically speaking, he supposed it was just about possible – but unlikely.

"Does she usually catch the bus to school?"

"Not always. Sometimes she walks with her friends. But she had quite a lot to carry today and she was a bit late, so she decided the bus would be better."

"What did she have to carry?"

"Sports equipment. And some home-made biscuits for the netball team. Mothers take it in turns to supply them when there's a match."

"Was it a spur-of-the-moment decision to go by bus, or did she mention it last night?"

"She said that she might catch the bus, but she'd wait to see how much time she had this morning. If she'd got up earlier, she'd probably have phoned one of her friends and asked them to come and help her carry the things."

"She didn't phone her friends to say she wouldn't be walking?"

"I don't know. I didn't hear her use the phone, but she'd have been more likely to text. I'm not one of those mothers who checks up on her children all the time. Besides, I've never needed to. Cassandra is as good as gold." Mrs Knipes uttered these last few words with some defiance, as if her credentials as a parent were being challenged. Tim steered her back to less controversial territory.

"So she ate her breakfast as usual, except that she was a little late?"

"Yes."

"You told Superintendent Thornton you always watch

her on to the bus when she catches it. From where do you do that?"

"It's a dormer bungalow. There's one upstairs room, up in the eaves. We gave it to Cassandra after Arthur became ill. He can't climb the stairs to it now and I thought it would allow her more privacy. Not that she's ever asked for it," she concluded, as if to anticipate Tim's next question.

"So you saw her off from her own bedroom window?"

"Yes."

"Tell me exactly what you saw. Did you go upstairs before she left the house or afterwards?"

"At the same time. I kissed her goodbye and began to climb the stairs while she collected her things from the kitchen. I heard the door close as I got to the top of the stairs. By the time I'd reached the window, she'd crossed the road. She turned to smile at me and I waved back. She couldn't wave herself, because her hands were full."

"What was she carrying? Exactly, I mean, as you saw it from the window?"

"She was wearing a rucksack containing her sports gear. She had her briefcase in one hand and a shoe-box containing the biscuits in the other. She was probably holding her bus pass ready in one hand, though I couldn't see it. She wouldn't have wanted to start fishing about for it when the bus arrived."

"So she looked up at you and smiled and walked up the road towards the bus stop. How light was it?"

"Not very. It was getting light, but it was a bit foggy. The street lamps are quite good here, though. I could still see her when she reached the bus stop."

"How long would she have had to wait for the bus to come?"

"Not long at all – in fact, I think the bus must have been

late. Cassandra herself was late, as I've mentioned. She was cutting it quite fine."

"What happened next?"

Mrs Knipes passed the back of her hand across her eyes.

"A large van passed the house. The driver was driving fast – too fast for a residential road. After he'd got round the dog-leg in the road, he crossed the white line, so when he pulled up he was right next to the bus stop."

"What did Cassandra do?"

"I couldn't see her face. She just stood there."

"And then?"

"He opened the rear doors of the van. Then he grabbed her and lifted her up and bundled her in. He was much stronger than she was."

"You're quite sure it was a man?"

"Yes, I'm certain. He was too tall and broad-shouldered to have been a woman. I was too far away to see his face. He was dressed completely in black – black jeans, black jacket, a black woollen hat."

Mrs Knipes gazed down at her mottled brown hands. Tim saw the tears come splashing down on them.

"He lifted her in just as she was, carrying the box and the briefcase? She didn't drop either of them? She didn't try to struggle?"

"It happened very quickly. She didn't struggle at all – I suppose she was too surprised, or too frightened. I don't know." Mrs Knipes fixed her red-rimmed azure eyes on Tim.

"Why do you think she didn't try to fight him? Why didn't she drop everything and just run away?"

"I wish I knew the answer to your question, Detective Inspector. But I don't think Cassandra's reaction was unusual: if I try to put myself in the same situation, I think I'd probably just freeze with fright, like in those horrible nightmares where

you're trying to run away from something and suddenly you can't move your legs."

"Indeed," said a voice from the doorway. Tim turned to see that a lightweight wheelchair had glided noiselessly into the room. Its occupant was a tiny wizened man whose head was twisted away from his body at an unnatural angle. His emaciated face had shrunk to a collection of features printed on taut skin and the eyes behind the wire-framed spectacles were hugely magnified: he must have been almost blind. But his voice was strong and firm, well-modulated, even wry.

"I can quite empathise with that sentiment, Susannah." He turned to Tim. "As you can see, I have no need to use my imagination on the point."

He fingered the controls on the arms of his wheelchair with clenched but dexterous fingers and manoeuvred himself further into the room. Verity followed, bearing a tray laden with teapot and tea-cups, which she placed carefully on the small table nearest his wife.

Tim's mobile rang.

"Excuse me."

He strode rapidly out to the hall and closed the door, briefly glimpsing Susannah Knipes staring after him as he did so.

"DI Yates."

"Tim? It's Juliet."

"Hello, Juliet. I'm sorry, I should have thought to call you and Andy. Can you tell him that Cassandra . . ."

"We know about Cassandra Knipes, Tim. Superintendent Thornton has briefed everyone here – we've been setting up the road-blocks. And I've just told Andy, who called a moment ago to say that Philippa Grummett has disappeared."

"What . . . ? I'm coming back to the station, Juliet."

Chapter Thirty-One

TIM HAD ASKED Verity Tandy to stay with the Knipes until a liaison officer could be appointed. He'd instructed her not to mention that Philippa Grummett had disappeared until he'd got a statement from the Cushings. He spoke to Andy, who was taking the call out of earshot in the Cushings' garden. Patti Gardner was still examining the remains in the old pigsty.

"Where are the Cushings?"

"They're in the house. They're pretty shaken up."

"Where's the daughter?"

"She's with them. She's the one who discovered that Philippa was missing this morning. Obviously they didn't send her to school."

"They wouldn't know about Cassandra Knipes' abduction, would they?"

"No. I certainly haven't mentioned it."

"Well, try to keep it like that. Don't let any of them leave the house. You'll have to interview them as thoroughly as possible. And for God's sake, keep the media out of it if you possibly can."

"I don't think the Cushings want to go anywhere. They seem to be pretty shaken up. We need at least one copper back at the accident site. Ms Gardner's there by herself at the moment. I could do with some help here, too, if you want me

to deal with the Press as well as interviewing the Cushings."

"I did ask Boston to send two coppers; they should be there by now. Let me know if they don't turn up. Make sure you interview all the Cushings separately, especially the girl. Find out if Philippa Grummett said anything strange or seemed worried or preoccupied last night. Ask when she was last in touch with her parents. And get some item belonging to her from the Cushings that can give us a DNA sample."

"If you want me to interview Alice Cushing on her own, I'm going to need a policewoman here as well."

"Good point. I'll ask Juliet to come. We've got a meeting with Thornton now. I don't know exactly how long it'll take, but I think Juliet can be with you in about an hour and a half. Interview the parents in the meantime. I'm going to join you as soon as I can. The tighter we can keep this case, the better. I'll try to make sure we're all briefed about new developments as they happen. Otherwise we might miss stuff that's common to both disappearances."

"You do think they're connected, then? That both are kidnappings?"

"Well, it seems more than likely, doesn't it? I don't believe in coincidences. Besides, I haven't forgotten what Verity Tandy said about Cassandra Knipes' resemblance to the Grummett girl. I've got a photo of Cassandra now. It's not a very good one, but I can see what Verity means. The hair colour alone is rare, especially in this area. There's almost certainly some connection."

"What about the train accident? Do you think that has anything to do with it?"

"I need more time to think about that. It strikes me that it could have been the catalyst for all of these events, but I can't see why. It was an accident, after all. I can't see how anyone could have engineered it, least of all one of the Grummett

family. Has someone notified the Grummetts that Philippa's missing?"

"Not yet. I waited to speak to you first."

"I'll do it. We'll need to interview them again urgently, as well. It would be better to see them face-to-face to tell them about her, but I'll have to do it by phone now. They're Philippa's next of kin and they mustn't hear about this from someone else first. Cushing hasn't told them, has he?"

"No. I think he's terrified of facing up to them. He regards himself as responsible because Philippa was staying under his roof."

"Well, he has a point there. Was there any sign of forced entry, or do you think the girl left the house of her own accord?"

"I don't know. They seem to think she walked out, but I'll need to probe further when I talk to them. And we'll have to get Forensics in to examine the house."

"You're right. As soon as possible, too. How's Patti getting on with what the contractors found? Do you think she could leave that for a while, or is it crucial she stays with it?"

"I don't know. I left her to it when Peter Cushing showed up."

"Right. Leave her where she is for now. I'll speak to her when I arrive. I'd better go. Sorry to repeat myself, but please don't speak to the media. We'll need Thornton's take on what to say to them. He may want to tell them we only know for sure that one of the girls has been abducted, though they won't believe it."

Superintendent Thornton was closeted with Juliet and DC Ricky MacFadyen when Tim reached his office. As Tim raced up the stairs, he could see Thornton holding forth through the internal window. He spotted Tim and beckoned him to join

them. Tim couldn't imagine what had got into his boss since the day's dramas had begun to unfold. Masterful would have been the word that sprang to mind, if he hadn't known Thornton better. He would have to look to his laurels if Thornton continued to up his game like this, but Tim suspected that his sudden self-galvanisation was prompted by some political manoeuvre and therefore likely to vanish as quickly as it had materialised.

"Ah, Yates. Thanks for returning pronto. I'd hoped you would. All the road-blocks have been set up now. Carstairs will stay with the Cushing parents until you reach him. I gather that you've spoken to him about it. PC Tandy's still with the Knipes parents, is she? Good. Urgent next steps are to talk to the Grummett parents and then enlist the help of the media. Which means designing a press release that isn't too lurid and then calling a press conference."

"I'm quite happy to . . ."

"Good Lord, Yates, not you. If you don't mind my saying so, tact is not your forte. I believe I have quite a way with words myself, but my prowess is not equal to DC Armstrong's. I've asked her to draft something for us. It won't take you too long, will it?" He turned to Juliet.

Juliet flushed and gave Tim a little sidelong glance. "No, sir, but I'd prefer to work on it alone."

"Of course, of course. Off you go."

He favoured Tim with a quick aside.

"I've decided that MacFadyen should break the news to the Grummett parents, Yates."

"But Ricky's not been involved in this case so far. I'd be grateful for his help, of course, but I'd really like . . ."

"He is involved in it now. You can go, MacFadyen. Let us know when you've spoken to the Grummetts. Hopefully you'll find them both at the hospital. If not, check with the ward staff

that Mrs Grummett is mentally stable enough to hear the news by herself."

"Yes, sir."

Ricky flashed Tim a quick smile of sympathy as he left the room. The Superintendent continued.

"You can't do everything yourself, Yates. You must learn to delegate. Besides, I want you to talk to the Cushings as soon as possible. You can take Armstrong with you. I know that Carstairs is already at the scene, but he was detailed to support Ms Gardner, and I don't want him to lose sight of that. He can go back to her once you've arrived. You and Tandy, MacFadyen, Carstairs and I will have to co-ordinate carefully, so that the victims' parents and guardians all know what's going on before I talk to the media."

"You're going to talk to the media, sir? But I thought that I was the SIO for this case."

"You're the SIO for the accident and whatever else has been going on at the site of the accident. As far as we know, the kidnapping of Cassandra Knipes and the disappearance of Philippa Grummett are not related to that. We also have no proof yet they are connected."

"I think it's unlikely they're not, sir."

"So do I, Yates, very unlikely. And if you want my opinion, it is that all of these happenings are related. But I'm not going to waste time thinking about exactly how at the moment. My priority is to find those girls unharmed and restore them to where they belong. And to preserve the credibility of this police force while I'm at it. I suggest to you that I'm unlikely to achieve either by giving you an enormous SIO caseload. Do you agree?"

"Yes, sir," said Tim reluctantly.

"Good. Nevertheless," Superintendent Thornton continued in a silky voice, "naturally I shall be relying on you to do a great deal of the work on all the cases."

"Thank you, sir."

"And I'm quite well aware that you're more au fait with the minutiae than I am. So I want to know if I've missed anything? We've been going at quite a pace this morning."

Tim wracked his brains for some flaw in the Superintendent's arrangements.

"There's just one thing, sir. PC Tandy had been going to Spalding High School to see Mr Lennard, but she's been detailed to stay with the Knipes now. And we should send someone to Boston High School: Philippa Grummett is a pupil there."

"Good point. Chakrabati visited Spalding High School with Tandy last time, didn't he? Send him again. And get Boston to send someone to the school there. In both cases, immediately. And tell them not to talk to the media."

"Yes, sir," said Tim. "I'll do just that – I want to find out why they haven't yet got my requested support out to Dowdyke Road."

Chapter Thirty-Two

GIASH CHAKRABATI EMERGED from his car, which he'd parked in the front drive of Spalding High School, to see Richard Lennard walking briskly towards him. Giash smiled inwardly. He was going to enjoy this encounter.

"Oh, hello," said the headteacher in an offhand way. "I'd been expecting PC Tandy. I'm sorry, I've forgotten your name."

"PC Chakrabati. PC Tandy's been detailed to remain with Cassandra Knipes' parents. I've come in her place."

Lennard's urbane mask fell away. He looked alarmed, confused almost.

"With *Cassandra's* parents? But why?"

"I'm sorry, sir, I had thought you knew. Can we go inside? It's not something we can discuss out here." Giash glanced across at the road at a small car that had just pulled up.

"Certainly. We can talk in my office." He gestured to the door and, leading the way, opened it for Giash. As they walked down the corridor, the bossy school secretary whom Giash had encountered on his previous visit came rushing up to them. Ignoring Giash, she launched into a breathless rigmarole.

"There you are, Headmaster. I've been ringing round the whole school for you. Councillor Start's here. He's most annoyed that the meeting booked on Saturday coincides with a netball match. *Most* annoyed. He says that the school is paid

to guarantee privacy for his society's meetings and it's not good enough. He says . . ."

A withering look from Lennard stopped her in her tracks.

"Hello, Mrs Hargreaves. Where is Councillor Start?"

"He's waiting in your office. He . . ."

"Please ask him to leave my office and wait in yours. We're going into the staff room for a couple of minutes to get some coffee. By the time we're ready to take it to my office, I expect him to have moved. Tell him that I'm with PC Chakrabati," he finished, enunciating Giash's name very distinctly.

"Yes, Headmaster," said Mrs Hargreaves, still looking dubious; but Giash also saw the gleam of curiosity dawning in her eye. She scurried away, her large bottom straining against the panels of her tweed skirt.

"You'd like coffee?" Lennard said to Giash.

"Thank you, sir. But what I've come to talk to you about is urgent."

Richard Lennard shrugged.

"Have coffee or not, as you wish. As you see, coming briefly into the staff room with me will be the quickest way of ensuring you get my attention."

"Yes, sir. I think I'll stay here, if you don't mind."

"Very well. I will fetch the coffee."

He disappeared through the staff room door while Giash waited in the corridor. As he'd expected, Councillor Start emerged from the office almost immediately, with Mrs Hargreaves waddling in attendance. He was expostulating in a loud voice and very red in the face. As he turned to take the two steps to Mrs Hargreaves' office, he cast a brief glance behind him and met Giash's eye. Quickly he looked away. Giash noticed that he fell silent immediately.

Richard Lennard emerged from the staff room as soon as Start had disappeared, as if their actions were co-ordinated.

He was carrying two Styrofoam cups of coffee. He pushed against the door of his office, which the Councillor had left ajar, and entered.

"Come in, Constable Chakrabati. Shut the door behind you."

Lennard didn't retreat behind his desk, as Giash had expected, but instead set down the coffee cups carefully on the small oval table and seated himself there, waving to Giash to join him.

"I apologise for the fuss," he said. "I'm all yours now."

"As I said, sir, I thought you'd been briefed. I'm sorry to shock you: Cassandra Knipes has been kidnapped."

"Cassandra! But why?" He paused. "And how can you be sure?"

"I have no idea why, sir. That's what we're trying to find out – and quickly. We know that she was abducted because her mother saw her being bundled into a van."

"Her parents are quite old."

"Mrs Knipes has not made a mistake, if that's what you're suggesting, sir. We'd like you and the staff and students here to help us as much as you can. We have twenty-four hours, forty-eight at most, before the trail goes cold. And Cassandra's chances of survival are decreasing all the time."

"Of course everyone will help. What should we do?"

"I'd like to speak to Cassandra's two friends – the girls that PC Tandy and I saw last time we were here. And would you ask the teachers who taught Cassandra yesterday if she seemed subdued, or they noticed anything unusual in her behaviour."

"Yes – although it will mean taking them out of their classrooms. Should I close the school?"

"I don't think that will be necessary at the moment, sir, or even advisable."

"But if Cassandra's been kidnapped, shouldn't we issue

some kind of warning to the rest of the students – and to their parents?"

"Superintendent Thornton, my boss, will be giving a statement to the Press, TV and radio shortly. I suggest you write a letter to all parents, based on what he says. After I've talked to Cassandra's friends, you might like to gather the school together to offer advice and reassurance. We'd be extremely grateful if you wouldn't discuss Cassandra with the media just yet. They're bound to turn up here, sooner rather than later, I'd say, and it'd be best not to treat them in a hostile way, as they might be helpful later. But we'd like you to work with us on exactly what you say to them."

Chapter Thirty-Three

KATHLEEN HARGREAVES SHOWED the two girls into Richard Lennard's office. Both were pale and subdued. Leonora Painter scuttled into the room and looked around nervously, as if unsure what to do next. The skin around her eyes was puffy, as if she'd been crying. Isobel Baxter was sad in a dignified way. Giash guessed she probably had superior powers of imagination and better understood than Leonora the dangers that Cassandra might be facing.

"Do you want me to stay?" said Kathleen Hargreaves brusquely, addressing the question to the headteacher.

"Please, Mrs Hargreaves, if you would."

She took a chair beside Richard Lennard's large desk, behind which he'd now retreated. Giash found this curious. On his previous visit, when the girls weren't upset, Lennard had fetched chairs and sat with them. Now, rather awkwardly, they and he were obliged to remain standing.

Richard Lennard waved a hand in Giash's direction.

"This is PC Chakrabati," he said. "You probably remember him – he accompanied PC Tandy when she visited a few days ago. I know that Mrs Hargreaves has told you about Cassandra's disappearance. PC Chakrabati would like to ask you a few questions."

Giash smiled at the two girls before scrutinising Lennard.

The latter held his gaze. Giash thought he could read contempt in the headteacher's expression.

"Cassandra hasn't merely 'disappeared'," he said quietly but firmly. "We have an eyewitness account that she was abducted while waiting at the bus stop a few yards from her house."

"Why would anyone want to abduct her?" asked Isobel.

"That's one of the questions I'd like to ask you. Does Cassandra have any enemies that you know of?"

"No," said Leonora. "Everyone likes her. She's a really nice person."

"What about boyfriends?"

"We go out in a group with some of the boys in the sixth form at the Grammar School."

"Is she friendly with one of them in particular?"

"I'm not sure," said Leonora, looking down at her feet.

"It's all right, Leo," said Isobel. "I don't mind telling the truth. Cassie has a kind of on-off relationship with my brother, Jack. But if you think Jack would kidnap her, you're barking up the wrong tree."

"Remember your manners, Isobel," said Kathleen Hargreaves, glowering.

"It's OK," said Giash quickly, inwardly cursing the woman for slowing the momentum of the conversation. "Why do you describe Cassandra's relationship with your brother as 'on-off'? Do they argue frequently?"

"No, I don't think so. But I don't think Cassie's parents like her to have a boyfriend."

"Were you with her yesterday?"

"Yes, in lessons and at the end of the day. We walked part of the way home together."

"What about you, Leonora?"

"I saw her in lessons, too. I didn't walk home. My mum came to pick me up."

"Thank you. Isobel, what did you talk about when you were walking? Did Cassandra seem upset in any way?"

"Not really. She worries about her Dad a lot – he's old, and not well. I think she worries about both her parents, actually. But last night was no different from usual. She mentioned that her Dad had had a bit of relapse, then we started talking about tomorrow's netball. It was Cassie's turn to bring in the food for it. Her mother was baking biscuits. Cassie said she'd have a lot to carry and she'd probably take the bus. That's why I didn't think it odd when she didn't call for me this morning."

"Of course we'll be cancelling the netball match," Richard Lennard said eagerly. "It wouldn't be seemly to carry on with it after this has happened."

Giash recalled vividly Lennard's brief but fraught exchange with Mrs Hargreaves and Councillor Start's departing glance over his shoulder.

"I'll check with my boss," he said evenly, "but I think he'll say that he'd like the netball match to go on as planned. We may have found Cassandra by then, and if we haven't, the match itself might give us more clues."

"I fail to see . . ."

"Sometimes people who've committed crimes hang around places associated with the victim. By mingling discreetly with those attending the netball match, we may be able to spot unusual behaviour and we'll be asking you and your staff to look out for anyone who comes that you don't know."

"Have you finished talking to Isobel and Leonora now?" asked Mrs Hargreaves icily. Lennard shot her a swift look of . . . what? Admiration? Gratitude?

"Yes, I think so," said Giash. "Thank you both. You've been very helpful. Can I just caution you not to talk to the Press, if anyone should try to contact you? And please tell your parents that we may need to talk to you again."

Both girls nodded.

"Thank you for looking for Cassie," said Isobel. "Please find her."

Leonora gulped back a sob. Mrs Hargreaves practically shooed them out of the room.

"Now," said Richard Lennard, when he and Giash were alone again, "all this talk of strangers lurking among the netball supporters seems rather far-fetched . . ."

"With respect, sir, a prowler has already been reported loitering near the school."

"In any case, we made a mistake when we fixed the netball match for tomorrow. There's a charitable organisation run by Councillor Start booked to meet at the school tomorrow and it's very inconvenient for them to have the match taking place at the same time. You probably heard a snatch of conversation about it when you came in."

"Yes, sir. But I'm certain that Councillor Start will want to aid police enquiries. I understand he's a very public-spirited gentleman and does a lot for the school. He'll surely consider it worth putting up with a minor inconvenience if it means helping us to bring Cassandra home, won't he?"

"Let me know what your superior thinks. I'm not convinced."

"Certainly, sir."

Richard Lennard escorted Giash to the school's main entrance with barely restrained impatience. Suddenly Giash sensed the headmaster tensing up behind him.

"You're going to have an opportunity to put your strictures about the Press into practice sooner than perhaps you'd anticipated," Lennard muttered. He was pointing at a tall, lithe young woman currently loping round the horseshoe sweep.

"Good morning, Mr Lennard," she said. She had a pleasant, open smile, though Giash detected a twang of irony in her voice.

"If you've come about Cassandra Knipes . . ."

The young woman looked curiously from Lennard to Giash and back to Lennard again.

"What about Cassandra Knipes? She's your head girl, isn't she?"

"Yes, but . . ."

Swiftly, Giash interceded.

"I'm PC Chakrabati," he said. "Could you tell me who you are and why you're here?"

"I'm sorry," she said, holding out a slim hand. "It was rude of me to jump straight in. My name is Jocelyn Greaves. I'm a freelance reporter."

"I believe the accurate term is 'investigative journalist'," said Lennard sourly. "Ms Greaves has been asked to leave these premises on a number of occasions."

Giash gave a nod in his direction.

"But answer my question, please," he said, taking the hand briefly. "Why have you come?"

"I've come to ask whether it's true that The Bricklayers are planning to meet here tomorrow morning," she said, fixing the headmaster with her eye. He wouldn't meet it, but stood blinking rapidly before he replied.

"It's none of your business and I don't have to answer the question. The school governors have approved the hiring out of the premises when they're not in use. We're not obliged to publicise which organisations have chosen to take advantage of this arrangement."

"May I take it, then, that the information I've received about a Bricklayers meeting here tomorrow is correct?"

"No, you may not! Constable Chakrabati, can you please tell this woman to remove herself from the site? She's causing a nuisance."

"I think it would be better if you left Mr Lennard in peace

at the moment, Ms Greaves," said Giash quietly. "Mr Lennard is a busy man, and, as he says, you don't have an automatic right to be here."

"OK," she replied, still smiling pleasantly. "But I'm pleased you saw how unco-operative Mr Lennard is. Almost as if he has something to hide, wouldn't you say?"

"Oh, really, you are insufferable. Goodbye, PC Chakrabati. I look forward to hearing your boss's opinion about the matter we discussed as soon as possible." He had re-entered the school before Giash could reply.

"May I walk with you?" asked Jocelyn Greaves.

"If you like, but I'm only going to my car. It's parked over the road," said Giash a little stiffly. Much as he disliked Richard Lennard and was inclined to agree that he was trying to hide something, Giash understood that she was a troublemaker. He wondered if she'd really come about the meeting, or whether somehow she'd got wind of the kidnapping and invented a pretext to obtain information about Cassandra Knipes before the press conference. He braced himself for her next question. When it came, it surprised him.

"Do you know Andy?" she said chattily.

"Andy? Which Andy?"

"DC Andy Carstairs. I had a drink with him last night.

Chapter Thirty-Four

As soon as Juliet had drafted the press release, Tim drove them both to Sutterton Dowdyke. Tim himself was in a sombre mood: he could imagine only too well the histrionics and hand-wringing they would experience at the Cushing household. He also knew that Patti Gardner would have some gruesome evidence to show to him. He noticed, however, that Juliet was transmitting quiet serenity, almost happiness, even though she usually hated such encounters even more than he did.

"You seem very calm. I have to confess I'm apprehensive, myself. I think the Cushings will make a scene."

"I'm sure you're right, sir. There's nothing like a guilty conscience to provoke an outburst – and they're bound to be feeling that Philippa's disappearance was their fault. They'll probably try to wriggle out of the blame in some way – say it was because we didn't provide proper police protection, or something."

"You may be right, although we had no reason to suspect that Philippa was at risk – or any of the Grummetts, for that matter. I'd say that if Philippa had anything to fear, it would be from her own family. They don't seem to like her very much, do they?"

"She wasn't cast in the same mould as any of them, that's for sure. But I don't think any of them would have deliberately

set out to hurt her. The person who shows most animosity towards her is the sister, and I wouldn't have thought she had it in her to plot a kidnapping."

"I agree – though it *is* rather convenient for her that she decided to decamp from the Cushings' house and stay with her uncle and aunt instead."

"That's easy to explain. Philippa and Alice Cushing showed nothing but contempt for her while we were there. They were probably quite horrible to her while she was staying with the Cushings. And she obviously likes her aunt."

"Elsie Grummett, you mean? Yes, they're two of a kind, aren't they? Despite the fact that they aren't blood relatives." Tim paused for a moment. "But coming back to my earlier point, you seem to be taking a very balanced view about all of this. Have you been trying something out to help you cope better? Pilates, or whatever?"

Juliet almost burst out laughing. The comment was so typical of Tim – and so wide of the mark.

"No, not Pilates. Not really my sort of thing. But recently I resolved to make more space for myself. That's why I asked you about Fenland Folklore. I did join it, by the way – and it's not as amateurish as you thought."

"You shouldn't take any notice of me," said Tim, colouring slightly. "I'm full of prejudices, as you know. Still, it would seem that you didn't. I'm glad you're enjoying it. Perhaps I might reconsider. The Historical Society meetings seem to be increasingly far between and some of them are too self-consciously academic for my liking. Who are the other members? Anyone I know?"

"I don't know if you know any of them, but there are certainly some that you know of. Richard Lennard, the head-teacher at the High School, is the President. And Veronica Start, Councillor Start's daughter-in-law, is the Secretary."

"That *is* interesting. What's Lennard like as the President? Do the other members get on with him?"

"I don't know about the other members. I've only been to two sessions so far and I haven't had much opportunity to speak to them. He chaired the first meeting and if I'm honest I found his attitude quite insufferable – he was definitely patronising, both to the speaker and members of the audience who gave their views. But he wasn't there last night. It was rather odd, actually. He was supposed to meet the speaker from the station and didn't show up. She arrived somewhat late and more than a little annoyed."

"I'm not surprised. Did he offer any explanation?"

"He may have done to her, but not to the rest of us, as he didn't come to the meeting at all."

"Even more interesting. What about Veronica Start?"

"Oh, she was there, trying to hold the whole thing together. She's quite a nervous sort of person. And Louise spotted a burn mark on her arm which she thought was probably inflicted by somebody else."

"Do you mean she's a battered wife?"

"I think she could be. Or it could have been an accident."

Tim was turning the car into Dowdyke Road as Juliet spoke. PC Walton was standing at the top of the road. Recognising Tim, he gave a mock salute and waved them through.

"Here we go again," Tim said. "Brace yourself. I'd like you to interview Alice Cushing – without anyone else present, if the parents will allow it. You'll get more out of her that way, if she has anything worth telling us. As well as all the usual stuff about how Philippa seemed over the past few days, whether anything was worrying her, whether she showed any sign of intending to run away – you know the drill, I don't need to tell you. Try to find out how long they've been friends. Given

that they're neighbours, they may have known each other at primary school or even earlier."

"OK. But I'm intrigued – why do you want to dig back so far?"

"It's obvious, really," said Tim, regretting immediately that this sounded patronising. Too late to rephrase now. "Everyone thinks that it's extremely odd that the Grummetts have a daughter like Philippa. They even seem to think so themselves. She doesn't fit in with that household. Now Cassandra Knipes has also disappeared. She's also a girl from a background that doesn't seem quite to fit – though I admit her circumstances aren't as incongruous as Philippa's. And to cap that, these two girls could pass for identical twins."

"I agree it's all very odd. Even Superintendent Thornton seems to have picked up on some of the links, though he's told us to treat them as different cases, hasn't he?"

"Yes, but you know as well as I do that's for the benefit of the media – and it won't last long. Some reporter will look at the photos and put two and two together. Fortunately, the photo we've been given of Cassandra Knipes isn't a particularly good one – though it's ironical that I should be saying so. And I don't think we have one of Philippa Grummett at all yet, but that'll be one of the things Ricky will be asking the Grummetts for."

"And I'm almost certain I know where they'll tell him to find it," said Juliet, smiling wryly.

"How do you . . . . Oh, you mean in the police warehouse? With the 'contaminated' items."

"Exactly. And it could take some time to find if there aren't photographs of her anywhere else. Let's hope that Alice or Boston High School can help out."

"Yes," said Tim, with a sigh. "Nothing's ever simple, is it? We're here now," he added, as he parked on the grass verge

beyond the Cushings' hedge. "You go first. I'll follow you."

Juliet climbed out of the car. It was late morning, but the daylight was a sluggish yellow-grey. A vicious wind came whipping in over the marshes. She shivered and turned up the collar of her coat.

"Let's hope that neither of those girls is outside somewhere. They'll perish of cold before we can get to them."

She turned and quickly made the short walk to the Cushings' back door.

Tim followed her, congratulating himself on his exquisite tact. He hadn't even raised an eyebrow when Juliet had mentioned Louise, let alone remarked on it. He reminded himself to tell Katrin that evening and ask what she thought about it.

The meeting with the Cushings wasn't as difficult as Tim had feared. Peter Cushing was a little tearful and blamed himself for Philippa's disappearance, though why was not apparent. His wife was almost as cheerful as on the first occasion that Tim had visited her house; her mood would have seemed inappropriate were she not trying to jolly the rest of her family along. Alice's reaction was hard to gauge: there was a defiance underlying her moroseness that Tim couldn't quite explain. She agreed, however, to be interviewed on her own – even seemed pleased at the prospect – so Juliet accompanied her into the little living room while Tim remained with her parents in the kitchen.

Juliet began gently, with the sort of questions she was certain Alice would have been expecting.

"When did you last see Philippa?"

"When we went to bed last night."

"You were sharing a room, weren't you?"

"Yes."

"And you both went to bed as usual?"

Alice nodded.

"Did you talk before you settled down? Or did either of you read or do anything else – text someone, for example?"

"I didn't. I turned my light out straight away. I was tired. I think I fell asleep right off."

"And Philippa?"

"How would I know?" Alice frowned. "I don't think she turned her light out at the same time, but I can't be sure."

"And when you woke this morning she'd gone?"

"Yes. But I wasn't worried at first. I thought she was in the bathroom. I waited quite a while, until Mum called out that we'd be late for school. I was going to bang on the bathroom door, but when I got to it, it was open. Dad and Mum were both downstairs – I told you she'd called me, and I could hear him talking to her."

"What did you do then?"

"I went down in my pyjamas and asked them if they knew where she was. We looked in all the rooms – it doesn't take long! Dad was worried straight off, but Mum said that perhaps Philippa had decided to go to school early for some reason. Dad said she couldn't have – the front door was still bolted from the inside and he'd been in the kitchen since six-thirty. Besides, the quickest way of getting to school is by catching the bus and it doesn't come by the end of the road until eight-thirty."

"Do you know what the time was when you went downstairs?"

"It must have been just after eight, because that's when Mum would have called. When I'm late up she always shouts up then. Half an hour is exactly long enough to get washed and dressed and eat some toast before the bus comes."

"Did your parents get in touch with the school?"

"Yes, Dad kept phoning until one of the secretaries an-

swered. People were still arriving then. She said she'd ask Mr Wellington – the teacher on gate duty – to keep a look out for Philippa. But she still wasn't there when school had started. That's when Dad walked down to the lodge house to talk to the policeman. He'd seen him go past while he was phoning."

"Thank you. And you didn't wake up in the night, hear any movement in your bedroom?"

"No. I'm a heavy sleeper. I don't often wake up."

Juliet reflected that Alice would have had to be more than a heavy sleeper if Philippa had been abducted against her will. She must have chosen to leave the house and, if the times that Alice mentioned were roughly correct, she'd probably left in the early hours of the morning. What could have persuaded her to venture into the dark inhospitable lanes of Sutterton Dowdyke at this time of year? She knew the area well, certainly. And she might have been accompanied: someone might have met her at or near the Cushings' house. But her motive was the biggest puzzle. She surely couldn't have been unhappier staying with Alice than at her own home, yet, as far as Juliet knew, she had no history of running away from there.

"Did you argue with Philippa last night?"

"No, we've never argued. We get on really well." Alice said this calmly, without over-protesting.

"Did she seem sad or upset about anything? Apart from the accident, I mean?"

"No, and to be honest she wasn't all that upset about that. You've seen what her family's like. She's always thought she must have been adopted. She hates Kayleigh, in particular. She was glad to be here for a while."

"Kayleigh stayed here on the night of the accident, didn't she?"

"Yes. She had a mattress on the floor. Then she decided to go and stay with her aunt Elsie."

"And Philippa was pleased?"

"We all were, if you want to know the truth. Kayleigh's not just stupid, she's sly. It makes her unbearable."

"I see. Do you know what Philippa was wearing when she left?"

"Her school uniform. She's very neat. While she's been here she's hung it all on a wooden hanger every night, at the side of the wardrobe. I saw it had gone as soon as I went back in the bedroom to get dressed."

"Has her coat gone as well?"

"Mum thinks so. She hasn't been able to find it."

"How long have you known Philippa? Were you at primary school together?"

"Most of the time. I think we came here when I was six. We moved from Spalding. I went to school there before we came here. Then to Kirton Primary."

"That's when you met Philippa?"

"Around that time. I think we may have met before then – Mum walked down to their house with me because she'd seen there was a girl living there who was about my age. But I can't remember if that was before or after I started at the school. She was there already."

"So you've been friends ever since?"

"Yes. She comes here a lot. She's like my sister."

Alice's blue eyes swam with tears. Juliet patted her arm.

"It's all right Alice, we'll take a break now. You've done really well. Shall we go and find your Mum and Dad?"

Chapter Thirty-Five

IT WORKED!

Why did he choose not to kill us both? He'd be rudderless without me, though he has his above-world life as well. And Ariadne? He's never shown the slightest affection for her and I believe feels none. But when I said he'd have her death on his hands, her murder by negligence, he was spooked.

I say this without irony, because I know he is continually at war with himself. It's not that he has no moral compass; he has, though it's hideous and crazy. He works to no normal code of human conduct, but still he's influenced by what his mother taught him. I'm not suggesting his subconscious tells him he'll face the wrath of God if he goes too far, but despite all his clever precautions he may have felt an irrational unease that 'something would happen' if he let Ariadne die. And he can't bear mess. There would have been the untidiness, the stench, the distastefulness of a decomposing body. The horror of how to rid himself of it without getting caught.

Two days ago, when at last he came, Ariadne was failing. Previously, he'd taken one look at her and threatened to beat her if she didn't stop pretending and he said he'd beat me if I didn't nurse her back to health. I'd seen him like that before: raging in his impotence, running scared. But not as scared as he was when he took her limp hand to feel her pulse. It was weak and fluttery: I know, because I'd been taking it obses-

sively myself. Her whole body was bathed in sweat. She drifted in and out of delirium, sometimes muttering words I could not hear. She was barely aware of either of us.

I see the panic flare in his eyes as he drops her wrist and grabs mine.

"What have you done to her?" he demands, in a voice meant to sound angry but is squealing with fear. I stand my ground. I've been planning this for hours. I have to get it right.

"I haven't done anything," I say. "She's ill. I've done all within my power to help her. She can't rally. We don't have the medicines or the knowledge."

"I suppose we don't," he says thoughtfully, as if he's just stumbled upon a shared flaw.

"I know . . . I know . . ." I say, faltering.

"What do you know?" he shrieks.

"I know I can rely on you not to let your daughter die. I know you have enough kindness in you – enough goodness – to get help for her before it's too late."

"What do you mean?" He knits his brows. There is a deep furrow at the top of his nose and there are crows' feet around his eyes. The Lover is ageing: he is weary. "I won't bring a doctor here, if that's what you want."

"You know I wouldn't ask that. This place is special, private to us. Besides, it's too late for a doctor. Ariadne needs to go to a hospital."

"In your dreams!" He flings my hand away, turns his back on me. I am terrified he will leave us. I skirt the end of Ariadne's bed so I can reach out to him. I put my arms around him, hug his back.

"We won't betray you," I say. "Ariadne can't speak. I'll say she suddenly fell ill, that we didn't know what to do, that we're travelling in the area, so that's why no-one knows us. I'll say you're an old family friend, that I called you because I had

no-one else to turn to."

He twists round in my arms, pushes his lips against mine, forces his tongue between my teeth. That ancient smell of mint.

"Do you love me?"

"You know that I do."

"You were wrong about me, weren't you, all those years ago?"

"Yes. Yes, I was wrong. Forgive me."

"Perhaps we can have a normal life together. I've been planning the stages, but we don't pass them. Perhaps we can try again."

"Yes. Yes, we can. I promise, we can."

"And you promise you'll be good? If we go to the hospital?"

"I promise. It will be all right, you'll see."

He is suddenly preoccupied with the logistics of getting Ariadne outside.

"You'll have to dress her," he says. "Does she have proper clothes?"

I nearly laugh in his face.

"She has what you've brought. Supermarket clothes. Mainly cotton dresses, some too small for her. We both spend our time wearing sweats, because we feel the cold. You know that."

"The supermarket clothes won't make a good impression, especially if they don't fit. They'll look cheap, as if she's been neglected. Don't you have any other clothes?"

"Yes. The ones from my suitcase when you first . . . when I first came here. I've barely worn them. They aren't practical."

"Will they fit her?"

"Probably. She's tall, but so am I. They're dated, though."

He looks at me shyly through his neat little fringe, like a boy on his first date.

"You always had classic taste. They won't look so out of place. Choose something easy and get her into it. Something good quality. And change into something smart yourself. I'm going out for a bit. I'll come back . . ."

"No!" I say, my heart lurching with alarm. "Please don't go. I won't be long. I'll change now and bring the clothes for Ariadne. We won't be more than a few minutes."

"All right," he says. He looks at his watch. "But you'll need to hurry, because it'll be daylight soon. I don't think Ve . . ." He pulls himself up short, fakes a coughing fit.

"What don't you think?"

"Nothing. Get yourselves dressed. I'll wait."

Chapter Thirty-Six

THE JOHNSON HOSPITAL was a low-slung, futuristic building set at the end of a wide white sweep of approach road. It had been built in 2009 and, although also called the Spalding Community Hospital, it was sited in Pinchbeck, the large village due north of Spalding. Pinchbeck was arguably even older than Spalding itself. In the past there had been competition between the two communities, but town and village were now virtually one: the main Spalding Road to Pinchbeck was dotted with houses all the way. The hospital was smart and efficient, proud of its record for treating A & E patients with minor injuries. It didn't pretend to offer specialist treatments and couldn't deal with serious accidents or patients who were critically or chronically ill.

Staff Nurse Marianne Burrell was standing in the reception area, feeling pleasantly tired and waiting for the last few minutes to elapse before she could go off duty after a busy but not traumatic shift. She'd spent the night supervising the usual flurry of cuts and bangs on the head sustained by those who 'had only had one drink' and helped to reassure the insomniac worried well who'd come in panicking about irregular heartbeats or because they thought they weren't breathing as easily as usual. She glanced idly out of the window. An interesting little tableau caught her eye.

A man had parked his car as close to the hospital entrance

as he could. Under the glow of the street lamps, the nurse observed him as he climbed out of it and tried to remove a very large bundle from the back seat, aided by a painfully thin woman who could barely stand. She kept stumbling and clutching at the open rear door for support. The watching nurse wondered if she was yet another drunk.

Together the couple managed to slide the bundle from the car. The man hoisted it into his arms. Apparently it was awkward to carry rather than heavy: he seemed not to flounder beneath its weight. The woman held on to one of his arms and haltingly walked beside him, peering into the top of the bundle now and then. It was only a short walk to the automatic doors, but twice they had to stop for her to rest and regain her balance before they finally entered the building.

Staff Nurse Burrell, rushing forward to help, recognised the man.

"Mr Start!" she said. "Matthew, isn't it? Let me help you. I hope that isn't . . ."

"I'm fine," he said brusquely, cutting her short. "I can manage perfectly well, thank you. Just tell me where to take her. This is her mother," he added in a rush. "She's someone I met years ago. They were travelling in this area when the daughter was taken ill. They came to my house and I offered to help. I . . ."

"Steady on!" The nurse smiled. "First things first. Follow me. We'll get her onto a bed first, shall we, then you can tell us what's wrong." Her eyes swept the face of the woman who'd been described as the mother. She was looking down at the floor. The woman was fair – very fair – but the nurse had never seen anyone with such a chalk-white complexion. Her skin was like paper, with an unhealthy, pearl-like sheen. And her pinched features and emaciated body were shocking when viewed close to. Staff Nurse Burrell touched the woman's arm.

"Are you all right, lovey?" she said. "Not sickening for the same thing, are you? I think we'd better have you examined as well."

"She's fine," snapped Matthew Start. "Just a bit worried about the girl, that's all."

"Even so . . ."

"I don't need any help for myself," said the woman in a voice at once colourless and inflected. She spoke English well, but Nurse Burrell would later hazard a guess that English wasn't her native language. "Please, just show us where to take Ariadne. I think she's quite sick."

"Follow me, if you can manage to carry her further."

She led them through some double doors to an A & E treatment area and took them to a cubicle, pulling the curtains around it deftly as she pointed to the bed.

"Put her down there. Take the blanket off her. Is she dressed?"

The woman identified as the mother nodded. The nurse took in her whole appearance for the first time. She was wearing a black suit with a fitted jacket and quite a short skirt and a purple blouse made of some very shiny material. The suit looked as if it was meant to be tight-fitting, but it hung off the woman, as if she'd lost a lot of weight since she bought it. The stockings that encased her stick-thin legs were sheer – the nurse noted a ladder in one of them – and she was wearing black suede high-heeled pumps with cut-out toes. She carried a shiny red handbag with a thick strap. It was dark and cold outside and the woman was shivering, but she had no coat.

Her clothes were smart enough, but there was something strange about them that the nurse couldn't quite put her finger on. The same went for the woman's silver-blonde hair, which had been smoothed down against her skull and kept in place with metal pins in several neon colours. Her long pony-tail

was fastened at the nape of her neck with a multi-coloured 'scrunchie'.

The man stood back while the woman slowly unwound the blanket that shrouded the patient, untangling it with some awkwardness. What she revealed was not a child, as the man had implied, but a young woman. Like her mother, she was very pale and thin. Also like her mother, she was dressed in a shirt of shiny satin material, predominantly green, with a swirling paisley pattern and a dark skirt.

The similarities ended there. Staff Nurse Burrell took one look at the supine patient and understood that she was very ill indeed. The young woman was holding her arms rigidly to her sides and appeared to be deeply unconscious. Her face was greasy with sweat.

"How long has she been like this?"

The man shrugged.

"A day or so," the woman said carefully.

"But I mean how long has she been unconscious?" The woman did not reply.

"I don't want to alarm you, but I think she's critically ill. I'm going to fetch a doctor right now. I'll send in another nurse to cover while I'm away. Don't leave her."

Half an hour later, the young woman had been hooked up to drips and a sac of blood and was being rushed by ambulance to the Pilgrim Hospital in Boston. Dr Sharma had explained that although he couldn't provide a diagnosis, Ariadne's symptoms indicated she was suffering from a condition too serious for the Community Hospital to treat. She needed help from the best-equipped hospital in the region, and as soon as possible. He didn't spell it out, because the mother seemed so fragile, but privately he thought the girl was close to death. He was very puzzled by her condition. On the face of it, she seemed well

cared for in a basic way, in that she was clean and there were no signs of physical abuse on her body. Nevertheless, some of her symptoms indicated prolonged privation: her muscles were wasted as if she never exercised them, the poor condition of her teeth suggested that she'd been malnourished over many months, if not years, and her extreme pallor suggested that she was not only habitually confined indoors, but had had little or no access to natural light. Her mother said they'd been travelling when Ariadne was taken ill, but he couldn't believe that this young woman had recently been in a fit state for a holiday. The mother herself seemed too frail for such a venture.

Curiously, her mother did not accompany her to the Pilgrim Hospital, even though Dr Sharma explained the gravity of the situation as clearly as he could. Matthew Start, the man who had introduced himself as the mother's old friend, said she needed to return to where she came from because she had other children to look after. He said he would take her back to them and then himself drive to the Pilgrim Hospital to check on Ariadne. The mother seemed to be briefly angered by his words, but she didn't contradict him. In fact, she said nothing at all. Yet she was clearly distraught about the girl.

"Before you go, I'll need you to sign a consent form as her next of kin and we'll also need Ariadne's address, and your own," said Dr Sharma. Wordlessly, the woman took the pen that he held out to her. The staff nurse had fixed the form to a clipboard, which she passed across. The woman hesitated and frowned, knitting her pale brows.

"I don't know the address . . . of the boarding house," she said to Matthew Start. "Perhaps I could use your address?" Her manner was tentative, as if she were afraid of him.

"No, don't do that, Lucy," Matthew Start said cheerfully. "It's bound to cause confusion. I think I know the name of the guest house. It's called Twelvetrees. It's in Surfleet. I'll find out

the rest of the details and phone them into you later." His final sentence was addressed to Nurse Burrell.

"Could you give me a contact telephone number?"

"I . . ."

"You'd better use my mobile number," said Matthew. "Lucy's might not work here."

"Am I to understand that you're not a British citizen?" said the doctor, addressing himself to 'Lucy'.

"Lucy's Dutch," said Matthew affably.

"If she's from the Netherlands, her mobile number probably will work."

"Better have my number to be on the safe side," he said, taking the clipboard from her and scribbling it down. "We have to go. We don't want to get into trouble for leaving the other children on their own."

"Just a minute," said Dr Sharma to Lucy. "We still don't have your signature."

Silently she took the clipboard from him and carefully inscribed something. Matthew Start watched impatiently. Staff Nurse Burrell, anticipating that he intended to take the clipboard back again, quickly relieved Lucy of it herself.

"Here's the number of the Pilgrim Hospital," she said, handing her a slip of paper. "It's a generic number for patients' relatives to call. After the first time, they'll probably let you know how to get through to the right ward."

"Thank you," said the woman called Lucy in a barely audible voice. She opened the red handbag and tucked the number inside.

"Come on," said Matthew Start. He crinkled his face into a grimace of a smile.

"Thank you for all your help," he said. "I'll get to Boston as soon as I can." He took hold of Lucy's elbow and steered her towards the door. Dr Sharma followed them out into the

reception area, Marianne Burrell behind him.

Lucy turned and held his eye. He had seldom seen anyone in so much despair.

"They will look after her, won't they? They will make her better?"

Faced with such a direct question, he felt unable to offer false hope.

"Lucy," he said gently, "I'm sure my colleagues at the Pilgrim Hospital will do everything in their power to help Ariadne and as I've already explained they have much more equipment than we do. But you must understand that she's very seriously ill. Since I can't give you a diagnosis I can't quantify the danger, but my advice is to find someone to look after your other children as quickly as you can so you can go to the hospital to be with her yourself. You may regret it if you don't."

The woman burst into tears immediately and lost her footing, as if she was about to faint. Marianne Burrell went to her aid, but Matthew Start got there first. He caught her and held her upright. For an instant she beat feebly on his chest, but he took both her wrists in his own and held her still.

"Thank you," he said again, bowing his head slightly in an incongruous gesture of courtesy. Gripping Lucy firmly, he half-carried her back through the automatic doors. Dr Sharma walked forward to observe them. He watched Matthew Start fix Lucy's seat belt. She was swatting him with her hands and sobbing. He was shouting at her.

"What do you make of that, Dr Sharma?" asked Staff Nurse Burrell. She was shaken both by the state of the girl patient and the bizarreness of the scenes she'd just witnessed.

"I have no idea what to make of it, but I'm certain of one thing: we need to tell the police. I think it's unlikely this girl's

life will be saved, but if it is she'll have to be protected from whatever it is that's made her so ill. And whether she survives or not, we have to find out the truth: I've never been so convinced I've just been told a pack of lies."

Chapter Thirty-Seven

TIM AND JULIET had gleaned as much as they could from the Cushing family. Before leaving, Tim asked them to stay indoors and not talk to the media. He said they shouldn't get in touch with Bob and Ruby Grummett and, if the Grummetts contacted them, to let their family liaison officer (Ann Bridges, a policewoman from Boston) listen to the call. Peter Cushing didn't argue.

"If Philippa calls, don't alarm her. If you think she's on her own, try to persuade her to come back. If there's evidence that someone else is with her, keep her talking as long as you can, so we can try to trace the call. And put the phone on speak so that WPC Bridges can hear."

Andy Carstairs had returned to Patti Gardner and remained with her while she worked. As far as Tim could tell, Peter Cushing had no inkling that human remains had been discovered in the old pigsty. That was how he wanted to keep it for the time being.

He knew that he and Juliet would have to visit Patti before they went on to the Pilgrim Hospital. The prospect of having to view the remains of a dead baby unnerved him, even though he now knew that the corpse had been interred for so long nothing was left but bones and a few fragments of pathetically tiny garments. He trudged along a few paces behind Juliet, his hands thrust into the pockets of his overcoat, his head bent against the vicious wind.

He was surprised to find the two workmen were still there, sitting in the cab of their lorry. One of them swung open the door and jumped down to greet him as he approached.

"Are you the boss? Is there any chance we can go home now, squire? My mate Tom's still shook up and your detective says we can't do no more work at the moment. We're fucking frozen and Tom needs a hot drink."

"I'm sorry we've kept you here for so long. I'll check with DC Carstairs, but I think it should be OK for you to leave now. You mustn't tell anyone what you found here today, or talk to the Press at all. Is that understood?"

"Sure, we've been told that already."

"Just wait here a bit longer, then. I'll be back as soon as I can."

He turned into the narrow path that breached the wrecked lodge house and its outbuildings. Juliet was standing outside the pigsty talking to Andy, who was flapping his arms and blowing on his fingers.

"Hello, boss. Am I glad to see you. It's fucking freezing here."

"That's what the construction guy's just said to me. I can't remember his name, but . . ."

"It's Nick Peat. Mate's called Tom Crosby."

"Why are they still hanging around? Did you ask them to stay?"

"Yes. I didn't know whether you'd want to interview them. And I thought you might be worried about them talking to the media."

"You've taken a statement, haven't you? Did they say anything that struck you as being odd?"

"No, it was straightforward. They started to move the floor covering and discovered some bones . . ."

"Well, tell them they can go, then. I've asked them not to talk to the Press, but you might like to say it again. I take it you have their contact details?"

"Yes."

"You'd better offer them counselling. Tom – I gather he's the one who found the remains – isn't looking too good. Recommend that he goes to hospital for a check-up, too. I don't want that coming back to bite us later."

Tim turned to Juliet.

"Have you spoken to Patti?"

"Only to say hello. She's in there packing up at the moment. She'll be pleased you're here."

Tim smiled wryly and involuntarily took a deep breath before going into the pigsty. Juliet saw, but pretended not to notice. Like Andy, she suspected that Tim and Patti had once been more than just colleagues. She'd observed awkwardness between them on several occasions.

Patti was squatting on the floor sweeping dust into a plastic bag. She had stacked several other plastic bags neatly to one side of the gap on the floorboards. There was also a small cardboard box, little bigger than a shoe-box, which she'd placed beyond these. She must have heard Tim talking to Juliet and she reacted to his presence in her usual manner, concentrating for some seconds with furious intensity on the job in hand before looking up at him. Her hair had been pushed into the hood of her plastic suit, but one stray strand now fell across her forehead. She tried to sweep it away with the back of her latex-gloved wrist. The action struck Tim as both vulnerable and endearing. Mentally he pinched himself for giving way to sentimentality.

"DI Yates," she said archly. "We've been expecting you."

"Yes, I'm sorry it's taken me so long. As you know, Philippa

Grummett has disappeared. I had to interview her friends up the road."

"She lived here, didn't she? I mean, in the lodge house."

"Yes, she's one of the two daughters."

"Do you think her disappearance is connected with this?" She pointed at the cardboard box.

"I don't know what to think at the moment. Possibly not directly connected, but the Grummett family is strange. I'm convinced they're doing something illegal, but – with the exception of Philippa – they're not very bright. Is that the . . . are the bones you found in there?"

"Yes. I took as many photographs as I could before I removed them. I think the skeleton's intact. It's certainly that of a child. Not newborn, but I'd guess less than a year old. Do you want to see it?"

"No," said Tim. "It's best disturbed as little as possible. I assume you'll carry out some tests on it?" He sensed that Patti understood his reluctance to inspect the remains.

"Yes." She indicated the plastic bags. "And on the fragments of clothing. There are some scraps of wool from a garment that's mostly rotted away, but there's still enough to analyse. And there's part of an item in synthetic material – it may have been a dress – that has survived rather better."

Tim blenched.

"What are you likely to be able to find out?"

"The sex and approximate age of the child. About how long the remains have been buried here. Whether it lived in this area or somewhere else. I could also match its DNA to that of parents and siblings, if we knew who they were."

"What about cause of death?"

"Unlikely. I'd only be able to do that if it'd been murdered and even then it would have to have been in a certain way –

trauma to the skull, for example. But I can see no evidence of deliberate damage of that kind."

"It must have been murdered, though, don't you think? Otherwise, why not give it a proper funeral?"

Patti smiled.

"I'd agree with you, if the bones had been found in a city. But there are still some deeply-held social taboos and superstitions in rural areas like this. For example, illegitimacy is still regarded as a disgrace by some local people, particularly if they follow one of the more evangelical brands of religion."

"Well, at least one crime has been committed. The death can't have been registered properly and, from what you're saying, possibly not the birth, either."

"Correct. I'm just telling you that even if you discover who concealed the body of a baby here, you'll probably find it difficult to make a murder charge stick."

"Thanks for the warning. You said that you could identify the parents of the child if you had their DNA. What about the Grummetts?"

"If the date of their tenancy of the lodge house precedes or coincides with the likely date the corpse of the child was buried, I'd say you'd be bound to want to start with them. Unless they confess upfront, of course."

Suddenly preoccupied with something he'd just remembered, Tim didn't reply. In his mind he was going over Ruby Grummett's statement after the accident. He had no doubt they'd deny all knowledge of the remains in the pigsty. If they did, Bob would have quite a lot more explaining to do.

"Thanks, Patti. I'll put a police guard on the pigsty for now, in case you want to come back. It'll stop ghouls from visiting, too."

Chapter Thirty-Eight

TIM AND JULIET'S journey to the hospital had taken place in silence. Tim's mood was unusually sombre. Juliet knew he was distressed by the dead baby, but she wondered if he'd also been disturbed by meeting Patti Gardner. Patti seemed to withdraw ever more into her shell these days. Each time Juliet met her, her figure was more angular and her tongue sharper than on the previous occasion. Juliet didn't suspect Tim of hankering after a renewal of whatever intimacies he and Patti might once have shared, but she wondered if he felt guilty about the colourlessly austere way in which Patti apparently now lived her life. She sympathised with Patti: she could so easily have fallen into a similar two-dimensional existence herself. She thought again of the evening she'd spent with Louise and her spirits lifted. Louise would probably be at the hospital now. Juliet smiled to herself before glancing sideways at Tim, hoping he hadn't noticed. She needn't have worried: he was staring straight ahead, his jaw set, his expression stern, gripping the wheel of his car so tightly his knuckles were white. Only when they'd turned into the hospital gate did he break out of his dark reverie.

"Could you text Ricky MacFadyen and ask him if he'd like to meet us outside? We may not be able to find anywhere private to talk to him in there."

Juliet tapped away nimbly at her smartphone. Ricky replied almost as soon as she'd sent the message.

"That was quick!" Tim managed a bleak smile.

"He just says 'yes'."

"Admirably laconic, but we'll probably have to text him again to ask where."

However, when they drove into the car park Ricky was already at the entrance, anxiously waiting for them. Tim halted and gestured to him to get into the back of the car.

"There's a parking space over there, near the path," said Ricky. "God, am I glad to see you."

"Everyone seems to be pleased to see me today, with the possible exception of Superintendent Thornton," said Tim drily. "To what do I owe your particular joy at my arrival?"

"It's the Grummetts," said Ricky. "They're doing my head in. They seem upset the girl's gone missing, but they don't appear to be worried about her, if that makes any sense. I know it sounds stupid. And I can't make them out – any of them. I can't decide whether they're really obtuse or just using the appearance of being thick to cover something up."

"When you say 'any of them', what do you mean? Who's there, exactly – apart from Ruby Grummett, I mean?"

"Ruby was alone when I arrived. I told the duty nurse why I was there and he said I should wait until the husband came before I told her about Philippa. Apparently her mental state still isn't good after the accident. He showed up quite quickly. At first, I saw him without her. He was unhelpful, aggressive. He said that he'd told you Ruby wasn't to be interviewed about the accident without her solicitor present. I said it wasn't about the accident and explained to him that no-one knew where Philippa was. He was gobsmacked by this, but in a strange way, as if he was afraid of something. I don't mean afraid something bad had happened to Philippa, but afraid for himself. But I might have imagined it, I suppose. I asked him if Philippa had got in touch with him since yesterday and he said

she hadn't. I said we should ask Ruby if Philippa had called her, perhaps to ask how she was, and he said she wouldn't have. He seemed sure of that, as if the idea was inconceivable. I asked if Philippa could have phoned her sister and again he said quite flatly that she wouldn't have. I said I'd need to see the sister even so and he agreed to call her. It took half an hour for the sister to arrive. Her name's Kayleigh. I said we should tell Ruby and Kayleigh about Philippa's disappearance at the same time and he agreed to this as well, but then he left me in the waiting room while he went to see Ruby. He said she'd get upset if he didn't go to her straight away."

"So you let him see her on his own first?" Tim hoped he sounded as annoyed as he felt.

"He said he wouldn't tell her about Philippa," said Ricky feebly.

"If I'd been you . . ."

"Ricky couldn't really have done anything else, Tim," said Juliet quietly. "In the eyes of the world, the Grummetts are now double victims: first they've suffered the loss of their home and Ruby's been mentally damaged by an accident that has yet to be proved her fault; now they've lost their younger daughter. Whatever we may think, at the moment we have no reason to treat them like suspects."

Tim sighed.

"I suppose you're right. I'm sorry, Ricky – I'm not having a good day. Carry on with your story. What happened when Kayleigh Grummett turned up?"

"She didn't come on her own. Her uncle and aunt were with her. God, that woman smells awful. Kayleigh's staying with them, apparently. They live at Spalding Common and she works in Boston, but she's got herself signed off sick. She hardly spoke, actually. Uncle Ivan did most of the talking. I asked both Ruby and Kayleigh if Philippa had been in touch

with them and Kayleigh looked at me as if I was mad. The uncle said that no-one had phoned his house recently except Bob, to report on Ruby. I asked Kayleigh if she had a mobile. She said she did, but Philippa didn't know the number. Very strange. I asked her if she knew where Philippa might have gone and Uncle Ivan intervened again to say that the sisters weren't close."

"What about Ruby?"

"She was just hunched up at the top of the bed, staring at everyone with her little black eyes. Bob had obviously spilt the beans about Philippa. Ruby didn't register any surprise when I said the girl was missing. She didn't say anything at all and I didn't push her. I was afraid of provoking some kind of outburst."

"I suppose that was wise," said Tim. "She's thrown a wobbly once already. Put on, most likely, but even if the hospital staff think so, their first duty will be to look after her. Where are all the Grummetts now?"

"Still up there. I asked them to wait until you got here. I know you want to speak to them about the child's skeleton."

"They don't have any inkling about that, do they?"

"No. I don't see how they could have, unless Peter Cushing told them."

"He doesn't know. And I've asked him not to contact them. He won't, either – he doesn't seem at all anxious to speak to them."

"I think we should go in," said Juliet. "Nothing we've done so far can make them stay if they don't want to. I think Ivan Grummett could do a lot of damage if he talks to the Press about them being shabbily treated – not to mention the lawyer they seem to have hired."

"You're right," said Tim. "And the lawyer's bound to show

up sooner or later. We need to talk to them before he gets involved and puts a brake on everything."

When Tim, Juliet and Ricky entered Ruby Grummett's ward, the four other members of the Grummett family were still huddled around her bed. Tim thought they made an incongruous group. Ruby was lying back on her pillows saying nothing to Bob, who was stroking her hand and whispering to her. Her small black eyes were sharply focused, however, and she spotted Tim first. Elsie was sitting opposite Bob on the other side of the bed chattering inconsequentially to Ruby, who appeared to be ignoring her. Ivan was prodding Bob to attract his attention, but either Bob hadn't noticed or he'd chosen not to. Kayleigh was engrossed in carrying out some activity on her mobile phone.

Ruby sat up when the three police officers approached. All the others except Kayleigh registered and turned to look.

"Mrs Grummett," said Tim. "I'm sorry about your daughter, but please rest assured we are doing everything in our power to find her. I'd be grateful if you'd let me check on just one thing, since DC MacFadyen didn't have the opportunity. I'm sure you would have mentioned it if it had been the case, but she hasn't tried to contact you, has she?"

Uncle Ivan jumped in immediately.

"She wouldn't have done that. Little madam, she is. Thinks we're not good enough for her."

"Now, Ivan . . ." Elsie began weakly.

"Shut up, woman."

"Mr Grummett, I must ask you to let your sister-in-law speak for herself."

"No, she hasn't been in touch with me," said Ruby dully.

"Thank you." There was a slight pause while Tim thought how best to put what he had to say next. He was aware of

four pairs of hostile Grummett eyes scrutinising him intensely. Kayleigh put down her phone and stared as well, emulating the others.

Tim cleared his throat.

"This isn't going to be easy," he said, "and I do understand that you've had an unbelievably tough time already this week, but there is something else I need to say to you – to Bob and Ruby, anyway." He turned to them. "It's a sensitive matter. You may want us to speak in private."

"Send us away, you mean?" said Ivan belligerently. "We're family and we stick together. Whatever you've got to say, Bob wants us here, don't you, Bob?"

Bob Grummett nodded obediently.

"Mrs Grummett?" said Tim, looking at Ruby.

She shrugged.

"I don't mind them staying if they don't want to go."

Bob had moved closer to Ruby and clasped her hand in his. It made it easier for Tim to observe how both of them reacted to his next sentence.

"I'm sorry to have to inform you that we have discovered the remains of an infant at the site of your home, in one of the outbuildings."

Bob looked alarmed. Ruby just stared him out.

"Do you have any knowledge of how they might have got there, or the identity of the child?"

"Of course they don't . . ." Ivan Grummett began.

"Mr Grummett, I must ask you to let me speak to your brother and his wife without interruption. Otherwise I shall have to insist on seeing them alone."

"The house was more than a hundred years old. They could have been put there at any time," said Ruby.

"That's right," said Bob, leaping in to reinforce her argument.

"How many outbuildings are there, Mr Grummett?" said Tim.

"Two. The old kennels and the old piggery."

"Do you use either of them?"

"Yes. I keep my tools in the kennels."

"And the piggery?"

"No. It's empty."

"Why don't you use it? It seems to be quite a strong building. The roof doesn't leak."

"Haven't had much call for it. The kennels is big enough for . . ."

"But you do keep a pig, don't you, Mr Grummett?"

"Come again?"

Tim felt a surge of irritation which he suppressed with some difficulty.

"You do keep a pig. When you gave a statement to the police about your whereabouts at the time of the accident, you said that you were out on your bike, visiting your pig."

"Oh, ah. Percy, you mean."

"No doubt, if Percy's the name of your pig. Where do you keep Percy?"

"Eh?"

"Where does Percy live?" said Tim, trying not to sound testy.

"Oh, at my mate Bill's. Out Algakirk way. Bill lets me use an old pigsty on his land."

"Why do you need to use Bill's pigsty?"

Bob Grummett's face assumed a look of intense concentration, though whether he was trying to remember why he kept his pig at Bill's or was thinking up a plausible reply was impossible to tell.

Kayleigh suddenly chirped up.

"It's because our pigsty gives him the willies, that's why.

He's never liked it, not since I can remember. And we was never allowed to play in there."

"Shut your mouth," said Ivan savagely.

"I'm not saying any more without my sollicingtor. I need to speak to Mr Dixon."

Tim asked Bob Grummett for his current address – he was still staying at his brother David's house in Boston – and warned him not to leave the area. He gave Bob his card and said he'd be setting up a formal interview at Boston police station the following Monday, so if he wanted Dixon to be in attendance he should make the necessary arrangements. The other Grummetts sat and stared in silence during this short interlude. Bob himself barely replied, except to say, "Where do you think I'm going with Rube in 'ere?", jerking his head in the direction of his wife. Ruby herself had closed her eyes.

"What now?" asked Juliet, after the three police officers had left the ward and were walking along the corridor.

"I'd like you to try to find Dr Butler. Ask her if she's got any plans to discharge Ruby Grummett in the near future. I'm hoping that the answer is that they aren't ready to release her yet, but you know what hospitals are like at weekends. Can't wait to get rid of people."

"I'm sure Louise – Dr Butler – wouldn't discharge someone just because it was convenient," said Juliet, flushing.

"You're probably right. But no offence – it's not Dr Butler's ethics that interest me, it's making sure I know Ruby Grummett's whereabouts."

"What do you want me to do now?" Ricky asked.

Tim smiled mischievously.

"I'd like you to go and talk to Philippa Grummett's teachers. That shouldn't take you all afternoon. After that, there's a little job that I'd asked Andy to do that I'd put on the back burner,

but now we've established that those are a child's remains at the lodge, it's moved a bit higher up the list of priorities."

Ricky groaned.

"I think I know what you're going to say. It's about sifting through the Grummetts' shitty possessions, isn't it?"

"You got it in one," Tim grinned. "But go to the school first. And be as thorough as you can. We think there's something dodgy about Richard Lennard, the headteacher at Spalding High School. If you smell something fishy about the head at Philippa's school, we may have found our connection. In which case you may be spared the shitty possessions, at least for today."

Ricky smiled ruefully despite himself and made for the stairs. He was just out of earshot and Juliet had started walking down the corridor in the other direction, when Tim's mobile rang.

"Superintendent Thornton," he said. "Hello."

"Yes, hello, Yates, I'm glad I've managed to get hold of you. Where are you?"

"At the Pilgrim Hospital. Is something wrong?"

"I'll treat that question with the contempt it deserves, Yates. A few minutes ago I might have replied that we've only got two missing schoolgirls and a dead child on our hands, but now I wish that were true."

"Has something else happened?"

"Oh, well done, Yates, quick on the uptake today, aren't you? Yes, something else has happened. A young woman was taken to the Johnson Hospital early this morning. She was very ill – it's only a kind of cottage hospital, as you know – and they couldn't cope with her. She was transferred as an emergency case to the Pilgrim Hospital. Where you are now," he added, with a hint of satisfaction.

"But I don't understand why this is a police matter. Was the woman attacked or involved in an accident?"

"Not as far as we know. But the doctor and nurse who saw her at the Johnson Hospital said the man and woman who brought her in were behaving strangely. Apparently the woman, who claimed to be the mother, also looked unwell. And they didn't accompany the young woman in the ambulance, even though they were told her condition was serious. The doctor on duty was sufficiently concerned to report all this to us. And now the Pilgrim Hospital's apparently called him back for more details. They say the woman's suffering from total organ collapse caused by extreme and prolonged privation. She's probably been kept within a confined space, with little or no access to sunlight, for months, if not years."

"You mean she's been *imprisoned* somewhere?"

"That's what they seem to think. I want you to find the doctor in charge of the woman, see if you can find out any more. While you're doing that, I want MacFadyen to get back here to interview the couple who brought her in. He's with you at the moment, I take it?"

"No, he's just left. I've asked him to go to Boston Grammar School to question Philippa Grummett's teachers."

"Oh. Oh well, I suppose that's a priority. We're so damned short of bodies at the moment, Yates. Who would you send to talk to these people?"

"I think it's a probably a job for uniforms at this stage, sir.

"You're probably right. I saw PC Chakrabati hanging about just now, looking for you, probably. He might as well make himself useful."

"He's a good copper," said Tim. "His partner's shaping up, too."

"Yes, I've noticed her," said the Superintendent approvingly. "Smartened herself up a bit since she came to us, hasn't she? Lost some weight as well."

"I hadn't noticed," said Tim blandly. "What's the name of the young woman who's been brought here?"

"Ariadne something." Tim could hear papers rustling at the other end of the phone. "Ah, yes, I knew there was something else that was strange. The mother provided no proper surname, either for herself or the girl. The nurse who gave her the consent form to fill in didn't notice until afterwards. She wrote the girl's name as Ariadne Helen and her own name as Helen. That was all. And in itself strange, because the man who accompanied her addressed her as 'Lucy'."

"What about the man? Was he the husband?"

"No, and because he said he wasn't related to the girl he wasn't required to sign anything. He said he'd known the mother years ago and offered to help when she turned up out of the blue on his doorstep with a sick daughter."

"Sounds a likely story to me. But what is his name? Do we know him?"

"I don't know if he's known to the police. If he is, I doubt it's in the sense of having a record. He comes from quite a prominent local family. His name's Matthew Start."

Tim whistled. "Councillor Start's son!"

"In all probability. I don't have time to start worrying about his genealogy. Find out as much as you can about that young woman's illness and get back here soonest, will you?" said the Superintendent, suddenly testy. He terminated the call abruptly.

Tim looked both ways down the corridor. It was deserted. Damn, he thought, it would have been easier to get information from the hospital about the girl if he'd gone with Juliet to talk to Louise Butler. He headed swiftly for the lift, hoping to catch up with her.

Councillor Start's son, he mused to himself as the lift made its jerky descent to the ground floor. It was a coincidence too far.

Chapter Thirty-Nine

JULIET WAS STILL waiting patiently in the reception area.

"Is Dr Butler off duty?" he asked.

"No, she's dealing with an emergency. She's sent a message that she may be able to see me in half an hour or so. Otherwise she'll ask one of her colleagues to help."

"It would be better to see the colleague now, wouldn't it, considering how much we've got on at the moment."

Juliet flushed crimson.

"Anyway," Tim continued quickly, "You're probably right to wait for her, because I have a favour to ask of her – or that I'd like you to ask. A patient was brought here from the Johnson Hospital this morning – a young woman, unconscious, I believe. Thornton's asked me to find out as much as I can about what's wrong with her. An abusive relationship is suspected. I thought your Dr Butler would be more likely to help you than just some uniform we might send in off the street – or me, if it comes to that." He smiled at her.

"That may be the emergency case she's with at the moment," said Juliet. "What's the woman's name?"

"Ariadne, apparently. Strange name, isn't it?"

"Strange for round here, certainly."

"According to Thornton, she isn't from round here – though there's some doubt about that. Finding out who she really is is part of what Thornton's after. The mother told some

cock-and-bull story about being on holiday when the girl was suddenly taken ill. It doesn't fit with the symptoms, apparently. The medical staff at Spalding smelt a rat. Something that will intrigue you is that it was Councillor Start's son who brought her in. At least I think it was him. Matthew Start. Claims that he knew the mother years ago and had never clapped eyes on the girl before."

"The son's name *is* Matthew. I found it on the website when I was trying to discover more about the Starts."

"Yes, why was that? I can't remember now."

"Well, I admit it seems a hundred years ago, but I was making a – sorry for the pun – start on the Superintendent's cold case file. I was interested in the au pair girl who disappeared in the early nineties. She'd been working for the Starts. I didn't find out much more than that. Matthew Start lives quite close to the Johnson Hospital – in Pinchbeck."

"I suppose that figures, since he took the girl there. Logically, he would have taken her to the nearest hospital to him."

"Funny that he says the woman just turned up at his house, though. I wonder what Veronica thought about it?"

"Have you met Matthew?"

"No. I've only seen pictures of him on the website. He and his father both come across as wide boys. The houses they build are poor quality, crammed into estates with virtually no gardens and that matchboxy sort of look that goes with cheap building materials. But there's a more upmarket side to the business, as well. They also do restoration work and renovations for the well-heeled: underground swimming pools and games rooms, that sort of thing."

"I didn't take to the father when I met him. And it's odd how they keep on cropping up. Councillor Start was at the railway lodge just after the train was derailed – said he was enquiring after Philippa Grummett – and now his son happens to be

asked for help by a woman whose daughter is dangerously ill."

"Juliet?"

A voice coming from behind them startled them both, although it was quiet and somewhat weary. Juliet and Tim both swung round to see Louise Butler standing a few feet away. She was wearing green scrubs and a blue hairnet. She was both slighter and prettier than Tim remembered.

"Hello, Louise. We're sorry to bother you. We won't keep you long."

"No need to apologise, but I don't *have* long. If it's about Ruby Grummett, from a clinical point of view there's no reason why she shouldn't go home now. Psychologically, though, she's far from ready for it. She's being treated by one of our resident psychiatrists for trauma and of course he won't breach patient confidentiality by telling me what her problems are. From my own untutored perspective I'd say she connects leaving the hospital with the prospect of some kind of punishment. Not necessarily relating to the accident, but that would be the obvious trigger."

"So you intend to keep her here for longer?" said Tim.

"For a little longer, simply because she suffered such a horrific experience. We have to be careful about that. She could still present delayed shock symptoms. And I understand her daughter has now disappeared, so we'll have to watch to see if that has a further effect on her health. But the general consensus among the nursing staff here is that she's exaggerating how ill she is."

"Putting it on, then?"

"I wouldn't like to say that. The mind works in strange ways, especially when under duress. But unless she presents some definite physical illness, we shall certainly discharge her at the beginning of next week. I'm sorry if you'd prefer it to be earlier than that."

"It suits our purpose very well if you need to keep her a bit longer."

Louise Butler regarded him with a certain amount of irony. For the first time, Tim wondered whether Juliet talked about him to others and if so how she described him.

"We're not here to 'serve your purposes', DI Yates. I suppose you may find it convenient to keep Mrs Grummett here because you know where she is. But we're not her gaolers. If she chooses to leave, we can't make her stay. As I've indicated, however, I think that's unlikely. Is that all?" She turned to Juliet.

"As a matter of fact there is something else we hoped you might help us with," said Juliet rather timidly, "but if you need to get back to work we can come again later."

Chapter Forty

ALEX COOPER GREETED Ricky cordially. He was obviously extremely worried about Philippa Grummett. By the time Ricky had arrived at Boston Grammar School, Superintendent Thornton's news bulletin about the abduction of Cassandra Knipes had been broadcast and Cooper had made the connection.

"Do you think this is something to do with the kidnapping in Spalding?" he asked Ricky.

"We have nothing concrete at present, but my boss thinks it's highly likely. That's confidential, of course, sir."

"I think I know your boss. I tried to help him when he was investigating the disappearance of a former pupil at Spalding High School, Bryony Atkins."

"I was involved in that case myself, sir."

"I'm afraid I don't remember you, but I was the head there at the time. I moved to Boston a couple of years ago."

"Promotion, was it, sir?"

A shadow crossed Alex Cooper's face.

"Sort of. Well, no, not really. If you must know, I crossed swords with some of the governors. Both they and I thought it best if I applied for a post elsewhere. Anyway, we have more urgent things to discuss. How can we help you to find Philippa?"

"We want you to contact us immediately if she gets in touch

with anyone here, pupils or teachers. Please impress on everyone how important that is. If she telephones anyone direct, let us know straight away – I'll give you an emergency number – and try to keep her talking as long as possible, so we can trace the call. A uniformed police officer from Boston will be arriving shortly, to talk to anyone who thinks they might have useful information. Tell him as soon as you can if anything happens, but your first priority must be to keep Philippa talking."

"I understand. Other than that, do we carry on as usual?"

"As much as you can. I'll stay until the officer arrives. I'd like to speak to any special friends that Philippa has. We've already interviewed Alice Cushing. Is there anyone else she's particularly close to? Or any teacher in whom she might have confided?"

"Philippa's quite a popular girl, but I'd say she was closest to Alice. Among the teaching staff, Mrs Clay might be able to help. She's their form teacher. I asked her to talk to Philippa a few days ago, after the railway accident, just to make sure she wasn't traumatised by it."

"Can I speak to Mrs Clay now?"

Susan Clay was a motherly, slightly plump woman in her midfifties. She had a pleasant, open face and greying curly brown hair. She entered the headteacher's office quietly and with a certain amount of deference. It was apparent that she liked her boss. Ricky was impressed by her matter-of-factness. Although obviously aware that they were dealing with a crisis, she made no attempt to melodramatise the situation. Alex Cooper motioned to her to sit down.

"Mrs Clay, I know you're aware that Philippa Grummett has disappeared from the home of Alice Cushing, with whom she was staying after her home was destroyed by the derail-

ment earlier this week. Mr Cooper tells me that he asked you to talk to her about it, see if she was all right. When was that?"

"I think on Tuesday or Wednesday. I'm pretty sure it was Wednesday, because yesterday she needed some time off, to visit her mother at the hospital."

"So you spoke to her quite soon after the accident?"

"Yes."

"How did she seem?"

"Quite pleased to be staying at Alice's. I wouldn't say she was upset."

"Was there anything at all in her behaviour that gave you cause for concern?"

"Only that she was almost unnaturally calm about it all. I did wonder if she might be in denial, and therefore suffer some kind of delayed shock reaction later on. I told her to come and see me if she wanted to talk again, or if she needed any help at all."

"Thank you. My next question is rather delicate. I'd like to ask you both what kind of impression you've formed of Philippa's parents. I don't mean to sound prejudiced, but have you ever thought there was anything . . . odd . . . about their relationship with Philippa?"

There was a pause. At length, Alex Cooper said, "I don't think I've ever met them, have you, Susan?"

"No, I'm sure I haven't. They've never been here, as far as I know."

"But you have parents' evenings, open days, that sort of thing?"

"Of course we do. But we can't make the parents come to them if they choose not to," said Alex Cooper.

"Isn't it rather unusual for the parents not to show interest when their children attend a school like this?"

"Yes, it is. Unusual, but not unheard of. And as I've said, there's nothing we can do about it."

"Thank you," said Ricky. "I think you've answered my question."

Chapter Forty-One

"YOU'D BETTER COME to my office," said Louise Butler. "This isn't something I want to discuss in the public waiting area." Tim and Juliet followed her back to the lift.

"Take a seat," she said wearily. "We're going to have to be quite quick about this. I must get back to the patient soon. There's also the question of confidentiality, although I have concerns that the young woman you're interested in has been subjected to abuse. Perhaps you can advise me."

"If you think that someone has put her life in danger, or that she'll be in danger if she's returned to that person, you have a duty to tell us all you can," said Tim. Louise Butler gave Juliet a quick question-mark look. Juliet nodded. The interchange was not lost on Tim.

"OK. The woman who was sent here from Spalding's Johnson Hospital earlier today is principally suffering from kidney failure. I'd say she's been afflicted with it for some time. Undoubtedly she will have had symptoms several days ago, perhaps longer, and these have become acute. She's now in a coma. It's an extremely serious condition. Her case is so advanced that I'm worried all of her organs might shut down. If that happens, we probably won't be able to save her."

"Can you tell what caused it?"

"There are several possible explanations, but in her case there are other clues. Her gums are bleeding and some of her

teeth appear to be loose. Her hair is in poor condition and her skin is unnaturally white. And she is very underweight, with under-developed muscles. She's almost certainly malnourished. Putting all these things together, I think that she's been living in conditions of acute deprivation for a very long time."

"What do you mean by that, exactly?"

"It's difficult for me to be more precise without straying into conjecture, but I think she's been held in a confined space with no access to natural light, possibly for many years."

"About how old is she?"

"She's probably younger than she looks at the moment. The mother gave the year of birth as 1995 on the consent form provided by the Johnson Hospital. I've no reason to doubt that's correct. Odd, of course, that no day or month was included. And the name the mother gave is also strange: Ariadne Helen, with Lucy Helen in the space for details of next of kin."

"I understand the man who took her to the Johnson Hospital said he'd come to visit her here after he'd taken the mother home. Has he shown up yet?"

"No. We wouldn't let him see her at the moment, anyway, unless he's a relative."

"Do you have the form the mother signed?"

"We have a copy of it. The Johnson Hospital kept the original."

"Could you copy it again for us?"

"I'll have someone do it, if you wait here. And now I really must go."

Tim cleared his throat.

"Thank you very much, Dr Butler," he said. "I suppose there's no chance we could see this patient, is there?"

"None whatsoever," she replied sternly. "It wouldn't help you, in any case. She's in a deep coma. If she comes round, naturally we shall allow you to speak to her then."

Chapter Forty-Two

"We'd better touch base with Thornton," Tim said, as he and Juliet drove away from the Pilgrim Hospital. "Then I think it's time we paid Matthew Start a visit. Do you have his address?"

"Yes. He lives in Blue Gowt Lane. It's quite a substantial house: I've looked it up on Streetview. Part of it is Victorian, but there's a large extension, integrated impeccably with the original structure. It's a good advert for the Start construction company – the upmarket bit of it, anyway."

"Let's call in there before we go back to the station. It's on our way, isn't it?"

"Yes, but he might still be at work. It'll only be late afternoon when we get there."

"It's Friday. Most firms round here knock off early on Fridays. I think it's worth a try."

"Veronica might be at home. I think the school day finishes at 3.30."

"Will that make it tricky for you?"

"I don't know her well. And I don't know him at all. Besides, we're not trying to charge him with anything, are we?"

"Not at the moment. But he's got quite a lot of questions to answer about that girl in intensive care. The tale he told the nurse doesn't hang together at all."

"I don't see how he could be responsible for the girl's condi-

tion. He . . ." Juliet suddenly stopped speaking.

"What's wrong?" said Tim, looking across at her.

"I've just remembered some of the details of that cold case I started looking at. Matthew Start was the last person to see the Finnish au pair who disappeared. He said he'd taken her to the station to catch the train to London. He claimed not to know what her plans were."

"I'm sure you're leading me somewhere with this, but I'm not quite with you yet. We want to see Matthew Start in connection with the sick woman now at the Pilgrim Hospital, don't we? We have no reason to suspect him of abducting Cassandra Knipes or Philippa Grummett."

"That's right. Not at the moment, anyway. But everyone who's seen them both has remarked on the physical similarity between Cassandra and Philippa. And Verity Tandy thought the photo in the cold case file of the missing au pair showed a resemblance to both of them."

"I seem to remember that we were both sceptical about that. I certainly thought Verity had Philippa lookalikes on the brain."

"OK, I agree it sounds far-fetched, but I'm convinced there's a link that we can't quite see yet. As you've always said, coincidences are suspicious."

"I do usually say that, but I'm not sure it applies to lookalikes. Both girls grew up in this area, but apparently they've never met and they come from quite different backgrounds. What are you suggesting? That they're each the product of donated sperm? I could believe it of the Knipes parents, but I don't think Ruby Grummett's the kind to go in for IVF."

"I wasn't thinking of IVF, but perhaps some other, hidden, familial link. The girls are unusual to look at: they both have silver-blonde hair and very pale skin and they're both tall and strong – and very dissimilar to their parents in both cases. I

was struck by something Louise Butler said when I was talking to her at the hospital the other day, about all the children in a village near Bourne being descended from the same great grandfather."

"Now you really have lost me, unless the point that you're making is that sperm travels in an occult sort of way."

"I suppose that is what I mean, but I'm trying to get at something beyond that. I'll have another look at that cold case file when we get back to the office. Perhaps I'll be able to think a bit more clearly then."

"Whatever, I'm sceptical. But you've sown enough doubt in my mind to persuade me not to call on Matthew Start without seeing Thornton first. We'll need to interview Start soon, and his wife, but separately. If you're right and he is involved in the abductions, we have to tread carefully – and the abductions are Thornton's case, as he'll be the first to point out."

As if on cue, Tim's mobile started to ring. Tim took the call on hands-free.

"Yates? Where the hell are you? You seem to have been in Boston all day. Get back here, will you? I want to have a briefing session. Is Armstrong with you?"

"Yes, I'm here, sir."

"Good. The way Yates is dreamboating around today, I thought he might have forgotten you and left you behind somewhere."

Chapter Forty-Three

SUPERINTENDENT THORNTON WASN'T as ebullient as he'd sounded when Tim and Juliet joined his briefing session half an hour later. He'd assembled all the officers involved in the case so they could report quickly on the progress of their various enquiries. This was essential in order to keep everyone up-to-date and avoid failure to connect linked pieces of information, an occupational hazard. Tim knew only too well how difficult it was to keep tabs on all the elements of major incidents as more officers were drawn into the investigation. Tim also suspected the Superintendent's keenness to hold the meeting stemmed from his having so far drawn a complete blank.

Thornton had decided to piece together the events of the day as the police had dealt with them. He started with Verity Tandy. She gave a brief account of what had happened after she'd been sent to the Knipes household. She mentioned Tim's visit and how he'd instructed her to stay with Cassandra Knipes' parents until police liaison arrived. She said that after that officer had come, she'd conducted a fingertip search around the bus stop in Woolram Wygate, but her search had produced no results that could be linked to the kidnapping.

"What were her parents like while you were alone with them?" the Superintendent asked.

"They were distressed and worried, of course. They showed it in different ways. The mother tried to be stoical, though she

got quite upset some of the time. The father reacted with a kind of anger. He's severely disabled, and I had the impression that in his mind he linked her disappearance with his infirmity in some way."

"Do you mean he was angry that he couldn't save her because he was physically incapable?" It was Tim speaking.

"Perhaps. But there seemed to be some underlying criticism of his wife involved: it was as if she'd made a decision that had caused the family to take a wrong turn."

"What makes you say that?" said Tim.

"He was clearly annoyed with his wife. She tried to pacify him, but they made no attempt to comfort each other. At one point he started to say, 'this wouldn't have happened if . . .', but she cut in."

"How did she do that?"

"She said that they were both upset and that he shouldn't say something he might later regret."

"Did she actually use that word? Regret, I mean?"

"I think so, yes."

"Oh, for goodness sake, Yates, this isn't an exercise in etymology. Thank you, Tandy; if that's all you have to tell us, we'll move on to Chakrabati. Well done." Superintendent Thornton added the perfunctory praise too belatedly. Tim and Giash Chakrabati both noticed Verity's dejection. Giash gave her a pat on the arm before taking over.

"I went to Spalding High School as you instructed, sir, and spoke to Richard Lennard. He was outwardly helpful, though cagey, I'd say. He was very keen to cancel tomorrow's netball match. He tried to say it was inappropriate for the netball to go ahead under the circumstances. But there'd been an altercation with Councillor Start earlier because of some kind of meeting he's organised at the school tomorrow. The Councillor doesn't want the netball event to coincide with the meeting. In

reality, Mr Lennard was keen to cancel the netball to ingratiate himself with Mr Start, who is the chairman of the governors."

"I'm not sure that this has any bearing on . . ."

"That's very interesting," said Tim, cutting Superintendent Thornton short. "Is the netball going to be cancelled?"

"I said I thought it should go ahead. Mr Lennard more or less said it wasn't my place to advise him and I said I'd check with Superintendent Thornton to see what he thought. And yourself, of course, sir. I said that you'd probably want the match to go ahead because we might get some clues from it."

"I think you're right. Superintendent?"

"Yes, I suppose so. I want to know what Councillor Start's meeting's for and this is one way of finding out. As the chairman of the governors, you'd expect him to be much more interested in locating the missing head girl of the school than in ensuring that he and his friends aren't disturbed. Do you know what he said?"

"I didn't speak to the Councillor himself, sir, though I did see him in the distance."

"So he was at the school earlier today?"

"Yes. Mr Lennard didn't tell me much about the meeting. He just said it concerned a 'charitable organisation' that the Councillor is involved with. I think it's not unusual for schools to hire out their premises out of hours."

"Quite. But I'm intrigued by this 'charitable organisation'. I'm surprised Lennard hasn't checked with me already, if he was as keen on cancelling the netball as you say. But I'll get on to him as soon as the briefing is over."

"I think I may know the name of the charity concerned, sir," said Juliet. "It's quite obscure – secretive, I'd say – so I haven't been able to find out too much about it. But it's called The Bricklayers."

"Really? It sounds like some kind of working man's guild."

"It may have started out like that, but from the very limited amount of information I have, I'd say it was more akin to the Masons."

"Oh." Tim thought he saw the mildest of flushes colour the Superintendent's face. "Well, nothing wrong with them, is there?"

"No, sir, not as far as I know. But I believe there are groups that have outwardly modelled themselves on the Masons to mask more sinister purposes."

"Really?" said the Superintendent again. "Well, try to find out more about this lot, will you? We'll need to be armed with fact tomorrow. Is that all you have to report, Chakrabati?"

"Almost all. There is one other thing, though it may not be of any significance. As I was leaving the school, with Mr Lennard escorting me – I got the impression he was glad to see the back of me – a female reporter appeared. He'd obviously clashed with her before. Their conversation was short and extremely hostile. He asked me to confirm that she was trespassing on school grounds and I had no option but to agree with him."

"Well, I can understand his annoyance. She'd probably got wind of Cassandra Knipes's kidnapping."

"I don't think she did know about the kidnapping, sir. She said she was there because she had evidence that the school premises were being used for unsuitable activities. That was why Mr Lennard was so annoyed."

"What was her name?" said Andy, suddenly joining the conversation from the back of the room.

"Jocelyn something. She gave me her card," said Giash, fishing in his pocket. "Here it is. Jocelyn Greaves. She . . . er . . . said she knew you."

"That's right, she does."

"In what context?" asked the Superintendent.

"She's one of my sister's friends. I took her out for a drink the other night." Andy ignored the smiles and knowing glances that flashed around the room.

"I see. I'm not sure that police officers should consort with journalists. However, on this occasion she may prove to be useful."

"In what way, sir?" said Andy tautly.

"She may be able to tell us a little more about these Bricklayers. I don't suppose she's mentioned them to you?"

"As a matter of fact, she has."

"Good. Well, after this meeting's over, get in touch with her and find out exactly what she knows about them." Andy's reply was inaudible, but the Superintendent didn't notice.

"Well, Yates, it seems you saw the Grummetts as well as the Cushings after all. Tell us about it. As quick as you can, please." He consulted his watch.

"DC Armstrong and I were present on both occasions, sir. I think the Cushings are above board . . ."

"What do you mean by that, exactly?"

"I think they're telling the truth and not holding back on anything. It seems that yesterday was a pretty normal day. Nothing unusual happened in the evening after the two girls returned from school. Philippa Grummett and Alice Cushing were sharing a bedroom. They went to bed at the same time, but Alice thinks she may have turned out her light first. When she awoke in the morning, Philippa had gone. Peter Cushing was downstairs at 6.30 a.m. and, although he didn't realise the girl had gone until Alice got up, Philippa almost certainly left the house before that. My guess is that someone arranged to meet her with a vehicle: she would have had to walk miles, otherwise."

"OK. And the Grummetts?"

"Ricky – DC MacFadyen – interviewed them first, as you

instructed, sir. DC Armstrong and I went to Boston to find out more about the woman in the coma as you instructed and DC MacFadyen met us at the hospital. He said he was having trouble getting a straight answer from Mr and Mrs Grummett."

"They were being obstreperous, MacFadyen?"

"I wasn't allowed to see Ruby Grummett until her husband arrived. I suppose that was fair enough, given her precarious state of mind. When Bob Grummett arrived he was clearly furious that I was there. He said he'd forbidden anyone to speak to her about the accident without a solicitor present. I told him I was there to tell them that Philippa had disappeared. This came as a bolt out of the blue – I'm certain he wasn't pretending – but he seemed to be shocked for the wrong reasons, as if the girl's disappearance would get him into trouble in some way."

"How could you know that?"

"I don't know it, sir, it's just a feeling. That's how it struck me."

"I thought the same thing when I spoke to him later," said Tim.

"OK, Yates, do you want to tell us the rest of the story now?"

"There's just one other thing," said Ricky. "I asked to see the other daughter – Kayleigh. Bob had already told me that Philippa wouldn't have tried to contact her mother and now he said he was certain she wouldn't contact Kayleigh. I thought this was very odd."

"Extremely odd. What did you think, Yates?"

Tim decided he wouldn't tell Superintendent Thornton that Ricky had allowed Bob Grummett to forewarn Ruby about Philippa's disappearance. As Juliet had said, Ricky hadn't had much choice and Tim didn't want to provoke Thornton's ire. It would be bound to make him go off at a tangent.

"By the time I spoke to them, the whole family had gathered. Kayleigh Grummett was there as well as her uncle and aunt, Ivan Grummett and his wife Elsie. I didn't get any more out of them about Philippa than Ricky did. I'd agree with him, though, that they seemed to be concerned about something other than her welfare. And that was before we told them about the infant remains."

"I'd almost forgotten about those. We're here to focus on the kidnappings, but just briefly, Yates, do you think the dead baby is connected with them?"

"We can't prove a link at the moment. The baby's skeleton was found in one of the Grummetts' outbuildings, but they're saying it must have been there since before their tenancy. We can't confirm this either way, yet: Ms Gardner has sent the bones and the other materials she found with the child to Forensics for testing. My guess is that there may be some connection, but not directly related to the kidnappings. The bones were almost certainly found after Philippa Grummett left the Cushing house."

"And did we get any further with sifting through the Grummetts' possessions?"

"Not yet, sir. Both DC Carstairs and DC MacFadyen have been busy with more pressing matters today, as you know."

"Yes. Well make it a priority now, will you? Sort out something after this meeting. I think there's just MacFadyen's account of his visit to Boston High School left for us to listen to now."

"There's not much to tell. Everyone at the school was extremely co-operative – more so, from what I've just heard, than at Spalding High School. Both Philippa Grummett's form teacher and her headteacher seemed to be genuinely concerned. They said they'd do everything we asked. They had no inkling there was anything upsetting her: rather the reverse.

They thought she preferred staying with the Cushings to being at home. Talking of people knowing each other, the headteacher said he knew DI Yates. His name's Alex Cooper."

"Oh?" said Tim. "That's where he went, then. I said to PC Tandy earlier this week that I didn't know he'd left Spalding High School. I'm surprised he's gone to Boston, though: it strikes me as a bit of a sideways move."

"He said he didn't see eye to eye with the governors, sir."

"We might like to find out a bit more about that, when we have time."

"Yes," said Superintendent Thornton, fixing Tim with his eye. "But that isn't now. My instructions are as follows: MacFadyen, I want you to make a start on working through the Grummetts' stuff. Chakrabati can come with you. Carstairs, I'm going to call Spalding High School to tell them to go ahead with the netball event. After that, I want you to visit the school with Tandy and find out who's going to be there tomorrow, as far as they know, and, if you can, who's going to be at the Bricklayers' meeting. And I'd like you to contact Ms Greaves to ask her what she knows about them. Yates, make sure that all the roadblocks will be manned all night and supervise the door-to-door enquiries we've started. Continue until about 8 p.m. We'll start them again tomorrow. Armstrong, you can help Yates."

The other officers began to leave. Juliet caught Tim's eye.

"There's just one more thing, sir," he said, when only the three of them were left. "I know we have to focus on the missing girls at the moment, but you asked me to find out more about the woman in a coma who was taken to the Pilgrim Hospital earlier today."

"As you say, we have other priorities. But was there anything?"

"Not a great deal, except that she's very ill – she may not

pull through – and she's been kept in conditions of extreme privation for a very long time. Imprisoned, probably."

"Good Lord! But she's safe for now, isn't she? So we can get on with . . ."

"She's safe as far as we know. It might be wise to put a police guard on her ward. But what I wanted to remind you of, even if you don't have time to bother with his genealogy, was that the person who took her to the Johnson Hospital this morning was Matthew Start, the son of Councillor Start."

Superintendent Thornton looked thoughtful.

"Councillor Start seems to keep on cropping up all over the place. And I know you feel the same way about coincidences as I do, Yates. By all means put a watch on the sick woman. And get on to Start as soon as you can. Not this evening, though. We have to focus on getting those girls back alive."

Chapter Forty-Four

Wearily, Tim and Juliet climbed the stairs that led to their office space. Directing operations from a desk was just the kind of work that Tim hated. He realised he had no cause for complaint, particularly as the Superintendent had now put him at the centre of the search operation, but he was champing at the bit. He wanted to involve himself in something more hands-on. He thought he might carry out some door-to-door enquiries himself later, though he knew Thornton wanted him to stay in the office to provide co-ordination and support. He sighed and looked at his watch. It was almost 6 p.m.

"It's going to be a long night," he said to Juliet. "I'd better give Katrin a quick call before we get started."

"Do you want me to leave you to it for a couple of minutes?" she asked, glancing up at him. He noticed with some curiosity that, although she'd switched on her computer, she'd actually started riffling through the cold case file again.

"God, no. I doubt we'll be exchanging intimacies." He managed a brief grin. "I'm much more likely to get an earful. But I'm sure you won't be embarrassed if you overhear." He moved a few yards away from his desk and was just in the act of speed-dialling his home telephone number with his back to Juliet when he heard her draw in her breath sharply. He cancelled the call.

"You OK?" he asked.

"Yes. But look at this!" She held out a sheet of paper. Clipped to the top of it Tim saw the photograph of the missing Finnish au pair they'd shown to Verity Tandy a few days earlier.

"What are you looking at that for? We need to . . ."

"Look at the name!"

Tim moved closer so that he could read where her finger pointed. "Helena Nurmi. Rings no bells. Should it?"

"Not the surname. But the mother whose daughter Matthew Start took to Spalding Community Hospital signed the girl's name as Ariadne Helen and her own name as Lucy Helen."

"Weird, I know – we agreed on that. But how . . .? Oh, I see what you mean." Tim whistled. "Matthew Start was the last person who saw Helena Nurmi before she went missing, wasn't he? And now he turns up with someone who calls both herself and her daughter Helen. Why not Helena, though?"

"I don't know. A clumsy attempt at a covert SOS message in case Start read what she'd written?"

"Could be. We'll need to speak to him this evening now. I'll go and find Thornton."

"As it happens, I'm right here, Yates. I've brought you these schedules. What was it you wanted?"

Tim jumped like a schoolboy caught in the act. When he'd recovered, he explained briefly.

"All right, Yates, I agree that what Armstrong's just found may put a different complexion on matters. But only because there's now a somewhat stronger case to fear the mother of that girl is being held by Start against her will. I still think your story's far-fetched. If he's been holding that woman for the past twenty odd years, where has he been keeping her? And I understand that he's married," the Superintendent concluded sagely, as if that exonerated Matthew Start from suspicion. "But you've sown the seed of doubt in my mind. You may go

and speak to him. But no histrionics with warrants etcetera, unless you're convinced – and I mean, *absolutely* convinced – that he's guilty. I don't want you barking up the wrong tree, chasing red herrings," he finished, mixing metaphors magisterially. "You'd better take Armstrong with you. She can pacify the wife."

"Yes, sir. Thank you."

"And come back here when you've finished. And, Yates, it's *Superintendent* Thornton to you."

Chapter Forty-Five

IT WOULD HAVE been pitch black as Tim drove his ageing BMW down Blue Gowt Lane if the fog hadn't returned, enveloping the whole landscape in smoky grey. It sprang out of the night like a spectre, hurling itself against the windscreen in flurries that alarmed him both by their intensity and the sudden obliteration of visibility they brought. Suddenly Tim saw a blurred shape dashing across the road, close to the car but still at the outer reaches of his vision. He stamped hard on the brake. Juliet lurched forward before springing back against her head restraint, mercifully held by her seat-belt.

Tim's speed had been around fifteen miles an hour. Now he stopped the car completely.

"Are you OK?"

She nodded. "What was that?"

"I don't know. Some creature I didn't recognise. I'd have said it was a sheep or a large dog, but it moved more like a wild animal. It was probably a deer."

"I didn't know there were deer round here." Juliet thought of the folk tale about the witch who had turned into a wolf that she'd heard at Fenland Folklore and shuddered.

"I believe so," said Tim absent-mindedly, starting up the engine again. "They've enjoyed a come-back. I think there's even some local group protecting them." The fog had begun flinging itself at the windscreen again.

"I think you've just passed the Starts' house," said Juliet. "There's a wall back there that looked very like the one on the Streetview picture."

"Fuck," said Tim. "If you're right, I'm going to have to turn round. I should have used this before. I did key in the address." He tapped his sat-nav. It took a while to prime itself. Then the chirpy Joan Baker voice instructed him to 'turn around when possible'.

"Can you see out of your side window?"

"Yes. There's a dyke there. A deep one."

"All the dykes in this area are deep. We don't want to end up in one. I'm going to drive very slowly. Can you keep a look-out for a bridge over the dyke, or a farmyard?"

Juliet pressed her face against the glass, shielding her fore-head with one hand.

"There's a kind of plank bridge alongside us now."

Tim stopped the car.

"How wide is it?"

"Tractor width, I'd guess."

"OK. Get out and direct me, will you? I need to reverse on to it. It'll be safer than doing a three-point turn."

Juliet climbed out of the car, taking a torch from the glove pocket, and went to inspect the bridge. The small areas she could illuminate in the circle of white light thrown by the torch looked slimy, possibly rotten, but when she kicked at the side of the one nearest to her it seemed solid enough.

Tim opened the driver's door and half-stood to poke out his head.

"What are you doing?"

"Just making sure this will take the weight. I think it's OK. If you want to drive forward now and start to reverse, I'll bang on the side panel if I think you're too far over."

Tim got back into the car and reversed carefully on to the

makeshift bridge, Juliet guiding him. He'd just swung the car round completely and was waiting for her to get back into it when a large shape came running from the road ahead of them and disappeared into the murk, in the direction of Matthew Start's house. Juliet clambered into the car quickly and shut the door.

"What was that?"

"I don't know. A big dog, probably."

"Was it the creature we saw earlier?"

"Could have been. I don't know."

"This place gives me the creeps. It reminds me of when I was bitten by the rat."

"I'm not surprised, but let's get on, anyway. I doubt if many cars come this way on a winter evening. I don't want Matthew Start to be too prepared for us when we reach him."

They drove the few hundred yards back up the road in silence. Matthew Start's house stood back from the road, on the other side of the dyke. It was accessed via a sturdier and more elaborate bridge than the one they'd just used, and surrounded by a high wall.

Tim parked at the side of the road. He and Juliet walked across the bridge, huddling into their jackets. It was bitterly cold. A tall and solid double gate opposed them.

"I'll bet this is locked," said Tim, eyeing the small silver intercom box built into one of the gateposts. "If so, we'll have to take our chance with the buzzer. Wait a minute, though, there's a pedestrian gate in the wall here, too."

He turned the black wrought-iron ring set into the smaller gate. The latch lifted and he was able to push it open. Through the swirling fog, he and Juliet caught glimpses of the house, still some distance away. A cacophony of barking erupted as they walked up the double sweep drive towards it.

"Dogs!" said Juliet.

"They can't be on the loose," Tim reassured her. "Otherwise they'd have been up here with us by now. Curious that the drive has a double sweep – there must be another gate and bridge over the dyke further back the way we came."

"I don't think there is. From what I saw on Google Earth, on that side it turns round the house in a kind of 'S' shape. There's another building at the back of the house. Quite a substantial structure, from the photograph."

"Nothing dodgy about that. I assume someone like Matthew Start understands the rules of planning permission," said Tim drily. They'd reached the front door of the house, which was protected by a porch and illuminated by a replica Victorian street lamp. The door was rather pretentious, a heavyweight white-painted portal with a massive central brass doorknob and flanked by two imitation Doric pillars. Tim could find no doorbell, but, looking up, he saw a large brass knocker set high above the doorknob. He had to stretch up his arm to reach it. He knocked twice, noting that a dim light was glowing through the small glass window above the door.

There was no response. Tim waited for a minute or so and rapped the knocker again. Listening carefully, he thought he could hear footsteps approaching.

The door opened. The woman who opened it was standing well back in the shadows of the hallway. Moving to one side of Tim, Juliet could see it was Veronica Start.

Tim took out his identity card and held it out.

"Mrs Start? I'm DI Yates, South Lincolnshire police. I think you know DC Armstrong. We'd like to have a few words with your husband. Is he at home?"

"I . . . No, no he isn't, I'm afraid."

"Could you tell us how long he's likely to be out? We'd like to call back this evening, if possible."

"I'm not sure. I don't think I can help you any further." Slowly she began to close the door.

Juliet stepped forward, putting her hand lightly against the edge of the door to halt its progress.

"Veronica?" she said. "Your husband isn't in trouble, as far as we know, but we have to speak to him about the young woman he took to the Johnson Hospital this morning. She's very seriously ill and he may be able to provide additional information that could save her life."

The door opened again. Juliet was now closer than Tim to Veronica Start and registered the shocked look on her face.

"Young woman? I know nothing of a young woman. Why was Matthew involved?" Her voice was hoarse and she spoke so quietly that Tim had to strain to hear her words.

"He didn't talk to you about it? He took a young woman and her mother to the Johnson Hospital early this morning. He said the woman's mother was an old friend who had called on him for help. We believe the mother's name is Helen. Perhaps you know her?"

Veronica Start shook her head.

"Matthew knows many people that I don't know. It's the nature of his work."

"Mrs Start, would you mind telling us where you were between about 6.30 a.m. and 7.30 a.m. this morning?"

"I was here, of course, getting ready for work."

"You're a teacher, I believe? At the High School?"

"Yes. I leave here at about 7.40. I usually arrive at school just after 8 a.m., which gives me time to do a bit of preparation before my first lesson."

"So you'd still have been here when 'Helen' called your husband?"

"I suppose I must have been," she said dully.

"But you weren't aware of the call? Did your husband tell

you he was going out?"

There was a long silence. Veronica Start was standing stock still, her eyes cast down. Juliet had seldom seen anyone so completely drained of energy.

"Veronica, please answer the question if you can," she said gently.

Keeping her eyes firmly fixed on the floor, Veronica Start finally spoke, quietly but coherently, concluding with a flash of asperity.

"DI Yates, my husband and I aren't close. If he went out early this morning, I didn't know about it. Do you require any more information about our personal arrangements, or may I leave it at that?"

"Thank you, Mrs Start," Tim said. "I assure you I didn't mean to pry, but I do need to find your husband. Have you seen him today? And are you able to tell us where he is now?"

"Yes, I've seen him today. He was here waiting for me when I got home at about half-past four. He went out shortly after that. He didn't tell me where he was going."

"Does he have a mobile?"

"Yes, of course he does. Do you want the number?"

"That would be helpful."

"You'd better come in for a moment. I'll have to look for it. It's his office mobile," she added quickly, as if anticipating the question. "That's why I don't know the number."

Tim and Juliet entered the hall. Veronica Start immediately turned away from them before closing the door.

"Wait here," she said. She was dressed in trousers and a lacy green jumper with batwing sleeves.

Tim and Juliet stood together in awkward silence. The hall was large; a semi-circular red velvet sofa squatted in one corner, but they hadn't been invited to sit down and neither took the liberty.

Veronica Start returned quickly. As she advanced, Juliet noticed a smell about her that she hadn't detected before. It was the scented odour of old-fashioned face powder, such as her grandmother used to wear. Strange that Veronica had paused at such a time to put on make-up.

Ignoring Tim, who was standing on Juliet's left, she walked up to Juliet with her head set rigidly forwards and held out a slip of paper. As she handed it over, the sleeve on her right arm fell back and exposed a series of ugly yellowing bruises stretching from the wrist to the elbow. There were fresh-looking angry red weals disfiguring the wrist itself.

"There's the number."

Juliet paused for a little too long before she took the paper. Following the line of her gaze, Veronica pulled down the sleeve to cover her knuckles. The action caused her to turn her head. It took all Juliet's self-possession not to cry out. The right side of Veronica Start's face, from the side of her cheekbone to the inside of her eye socket, was disfigured by a massive purple contusion that, pathetically and ineffectually, she'd tried to conceal under a thick layer of powder.

As calmly as she could, Juliet said, "Thank you. That's a very nasty bruise, Veronica. How did you manage to hurt your face like that?"

"Oh, it was just an accident that I had at school." She laughed awkwardly. "One of the hazards of being a teacher."

"What kind of an accident? It looks to me as if you might need to see a doctor."

Again the strained little laugh.

"No, it's nothing. Honestly. Just a small accident. I'll let you out now."

"Here's my card," said Tim. "When your husband comes home, please ask him to call me. We'll keep trying to contact him in the meantime."

Veronica Start nodded and took the card. She clicked the latch of the door and opened it, keeping both the detectives to her left as she did so and hugging her damaged face against the wood of the door.

Tim paused to allow Juliet to precede him before offering his hand. Veronica Start accepted it uncertainly. He noted that her own was cold but clammy with cooled sweat.

"Please accept my thanks, Mrs Start. We'll need to keep in touch, but we'll try to bother you as little as possible. By the way, did we hear dogs as we were approaching your house, or am I mistaken?"

"No, you're not mistaken. Matthew keeps two Alsatians. They have a kennel and a run alongside his office. They don't come into the house."

"I see. Is his office in the building that stands to the back of your house?"

"Yes. It isn't the company office – that's in town. But Matthew needs an office here as well, for when he's drawing up plans."

"She's a battered wife," said Juliet, once they were seated in the BMW. "Louise thought so. She spotted a burn on her arm yesterday evening."

"It certainly looks like it. Prima facie."

"I can't think of another way of accounting for such injuries, can you?" said Juliet, bridling a little. "And her explanation was feeble and evasive: typical of an abused woman."

"I'm sure you're right. Matthew Start may have more to answer for than we at first thought. Let's have a look at the note she gave you."

Juliet was still clutching the piece of paper. She smoothed it out and handed it to Tim.

"It's a business compliments slip," said Tim. "It has the business address and registration number printed on it, to-

gether with a landline number and Matthew Start's name and personal mobile number. She didn't write on it."

Juliet laughed. "What were you expecting, an SOS message? At least we know the number must be correct."

"I'm glad you said that, because I'd like you to call that number now and then keep on calling it every ten minutes or so until you get a reply. It'll help to relieve the tedium of co-ordinating the door-to-door enquiries. I want you to pass him on to me as soon as he answers."

"And if he doesn't?"

"We'll come back here early tomorrow morning, before we go to the school. We know that Start will have to return at some point, to feed his dogs."

"He may be at the school tomorrow himself. I'm pretty certain he belongs to The Bricklayers. We know that his father's one of them."

"Good point. So one way or another we'll catch up with him."

Chapter Forty-Six

I LET HIM take me back to my prison. It was part of the bargain: no struggle, no fuss. He swore he'd kill Ariadne if I tried to escape or ask for help. He'd have had to do it instantly, and he'd have been convicted of murder, but he knew I couldn't take the risk. I've always believed he wants to be punished and Ariadne's life is too precious to use as a bargaining chip. Alone, I could have run, screamed, kicked, fought, thrown myself on the mercy of strangers. I could have killed him and pleaded self-defence. I turn from this thought because it gives me too much pleasure.

Ariadne is gone from me, that I understand. If she can be saved, in return for her life I have given her up to the world she has never known. If she dies, I will have wrecked our life together, my reason for living, in vain. I had to try, God knows. I had to try. It tears me apart that I shan't find out, perhaps for many months, if she is still alive. The Lover has taken away the television. He said it wasn't to punish me, but to calm me down. By some malformed logic I think he believes this, because when he punishes me it means darkness and he has yet to take away the lights.

I struck a bargain with him. I promised not to betray him when we took Ariadne to the hospital if he would let me see the others. He agreed and I am waiting, in despair about Ariadne but still with a faint glimmer of hope that he may

keep the promise. I know in my heart of hearts it is almost impossible. Does he know where they are and if not how he will find them? If he can find them, what explanation can he give to persuade them to come here? Under what terms will they walk away again? If he shuts them up with me, their friends will contact the police. Did my own friends get in touch with the police? I'm suddenly pierced by a terrible guilt. Surely he would not try to keep the girls here, in this dungeon?

He has started talking again about a future life for us; this time, he says, with the girls. How can he believe this when we have never been a family? Does he think those three young women will have no minds of their own, like Ariadne? He is retreating again into a place where I can't reach him. He'll become vicious and cruel. I've managed his mood so well for so long I cannot bear it if that madness returns. Yet this time he has not struck me. He hasn't trapped my arms in his restraints. He hasn't laid a finger on me. I'm filled with a deep fear. It's almost worse to suffer a continual state of anticipation that the blows will come than to have to fend them off when they do.

The signs are all there, the insecurities, the uncertainties, the demons that make him lash out. Yet, if not calm, if not gentle, he has not been savage. I've not had to submit to his anger, not had to plead against his brutality nor submit to rape. Has he found someone else on whom to vent his scorn? Has he been shaken by Ariadne's illness? Is it possible that he has repented?

The quality of air in here is poor today, or perhaps I notice more how thin it is after my journey outside. I'm dizzy and have to lie down. I must save my energy to concentrate on Ariadne. I focus all my thoughts on her. She needs my willpower to help her to live.

Chapter Forty-Seven

TIM AND JULIET returned to the police station. Taking over from Superintendent Thornton, who shortly afterwards announced his intention of going home for a few hours' rest – 'and so should you, Yates, eventually' – Tim immersed himself in co-ordinating the door-to-door enquiries. He quickly realised that these had already been well-organised, with proper handover, feedback and back-up arrangements in place. Still, he and Juliet bore the crucial burden of maintaining and boosting morale in a double enquiry that had yet to achieve any leads or breakthroughs.

Juliet took her share of the load, breaking off only to call Matthew Start's mobile every ten or fifteen minutes. It went to message every time. She'd just recorded her fourth message and put down the phone when it started to ring. She grabbed it quickly without registering the caller's number, hoping that Start had at last responded.

"Juliet?" She recognised the voice immediately.

"Louise! Are you all right? You sound weary."

"Hello, Juliet. I thought you'd still be working. That's why I called you first." Louise Butler sighed. "I'm sorry to have to tell you that the young woman you enquired about – the one signed in as Ariadne Helen – died just over an hour ago. We tried everything we could think of to save her. Not knowing exactly why she was in that state didn't help, but I think the post mortem

will show that the internal damage was too advanced for her to have survived. She'd been neglected for too long."

"Are we talking about criminal negligence?"

"I can't give you a definitive answer before the post mortem, but I'd say you have at least a case of manslaughter on your hands, probably murder."

"Thank you. I'll tell DI Yates. We'll send someone to talk to you tomorrow – I'll come myself if I can. And I'm sorry, Louise. I know how hard it must hit you to lose a patient. Will you get some rest now?"

"I'll go home for a few hours. What about you? I hope you're not intending to work all night."

"Not quite all night, because I have to be able to function tomorrow. But most of it, probably. We have to find those two girls. Time's running out."

"Try to look after yourself. I hope that it will be you tomorrow. Good night."

"Good night."

As Juliet put the phone down, she looked up to see Tim watching her curiously.

"Not Matthew Start, I take it?"

"No, it was Louise Butler, to say that the woman admitted from the Johnson Hospital has died."

Tim whistled.

"Jesus. We'll have to find Matthew Start now. And the woman's mother. We can't spare anyone tonight, but we'll go to Start's house again tomorrow, and to the hospital. We'll need to talk to the nurse who saw Start and the mother."

"Staff Nurse Burrell? She works nights."

"We'll get there before the night shift's finished, then."

Tim's personal mobile rang.

"Hello? Oh, Katrin, God, I'm sorry, I meant to call you hours ago."

Juliet returned her attention studiously to her computer screen and continued to mark the streets that had been covered by the house-to-house enquiries. They had only a few hours left before they'd have to stop for the night. Superintendent Thornton now agreed they could continue until midnight, but after 10.30 p.m only to knock on the doors of houses where the lights were still on. After that, all they would be able to do was continue to man the roadblocks, look after the girls' families and the Cushings and wait for the morning to arrive.

Ricky MacFadyen and Giash Chakrabati had hurried to arrive at the police warehouse just before 6 p.m., the time at which its manager went off duty. Ricky had warned him they were coming. He'd met the manager, Ian Tucker, on several previous occasions. A taciturn and somewhat surly man, he seemed to take it as a personal affront when he was asked to allow access to the often grisly effects that he and his team had to store as neatly as possible. As if, Ricky reflected, the police got some kind of weird personal kick out of unpacking blood- and semen-stiffened garments to take away for further analysis or be baled up again.

At least this evening's mission didn't involve sifting through the detritus of rape or violent death, though in its own way it would be equally unpleasant. Many of the Grummetts' possessions would be encrusted with human waste from the tanker lorry. He hoped Ian Tucker had sorted out some protective clothing.

The warehouse was a drab, faceless building with no windows. A former wartime aircraft hangar, it stood on the edge of reclaimed fen land at the end of a long, narrow concrete road that was cracked and uneven, the runway beyond

it long overgrown and now barely visible. The huge hangar door, still in use by the lorries that delivered its grim wares, was illuminated on either side by a row of lamp-posts that also lit up the small car park. At present, the latter contained only Ian Tucker's shiny red pick-up truck. An ordinary door which looked tiny but was in fact of standard size (dwarfed by its parent) was let into the far right hand side of the main entrance. Ricky and Giash parked the police car next to Ian Tucker's truck and headed for it.

Inside, the hangar was cavernous and shadowy. Huge racks of shelving extended from floor to ceiling. There were rows of dim lights set into the floor between the bays. Four fork-lift trucks were lined up with military precision opposite the manager's office, which consisted of a kind of large wooden kiosk set just inside the door. Ian Tucker emerged, displaying a friendlier smile than usual. He held out his hand.

"DC MacFadyen, hello." He pronounced Ricky's title with some archness. "Not a very pleasant job you've got this evening, I'm afraid. Quite a shitty one, really." The grin widened.

Ricky immediately understood the cause of Tucker's good mood. He didn't rise to the bait.

"Hello, Ian. This is PC Chakrabati – Giash Chakrabati. He's come to help me. Not a nice job, I agree, but it needs doing, and the sooner the better. Did you manage to find us some suits?"

"They're in the office, on a chair in front of the desk," Ian Tucker said, jerking his head in the general direction. "And some masks. There's tea and coffee and a kettle in there, too, and I've left out the rest of today's milk. If you come with me, I'll show you where the stuff you want is. We've put it in an area by itself because it's probably still contaminated. There are disinfectant sprays and hoses and hand cleaner there. Do

you want me to run through the health and safety protocols?"

"We probably know them, but it might be useful, just to be on the safe side."

Ten minutes later, Ricky and Giash were kitted out and had begun on the first of the crates. Ian Tucker had gone home, having left them with his mobile number and instructions on how to lock the building when they'd finished.

After two hours, they'd searched through six of the eight boxes. They'd worked through fragments of smashed china, shaken out ordure-covered soft furnishings and flipped through stained copies of *The Pig Breeder*. Giash's knees were numb and cold from kneeling on the concrete floor. He stood up painfully and rested his back against a corner of the adjacent shelving.

"Do you know what's funny about this?" he said. Ricky was also standing up, a claw hammer poised in his hand to remove the lid from the seventh packing case.

"I assume you mean funny 'peculiar'," he said, "because otherwise I'm struggling to find anything hilarious about being stuck in an aircraft hangar on a winter's evening more or less immersed in shit."

Giash laughed.

"Yes, indeed. Funny peculiar, as you say. What I mean is that there aren't any papers – insurance documents, utility bills, birth and marriage certificates. Nothing. Don't you think that's odd?"

"I would do, if Tim hadn't told me that Ivan Grummett took away a separate strong-box which contained stuff like that."

"In that case, aren't we wasting our time? I'd have thought if we were to find anything incriminating, it would almost certainly be in writing."

"Ivan Grummett took the strong-box before we could get a warrant. I'm sure Tim'll be asking for one. Meanwhile, there may be something amongst this lot. Give us a hand, will you? I don't know who nailed this on, but they certainly didn't mean us to get it off in a hurry."

Giash moved across to Ricky and helped him to attack the nails.

"I've just noticed this box is labelled," he said. "Were there labels on the others?"

"I don't think so. What does the label say?"

"Main bedroom."

"That may be because, from the photographs I've seen, the main bedroom was the only room at the lodge that was more or less left intact. This other stuff we've been ploughing through was just about literally scraped up off the floor."

Giash was yanking out the last of the nails.

"Come on, you bastard!" he muttered as he prised off the lid of the crate. He peered into it. "I don't think we'll find much here. It seems to be full of clothes." He flipped back the two or three garments on the top, inspecting them gingerly. "At least there doesn't seem to be any shit on them. Should we take them out?"

"Yes, but since they're not 'contaminated', we'd better carry them over there." Ricky indicated one of the narrow corridors that ran between the ranks of shelves. "We don't want to be accused of damaging the Grummetts' property."

They pulled the clothes out in armfuls and placed them at intervals in piles along the gangway. Giash wrinkled his nose.

"They may not be covered in shit, but they still don't smell very sweet. Don't those people have a washing machine?"

"I don't know the answer to that question, but I suspect it may be 'no'," said Ricky. "The Grummetts strike me as being backward in pretty much every way."

They worked diligently through the piles of clothing. Most of it evidently belonged to Ruby Grummett and consisted of blouses, skirts and cardigans, with some horrific-looking foundation garments and voluminous vests and knickers. There was also a man's suit and two or three shirts and ties.

"What's this?" said Giash. He had unwrapped a bundle folded into a piece of flannelette sheet sewn to form a flap-over pouch. "Baby clothes!"

Ricky paused to look before resuming his rummage through the pockets of the suit. "Yeah," he said. "I suppose even the Grummetts had to dress their babies in something."

"These are all in pairs. Two of everything. All hand-knitted. All in pink."

"Well, you know more about kids' clobber than I do. I suppose you need more than one of everything?"

"Of course. But generally if someone's made them you wouldn't expect them to use exactly the same pattern and wool."

"No? Well, Ruby Grummett doesn't strike me as being very imaginative. I'm surprised she had the nous to make baby clothes at all." Ricky leaned across to take pluck two salmon pink matinee jackets from the old sheet. "They're not identical, anyway. Look here: there's a 'P' worked into the yoke of this jacket . . ."

" . . . and I'll bet a 'K' worked into the other one," said Giash. "For Philippa and Kayleigh. Ruby Grummett must be more sentimental than you'd give her credit for."

"Except that it isn't a 'K'," said Ricky. "It's either an 'O' or a 'D'."

"Let's see," said Giash. He walked to the end of the gangway and held the tiny garment close to one of the lights. "You're right," he added. "It's a 'D'. How would you explain that?"

"We may be discovering mysteries where there aren't any,"

said Ricky briskly. "Perhaps someone gave them some cast-off clothes – they may have belonged to twins. Or Ruby Grummett bought them in a charity shop."

"I guess you're right," said Giash. "Have you found anything in those pockets?"

"Plenty, but it's only rubbish. Old sweet wrappers, some loose cash, used betting slips, a biro, that sort of thing. Nothing of interest."

"Let's pile all this back into its box, then, and start on the last one. Then perhaps we can get some sleep before the fun starts tomorrow."

~

Andy Carstairs had called Jocelyn Greaves immediately after the debriefing and asked her if she could meet for a drink.

"I'm surprised you've got the time," she said; a little warily, he thought. "Aren't you busy looking for those two missing girls?"

"I'll come clean," said Andy. "This isn't just a social call, much as I'd like it to be. I'd like to pick your brains for some more information about The Bricklayers, if you're up for it."

"You've changed your tune. I seem to remember last time I brought them up it almost led to a quarrel."

"I know. I'm sorry. We now think they may be involved in this enquiry in some way. Strictly confidentially."

"It wouldn't surprise me in the slightest. Where should we meet? The Pied Calf?"

"If that's OK with you."

Andy headed for the Pied Calf as soon as the call was finished. Jocelyn arrived a few minutes later. She had rather a distracted air about her. Her long dark hair was tangled, as if she'd been running. It was damp at the front.

"Are you OK?"

"Yes, why shouldn't I be? It's Friday night, that's all. Knackered after a week's work."

"Well, I'm sorry to add to your workload. I hope it won't be entirely a chore."

"No use fishing for compliments. But you can buy me a drink."

"Large red wine?"

She laughed. "How did you guess?"

Andy returned from the bar with the glass of wine and a small shandy. There was no chance he would be able to unwind with a decent drink this evening.

"So," he said, sitting down opposite her, "you told Giash Chakrabati we were friends."

It took her a moment to register.

"Oh, you mean the Asian policeman I saw at the High School this morning. I'm afraid I didn't take to him. He was on Richard Lennard's side."

"Just doing his job. Technically, you were trespassing." She tensed up immediately.

"Yes. Well, I didn't come here to be lectured . . ."

"Of course not," said Andy quickly. "Actually, I was quite pleased you said we were friends."

"I'm not sure I did say that. I think I said I knew you."

"Whatever. Anyway, even if Giash did give the impression of not being on your side, we're increasingly suspicious about what's going on at those Bricklayer meetings. I'd be grateful if you could tell me what you know."

Jocelyn eyed him doubtfully.

"This is my story. I've been working on it for months."

"We won't share it with anyone else."

"I daresay not, but if I tell you something that leads to early convictions, I probably won't be able to publish anything at all

at first. Then every hack'll get hold of it before I'm allowed to write about it."

"I admit that's a possibility. But from what you've told me, your findings are inconclusive at the moment, so you can't publish anyway. And if you're right and The Bricklayers are prosecuted, you'll have a much bigger story to tell."

She toyed with her glass.

"OK. I'll tell you what I know. I first became interested in The Bricklayers when I was covering the local elections. Councillor Start stood again – he's been a councillor for years – and I was looking for some kind of angle about him. He's very right wing and I was hoping to uncover something that could discredit him."

"You mean, like Nazi sympathies or evidence of fraud?"

Jocelyn looked up sharply and smiled uncertainly.

"It isn't a joking matter."

"I know that. Carry on."

"I just found one reference to The Bricklayers, on the Start construction website. I think it was put there by mistake, because the next time I looked it had gone. I tried to find out more about them, but drew a complete blank. They aren't a registered charity. I couldn't find any record of their activities. The elections came and went and Councillor Start was back in post again, but by this time I was intrigued and decided not to drop my investigation, such as it was. I was convinced there was something very sinister about Councillor Start and his family and it was confirmed when I had a bit of a breakthrough."

"Why do you say 'and his family'? Do you mean Matthew Start? Or his wife?"

"I don't know much about her, except that she's a teacher at the school. Matthew Start's an unpleasant piece of work. He has a little sideline, letting sub-standard flats to immigrants."

Andy paused for a second before deciding it was only fair if he confided in Jocelyn.

"Did you know that twenty years ago the Starts had an au pair who disappeared?"

Her eyes widened.

"No, certainly not. What was her name? Who was she looking after? Au pairs usually work with children. Surely it wasn't Matthew himself: he would have been in his early twenties then."

"Steady on! I can't keep up with all the questions and actually have no answers. Tell me about your 'breakthrough'."

"I went to Boston High School to interview the headteacher there about a new training programme the school was setting up. It was a cross between an Outward Bound course and the OTC. He's a nice man. His name's Alex Cooper. The story wasn't my kind of thing – I'm not big on training kids to be soldiers – but I was getting paid for it and I decided to make it more interesting by including a bit more about Alex Cooper himself. It turned out he used to be the Head at Spalding High School. I asked him why he'd left and he blurted out this story about The Bricklayers and how they'd been using the school premises for their meetings. He was unhappy about it and tried to put a stop to it. From what he said, the governors more or less forced him to resign."

"It doesn't sound like a resignation issue."

"No, but Councillor Start is the chairman of the governors."

"Did Cooper say why he didn't like The Bricklayers?"

"He didn't give me any specific information. He said something about the Minnesota Study. Then he clammed up. I think he's afraid of them."

"Go on," said Andy.

"Go on with what?"

"You don't mean to tell me you got that far and then didn't bother to find out what the Minnesota Study was about?"

For the first time that evening, she seemed to relax properly. She laughed again, this time with real mirth.

"You're getting to know me very well! Yes, I did find out more. It wasn't difficult: it's quite well-documented. It's a nature / nurture thing. Experiments with siblings, particularly twins, to see if they develop in similar ways when they're separated. I can send you some stuff about it if you're interested."

"Thank you. I might take you up on that. But there's nothing sinister about it, is there?"

"Not the Minnesota Study itself. But it's a bit creepy if you think about it. The siblings it studied had been separated by accident, but a warped mind might try to take it further than that."

"You mean like Mengele?"

"I wasn't thinking of that, though I suppose it's possible. I was thinking more of separating siblings deliberately, to see how they developed."

"That couldn't be done legally unless their parents gave them up for adoption. And in this country social services would try to keep them together if they possibly could."

"Precisely," said Jocelyn.

Chapter Forty-Eight

IT WAS VERY early on Saturday morning. Tim had been working through the night. After shutting down the door-to-door enquiries at almost midnight and checking on the police manning the roadblocks, he'd revisited all the information they'd gathered so far about the kidnappings. There was pitifully little about the actual events: no witnesses to Philippa Grummett's disappearance or even proof that she had indeed been kidnapped, and only Cassandra Knipes's mother's account about her daughter's abduction. Could Mrs Knipes have been mistaken, or lying? Tim doubted it. He had himself seen how distressed the woman was and she didn't strike him as a liar.

The cases had to be linked, he was pretty sure about that, although the supporting evidence was slender, consisting mainly of the missing girls' physical similarity. Nevertheless, it gave him hope, as it suggested they had not been seized at random by a serial killer or rapist. There were other, more tenuous links if you looked hard enough for them: both girls were clever, both brought up in unusual households where they didn't altogether seem to fit and both attended local grammar schools. Another factor, although it was circumstantial, was the peripheral presence of Councillor Start at both investigations. He'd turned up at the Grummetts' house on the night of the rail accident and he'd been at Spalding High School, protesting about the threatened privacy of his Bricklayers' meeting, when

Giash Chakrabati had spoken to Richard Lennard after Cassandra Knipes was taken.

Juliet's preliminary re-opening of the cold case concerning the disappearance of the Finnish au pair established that Matthew Start was last person to see her alive. Start had also delivered the sick young woman to the Johnson Hospital, a coincidence too far even if he'd offered a convincing explanation for it. That he had himself since disappeared convinced Tim that he held the key to the fate of all of these women, though at present the police had no grounds to arrest him.

"Tim? Are you OK?"

Tim raised his head from where it was resting on his folded arms. He must have fallen asleep at his desk. He groaned and looked at his watch: 5.45 a.m. Juliet was standing beside him.

"I'll make you some tea," she said. "Then we need to leave for the hospital, if you want to see Staff Nurse Burrell. I called her on my way in, so she's expecting us."

"Thanks. God, my neck's stiff. Just let me get a quick wash, will you, and change my shirt? Some tea would be great."

It would still be dark for several more hours, but when they left the police station Tim looked at the sky and could see the stars. The fogs that had haunted the Fens for the last few days had dispersed. In their wake a cruel coldness had set in. It was a raw day for a netball match.

The cold stung his cheeks but prodded his brain into alertness. He was aware, however, that he was probably still too groggy to drive.

"How much sleep did you get?" he asked Juliet.

She shrugged.

"Don't tell me you carried on working after you went home." He changed his mind about offering her the car keys.

"Only for a while. I wanted to find out more about the Starts. I'm convinced they're at the root of all these cases."

"You and me both. Any joy?"

"Just a couple of things. Councillor Start describes himself as a widower, but in fact he was divorced from his wife, whose name was Carol, more than twenty years ago. They had a daughter quite late in the marriage: ten years younger than Matthew."

"That would explain the au pair: to look after the daughter, not Matthew. Do you know the daughter's name?"

"Yes, it was Elizabeth. Nothing exotic. I understand why you're asking: in case it was another of those Greek-sounding names. The other thing I discovered relates to the names, though only in a way. Matthew Start studied classical architecture at Sheffield University."

"That's interesting, but it doesn't explain much. He couldn't have been responsible for naming Cassandra Knipes or Philippa Grummett. And certainly not Helena Nurmi."

"I agree with you about Helena. I'd like to keep an open mind on the other two."

Tim shot her a quizzical look.

"Go on," he said.

"I don't have anything to add at the moment. I just have a hunch that those names were chosen by the same person."

"OK. What about Start's wife? Do we know she's alive and kicking? And the daughter?"

"Both very much so. They moved right away from Spalding, which may be significant. Carol Start was a teacher. She moved to a school in Nottingham and eventually got married again, to another teacher. Elizabeth moved with her, and later took her stepfather's name. She studied languages and is now also a teacher."

"There seem to be a lot of teachers involved in this! Veronica Start teaches languages as well, doesn't she?"

"Yes. I don't know whether that's a coincidence or not. You're the one who's interested in psychology."

Tim looked across at her sharply but could detect no glimmer of irony.

"I suppose when he married Veronica he could have been trying to compensate for something that he'd missed out on," he said sagely.

"That's what I thought you'd say."

Staff Nurse Marianne Burrell was waiting in the hospital foyer, standing in much the same spot from which she'd seen Matthew Start approaching with the terminally-sick woman the day before. She was tired and still feeling shaken by the news that the woman had died. She watched Tim and Juliet cross the path and enter through the sliding doors. In her mind's eye, she saw the young woman's mother walking towards her again and in that instant grasped what it was that had been nagging at her.

"Good morning. DI Yates and DC Armstrong," said Tim. "We've come to see Staff Nurse Burrell."

"I'm Marianne Burrell. I spoke to you earlier," she said, addressing Juliet. "I've just remembered what it is that was bothering me – the thing I mentioned to you on the phone."

"I'd prefer it if we could start at the beginning," said Tim.

"Do tell us what's troubling you first, if you want to," Juliet was quick to counteract Tim's early-morning negativity, sensing something important. "Is there somewhere comfortable where we can talk?"

"Of course. Come with me."

Marianne Burrell led them to a small office off the reception area. She had become animated, almost excited.

"I knew there was something odd about those two women as soon as they came in," she said. "I don't just mean that the daughter was obviously very ill. They seemed not to belong, somehow. I've been thinking about it ever since. I just realised what it was when I was watching you walk up the path. It was

their clothes. They were twenty years out of date. The mother's red patent handbag was exactly like one my friend used to have years ago."

"Have women's clothes really changed all that much?" said Tim.

"That's the point, they haven't. If a woman of my age still had clothes from back then, she could get away with wearing them – assuming she could get into them – they'd just look slightly odd, at least to another woman. That was why I couldn't put my finger on it."

Juliet saw immediately that Tim was sceptical. Marianne Burrell's comments made sense to her and she'd have liked to explore them further, but she knew that at the moment it was important to get the rest of the nurse's account, before Tim's doubts put her off.

"Would you mind taking us through the whole incident step by step? You say you were standing near the door when the man and woman brought in the sick girl. What kind of vehicle did they come in?"

"It was a 4×4. A Land Rover, I think."

"Did you get the number?"

"No. It didn't occur to me. But in any case I recognised the driver. It was Matthew Start."

"You're quite sure of that?"

"Yes. I live round here, and so does he. Besides, I called him by his name. He didn't try to pretend it wasn't him. But he was quick to explain how he'd come to be helping the two women."

"What did he say? Can you remember his exact words?"

"He said he'd known the mother years ago. That she'd been travelling in this area and asked him to help her when the girl fell ill."

"He was implying they'd lost touch in the interim?" Tim asked.

"I suppose so. I was more interested in helping the girl than trying to pick up anything he might have been hinting. I did think it was odd that he was so keen to tell me why he was involved."

"Can you describe the mother?"

"She had fair hair. It was very fair. And her skin was pale – abnormally pale, even for a blonde. The girl was very pale, too. And thin, dreadfully thin. They both looked malnourished. I did think . . ." Marianne Burrell paused.

"Go on," said Tim. "What did you think?"

"I did think it seemed unlikely that those two women could have been taking a holiday in this area in the middle of winter. Dr Sharma thought the girl had been ill for several days at least. And the clothes they were wearing were too summery. Neither of them had a coat."

"So their clothes were inadequate as well as old-fashioned?" Tim smiled. Marianne Burrell looked at him suspiciously. "Did you notice anything else about them?"

"When I got closer to the mother, I thought I noticed a kind of musty smell about her. But I could have been imagining it," she concluded rather crossly.

"Where is Dr Sharma? Would it be possible to talk to him?"

"Not today. He often works at weekends, but he's away at a conference. I'm sure he'd be happy to talk to you one day next week."

"We'll have to talk to him, but if you were with the women the whole time it will only be to ask him about his initial diagnosis. I'm sure your own observations will be accurate."

She managed a small smile.

"Did you admit the young woman?"

"Yes. I could see straight away that she was extremely ill. She wasn't conscious and she was running a high temperature. I told the mother how ill she was. It didn't seem to surprise her."

"What did she say?"

"Now that you mention it, she didn't say very much at all. Matthew did all the talking."

"I see." Tim looked at Juliet. She'd been taking notes. She underscored the last sentence she'd written.

"When you realised the girl needed urgent treatment, what did you do?"

"I took them into an emergency recovery room and asked one of the nurses to stay with them while I went to fetch Dr Sharma."

"Is the nurse here?"

"No. She doesn't work weekends. She told me they didn't speak to each other at all while I was gone, which couldn't have been more than a couple of minutes."

"Can you give us the nurse's name?"

"Julie. Julie Pack."

"And when you returned with Dr Sharma, what happened?"

"We gave her the usual recovery drugs and he put her on a saline drip and began to give her a blood transfusion – we sent Boston an exact description of what we did, but I can get a copy of it for you if you like – and he called Boston to ask them to admit her as an emergency. We had a spare ambulance here and it took her as soon as he'd inserted the drips."

"But the mother didn't go with her?"

"No. Matthew Start said she couldn't. He said she had to go back to her other children. He said he would take her to them and himself go on to the hospital as soon as he could."

"But she didn't speak for herself?"

"No. I thought she was angry with him, but she could just have been upset. She spoke when I asked her to sign the consent form. : She said she didn't know the address of the boarding house where she was staying. Matthew said it was

called Twelvetrees and he would find out and send the exact address later. That's also when he said she was Dutch."

"Did he call you?"

"No. He gave me his mobile number – he said her mobile might not work. I've tried calling the number he gave, but it always goes to message."

"May I see the number?"

"I wrote it on the consent form." Marianne Burrell handed the form to Tim. A row of figures were scrawled at the top of it in a childish hand. It was the same number Veronica Start had provided.

"Did the woman hesitate when she wrote the name on the form?"

"No. She wrote it quickly and handed it to me."

"Did you think the name was strange?"

"I didn't think that Lucy Helen was a particularly strange name, though it didn't sound very Dutch. Of course I thought the girl's name – Ariadne – was unusual, but I didn't look at the form properly until they'd gone. I was trying to console her. She suddenly became very agitated and begged Dr Sharma to make sure the girl survived. She almost passed out. Matthew Start caught her. She seemed to lash out at him at first, but that could have been because she was upset."

"Did you watch them as they left?"

"Yes. When they got back in the 4×4, she seemed to try to hit him again. She was crying."

"And you were concerned enough about the way in which they both behaved to report it to the police?"

"It was Dr Sharma who said we should call you. It was because of her medical condition. He was convinced that she'd been criminally neglected over many months, if not years.

Chapter Forty-Nine

"WHERE CAN MATTHEW Start be?" said Tim as he and Juliet drove away from the hospital.

"You told Veronica we'd be calling again this morning."

"I know. If she's seen Start since then, she'll have told him."

"Well, that's what we asked her to do."

"Agreed. We'll go straight there."

"Do you think we need back-up?"

"There isn't time. Why do you ask? Do you think Start's mad enough to attack us?"

"I don't know, but everything we've found out about him says he's unstable."

"I think we should chance it," said Tim. "My hunch is he won't be at home. We know he's trying to avoid us. If we can't speak to him now, we've got enough on him to tell the media that we're looking for him."

"If he's holding those girls, that could spook him into harming them, if he panics."

"You're right, but I don't see what the alternative is. If we take too long to find him, he may harm them anyway. We don't know what happened to Helena Nurmi. We can't be sure that the woman who called herself Helen is the same person. And we need to find her, as well. Can you look for a guest house called Twelvetrees?"

Juliet took out her mobile. They were both silent while she carried out some searches.

"If there's such a place in this area, it isn't listed."

"There's a surprise!"

They'd reached the beginning of Blue Gowt Lane. Tim slowed the car.

"If Veronica opens the door, I'd like you to talk to her. You'll make more headway with her than I will," he said. He parked the car on the ramshackle bridge where he'd turned it round the previous night. "We'll walk from here. If Start's watching from the house, we stand more chance of taking him by surprise if we're on foot."

"Don't forget the dogs," said Juliet nervously. "They'll hear us as soon as we open the gate. They may not be tied up this morning."

They trudged along the narrow lane. It was still dark; there were no street lamps and a bitter wind was sweeping across from the fields.

When they reached the Starts' house, Tim opened the same small gate and motioned to Juliet to precede him. She entered the garden hesitantly, listening out for the dogs, but could hear nothing. A few yards further on, they encountered a vehicle: a black 4×4.

"This looks promising," Tim whispered. "Perhaps I'm wrong and he's here after all."

Juliet rang the doorbell. Veronica Start opened the door almost immediately.

"Hello, I thought it would probably be you," she said briskly. She didn't invite them in.

"Mrs Start, we've come to speak to your husband. Is he here?" said Juliet.

"No, unfortunately not. I did tell him you wanted him. He's

been back. He says he's got a busy day ahead of him. And his father wants the dogs. To guard a building site, probably. That's what they're trained to do."

"That's his car standing on the forecourt, isn't it?"

"Yes. He's driving one of the works vans now. He usually does when he has the dogs with him. He doesn't like them messing up his own vehicles."

"So he knows we're looking for him. Did he say when it might be convenient to see him?" Tim couldn't resist taking over from Juliet. If Veronica Start noticed the question was laced with sarcasm, she didn't show it.

"He's bound to be back tomorrow. He always spends Sunday afternoons working in his office, preparing for the week ahead."

"You said yesterday that his office is round there, behind the dog compound?"

"Yes, it's always been his office. Since before we were married."

"I see. Did he own this house before he met you, then?"

"His father owned it originally and gave it to Matthew after his mother left. Matthew grew up here: he's never lived anywhere else, except when he was a student. Matthew's obsessive about this place. He'll never leave it. He doesn't even like going on holiday. Now, if you'll excuse me, I'm running a bit late. There's a netball match at school today and I'm supposed to be helping."

Tim took a step back.

"Certainly," he said. "We'll probably see you there. We'll be continuing our search for Cassandra Knipes; attending the netball event is one of our lines of enquiry."

"Really? Well, you know best, I suppose."

Juliet was still standing on the doorstep.

"How's your face today, Veronica?" she said. She moved

a little closer. "It's still looking rather nasty. I do think you should see a doctor."

The violence of Veronica Start's reaction was unexpected. Her face crumpled.

"Why don't you leave me alone? Don't you understand that your snooping only makes things worse. It should be obvious to you by now that I have no control whatsoever over Matthew or his comings and goings."

She slammed the door shut.

"Should I ring the bell again?" said Juliet.

"No. Leave her to it. Whatever hell it is she's living in, I think we'll be able to help release her from it very shortly."

Chapter Fifty

HE'S LOCKED ME in our bedroom. They're in Ariadne's room. I asked him to bring all of them. That was part of the bargain and I think he's kept his promise.

I am impatient to see them, but I know I mustn't annoy him by showing it. He hasn't switched off the light. I look in the mirror. I am still wearing the suit. I think I look passable. I don't want them to be scared by me. I couldn't bear it if they think me ugly or repulsive.

He's been alone with them for a very long time. Once I think I hear a raised voice. Then there is silence. I dread that he'll hurt them. If he injures them it will be my fault. I sit on my bed and wait. I pick at my nails. I can't bear the suspense.

Seeing them was everything to me. I didn't think about what he would do afterwards. What will happen to them now? What will happen to us? Ariadne will always be damaged. But my other girls are bright and strong and full of hope. Have I stolen their freedom? Surely he wouldn't try to keep them here.

The door is being unlocked. Usually I dread the sound. Today I am jubilant.

He enters my room. Our room.

"You can see them soon," he says. "But first listen to me." He grabs hold of my ear and pulls it. I know better than to cry out. "I don't want you to mention Ariadne. And I don't want you to ask them about anything to do with them. Where they

live, who they live with, where they go to school. Anything. Do you understand?"

I nod. "But they know I am their mother?"

"Not yet, they don't. You can tell them that if you want you. It'll be interesting to see what kind of reaction you get." He sniggers. "You're a little bit shop-soiled these days."

Then they are there, standing in front of me. But just two of them.

"Only the twins? But I thought . . ."

"We aren't twins," says the shorter one. "We don't know each other." She is calm and self-possessed, but angry, I'd say. The other one has been crying.

"What is your name?"

"Philippa."

"But where's Diana? Are you Diana?"

"My name's Cassandra. Will you please tell me why I've been brought here? My parents will be looking for me." She turns to The Lover. "If you let me go, I won't tell anyone. I'll . . ." she starts to cry.

"Shut up!" he says savagely.

"Will you tell me why you've brought us to this fucking awful shit-hole," Philippa says to him. "You told me you would take me to my real mother."

"She's your mother!" he jeers, pointing at me. I stand up, move forward to embrace her.

"You're so beautiful . . ." I say, stretching out my arms.

"Keep away from me!" she shouts, brushing my arm away with hers.

Chapter Fifty-One

TIM LOOKED AT his watch. It was still only 8 a.m. – too early to head to the school.

"We could get some breakfast somewhere," he said. "I'm frozen."

"Good idea, but I'm not sure where at the moment. The supermarket café won't be open yet. We could try Greggs, but there's nowhere to sit there."

"Let's give Katrin a call."

"I'm sure she won't want . . ."

"Hello, it's me. I've got Juliet with me. Yes, most of the night. We've just made a couple of calls. No, nothing immediate. Some leads, maybe. We were wondering about some breakfast? Nothing special, toast will do. And some hot tea. Great. We'll be there in a few minutes."

Juliet had turned pink.

"Tim, that's disgraceful! She had to agree; she wouldn't have been rude enough to say no."

"Sure, but I know she'll be pleased to see you and you haven't made friends with Sophia yet. And it'll probably be my only opportunity to see either of them today. Besides, you know what Katrin's like. Her ability to spot solutions that are staring us in the face is uncanny – almost as good as yours. If you put your heads together, we might get somewhere!"

"Well, we'll have about an hour to do it before you and I

have to leave again. I doubt if there'll even be time to tell her everything."

Katrin was wearing her dressing-gown and looked tired and dishevelled. She opened the door carrying Sophia in her arms.

"Sorry, we were up twice in the night and we haven't got started yet," she said, handing his daughter to Tim. "Hello, Juliet, it's nice to see you. I've put the kettle on and I'll make some toast. There's bacon if you want it."

"Cor! Yes, please," said Tim, holding Sophia high above his head. She crowed with pleasure.

"That's right," said Katrin wryly. "Tell Daddy how wonderful he is! I wonder if he'd have got up for you when you were screaming at 3 a.m."

"I will do next time," said Tim, "because I'll know that it's better than trying to piece together a bunch of clues that don't fit, which is what I was doing then."

"I almost feel sorry for you! Would you like a bacon sandwich, Juliet?"

"I'll come and help you. How much has Tim told you about this case?"

"It depends what you mean by 'this case'. Tim says his case is really the accident at the crossing. Superintendent Thornton told him to concentrate on that, didn't he? But now I gather that two girls have disappeared, one of them the daughter of the crossing-keeper, and that they've found a child's body at what's left of the ruined lodge house. Tim told me all this when he called last night," she added. "I know it was partly because he didn't want me to find out about the dead child from the news. I don't think you've released any details about that yet, have you?"

"No. Did Tim tell you that we think it's all part of the same case, but we can't decide how?"

"No, but I'd be thinking the same thing if I were you. Have you tried creating a story-board?"

Setting out the details of a case on a transparent glass screen and adding to it as many photographs, maps and diagrams as she could gather was one of Juliet's favourite ways of cracking refractory evidence. It was an enthusiasm she'd shared with Katrin.

"No. No time."

"If you've got time later today, I'll come in to the station and help you."

"Thanks. I'd appreciate it." Juliet meant it, but privately she was thinking that if she and Tim hadn't found the missing girls by the end of the day, their chances of being recovered alive were minimal. She remembered she'd told Louise Butler she'd return to take her statement that afternoon. She supposed that the story-board was more important: a uniform could as easily talk to Louise.

"What's the matter?" said Katrin. "You look furious!"

"Sorry! I was just thinking about the case. I've never had to deal with such a hodge-podge of contradictory details. Did Tim tell you about the woman who died at The Pilgrim Hospital yesterday, by the way?"

"No."

"An emaciated young woman was taken to the Johnson Hospital by Matthew Start, Councillor Start's son, and a woman who claimed to be her mother. She was desperately ill and they transferred her to Boston, where she died. Louise Butler says the death was suspicious. Matthew Start was the last person to see the Finnish au pair in the cold case I told you about. I know it's far-fetched, but I 'm convinced that he's up to his eyebrows in all of this."

"So there are how many possible victims altogether? I'm losing count." Katrin put down the packet of bacon she'd been

holding and counted them off on her fingers. "The Finnish au pair. The baby. The two schoolgirls. And the girl who died at The Pilgrim Hospital, if it wasn't of natural causes."

"Correct. Any ideas?"

"You're much more familiar with the detail than I am. I can only state the obvious: that if I were you, I'd get some DNA tests done, and quickly."

"Patti Gardner's already sent the baby's remains for testing."

Katrin winced. "I'd get the others done as fast as you can. Is there still stuff belonging to the Finnish au pair that can be used?"

"I don't know. I think that some of her possessions were collected at the time. I'll have to see if they're still in storage."

"And presumably getting DNA for the others won't be a problem?"

"I think we already have it. We've taken the toothbrushes of both the missing girls."

"There's a lab I use sometimes for emergencies – not very often, because they know how to charge and Superintendent Thornton loathes paying. But they'll work fast, and at weekends. If you have the samples ready today, you might have the results by Monday."

"How's the bacon doing?" Tim called from the sitting room.

"Coming!" Katrin shouted back. She tore open the packet and shoved a row of rashers under the grill.

"Incidentally," she said casually. "You mentioned Dr Butler. How is she?"

Chapter Fifty-Two

DAYLIGHT STRUGGLED WITH darkness and insinuated itself haltingly and without enthusiasm over the netball courts at Spalding High School. Small knots of people had already begun to gather. Two girls dressed in school uniform were serving tea and coffee from urns on a table. The modest crowd was huddled there, clasping steaming Styrofoam beakers in gloved hands. Verity Tandy and Giash Chakrabati were standing on the periphery, largely ignored by the adults. A few students drifted about – evidently spectators rather than participants in the forthcoming event – and eyed them curiously. The mood was subdued. Some of the parents were speaking to each other in low tones. One or two members of the netball team arrived by bicycle and emerged from the bike sheds carrying holdalls. They entered the building rapidly, brushing importantly past the girls at the refreshments stand.

Tim nodded briefly at Giash and Verity and Juliet gave them a half-wave. More uniformed police would be arriving, as well as Ricky MacFadyen and Andy Carstairs, but he didn't want the crowd to know the extent of the police presence.

Juliet asked for two teas and posted two pound coins in the voluntary donations box. She noticed a scrawny woman engaged in animated conversation with Verity Tandy.

"Do you know who that is?" Tim asked.

"No, but at a guess I'd say it's Mrs Painter, the mother of

one of the girls who saw the prowler. She fits Verity's description of the woman."

"Well, I wish she'd leave Verity alone. I don't want people to take any more notice of her and Giash than we can help."

"She's bound to feel involved. She protected the girls from the prowler and her daughter is one of Cassandra Knipes's best friends."

"I suppose you're right," said Tim grudgingly. "I'm going to find Richard Lennard. He said he'd be here by 9.30. I expect he'll have a high profile today – it's his style. But I want to make sure he doesn't make any unhelpful announcements. I also want to know when The Bricklayers are expected to turn up. Have a walk round the back of the school, will you, while I'm gone. Make sure there aren't any girls wandering about there on their own – or other loiterers with no business to be there."

"You can't think there'll be another kidnapping?"

"Not unless I spot an extremely fair girl with incongruous-looking parents. But I'm not prepared to take any chances. The media would make hay of it if another girl was taken from under our noses. And I can't even think about what Thornton would say."

Tim passed the knot of spectators, noting that Verity Tandy was still talking to the animated, rather strangely-dressed woman. A girl had now appeared at the woman's side, a pudgy teenager. As he entered the front door of the school, he saw a minibus drive slowly round half of the sweep and park in one of the bays on the far side of the building, next to the small chapel. He guessed this contained the netball team's opponents. The match was scheduled to start at 10.00 a.m., so he would need to find Lennard quickly.

Turning left in the direction of the headteacher's office,

he saw a balding, thick-set man walking ahead of him. Although he'd seen the man only once, at the accident at Sutterton Dowdyke, and then spoken to him only briefly in the darkness, he recognised him immediately. It was Councillor Start. No great surprise to encounter him here, Tim thought: he'd known the Councillor would be on the premises today to conduct his mysterious meeting.

He was more than a little frustrated when, instead of heading for the hall, as Tim had expected, the Councillor turned left into the corridor leading to the headteacher's office. He had no intention of passing up his conversation with Lennard because he was closeted with the Councillor. He decided to allow them just a few minutes alone before he announced himself. Impatiently, he waited at the top of the corridor, looking at his watch.

"Can I help you?"

Tim looked round to see an exuberantly fleshy woman with a dour face bustling towards him.

"I'm Kathleen Hargreaves, the school secretary."

"DI Yates, South Lincolnshire Police." Tim held out his ID card. He was sure she was the sort of woman who would want to see it. "I need to speak to Mr Lennard before the netball match starts."

"I'll just go and see if he's available." Her voice trilled up the scale as she spoke. Tim knew she'd return to announce that the headteacher was engaged with another visitor.

"It's not a question of whether he's available. I've waited here several minutes, as a courtesy, because I know Councillor Start is with him, but I need to see him now, before the match begins. I'm investigating the abduction of one of your students, not queueing up for the bran tub. Is that clear, or should I tell him myself?"

"Perfectly clear," she replied, her voice once more a deep

contralto. She shot him a look of deep loathing. "Please wait here."

Tim didn't have to wait long. Richard Lennard came striding swiftly down the short corridor. He was attempting to smile, but clearly agitated. He held out his hand.

"DI Yates! I'm sorry to have kept you waiting. As you know, part of the school has been hired out today for an external client's meeting – rather an unfortunate double-booking – and I've just been trying to sort out some details. We have to make sure that none of the students or their parents interrupts the meeting. Will you come this way?"

He almost pushed Tim into a small meeting room that faced the end of the corridor. As Lennard shut the door, Tim turned to see Councillor Start go lumbering into the school hall.

"Is there any news?" Lennard continued as he motioned to Tim to take one of the seats in the room, his mobile features assuming a look of compassion.

"No. We've continued the investigation through the night. I'm sure I don't need to tell you that the next few hours are crucial. If we haven't found Cassandra – and Philippa Grummett, the girl from Boston High School who has also disappeared – by the end of the weekend, our chances of getting them back alive are slim indeed."

Lennard's face contorted briefly and then reshaped itself.

"If there's anything at all that the school can do . . ."

"Well, of course there is quite a lot you can do, Mr Lennard. Thank you for offering. As you know from your meeting with PC Chakrabati and subsequent conversation with Superintendent Thornton, we're pinning some of our hopes on this netball match. We don't know what kind of perpetrator we're looking for, but we do know that sometimes kidnappers – and, unfortunately, also murderers – are drawn either to the scene of the crime or some place that's important to the victim, even

if it means taking the risk of getting caught. You and your staff should be aware that there will be several police officers among the spectators here today, some in uniform, others in ordinary clothes. We'll be on the look-out for anyone who's acting strangely, any talk that seems suspicious. You and the other teachers can help us best by just leaving us to it. Don't draw attention to us and don't talk to us unless you really need to."

"That's quite clear, DI Yates. Rest assured we won't stand in your way."

"Thank you. May I ask if you're intending to make some kind of speech at this event?"

"No more than usual. I'll welcome the guest team – they're from Ken Stimpson Community School at Peterborough – and just say a few words of encouragement before the match starts."

"Do you intend to mention Cassandra Knipes?"

Richard Lennard's eyes swivelled around the room before finally meeting Tim's own.

"I'm . . . not sure. What would you recommend?"

"I think you should say very briefly that the school is saddened by her disappearance and doing everything to support police enquiries. If you don't mention her it will look odd. I'd appreciate it if you'd also ask the parents to be discreet and not try to discuss her with staff or students. I believe that PC Chakrabati has already asked you not to give statements to the Press. Please continue to observe that."

"Certainly. I'll brief the other staff."

"How many of them are there?"

"Just the games staff – there are three of them. And I asked Veronica Start to come in. She has a pastoral job as well as being the head of languages. I thought her presence might be useful." Lennard concluded virtuously.

"Good," said Tim briskly. "I'm glad you mentioned Mrs Start, because you've reminded me that it's her father-in-law who's organised the 'client' meeting here today. That's correct, isn't it?"

Richard Lennard frowned.

"Yes. But don't worry about it. I've made it clear that the meeting mustn't be disturbed. I've promised Councillor Start his party will be left in peace."

"You may have promised that, Mr Lennard, but I'm afraid I shall have to over-rule you. We won't intrude on the actual meeting without good reason, but I shall want to speak to those attending it before they leave. I shall tell them that myself – there's no need for you to involve yourself further. Do you know what time they plan to start?"

"I believe at 10.00 a.m., the same time as the netball."

"Good. As I said, I shall want to talk to them. Do you know how many of them there'll be? Approximately, I mean?"

"No. The minutiae of how they operate doesn't concern me."

"Of course it doesn't. So I'd be grateful if you'd steer clear of them and leave any interaction to me. Shall we go outside now? It's almost ten o'clock."

"But . . ." Richard Lennard met Tim's eye again. Tim detected defiance, but also a look of real anguish. "Very well. Just let me get my coat."

Chapter Fifty-Three

JULIET SLIPPED PAST the gathering crowd and, skirting the netball courts, walked along the edge of the playing fields that backed on to the main school building, which was broadly E-shaped. She scanned the horizon. There wasn't a soul in sight. Turning up the collar of her coat, she carried on walking until she reached the square semi-garden that lay just beyond the main entrance. She knew from the plans she'd studied that the school hall faced the garden. Next to it were the changing rooms. A stream of girls dressed in shorts and sweatshirts emerged from the latter as she approached, carrying their day clothes. Walking past her, they crossed the garden to the back entrance, going in the direction from which she had come. Beyond this entrance was a kind of foyer area and beyond that a second set of doors, in front of which stood the refreshments table.

Pausing, Juliet could hear someone begin an address from a loudspeaker. She wasn't close enough to hear the words. Glancing across at the full-length windows which ran the length of the hall, she saw two people looking out. One of them was Councillor Start; the other was his daughter-in-law, Veronica. Veronica Start turned away, but not before Juliet saw the Councillor make a grab for her arm. Juliet was debating whether to go to Veronica's aid when she saw her hurry from the hall into the corridor and disappear through the front

door. Turning back to the window, Juliet saw that Councillor Start had also vanished.

She continued walking, making her way to the far side of the school, where there was a small visitors' car park beside the chapel. She heard a car door slam and voices issuing from the car park. Peering warily round the far corner of the main building, she spotted an elderly man in an automated wheelchair shrugging off the attentions of a mature but distinguished-looking woman. It took the man a little while to arrange himself in the wheelchair, the woman standing by patiently until he was ready to move. Eventually he set off at a cracking pace, careering round the side of the building, on to the main sweep, and finally out of sight. The woman followed.

Cautiously, Juliet walked in the same direction. The visitors' car park had filled up rapidly. She inspected the row of vehicles as she walked past them. Stationed at the end of the rank of neatly-polished cars was one incongruous addition: a rusty, mud-splattered pick-up truck. Juliet recognised it immediately as Ivan Grummett's vehicle. Briefly she was puzzled by why he should want to attend a girls' netball match: it wasn't being held at his missing niece's school and as far as she knew he had no links with Spalding High School. The explanation was obvious: he must have come for The Bricklayers meeting.

As she reached the main sweep, she saw it also was being used as a car park. The female teacher supervising turned to face Juliet as she heard her approach. Juliet had already recognised Veronica Start.

"Good morning, DC Armstrong," said Veronica brightly, as if the two recent taut interviews at the house in Blue Gowt Lane had never taken place. Looking over her shoulder, Juliet realised that several students and their parents were within earshot.

"Good morning, Mrs Start. I hope the weather brightens up a little. I think the match's about to begin, isn't it?"

"Yes. I suppose we can't complain about the weather. At least it's not raining." She attempted a smile. It warped uncontrollably into a rictus. As Juliet came closer to her, she saw again the bruise on the side of her face. It was massive and livid. Veronica's attempt to cover it with make-up had, if anything, made it more unsightly. Juliet waited until the knot of people who'd left the parked cars headed off to the netball courts.

"Veronica, are you sure you're all right? That bruise really does look nasty."

"I'm fine," she said. Juliet thought her lip wobbled slightly. "If you'll excuse me, I need to close the gates now."

"Do you usually do that when there's a match? What if some of the spectators arrive late?"

"No, we don't usually do it, but it was one of the conditions that Mr Lennard agreed with Councillor Start when we discovered there was a clash in use of the facilities. Anyone who arrives late will be disappointed, I'm afraid."

"I see. Did Councillor Start demand other conditions that you know of?" Juliet didn't comment on the fact that this was an odd way of referring to one's own father-in-law.

"Only that the hall is out of bounds to everyone attending the match," Veronica Start replied warily. "The home team was allowed to use the changing rooms, which are near the hall, because their kit was there, but the door to the corridor connecting them to the hall and the outside door have now been locked. The girls can't return to the changing rooms. The foyer opposite has been turned into a temporary changing room for both teams. "

"Isn't the hall rather a strange place to hold a meeting for just a few people? Surely the staff room or one of the class-

rooms would have sufficed, and probably been more comfortable to use."

"I think they're intending to occupy the stage area only. The advantage of the hall is that all the doors leading into it can be locked. Now, if you'll excuse me, I have to get on."

Juliet watched Veronica hurry away, hands thrust deep into the pockets of her coat, head bowed. She decided to complete her circuit by returning to the netball courts. The first games would have started by now. She'd hover right on the periphery of the crowd so that she could watch the main entrance as well as the spectators. She was looking back at the main door whilst still walking when she bumped into someone. Jerking round sharply, she saw it was Andy Carstairs.

"Ow!" he said ruefully. "That was my shin!"

"Sorry, I was trying to do two things at once. I'm glad you managed to get in before they closed the gates. Councillor Start's orders, apparently."

"Wouldn't have stopped me," he said. "I know this area well. I grew up in Alexandra Road. I'd have just gone down Matmore Gate and then cut across the playing fields from the river bank."

"Show off! Interesting that's possible, though. Who else would know?"

"I suppose most of the people who live round here. And most of the students at the school, too. You can bet they sneak out to the shop in Matmore Gate during school hours. I'll move on. DI Yates will be annoyed if he sees us hanging around in gaggles, as he put it. Where is he, by the way?"

"You're right, he will. He's going to stay close to Richard Lennard. I'm not sure exactly where they are at the moment: you'll probably see them if you move further into the crowd. I'll stay here. Could you ask Verity Tandy to come across for a quiet word? I think I saw Mrs Painter talking to her earlier."

"Sure."

"Found out anything interesting?" she said to Verity when she appeared.

"Not much. I was surprised to see Cassandra Knipes's parents here. I know they're supporting the match because Cassandra was so keen on netball, but I'd have thought it would be too much of an ordeal for them. Most people have treated them with respect – even deliberately kept their distance, actually, almost as if misfortune is catching. I think only Cindy Painter has spoken to them at any length. She seems to be talking to almost everyone."

"Yes, I saw her talking to you. I didn't make the connection when I first saw him, but I assume Mr Knipes is the man in the wheelchair?"

"Yes. That's his wife standing beside him."

"Did they speak to you?"

"Only to say hello. He's in a really bad mood. I know he's got cause to be, but he's taking it out on her. He seems to be furious with her, for some reason."

"Really? I suppose everyone reacts to grief in a different way. Might be worth keeping an eye on him, though. Do you know anyone else?"

"I recognise the teachers and some of the students. I don't know any of the other spectators. I think they're mostly parents. DI Yates's hope that we'd discover a smoking gun was optimistic – though worth a try, of course," Verity added hurriedly, as Juliet's friendly expression faded. "I'd better go and stand somewhere else now. I know DI Yates doesn't want us to spend much time talking to each other."

She moved away. Juliet stood with her back against the wall and tried to keep watch on both the crowd and the main entrance. She was very cold and could have murdered another cup of tea. It seemed an age until a shrill whistle announced

half time. She watched the girls re-don their discarded sweatshirts and file off the netball court, past the tea table and into the 'changing room' in the foyer.

Tim appeared at her elbow bearing a fresh beaker of tea.

"Thanks," said Juliet. "Manna from heaven! But I thought you were glued to Mr Lennard."

"He's talking to Mr and Mrs Knipes. I've had a brief word with them myself. I thought I'd better leave Lennard to it for a little while."

"You don't suspect them of anything, do you?"

"Not really. But this whole thing doesn't make much sense. Who knows who's guilty of what? Have you found out anything worthwhile?"

"A couple of things. Ivan Grummett's pick-up's in the car park, so I'm assuming he's a Bricklayer."

"I certainly haven't seen him here," said Tim, looking round.

"And Councillor Start has made the hall out of bounds while his meeting is going on. That includes the adjacent changing rooms. The netball teams can't go back to them until the match's over."

"Lennard didn't tell me he'd agreed to that. How did you find out?"

"Veronica Start was supervising the car park. She told me. She was also instructed to close the school gates after the netball started. I assume all the Bricklayers had arrived by then."

"You didn't see any of them?"

"Could have done. Presumably they don't look unlike parents!"

"I'll ask Lennard if he thinks they're all here. We didn't check that side car park, did we?"

"No. But Giash and Verity may have done."

"Ask them, will you? I'm going back to Lennard now."

"Enjoy," said Juliet.

Chapter Fifty-Four

WE ARE LOCKED together in Ariadne's room. The sheets on the bed are foetid with her sweat. I realise that the room must stink. Cassandra gagged as he shoved her through the door. She and Philippa are huddled on the floor, sitting next to each other but not speaking. There's no rapport between them. They seem only to agree about one thing: they don't want me anywhere near them. We are separated by the bed. If I try to get closer, they tell me to keep away. Philippa says it menacingly, Cassandra is almost hysterical. It is worse than a nightmare. If I'd never set eyes on them, at least I could have pretended that I held a place in their hearts.

Chapter Fifty-Five

TIM HAD TAKEN only a couple of steps when he heard some angry shouts. His name was being called and straight away he recognised Richard Lennard's voice. Lennard sounded as if he was being attacked.

"DI Yates! DI Yates! Over here!"

Tim sprinted to Lennard's side, pushing his way through the crowd, most members of which were converging on the same spot. Lennard was still standing beside Mr Knipes's wheelchair. Red in the face, he was being challenged by a tall young woman standing aggressively close to him. He saw Tim and pointed accusingly at the woman.

"This woman is trespassing. Please ask her to leave."

Tim was about to intervene when Andy Carstairs came diving through the throng.

"Jocelyn . . . Ms Greaves. What's wrong?"

"I've come to report on the netball game. I have a perfect right . . ." the woman began indignantly. Tim disliked her immediately. He wasn't keen on people who insisted on their rights.

"You have no right!" said Richard Lennard furiously. "You are trespassing on school property. DI Yates, this woman's name is Jocelyn Greaves. She's a reporter. She's made several malicious attempts to discredit this school."

Tim had just reached them. He gave Andy a puzzled look.

"Let's all keep calm and sort this out in private, shall we?" he said. "Where can we go to talk?"

Richard Lennard was still glaring balefully at the young woman. Looking past her, he saw several parents staring curiously and was suddenly aware that he'd made a spectacle of himself.

"The German room is the first classroom to the right of that door," he said, indicating the side entrance grudgingly. "I suppose we could go in there."

He led the way. Tim shepherded Andy Carstairs and Jocelyn Greaves after him.

"Now," said Tim, turning to Jocelyn Greaves, "please explain why you're here, Ms Greaves."

"As I've said, to report on the netball match."

"For the *Spalding Guardian*?"

"No. I'm a freelance reporter."

"Who wants a report on a school netball match, if not the local paper? I wouldn't have thought it the sort of news that would travel far."

"Well, I . . ."

"Ask her how she got in!" Richard Lennard shouted. "Ask her about her snooping. If she wanted to cover the netball, why did she arrive so late?"

"Mr Lennard, please keep your voice down. Ms Greaves, I'd be grateful if you would answer Mr Lennard's questions. As you no doubt know, the school gates were closed when the match began, at 10.00 a.m. Its start time was well-advertised."

"I mistook the time."

"How did you get in?"

"I took the back way, across the river bank from Matmore Gate and over the playing fields."

"I see," said Tim, giving Andy a searching look. "That is actually trespassing. Mr Lennard is correct."

"I'd be obliged if you'd make her leave," Richard Lennard said, trying to re-summon his dignity. "If you'll excuse me, I have to be there for the second half." He left the classroom.

"Ms Greaves, I am afraid that I *am* going to have to ask you to leave. DC Carstairs will escort you to the gate. Mrs Start has the keys," Tim concluded, addressing Andy. "She's round the front of the school somewhere."

Jocelyn Greaves' eyes blazed fury, though she spoke with restraint.

"Well, that's the last time I help the police with their 'enquiries'," she said.

"Ms Greaves was very co-operative yesterday evening in supplying the information you requested, sir," said Andy uncomfortably.

"And I'm very grateful," said Tim, "but that doesn't mean I can help her to break the law."

"Then let me get out of here at once," she said, "but don't be surprised if you live to regret it. There's more going on here at the moment than you understand."

She left the classroom abruptly. Andy followed her.

"I don't doubt that she's right," Tim sighed to himself. "It's nailing it that's the problem."

The netball players had reconvened and begun the second half. Outside again, Tim noted swiftly that Richard Lennard was no longer among the spectators. Shit, he thought to himself. I've lost him now. Whatever Jocelyn Greaves' intentions, she could hardly have done the headteacher a greater favour. Tim glanced across to where Juliet had been standing and saw that she also had vanished. Perhaps she'd accompanied Lennard, or at least followed him. Tim hoped so. He thought of texting her, but decided against it. Scanning the crowd, he saw Giash standing on the far edge of the netball courts and Ricky Mac-

Fadyen standing just apart from a group of spectators. Verity Tandy was nowhere to be seen. In the distance he perceived Andy walking back to the netball courts. Veronica Start was beside him.

Tim had a sudden inkling that something had gone wrong. He'd hardly formulated the thought when he spied an uncouth figure lurking on the periphery, smoking a cigarette and staring hard at the crowd. He heard someone gasp close by and, looking across, saw that Mrs Knipes had also spotted Ivan Grummett standing there. Grummett grinned at her, making eye contact for some seconds, then turned on his heel and ambled back down the sweep. Mrs Knipes had quickly crouched down to tend to her husband. She was tucking his travel rug around him while he swatted petulantly at her with his hands. Either he hadn't seen Grummett, or the man's silent interaction with his wife held no meaning for him. Tim needed to question her urgently, but her husband presented an obstacle. He moved towards her as casually as he could and said quietly,

"Mrs Knipes, may I have a quick word?"

She nodded and walked backwards a few paces. "It'll have to be quick," she said. "I can't leave Arthur."

"Of course not," said Tim. "I just wanted to ask you whether you know the man who was staring across at you from the sweep?"

"Which man? I didn't notice anyone in particular." She clipped her words tersely. Tim knew that she wouldn't yield the truth.

"My mistake," he said evenly.

Chapter Fifty-Six

JULIET DECIDED TO walk round the building again. Meddling reporters didn't concern her, but she was suspicious that the Bricklayers had some secret way of getting into the school. She was convinced the Bricklayers had information about the two missing girls and agitated by Tim's failure to bust their meeting.

She turned the corner and saw Verity Tandy walking a few paces in front of her. Verity was moving cautiously, hugging the wall, evidently observing a small man leaning against one of the hall windows. The man stubbed out the cigarette he'd been smoking and let the stub fall to the ground. He stamped on it briefly before scurrying towards the other end of the building. Verity followed him, walking fast but nimbly. Juliet trailed them both, closing the gap between herself and Verity but still leaving a few paces between them. As the man turned the corner, Verity swivelled her head and saw Juliet; at the same instant, the man turned and spotted her. Verity rapidly focused on her quarry, herself cautiously rounding the corner. When Juliet caught up with her, the man had vanished. He was no longer on the path and the car park beyond was deserted.

She and Verity moved forward together silently. It was darker at this side of the building. As her eyes adjusted to the gloom, Juliet noticed a slight movement at the periphery of

her vision. A blue door set into a cranny in the building was swinging shut. She sprinted towards it and held it before the latch could close, praying fervently that the person who had just passed through it would not try to pull it from the other side or check to see it had locked. She waited, stock still, for a couple of minutes, Verity equally motionless at her side.

"What now?" Verity mouthed.

"We go in," Juliet whispered. "Have your baton ready in case someone's waiting for us."

She slipped through the door, her heart banging, Verity on her heels. The room they had entered was windowless. Reassured they were alone, Juliet took a small torch from her pocket and shone it around until she spotted a light switch and snapped it on. The low watt bulb barely served its purpose, but she and Verity could see they'd entered a store for lighting equipment. Several large round lamps, packed around with straw in lidless boxes, had been stacked along two of the walls. There were also larger boxes from which a jumble of cables protruded and a number of tripods.

"What do you think all this is for?" said Verity, still keeping her voice down.

"It's stage lighting. The hall obviously doubles for putting on plays as well as for gym and assemblies."

"I'm surprised they don't leave it in there all the time."

"Probably have to move it when the hall's hired out. But I wouldn't mind betting all this stuff is in here because there's a quick route through to the stage."

"I can't see another way out."

"There certainly isn't another door." Juliet turned her torch on again and shone it around, finally arcing the pool of light at her feet. "There's a panel set into the floor here. Could be a trapdoor." She knelt down, grabbed the piece of raised wood at one end of the panel, and pushed. It slid back smoothly.

Juliet peered into the cavity that she'd opened up and shone the torch into it.

"It's quite deep," she said. "Not room height, but almost that, I'd guess. I'm going to climb into it, see if it leads anywhere."

"Do you want me to come with you?"

"Stay here for a couple of minutes. If I don't come back, follow me. Do you think you can manage in the dark if you turn the light off first?"

"Sure. You're not the only one with a torch!" Verity hissed indignantly.

"Great. If you pull the lid back over after you're in, no-one will know we're here."

Verity hated confined spaces and understood the advantage of invisibility could be two-edged. But Juliet was being so matter-of-fact that she hesitated for only a second.

Juliet disappeared into the cavity. Verity monitored the passing seconds with religious accuracy. After two minutes had elapsed, she switched on her torch, turned off the light and followed.

Chapter Fifty-Seven

STILL SMARTING FROM Jocelyn Greaves's frosty departure, Andy Carstairs realised only gradually that Veronica Start had continued to walk alongside him. When he turned to speak to her, he noticed the huge badly-camouflaged contusion on her face. He paused and she also stopped, turning her face slightly away from him.

"Mrs Start, are you all right? That's a bad bruise on your face. Don't you think you should see a doctor?"

She searched his face with an intensity that disturbed him.

"Can I see your ID?" she said.

"I'm sorry, what did you say?"

"Can I see your ID? You tell me that you're a police officer and one of DI Yates' team. I only have your word for it."

Andy drew his ID card from his inside jacket pocket and flipped it open.

"Thank you. In answer to your question, no, I'm not OK. I want to seek police protection. Can you tell me how to do it?"

"Yes, but . . ."

"I understand that your priority is to find Cassandra Knipes and the other girl who's gone. Please believe me when I say I have no idea whether my husband is mixed up in either of their disappearances. I can tell you that he's dangerously unstable. He has been from the start of our marriage, but he's got worse over the past few days. I suppose that might tell you something

about whether he knows where those girls are. I'm terrified of him. And I'm ashamed: I've been behaving like a typical battered wife, too frightened to leave. Not much of a role model for young girls, am I?"

Andy was stunned.

"Of course we can help you," he said. "Stay with me until we're finished here. Then I'll arrange for a WPC to come and escort you to a safe unit."

"What about my job? Will I have to give it up?"

"Usually employers are sympathetic if people have to take time off in such circumstances. You'll probably have to confide in Mr Lennard."

She smiled sardonically.

"I'll have to think about that. Resignation may be preferable. But thank you. I'm sorry for getting in your way."

"No problem," said Andy, trying to summon a grin. Fate seemed not to be on his side today. He'd managed to exchange the company of a brave, independently-minded woman for one who was needy and damaged. He cast another sidelong look at Veronica. He still found her puzzling. He suspected that her plea for help might not be as straightforward as it looked.

"You say your husband's dangerously unstable. Do you know where he is at the moment?"

"No. And that's the truth. I know DI Yates doesn't believe me."

"Does he have weapons?"

"I don't know. That's the truth as well. I've never seen him with any: he prefers to use his fists on me. But a man like Matthew would certainly be able to get hold of weapons if he wanted to. Or think of ways to improvise."

Chapter Fifty-Eight

HAVING SEARCHED THE crowd in vain, Tim was worried about Juliet and Verity Tandy. He'd instructed his team not to use pagers but set their phones to silent so they could text each other. "Where are you? Are you OK?" he texted Juliet now. He waited five minutes for a reply, knowing that she would answer immediately if she could.

The spectators' enthusiasm for the game was dwindling noticeably. Returning to them, he saw Giash Chakrabati stationed unobtrusively near the side entrance and Ricky MacFadyen talking to Arthur Knipes. "I need to leave now," the old man was saying angrily. "I can't wait until the end." Ricky caught Tim's eye. Tim nodded as he approached them. Ricky understood the Knipes were free to go if they wished.

"Would you like a hand getting back to your car, sir?"

"Certainly not. I won't require help, but if I do there's always Susannah." Mrs Knipes had her back to Tim, so he couldn't see her expression.

"We'll arrange for the gate to be opened for you, Mr Knipes." Tim observed that Andy Carstairs and Veronica Start were deep in conversation. He beckoned to Giash.

"PC Chakrabati, would you mind asking Mrs Start to open the gates for Mr and Mrs Knipes? And when she's done that, I'd like to speak to her myself."

Tim was irritated when a few minutes later he saw Giash and Andy walking away with Veronica Start.

"Jesus," he muttered to himself. "It's not as if we're exactly overstaffed here."

He looked at his phone again. Still no message from Juliet.

The Knipes were moving more slowly than when they'd arrived. They seemed to be arguing. At one point, Arthur Knipes halted his wheelchair and stabbed a finger at his watch. Susannah Knipes bent to say something to him and they moved on again. Veronica Start had opened the gate and was patiently waiting for them to drive through it, Andy still at her side, Giash standing at some distance. Finally, the silver people-carrier edged along the far side of the sweep and through the gate. Veronica Start flicked her remote control tag and the gate swung back again smoothly. Tim and the trio converged outside the main entrance. He spoke to Giash.

"When did you last see PC Tandy?"

"About half an hour ago, sir."

"Try texting her, will you? Ask her where she is. Mrs Start, we need to get into the school. It's urgent. Can you open the door, please?"

She looked panic-stricken. "I'm sorry, I can't. Mr Lennard has the only set of keys we've taken out of the building today."

"We've lost sight of him for the moment. We think he's gone back into the school. I assume you know his mobile number. Can you call him?"

"I'm sorry, I can't," she said again. "When Mr Lennard came to the school, he had a mobile jammer system fitted, to prevent students from using their mobile phones here. It means the staff can't get reception, either."

"Right," said Tim. "We're going to go in. We'll need back-up. Armed police with a battering ram. I'll call Superintendent Thornton now. PC Chakrabati, we're going to stop the netball

match. Go and tell DC MacFadyen. I want you to take the names and contact details of everyone present, including the netball players. Then ask them to leave. Make sure no-one stays. Ask the visiting netball team to collect their kit from the foyer and go. Mrs Start, please open the gates for people as they leave but make sure you don't let anyone else in. DC Carstairs will help you."

Veronica Start stared at him like a trapped rabbit.

"DI Yates, a word," said Andy, drawing Tim to one side. "Mrs Start has requested police protection. I think she's traumatised."

"She will be fucking traumatised if we don't find Juliet and Verity Tandy soon," said Tim, sotto voce but furiously. "Get her organised. I'm going to call Thornton."

He moved to the shelter of the school porch and took out his phone.

Chapter Fifty-Nine

JULIET AND VERITY had crawled into a subterranean world constructed of elaborately-interlocking rafters propped up at frequent intervals by vertical posts. By the light of their torches, they could see thick drifts of dust amid which several cables snaked along the ground. The structure was about four and a half feet high; they could walk half-bent along the line of posts like miners toiling to a coal face. Roughly calculating the square footage of the area, Juliet was convinced her original hunch was right: they were underneath the school's stage. If indeed the storage room was used by The Bricklayers as a secret entrance, there must be another trap door somewhere. More nervous than she'd led Verity to believe, she hoped fervently that no-one would find them via that route. It would be impossible to beat a hasty retreat.

"Did you hear that?" whispered Verity.

Juliet paused and knelt down to ease her leg muscles. She listened intently. She heard a voice immediately above her. Although it was distorted by the poor acoustics, she was certain Councillor Start was speaking. She shifted her position so that Verity could sit alongside her. They both listened hard.

"It sounds as if he's giving a lecture," murmured Verity, as they accustomed their ears to the warped timbre of the voice.

". . . and now you see the differences," the disembodied voice was saying. "Intelligent, yes. Clever, yes. But consider-

ably shorter at the same age. Mathematical aptitude not as advanced. Social skills present, but not as developed."

There was a pause and some muttered conversation which was difficult to pick up.

"I agree, it's unfortunate that D didn't survive."

"What about A?" Someone else was speaking. "What's happening to her?"

There was another pause.

"I don't know, at present. Unfortunately, we haven't been able to collect the information."

"If you want my opinion, this is all fucked up now. They were meant to meet H, but not like this. They can't be sent back now. They're going to tell the cops where they've been."

"I know it's a problem. We could send them abroad somewhere, give them a new identity."

"And you think they'll just go along with that? Let us rip them away from what they know as their families and give them a fresh start? Agree never to come back?"

"It's worth a try. P would probably agree to it. She detests her 'family' . . ."

"Less of that!" said a rough voice.

"Well, she does."

"I said, shut it!"

"Stop it! We've got to agree on a solution to the problem."

"We all know who caused the problem. Without him there wouldn't have been one."

"Perhaps he can be the solution as well. The police already suspect him, but they've got nothing on the rest of us. Tell him to sort out the mess he's made and get rid of them. He's done it before, hasn't he?"

"You mean, keep them where they are?"

"That or dispose of them. One or t'other."

There was another pause.

"All right, I'll talk to him. We'll see what we can come up with."

"You'll have to do better than that. You make him do something about this. He's got until Monday. You can report back to us Monday evening. Use the e-mail address, it's too risky to meet again. Have we got all the stuff?"

"Yes, Ivan took it out earlier."

"Nothing left here of ours?"

"No, I don't think so."

"The meeting's over, then. Last one here. Let's go."

"Through the back entrance?"

Juliet looked at Verity. They both held their breath.

"No. The copper said he wanted to speak to us and we'll oblige him. At least, I'll oblige him. No reason to make him more suspicious. I'll listen to what he has to say. You can all leave through the French windows. You won't have to speak to them unless they stop you."

"Did you slide the bolts on the traps?"

"I fastened the one here," said a deeper voice. "The one at the other end hasn't been done."

"If there's no-one about, we'll do it from the car park. Otherwise we'll leave it. Kids'll get the blame, that's all."

"I'd like it done properly," came the deeper voice, sounding uneasy. "No trace of us using it. Not if we're not going to come here again."

Chapter Sixty

TIM AND SUPERINTENDENT Thornton were back at the police station. Thornton had refused to stay at the school, saying that Tim had mishandled events by terminating the netball match early and antagonising the headteacher. He was convinced Juliet and Verity would turn up shortly. Tim told Ricky MacFadyen and Giash Chakrabati to keep calling their mobiles, although he knew it was hopeless if Veronica Start's information about the mobile jammer system was accurate. The Superintendent seemed to think that her plea for police protection had nothing to do with the case.

"She's not married to her father-in-law, is she?" he said. "What are you going to do with her?"

"A WPC will take her to hospital to see if she needs treatment for that bruise on her face. Then we'll try to find her accommodation in the battered wives' refuge at Whittlesey. She won't need it long term, but she'll be safer there until we can locate her husband."

"Good, good," said the Superintendent. "But make sure someone keeps an eye on her, Yates. She could lead us to your man yet."

"What about DC Armstrong and PC Tandy, sir?"

"Put a trace on their phones. If you can't get a signal in the next hour, we'll ask for an emergency warrant to search the school."

"OK," said Tim doubtfully. If Matthew Start was trying to avoid the police Tim doubted that he'd risk going anywhere near the school. But what if he had, and was holding Juliet and Verity somewhere?

"You need to get your mind back on the case, Yates," Superintendent Thornton cut into his thoughts. "What are you going to do next?"

"Katrin was going to come in to the station to help Juliet build a storyboard. And she's got a contact who can get DNA results done quickly. I was going to ask Verity Tandy to go to the Pilgrim Hospital to get a sample from the woman who died yesterday. We've got samples from the two girls." He didn't add 'and the baby and Helena Nurmi'.

"I know about that contact," said the Superintendent. "It's a private lab. And its charges are exorbitant."

"Under the circumstances . . ."

"Yes, yes, Yates, I agree. Get on with it. We'll worry about the budget later. Send someone else to get the sample. Your wife can still come in and have a go at the storyboard, can't she? I seem to remember she's good at that sort of thing. Do her good to get back into the swing."

"I'm sure she'll still be willing to do it, though she's bound to be worried about Juliet. We'll have to find someone to look after Sophia."

"Who? Oh, your daughter. I was forgetting. Yes, well I'm sure a neighbour or someone will oblige. And of course we'll pay Katrin," the Superintendent added, as if his largesse would be impossible to refuse.

Once alone, Tim tried Juliet's phone himself. Still no answer. Immediately he made a call to the tracking unit. He was damned if he'd wait for Superintendent Thornton's stipulated hour to elapse. He asked for both mobiles to be tracked.

Wearily he sat down at Juliet's desk. He called Katrin, ex-

plained the situation to her and asked if she could get a babysitter. He'd no sooner put the phone down than it started ringing. He seized it.

"Juliet?" he asked.

There was the sound of tinkling laughter.

"Is that DI Yates? I thought I recognised your voice. It's Louise Butler here. I was actually calling Juliet. She said she wanted to come and pick up some tissue samples from the woman we know as Lucy Helen."

"Yes," said Tim. "I did know about that. It won't be Juliet now, I'm afraid. I'll arrange for a squad car to come for the samples, if that's OK with you."

"Fine by me. But is Juliet all right?"

Tim had a lightning debate with himself and decided not to dissemble. He wanted to keep Louise Butler on board.

"Very confidentially, Dr Butler, we're not sure of DC Armstrong's whereabouts at the moment. I'm certain there's been some kind of misunderstanding, but naturally we're concerned. Will you let us know if either she or PC Tandy gets in touch with you?"

"Of course. But . . ."

"I don't mean to alarm you, Dr Butler, but I think I should tell you the truth. Frankly, I'm very worried myself. Please, just keep calm. If she can't reach us, I think she may try to contact you. Can she reach you if you're not on duty?"

"Yes. But I shall be on duty for the next six hours, at least."

"I hope to God she'll have turned up by then."

There was a pause.

"Dr Butler? Are you still there?"

"Yes. Yes, I'm sorry, this is a lot to take in. I actually had another reason for calling Juliet."

"Anything that concerns me?"

"Yes. Yes, it is. We're planning to discharge Mrs Grummett

later today. There's no medical reason to keep her here any longer."

"Does she know this? Or her husband?"

"No. You asked me to tell you first. But . . ."

"Dr Butler, you'd be doing us an immense favour if you could hold her a little longer."

"As I told you before, DI Yates, we're not a prison. Or a charity, for that matter."

"Do you need her bed?"

"As it happens, we don't. Not yet, anyway. We try to send as many people home as possible at the weekend, as I'm sure you know. But we'll probably need the bed on Monday."

"Could you keep her until then? Please, Dr Butler."

There was a much longer silence.

"I suppose so. But I want you to know that it's not only against my principles, but probably breaking the hospital's code of ethics. I could get into serious trouble."

"I promise you I'll take the blame if anything goes wrong."

"I don't think you can do that. But all right. We'll keep her a little longer. To be honest, she doesn't seem to be in much of a hurry to leave."

"Thank you, Dr Butler. I'm grateful."

"You will do everything in your power to find Juliet, won't you?"

"Yes," said Tim. That goes without saying, he thought, as he put down the phone. And he didn't have time to consider it now, but at the back of his mind was the passing thought that Katrin's hunch about Dr Butler was correct.

Chapter Sixty-One

JULIET AND VERITY were listening to clattering footsteps, so loud they must be coming from just above the place where the two policewomen were crouching. Juliet waited until the noise receded before she spoke to Verity. She was still keeping her voice low.

"Did you hear what they said?"

"Yes. If they get a chance, they're going to bolt the trapdoor that we came through. We've got to get there first."

"We can try. But unless we can move fast enough to get completely outside the building before they come, we'll have to hide in the lighting store. Or we'll have to face them, but I don't fancy it. I think we know enough for them to want to shut us up in any way they can. We've got to get out of here unseen to make sure they're arrested."

Verity's hatred of confined spaces was taking hold and she felt close to panic, but for the second time that day took courage from Juliet's apparent calm.

"I'll go first. I'll move as quickly as I can. It's still going to take a few minutes to crawl back to the exit."

"OK. I'm going to text Tim. He may still be outside."

Juliet wedged her torch in the elaborate carpentry above her head and started texting. Verity began to slither back the way they had come. She'd gone only a few feet when she heard Juliet exclaim.

"Fuck!"

"Are you OK?"

"I can't get a signal."

"Leave it for now. Come on!"

Juliet put away her phone and plucked the torch from its perch. On her hands and knees, she crawled after Verity, holding the torch awkwardly as she propelled herself forwards.

Verity had reached the enlarged space immediately below the trapdoor.

"You can turn off your torch now," she said. "I'll light the way for you." She was speaking in her normal voice.

"I think we should still keep as quiet as possible," Juliet whispered. She heaved herself round the last corner and banged her elbow on one of the wooden pillars.

"Ouch!" she yelled, letting the torch fall. It hit the ground with a thud and rolled along the floor before she could grab it.

"What was that?" said a man's voice. It was uncomfortably close.

"I didn't hear anything."

"Well, I did. I think there's somebody down there."

Verity moved as far to one side of the trapdoor as she could and held her breath. Juliet, now motionless, was still lying on the dusty floor.

"Can't be. But if there is, we'll cook their goose for them," said the first voice, with a throaty chuckle. Heavy footsteps crossed above. The two policewomen heard the trapdoor bolt being yanked into place. The footsteps receded. The outside door banged and clicked shut.

Verity exhaled noisily.

"Thank God, they've gone," she said.

"Yes. But we're trapped in here now. We're going to have a job getting out, unless we can tell someone."

For a moment Verity looked at Juliet in wide-eyed horror. Then she put her hands over her face and started screaming.

Chapter Sixty-Two

CASSANDRA IS LYING on Ariadne's bed, her face like ash. The poor air is making her ill. She'll have to lie motionless and rest until it gets better. It's happened to me so many times that I'd forgotten how frightened I used to be. She's been crying, but she's quiet now, collapsed like a wounded bird. Her face is without expression, tear-stained but calm at last. I catch a fleeting glimpse of Ariadne, as if I can see the negative beneath a photograph. But Cassandra's cheeks are firm, her forehead smooth, her blue eyes clear and bright. She has the sweetest voice I have ever heard. Her silvery hair is tied back at the crown and cascades over her shoulders. She is tall and strong. She won't look at me. She has turned her face away from me. She closes her eyes.

Philippa is still squatting on the floor. The lack of oxygen hasn't affected her. She's wary, like a wild animal. She trusts neither of us and snarls when I try to speak to her. She's told me to keep away from her. When she raised her clenched fist to me she reminded me of her father. Is she also riven with broken emotions? She's shorter than Cassandra, but as beautiful. They are heartbreakingly lovely. My girls. My wonderful girls.

Chapter Sixty-Three

KATRIN HAD ARRIVED and was in the meeting room beginning to construct the storyboard. Tim left her with Ricky MacFadyen and called the tracing squad again. When he heard they'd had no luck in locating the two phones, his patience ran out. He stormed up the stairs, resolved to bulldoze his boss into giving permission to search Spalding High School. He met the Superintendent coming out of his office.

"Ah, Yates, I hear your lady wife is here. Excellent. I was just on my way to have a word with her. Any news of Armstrong and Tandy?"

"No, sir. As I've explained, the school is barred from receiving cellphone signals by a mobile jammer device. I'm convinced they must be in there and that's why we can't reach them."

Tim was expecting a battle, but the Superintendent merely looked grave.

"I see." He consulted his watch. "How long is it since you last saw either of them?"

"Getting on for three hours."

"All right, I agree there's cause for concern. Call Richard Lennard and ask him to let you into the building to search it. Take someone with you."

"I suspect that Lennard will be mysteriously unavailable when I call him. Then we'll need a warrant, which will take hours."

"Not necessarily," said the Superintendent unexpectedly. "If you have a good reason to force your way into the building without a warrant, I can authorise it. And I'm willing to do that. But just make damned sure you find them in there, because it'll be your head on the block. And call Lennard first."

"Thank you, sir."

"Now, I'm going to see if Katrin needs any help."

"From you, sir?"

The Superintendent arched an eyebrow.

"Yes, from me, Yates. Nothing strange about that, is there? I'm at least as familiar with the details of this case as you are. And, it strikes me, a damned sight more committed to finding those girls unharmed, beguiling though sideshows of disappearing policewomen may be."

He brushed past Tim and set off down the stairs.

Tim took out his mobile and called the number Lennard had given him. To his surprise, Lennard answered immediately.

"Mr Lennard? It's DI Yates. I'm afraid I'm going to have to ask you to return to the school to let me into it. I'll have a colleague with me. The two policewomen I told you about still haven't turned up and we have to make sure they're not trapped in the building."

"I can be there in fifteen minutes, if you meet me outside."

Tim was astonished. It seemed there'd be no need for another battering-ram drama or for Superintendent Thornton to risk being hauled over the coals by the Police Complaints Commission.

Andy Carstairs came running up the stairs.

"Any news?" he asked. "Of Juliet, I mean."

"No, but Thornton's just said I can search the school and, miraculously, Richard Lennard has agreed to let us in without a warrant. I'd like you to come with me."

"Sure. Do you need anyone else?"

"Ideally, yes, but we can't take anyone off the main case at the moment."

They headed for the car park. To Tim it seemed an eternity since he and Juliet had walked the same way early that morning.

"How's Veronica Start?" he asked, as he started the engine of the BMW.

"She's had a head X-ray and the hospital seems to think she'll be OK. She's got a nasty bruise and there is evidence of other, older, bruising. She wouldn't let the doctor she saw examine the rest of her body, but the weals on her forearms were hard to hide when they took a blood test. My guess is she probably has other scars she won't tell us about."

Tim winced.

"I've read about battered wives syndrome," he said. "I guess we all have. But I don't pretend to understand it. Is she at the refuge now?"

"Yes. A WPC from Peterborough came to collect her. She's going to spend the night there with Veronica in case Start turns up."

"I think that's unlikely."

"So do I, but as you said we can't afford to take chances. And I still think there's something odd about her."

"There's a lot that's odd about the whole Start family."

"Yes, but apart from the obvious. I've had the feeling all along that she's holding something back. Unless it's just that she's afraid of Start and traumatised by him."

"Here we are. And there's Mr Lennard, as good as his word."

Tim was still incredulous that Lennard was being so cooperative. He hoped they weren't walking into a trap.

Richard Lennard was all smiles. After an initial greeting he opened the main door of the school and ushered them inside.

"Do you want me to show you where everything is, or would you rather be on your own?" he said, unctuously. Tim's instinct was to get rid of him, but he realised that Lennard could probably save them some time, and if he was planning some kind of trap, it would be better to have him where they could see him.

"Thank you, sir. That would be helpful."

"Where should we start?"

"With the hall," said Tim, making Lennard meet his eye. Lennard stared back at him with childlike candour.

"As you wish." He led the way.

The hall door was unlocked. Tim and Andy followed the headteacher into the huge room, where a canvas cover was stretched across the floor. Several chairs had been set out on the stage, turned to face the wings on the left hand side. A screen had been suspended from the ceiling in front of the wings.

"The Bricklayers held their meeting on the stage?"

"Yes, that's what they usually do. The caretaker puts out the chairs for them."

"There's a screen but no AV equipment that I can see. Has it been removed?"

"They don't use the school's equipment. They always bring their own."

"Have you ever been to one of their meetings?"

"No."

Tim walked across the canvas to the far door and gave it a push.

"This door's locked."

"Yes. The Bricklayers asked for it to be locked. It leads to the changing rooms. They didn't want anyone to come through the changing rooms and disturb their meeting. The caretaker will unlock it first thing on Monday morning."

"I'd like you to unlock it now, please."

"All right. I'll have to look for the key. It should be on a board in the staff room."

While he was gone, Tim paced up and down the canvas floor covering several times before moving to the windows. He drew back the vertical blinds from one of them and looked out. If Juliet had walked along the path that skirted the rear of the school, she might have been observed from this window. Had someone followed her? If the door to the changing rooms was locked, where might she have entered the building?

Richard Lennard returned, still wreathed in smiles, bearing a ring from which several keys were suspended.

"It should be easy to find the right one. The caretaker's marked them all with tags."

He worked round the ring of keys before selecting one and inserting it in the door. It turned immediately.

Tim followed him into the changing rooms. In the first, there were lockers ranged round the walls and three racks of empty pegs with cages for shoes beneath them. Beyond were showers and two separate toilets. Tim pushed open the toilet doors while Andy searched the showers.

"Where does that door lead to?"

"Just outside again. Would you like me to open it?"

"Yes. Are these two doors the only way of getting in and out of the changing rooms?"

"Yes."

"What about the hall? Are there other ways of getting in and out, besides the doors we've used?"

"The windows open to the ground. And there's a sliding door through to the canteen."

"Go and have a look in the canteen, will you, Andy? I'm going to follow this path round. Mr Lennard, will you come with me? I might need you to use your bunch of keys again."

It was beginning to snow. Tim turned up the collar of his coat. Lennard was still dressed in the suit that he'd been wearing that morning. He shivered as he left the building.

"Would you like to fetch a coat? I'll wait here for you."

"I'm OK. It won't take long, will it?"

Tim found the headteacher's newfound co-operation suspicious, but he was impatient to get on and didn't reply. Lennard walked along tentatively at his side, almost but not quite a companion. They turned the corner of the building. Tim saw at once that the visitors' car park was deserted. He almost missed the small door set back in the L-shaped groove in the building.

"Where does that lead?"

"Just into a lighting store. Spotlights for the stage."

"Can you open it?"

Again Lennard worked methodically through his bunch of keys.

"I think it's that one," he said. He handed the bunch to Tim, who opened the door without difficulty.

"Is there a light?"

"I suppose so. I've never been in there myself."

Tim fished in the darkness until he found the light switch. It was as Richard Lennard had said: the room was full of lighting equipment. Lennard remained standing outside.

"There's no other way into or out of here?"

"No. It's just a store room."

Tim prodded the straw in which one of the lights was nestling. He removed the box from the pile to inspect what lay beneath it. The boxes were piled two high, the ones on the ground containing the larger lights. He could find nothing unusual and there was nothing to suggest that the room had been used recently. He replaced the box.

As he was turning to leave, he knocked against one of the

big tripods propped against the wall opposite the boxes. It fell to the ground with a clatter.

"Shit!" he exclaimed, scooping up the contraption – it was surprisingly heavy – and shoving it back against its fellows. He took one last look around and left the room, locking the door behind him.

Chapter Sixty-Four

JULIET SPENT TIME calming Verity Tandy down before she tried to text again. Verity's howls had gradually subsided and she was now propped against one of the wooden uprights, her eyes closed, occasionally letting out the aftershock of a sob like a distressed child.

When Juliet finally tried re-sending her short message, 'no network' came up on the screen immediately.

"Do you know anything about mobile jammers?"

Verity opened her eyes.

"I understand what they do, but not how they work. They put some kind of force field round a specified area to stop electronic signals getting through."

"A specified area such as a school, you mean?"

"Oh my God . . ."

"Stop it, Verity. I won't put up with that again. We've got to work through this together if we're going to get out."

"I'm sorry. Yes, some schools do use them," said Verity, concentrating hard. "They do a reasonable job, but they're not entirely reliable. There might be areas near the edge of a building – a window, say – where they don't work properly and a signal sometimes still gets through."

"Not many windows to choose from here!" said Juliet with a grim attempt at humour. Verity didn't answer.

"I'm going to crawl all the way round this space and see

if I can find anything at all that will help us. There might be something that we can use to bust the trapdoor at the other end. This one isn't going to budge."

"What shall I do?"

"Just stay here and keep your cool. If you hear any sounds overhead, shout and bang on the trapdoor as loudly as you can."

"What if it's them coming back?"

"I think that's unlikely, but's a risk we'll have to take. If you can bear to do it, turn your torch off. I'm going to have to use mine and we need to keep the batteries live for as long as we can."

Juliet began to crawl beyond the area beneath the trapdoor, keeping as near to the wall as the wooden joists would allow. It was much dirtier away from the main thoroughfare used by the lighting crews, and the floor was rougher. She felt the splinters sliding with vicious precision beneath the skin on her hands and knees.

It took longer to reach the far side of the under-stage than she'd expected, given the relatively small area she had to cover. Doggedly, she turned right and began her slow journey along its outer length. Now she was ploughing through great drifts of rank and sooty-smelling dust. This place must be a fire risk, she thought, before banishing the images the thought conjured up in her imagination. Her throat and nose were very dry, causing her to cough wretchedly. She felt nauseous. Her eyes were smarting and she was desperately thirsty. She knew that Verity hadn't yet contemplated what it would be like to spend the night here without water. She herself was afraid to think further ahead than that.

She'd almost reached the furthest limit of the underfloor space when she saw a piece of card sticking out of the dust. It was in front of her, but beyond her reach unless she moved

to her right and crawled into the network of joists. It was probably just some item of ancient rubbish and she debated whether it was worth expending her flagging energy on retrieving it. Logically she knew it wasn't, but, spurred on by a hunch and her natural curiosity, she wormed herself deeper into the network, inflicting another splinter on her knee as she did so, and reached out to grab the card. When she lifted it from the dust she realised it was bigger than she'd thought, a faded oblong cardboard envelope which, as she grasped it, swung open to let fall several squares of paper.

"Shit!" she muttered. Levering herself up on one elbow, she plucked one from the dust and shone her torch on it. It was a photograph of a small girl with very blonde hair. The child was seated, with a hideously fat girl, perhaps two years older than she, standing beside her. Juliet gazed at the photograph for some minutes.

"Philippa and Kayleigh Grummett!" she exclaimed. "It has to be."

She began scrabbling furiously through the dust in search of the other photographs.

"Juliet! Are you all right?"

"Yes, I've just found something, that's all. I'll be back with you in a few minutes."

"I think I can hear someone up above."

"Well, shout! Bang on the trapdoor with your torch!"

"I think they've gone again. I heard the door close."

"Did they say anything?"

"Just 'shit'. That was all I could hear."

There's a coincidence, Juliet thought grimly. She wondered if it could have been Tim. She was suddenly desperate to get her message to him. Abandoning the photographs, she crawled beyond the area under the second trapdoor as fast as she could. Although she knew there would be no window, it was

the nearest she could get to an outside wall. There was just a chance that this would be enough to weaken the effect of the mobile jammer.

Shining her torch meticulously up and down the wall, she noticed something had been set into it low down. Moving closer, she saw it was an air brick. Reaching it would be awkward: she'd have to haul herself over several of the criss-crossed joists. She flung herself into the task with a gusto born of desperation.

"Please!" she whispered to herself, "Please let this work." She launched herself full-length across the joists and lay with her head as close to the air brick as she could, clutching her phone in one hand. She found the message with shaking fingers and pressed 're-send'. Miraculously, it didn't bounce back. Dozens more messages came flooding in. Then the phone rang.

"Juliet? Juliet! Where are you?"

Chapter Sixty-Five

TIM LEFT JULIET and Verity Tandy at the A & E department of the Johnson Hospital and returned to the police station. He was shaken by how much they'd been damaged by being trapped for just a few hours under the stage. Verity was being treated for shock and Juliet's hands and knees were a bloody mass of splinters. Both were filthy, exhausted and dehydrated.

Richard Lennard had appeared to be horrified when Tim and Andy had pulled the two policewomen out. He'd said that he'd vaguely known that the space was there, but simply hadn't thought about it when they'd gone into the storeroom. On balance, Tim believed him and had allowed him to go home, but asked him to remain on call in case he was needed again. Tim kept the bunch of keys that opened the doors to the hall complex and asked for the key to the main door of the school. He promised to return them by Monday morning.

Juliet had told Tim about the photographs. He asked Andy to put on protective clothing and retrieve them; a police constable was sent to guard the lighting store while Andy was under the stage. Andy had yet to return with the photographs.

Reporting to Superintendent Thornton, Tim saw his boss had the grace to look sheepish.

"They're OK, you say?" he asked eagerly.

"Yes, but shocked. They didn't know how long they were going to be trapped there: their mobiles wouldn't work. They must have been terrified."

"Do you think someone shut them in there deliberately?"

"DC Armstrong says it's possible, but she isn't certain. It was clear to her that whoever slid the bolt intended to do it anyway. They didn't check to see if there was anyone in the cavity, but why would they? Though she did hear one of them say that if anyone was there, fastening the bolt would 'cook their goose'."

"Interesting. If we'd reported them missing, I wonder if anyone would have come forward?"

"Not if it was one of The Bricklayers. And we still don't know the identities of all of them or exactly what it is they do."

"Well, it's time we found out now, isn't it?" said the Superintendent, as if only Tim's reluctance to act was holding them up. "You'd better bring in Councillor Start. I'll question him myself."

"Yes, sir." Tim concealed his amazement.

"There's still no sign of his son. I'm going to push Start harder on that. He must have some idea where the lad's got to."

"Hardly a lad, sir. Matthew Start is in his forties."

The Superintendent didn't answer immediately, but scrutinised Tim for a long moment, looking peeved.

"Yes, well, we can't all boast your youth, can we? Have Councillor Start brought in, will you? And then check on the roadblocks again and see how the house-to-house enquiries are going. I want a breakthrough on these kidnappings, Yates, and I want it today."

"Yes, sir," said Tim again.

"Oh, and look in on Katrin, will you? I don't want her to

think we're leaving her entirely on her own. She is doing us a favour, after all. And she'll want to know about Armstrong."

A rush of indignation turned Tim's face scarlet. It had taken considerable self-discipline to head for Thornton's office on his arrival at the station, rather than going to update his wife first. He mumbled something unintelligible and left.

Katrin was serenely writing something on one of her glass panels when Tim entered the meeting room. She looked up at him and smiled.

"Hello. No need to tell me about Juliet and the policewoman. The staff sergeant's given me the whole story. Have you had anything to eat? There's a packet of biscuits and crisps if you're hungry."

Tim realised he was starving.

"Thanks! Shall I fetch some coffee?"

"The water from the dispenser will do me," said Katrin, indicating the plastic water-tank in the corner of the room. "I'm only going to be able to stay for another hour or so. I told Sally Dobbs I'd be back to collect Sophia by 5 p.m. She's going out this evening."

"How are you doing?"

"I'm making progress, but slowly. There's a lot I don't understand. And I've got a colossal timeline."

"What do you mean by that? How colossal?"

"I've started with the last sighting of Helena Nurmi, on July 9th 1993. Then there's the birth of Cassandra Knipes on 27th July 1997. Philippa Grummett was born on 13th July 1999. According to her mother, the young woman named as Ariadne Helen who was admitted to the Johnson Hospital on Thursday was born on July 31st 1995." Katrin had stuck the most recent photographs available against each of these dates. The one of Philippa Grummett had been taken from a blow-up of an old school photo supplied by Alice Cushing, so it was some-

what blurred, but, in spite of that, the likeness between the three was astonishing. There was no photograph of Ariadne Helen.

"All July dates, and all spaced about two years apart. More bloody coincidences. But I'm not sure how it helps."

"Neither am I, but there is one other date to add." The dates she'd already given Tim and the photographs were all on the same glass screen. Now she pointed to another screen.

"Matthew Start was born on July 9th 1970. Helena Nurmi disappeared on his twenty-third birthday. He was at home at the time, in the house where Helena was working as an au pair, looking after his younger sister. The year before, Start had completed a degree in architecture at Sheffield University and joined the family firm."

"That's fascinating! Go on."

"That's where the pattern ends, I'm afraid. Except for one more thing. As you know, Matthew Start was questioned closely about Helena Nurmi's disappearance. He was held in police custody at one stage. But he always maintained that he'd dropped her at the station as planned. She was estranged from her family because her stepfather had died in suspicious circumstances, so it took several weeks for a friend to report her missing. It was discovered that she never left the UK, as Start had claimed. He was on record as the last person to see her – no-one could remember her waiting at the station – which obviously made him a prime suspect. But in Start's favour was the fact that he'd paid for her ticket back to Finland. The police reasoning was that he wouldn't have done it if he'd been planning to kill her."

"Or he might just have been one step ahead in cunning."

"I thought you'd say that."

"So what's the final piece of your pattern? There's a welter of detail here, but I don't see that it adds anything new."

Katrin laughed. "Steady on! Is that how you usually talk to people when you want a job done?"

"Sorry! I'm just impatient to get to the results. I think you've done a brilliant job. You know that."

"Helena Nurmi applied very late to be an au pair in the summer of 1992. The agency that she registered with had more or less filled all the places available. They suggested that she reapplied in the autumn, when apparently there would be further opportunities because not all au pairs managed to stick it out, so the agency had to find replacements. She was adamant that she wanted a placement immediately. There was some suggestion during the police investigation that before he died her stepfather had been abusing her, but the Finnish police weren't co-operative and the police here gave up on that line of enquiry. If she was either being abused or mixed up in his death, it would explain why she was desperate to find a job immediately. Anyway, one of the few placements the agency could offer was in the Start household. They were dubious about it, because Mrs Start had left her husband a couple of years before. They had shared custody of the daughter, who was much younger than Matthew – still a primary school child when the parents split. Frederick Start wanted an au pair to help look after the girl when she stayed with him. The agency wasn't convinced this would be a suitable arrangement, as the au pair would frequently be in the house on her own with him or him and his son when the girl was with her mother; there would be no adult woman present. Extra interviews were held and the Starts went through a vetting process, which they passed with flying colours – Councillor Start being a pillar of the community, etcetera, etcetera. Helena herself didn't take much persuading: as I've said, she was keen to get away from home and the Starts' offer was attractive. Spending less time with the child would mean she'd have more time to devote

to polishing her English. They offered to pay for lessons at Boston College. She took the placement."

Tim whistled. "Do you think that would still happen today?"

"I'm not sure. The vetting process now is probably stricter. On the other hand, there are more laws about sexual discrimination. But coming back to the date pattern again: the police enquiry was very thorough in some respects. They went into Matthew Start's background in some detail. Apparently he was very cut up when his mother left and was referred to a psychologist. He was still receiving counselling. And the police account records that his mother left home on his birthday."

"Two years before Helena's arrival?"

"Yes. The pattern of events relating to the date of his birthday had not been started by him, but it seems to me that he decided to continue it. Those three birthdays were as close to his own as he could possibly have managed, given that gestation is an inexact science." Katrin gave an ironic smile. Sophia had been born almost two weeks later than anticipated. "The physical evidence that we have shows a strong resemblance." She gestured at the photographs. "I think that Helena Nurmi is probably the natural mother of both Cassandra Knipes and Philippa Grummett."

"Juliet may have come to the same conclusion. And the child who died?"

"Probably that one as well. But we'll need the DNA results to be sure. There is surviving DNA material from Helena Nurmi and the Pilgrim Hospital sent samples from the woman who died yesterday. They've been couriered to the lab that I told you about, along with samples from the missing girls. We should know the answer on Monday."

"If you're right about all this, Helena Nurmi could still be alive."

"If I'm right, she was still alive in July 1999, when Philippa was born. There's no proof that the woman who left 'Ariadne Helen' at the Johnson Hospital was Helena Nurmi."

"I know that. But the nurse at the hospital, Marianne Burrell, said that woman's clothes were old-fashioned. As if she'd dug stuff out of her wardrobe from twenty years back."

"Well, if it is Helena Nurmi, either she's created a complete new identity for herself or she's being held captive somewhere, because there's been absolutely no trace of her since 1993."

"Am I missing something?" said a bright voice. Katrin and Tim both turned to see Juliet come hobbling through the door. "Excuse the clothes. One of the nurses lent them to me. They keep spares for drunks, apparently." Juliet wrinkled her nose. She was wearing an A line skirt and a baggy sweater, both in nondescript colours, both extremely ill-fitting. Her knees and one of her hands were bandaged.

"What are you doing here? The doctor at A & E said he was signing you off until Tuesday at least," said Tim.

"I'm no more ill than if I'd fallen off my bike and I certainly wouldn't go sick for that. Besides, this looks fascinating. You've got a lot further with it than I would have," Juliet said, turning to Katrin with a smile. "Are you going to talk me through it?"

Katrin looked at her watch.

"I'm going to have to go. I'm sorry. I promised that I'd pick Sophia up by five."

"Why don't you go home with Katrin and take all this stuff with you?" said Tim. "You'll probably get a lot further with it together. And you can have a decent meal and a stiff drink, too, if you stay the night."

"And some better clothes," added Katrin.

"It would be the second time today I've imposed on you," said Juliet doubtfully. "And we'll need a van to shift these

screens. And what about Superintendent Thornton?"

"It'd be great to have your company and work on this with you. I imagine that Tim intends to work late again tonight. There's no guarantee he'll come home at all."

"And what about Thornton?" said Tim. "I can manage him."

"Can you, indeed, Yates," said a voice from the back of the room. "I'm looking forward to it already."

Chapter Sixty-Six

IT CONTINUED TO snow through the night. Tim stayed at the police station until after midnight, still painstakingly keeping tabs on the teams making the door-to-door enquiries and manning the roadblocks and helping to co-ordinate the intensified search for Matthew Start. Superintendent Thornton had grilled Councillor Start for two hours that evening, with Tim watching from a one-way window, but the Councillor was adamant that he had no idea of his son's whereabouts or who his associates might be. He also denied that Matthew Start had taken his dogs to guard the Start Construction Builders' Yard. A police check proved the dogs weren't there, nor was there anyone working either in the offices or the yard itself. Veronica Start had said that Matthew would be sure to return to their home in Blue Gowt Lane on Sunday afternoon and certainly the policeman stationed there had so far reported no activity. Veronica had given the police the keys to the house and permission to search it. Matthew Start wasn't there. The Superintendent detained Councillor Start until a warrant could be obtained to search his house, as well. Again, they drew a blank. Before he was released, Councillor Start was asked to provide a list of the men who'd attended The Bricklayers meeting that morning. The list he came up with was suspiciously short, but there were two names on it that they recognised: Ivan Grummett and Peter Cushing.

"We knew Grummett was there," said Tim. "We saw him. And Andy told me that Ms Greaves had said that Cushing was a Bricklayer."

"We'll lay off Grummett for the moment, though I think we should have him followed from tomorrow. Who's been detailed to the Cushings as family liaison officer?" the Superintendent demanded when they'd finally let the Councillor go.

"Ann Bridges, from Boston," said Tim. "I don't know her."

"Is she staying with them?"

"Yes, until the end of the weekend."

"Get on to her, will you?"

It took Tim some time to find PC Bridges' number. Not for the first time, he cursed himself for not being as well-organised as Juliet. The call itself did not take long.

"She says that Peter Cushing did go out for a few hours this morning. He returned in the early afternoon."

"Why didn't she stop him?"

"He's not under arrest, is he, or obliged to account for his movements? Not yet, anyway. And we had no good reason to put a stop to The Bricklayers' meeting."

"All right, Yates," said the Superintendent wearily. "Sometimes it's me doing things by the book on this case and sometimes it's you. Perhaps we both need to adopt a more maverick attitude. Put a round-the-clock watch on Grummett and have Peter Cushing followed every time he leaves his house. Ask Bridges to tell you when he goes somewhere. And tell her to try to find out where he's going."

"Yes, sir, but as I've said, she'll only be there until tomorrow."

"I imagine we can extend that if necessary. But, quite frankly, if we don't find those girls tomorrow, we may as well give up."

"Don't say that, sir." Tim disliked negativity in any of his

colleagues and always tried to cajole them out of it, but on this occasion his protest was half-hearted. He knew the Superintendent was right.

"Maverick!" he thought to himself as he drove home, in an attempt to cheer himself up. "As if."

Chapter Sixty-Seven

KATRIN AND JULIET had both gone to bed. Tim sank down on the sofa in the sitting room, having poured himself a large Scotch. The glass screens had been erected all around the room. Tim noticed that many more details had been added to them. He'd have to make sure that the van came back to collect the screens in the morning, in time for the next briefing meeting.

There was a sheaf of multi-coloured papers on the coffee table in front of him, torn from a pad that Katrin used for shopping lists. Each of the slips bore handwriting, mostly Katrin's, with some shaky additions by Juliet. (He remembered that it was her right hand that had been bandaged.) He picked them up. Along the top of each a name had been written in block capitals, with a sentence or just a few words in longhand beneath it.

HELENA / HELEN. Zeus's mortal daughter. Abducted by Paris.

ARIADNE? Means 'she knows'.

PHILIPPA. Lover of horses.

GRUMMETT. Common Lincolnshire name. Of seafaring origin. Naval rating of low status. Sometimes described as a 'workhorse' because served as a skivvy to the higher ranks.

CASSANDRA. Means 'doomed'.

KNIPES Scottish name for a hill. As a family name, used

in the North of England, Ireland. Diaspora in Australia. Site of a famous long barrow.

Tim sipped his whisky. He was half asleep, but his interest was piqued, nevertheless. He could see where Katrin and Juliet were going with this, or at least had some inkling. But were they solving word games that gave them insight into a disturbed mind, or just muddying the picture with a too-ingenious theory?

He mulled over this question, eventually falling into a disturbed sleep. He woke up a couple of hours later to discover that he had spilt what remained of the whisky down the front of his shirt. It was two days since he'd showered and the mixture of smells rising from his body disgusted him. Rousing himself, he staggered upstairs to the bathroom, where he peeled off his clothes and dumped them on the floor. With some relief, he stepped into the shower and put gel and water to work. Finally, he rolled into bed beside Katrin. She stirred slightly.

"Is that you, Tim?" she murmured, not really waking.

"Yes, it's me," he said tenderly. "Who else would it be?"

Chapter Sixty-Eight

TIM CLIMBED OUT of bed reluctantly at 6 a.m. and looked out of the window. The sky was bright with stars, the ground a blaze of sparkling white. He pulled on some clothes and stumbled, still half asleep, to the kitchen.

He found Juliet sitting at the kitchen table, sorting through the coloured slips while she waited for the kettle to boil.

"Good morning," she said. "I put the kettle on. I hope you don't mind."

"Of course not," said Tim. "But let me make the tea." He rather hoped she'd insist that she should do it.

"All right. I'll go and tidy up the screens a bit and then I can talk you through what we did last night."

"Great."

Tim entered the sitting-room a few minutes later, bearing two mugs of tea.

"Did you see it's been snowing?"

"Yes. Isn't going to help the search teams much, is it? I hope those poor girls have shelter somewhere."

"I hope they're still alive," said Tim grimly. "You know as well as I do that we're about to pass the forty-eight-hour threshold."

Juliet didn't reply. She looked so distressed that Tim was chastened.

"I didn't ask how you're feeling today. Did you sleep all right? Not in pain, I hope."

"My knees are sore, but it's not unbearable. Thinking about being shut under that stage is much worse. I'll probably have to put up with nightmares about it for a while." She managed to smile.

"You seem to have coped better than Verity Tandy. She was quivering like a jelly when she came out of there."

"She's claustrophobic. She can't help that. She did very well, considering."

Tim wasn't convinced, but there wasn't time to waste on discussing Tandy's performance. He waved a hand at the screens.

"You and Katrin seem to have done a good job piecing all this together. It's going to be great for the briefing."

"Thanks. A lot of it's conjecture, of course. Katrin created the timeline and that's sound. What we were trying to do last night was build a profile of Matthew Start."

"Go on."

Juliet picked up the slips of coloured paper and laid them out on the coffee table like a hand of cards.

"We know Matthew Start studied architecture at Sheffield University and that he was particularly interested in the culture of ancient Greece. Some of his work reflects this: for example, he has a penchant for giving modern buildings classical pillars, even though his are often made of plastic." Juliet gave a characteristic wrinkle of her nose. "There's evidence from the old police records that he developed a crush on Helena Nurmi. He didn't deny that. She was a very attractive young woman and he was rather a gauche young man, so no surprise there. He didn't choose her name, of course, but I wondered if it played some part in his fixation for her. He . . ."

Tim's mobile started to ring.

"Just ignore it," he said. Then, looking more closely, "Fuck, it's Thornton. I'd better answer it." He tapped the speaker so Juliet could listen.

"Yates? Glad you're up. I'm on my way to the station. I want you there as well. They've found a body in Bourne Woods."

Tim's heart sank.

"One of the two girls?"

"No. It's male. It hasn't been formally identified yet, but we think it's Matthew Start."

"I'm on my way." Tim pressed the red button.

"Oh, God!" said Juliet.

"I know what you're thinking. If he's captured those girls and imprisoned them somewhere, we've got to find them soon. And it'll be like looking for a needle in a haystack."

Chapter Sixty-Nine

MATTHEW START'S BODY was taken to the morgue later that morning, having been examined by Patti Gardner and a military expert on hanging. They agreed Start had taken his own life. Patti photographed the body and jointly they prepared a report for the coroner. Superintendent Thornton checked that nothing had been found that might associate Start with either of the missing girls. Patti said his pockets contained only keys and a wallet with credit cards and fifty pounds in notes, and some loose change. His mobile phone had fallen to the ground beneath him; the sim card had been removed.

They postponed the lunchtime briefing until later in the afternoon. Although there was no doubt the body was Start's, it would have to be formally identified. Whom to ask posed a dilemma. Start and his wife were estranged, but even Start himself might have been unaware of this and certainly no formal separation had taken place. Tim had no idea how Veronica Start would react to news of his death. Witnessing her response was an intriguing prospect, but he had a hunch it was Frederick Start's reaction to the news that he most needed to observe. He decided to ask Juliet to visit Veronica Start at the refuge and ask her if she wanted to identify the body or would prefer her father-in-law to do it. Veronica would in any case have to come in to the police station to answer questions about

what she knew of Start's movements. After that, she could return to her home if she wanted to. A family liaison officer would be detailed to look after her.

Tim himself set out for Councillor Start's house. Looking at the address he'd written down the previous day, he saw the Councillor lived in London Road, in Spalding, in a house called The Rookery. Unless he was mistaken, this was the large Elizabethan house that stood back from the river. Not the sort of dwelling he'd have expected Start to choose.

A woman answered the door. She was middle-aged and personable, neatly dressed in a black jumper and tweed skirt. Tim didn't think Start had remarried; nor did this woman behave like a wife or partner. She didn't introduce herself, but he deduced she was the housekeeper. She was polite but wary.

"Mr Start isn't up yet."

Tim looked at his watch. It wasn't quite 8 a.m. Early for rising on a Sunday.

"I need to speak to him urgently. Could you tell him I'm here?"

"He knows who you are, you say?" The woman had been unimpressed by Tim's identity card.

"Yes."

She showed Tim into a small room leading off the hall and left him, returning quickly.

"Mr Start will be with you shortly. Would you like tea?"

Tim accepted, thinking the Councillor himself would be in need of it after he'd heard Tim's news. The woman hadn't come back when Start entered the room. He was dressed in well-pressed grey flannels, a navy-blue blazer and striped tie. He didn't look like a man who had scrambled hurriedly from sleep into his clothes.

Tim broke the news as gently as he could. Like all police officers, he hated being the harbinger of death. Councillor Start

was shaken in an understated way. Tim had seldom seen a better example of the British stiff upper lip in action: he muttered something that Tim didn't quite catch.

"I'm sorry, sir?"

"No matter. Of course I will identify the body. There's no question of asking Veronica to do it. I'll get my coat."

Tim decided not to press it further, but he was pretty sure that Start had said 'it'd all got out of hand'.

Chapter Seventy

Councillor Start paused at the door of the mortuary and stumbled. Tim took hold of his arm, but was shaken away precipitately.

"Are you all right, sir?"

"Of course I'm not all right. But I can cope."

"I'll have to accompany you while you make the identification. Then I can leave you for a few minutes if you like."

He nodded tersely before preceding Tim into the small room. The body was still zipped into a body-bag; just the head, covered with a cloth, and the neck had been exposed. Tim had been warned by the mortician that the ligature was still in place. Another cloth had been placed around the neck like a scarf to spare the witness as much distress as possible.

Tim lifted the cloth. The lower part of the face was livid and purplish, the rest chalk white. The eyes had been closed.

Councillor Start stepped close to the mortuary table. He stared for a long moment before turning away.

"Yes," he said. "That's Matthew. You can cover him up again now."

"Would you like a few moments alone with him?"

"No. What would be the point?" The Councillor stared bleakly, even defiantly, at Tim before leaving the room. Tim followed him.

"Do you want to sit down, sir? A glass of water?"

"No. I just want to leave. I'll go home now. I want to be alone."

"I'm afraid that won't be possible. If you're well enough to come with us to the police station, we'll interview you there. If not, DC Armstrong and I will talk to you at home."

"I'll come to the police station. You'll understand that I have strong feelings about coppers tramping round my house. No offence," he added, scowling as if he had every intention of being offensive. "I want to know what it's about. Should my solicitor be present?"

"That's entirely up to you, sir. At present, you're not under suspicion. You're aware that two schoolgirls have disappeared. We have reason to believe that your son was involved. All his known associates will be interviewed to try to establish where he may have taken them. Obviously you and Mrs Start are at the top of our list."

"Mrs Start? You mean Veronica? She's as wet as watter." He pronounced the word coarsely, in exaggeration of his normal Lincolnshire dialect. "She won't be able to help you." His sneer would have been unpleasant under any circumstances; it was crass coming from a man who had just lost his only son.

Tim didn't answer him. Instead, he led the way to the door.

"After you, sir."

Veronica Start was escorted to the police station shortly before her father-in-law arrived. Juliet met her and took her straight to an interview room. She was very pale but calm, almost serene.

"Mrs Start – Veronica – thank you for coming to the police station. You understand why?"

"Yes. You've found a body. A suicide. And you think it's Matthew."

"We can't confirm that the cause of death was suicide until we have the results of the post mortem and the coroner's verdict. But I can confirm that the body is that of your husband. Your father-in-law has just identified him."

Veronica Start let out a bitter laugh.

"How very appropriate," she said.

"What do you mean?"

"Nothing. No, I'm sorry, that makes me sound like a child trying to get away with some kind of misdemeanour, doesn't it? It's just that Matthew has been his father's creature all of his life. Frederick gradually isolated Matthew from his mother so that he could see her only through his father's eyes. He was implacably hostile when she left him. Carol Start must have been a woman of some spirit. She not only managed to escape Frederick, she succeeded in getting custody of her daughter. Not like me."

"I didn't know you had children."

"We don't, thank God, though I never thought I'd hear myself say so. Perhaps if we'd been able to have children, Matthew would have released himself from his father's clutches, but I think it's more likely the children would have been damaged. I meant that I never had the guts to leave Matthew, though I knew I should have done it years ago."

Juliet was silent for a moment. Veronica Start's behaviour was typical of a battered wife.

"Why do you think he stayed with you?" she asked carefully.

"I don't think he enjoyed hurting me," Veronica said slowly, almost as if she were talking to herself. "Sometimes it seemed to hurt him almost as much. His cruelty came from some kind of inner compulsion, as if he'd been programmed. And of course," she added more briskly, "as a teacher, I gave him respectability. I don't know as much about Start Construc-

tion as I should, given that on paper I'm a director, but I'm certain not all of its dealings are above board."

"Veronica," she said gently, "I'm sure we'll want to talk to you again about that. We'll be grateful for any help you can give, even though I believe you when you say you've been kept in the dark. But for the moment our priority is to find those two girls. Do you think Matthew was holding them somewhere?"

"I think it's very likely. They're both blondes, for one thing. Matthew had a fixation with blondes, including me before we married. But if Matthew killed himself I think they're probably already dead."

"To be honest, I think the same. But we can't give up until we know it's hopeless. If they're not dead but held captive and no one knows where, they'll die horribly. Can you think of anyone he might have asked to help him?"

"Matthew didn't have friends. Apart from his staff, the only people he associated with were The Bricklayers, but I think they were really Frederick's friends. You'd have to ask Frederick about them."

"I'm sure DI Yates will do that. What about hiding places? Did Matthew have any lock-up sheds or secure buildings where he could keep someone imprisoned?"

"Not that I know about, but I'm sure he could find somewhere like that if he wanted to, at least on a temporary basis. He was a builder, remember. He and Frederick were famous for building their estates of 'affordable' little boxes, but Matthew's real passion was underground cellar conversions. Or new builds with underground room complexes – swimming pools, home cinemas, that sort of thing. Obviously in quite a different price bracket from the estate stuff, but I don't think Matthew just liked it because of the money. There was something he found deeply attractive about living and working underground."

"Does your house have one of these conversions?"

"There's a cellar, but nothing fancy. Just a small wine store and a little workshop. Matthew used the workshop when he was a boy and he still goes down there quite a lot, even though he has a much bigger and better one at the yard. He didn't build our house: it was a Victorian villa that Frederick bought when he married. Matthew persuaded Frederick to let him keep it a few years after his divorce from Carol, when Frederick decided he didn't want it any more. He doesn't mind building shoddy houses for other people, but he's much more into vintage properties himself. That house he lives in dates from the mid-sixteenth century."

"So Matthew never showed any interest in making improvements to your house?"

"I think he did some work on it before we were married. He'd been living on his own there for quite a while then. He certainly added the pillars. And he built the office, I think when he left university. But he hasn't made any major improvements since I came."

"When was that?"

"1998. It was Matthew's birthday. He had a thing about his birthday because it was the day on which Carol left. Oddly, he didn't avoid doing important things then: rather the opposite, in fact. It was as if he was trying to counteract the pain that he'd felt. He refused ever to see Carol again, probably encouraged by Frederick."

"Veronica, we're going to have to search your house again for clues. We'd like you to come with us, if you feel up to it. We'll be quicker with your help. There's no need for you to return to the refuge unless you want to: you can go home tonight if you like. We'll detail someone to stay with you."

"I'm fine, really I am. I know it's callous of me, but I feel happier than I have for years. I'll help if I can."

~

In a second room, Councillor Start was proving a tough nut to crack when Tim and Andy Carstairs interviewed him. Superintendent Thornton was watching from above through the one-way window and Tim was nervous about this. Although he believed the Superintendent was one hundred per cent committed to finding the two schoolgirls alive, he was also sensitive to Councillor Start's new status of bereaved father. Thornton was nothing if not politically correct.

"Mr Start," Tim began, "Please believe me when I say we're truly sorry for your loss. If it weren't for the urgency of the situation, we certainly wouldn't be troubling you at such a time. We must find Philippa Grummett and Cassandra Knipes."

"You have no proof that Matthew was involved."

"That's true. It's possible he wasn't. I believe you know Philippa Grummett yourself?"

"I've spoken to her. Her parents attend the same Methodist chapel as me."

"And Cassandra Knipes?"

"No. I don't know her."

"You are one of the governors at Spalding High School?"

"Yes. The chairman, actually."

"And you know Cassandra Knipes is the head girl?"

"Yes, of course."

"But you've never spoken to her?"

"Not that I can recall."

"Mr Start, could you give me a specimen of your handwriting?"

Frederick Start hesitated.

"I suppose so." He picked up the black rollerball pen that Tim gave him and scrawled his signature on the sheet of paper in front of him: *Councillor Frederick Start*. "There you are."

"I'd like you to write a few more words if you would, sir."

"Which words?"

"Two names. Philippa Grummett and Cassandra Knipes."

The Councillor tossed the pen back at Tim and folded his arms. "I think we're through playing games. I'm not doing anything else at all until I've seen my solicitor."

Tim nodded at Andy, who produced a faded and dusty cardboard packet from the folder he was holding. He removed a series of photographs from the packet and spread them out fanwise across the desk. Each captured a young girl playing, sometimes with companions. Andy turned them over. On the back of each a label and date was recorded in a sprawling hand. Andy selected three and read out the inscriptions.

"Cassandra Knipes, 9th July 2007. Philippa Grummett, 9th July 2008. Ariadne, 9th July 2005."

Frederick Start stared into space, his arms still folded.

"That's very like your handwriting, wouldn't you agree, Mr Start?"

"No comment."

"Especially the 'C'. The capital 'C' for Councillor you've written is very distinctive: just like the capital 'C' for Cassandra."

"No comment."

"And what about Ariadne? Who's Ariadne, Mr Start? She doesn't look as well cared-for as the other two, does she? How does she fit into the picture?"

"No comment. And if you keep on bullying me with your questions before my solicitor arrives, I shall make sure you pay for it."

As if on cue, a text message pinged on to Tim's mobile. Reluctantly, he extracted it from his pocket.

"Wait for the solicitor," it said. Tim looked up at the one-way window and gave it a wry nod.

Chapter Seventy-One

IT WAS SMALL surprise that Frederick Start's lawyer turned out to be Charles Dixon. Start's call to him was monitored; Dixon said he was at the Pilgrim Hospital 'with another client' and expected to get to Spalding police station in about ninety minutes. Tim seized the opportunity to accompany Juliet and Veronica Start to the house in Blue Gowt Lane. Andy Carstairs was left to guard the mutinous and now silent Councillor, with instructions not to continue the interview without Tim once the lawyer had arrived.

Veronica Start was chatty, almost cheerful, during the short journey.

"It seems such a long time since I left yesterday morning," she said. "Who could believe that your life could change so much in so short a space of time."

Tim was non-committal. He didn't like Mrs Start and still had an uneasy feeling about her. Juliet was more sympathetic, believing the languages teacher was behaving oddly because she was suffering from nervous exhaustion.

She faltered a little when she crossed the threshold of her house to turn off the burglar alarm. "Matthew's birthday," she explained, as she punched in the code. "He always used a combination of the numbers for passwords. I shall change it now."

They entered the hall, which was in semi-darkness.

"Could you turn on the light, Mrs Start?" Tim asked, as she

made no move to do so. He wanted to see if there was evidence that Start had been in the house since Veronica's departure on Saturday morning.

"Sorry. I wasn't thinking. Where would you like to begin?"

"First I'd like you to give us a quick tour of the whole house. Look carefully to see if you can spot anything that's different or out of place since you left yesterday."

She did his bidding, Tim and Juliet following close behind her. They explored the upstairs rooms first. All were immaculately tidy. In the master bedroom, a pair of neatly-folded overalls had been placed on an ottoman and topped with a white hard hat bearing the words 'Start Construction'.

"Were those there last time you were in here?"

"Yes, I think so. Matthew always keeps – kept – a clean set of work-clothes for emergencies, though most days he wore a suit."

Tim nodded. Juliet gave him a quick look, knowing that he had registered that the Starts had still been sleeping together in the same king-sized bed.

Downstairs, all the rooms were equally tidy, the small office almost obsessively so. The desk top was empty except for a leather pen-tidy containing a single fountain-pen. Immaculate identical plastic covers on the row of hanging files concealed the apparently uniform papers they contained. A floor-to-ceiling bookcase stood against one wall, mostly containing beautifully bound hardbacks including oversized volumes on architecture.

"Is this your office?" Tim asked.

"No. It's Matthew's. I prefer the kitchen."

"But he has an office outside, doesn't he?"

"Yes. This one's more of a study. The one outside's for working in. It's where he keeps his drawing boards and makes the models for big projects."

"If you can't see anything out of place in here, I'd like you to show us the outside office."

"I don't have a key," she said tremulously. "I've never been in there."

"Don't you know where to look for the key?"

"No."

"There was a bunch of keys found on the . . . with Mr Start," said Juliet.

Tim considered. It could take upwards of an hour to have the keys brought from the morgue: precious time he didn't want to lose.

"Mrs Start, would you have any objection to our forcing the door?"

"No. I suppose not. I don't want to come with you, though. I'll stay here if you don't mind. I've never been allowed in there. It seems distasteful – almost obscene – to pry now."

Juliet caught Tim's eye. She fervently hoped he wouldn't ask her to stay in the house with Veronica Start. He understood immediately. He needed Juliet with him, in any case. It was a pity they'd stood down the WPC from Peterborough, but all the local police forces were desperately short-staffed at the moment as the hunt for the missing girls continued.

"I understand completely how you feel, Mrs Start," he said, while intentionally conveying the opposite. "Please stay in the house with the doors locked and don't answer the phone. If you hear anyone at the door or trying to get in, call my mobile immediately. We'll call your mobile when we want you to open the door to us. Juliet has the number?"

Juliet nodded.

"The office is the building to one side of the rear of the house, Veronica? Is the door this side of it?"

"No, the far side. You can't see who is coming or going from the house."

"And there's only one door?"

"Yes."

"Strange that a builder should not add a fire exit to his own office," said Juliet, after they'd heard Veronica lock the door behind them.

"I'm sure he had his reasons."

There seemed to be nothing unusual about Matthew Start's office. It was a long, low building with large windows, built in the same materials as the house. There were no bars on the windows, which were fitted with black roller blinds, and the door was quite ordinary. A few shrubs had been planted around it. The only singular features were the empty dog run and a large tank to the rear with a number of pipes coming from it, some of them feeding into the ground.

"If that's the heating system, it's very elaborate for a small building," said Juliet.

"It probably serves the house as well. At a guess, I'd say it was there before the office. It's on the house side."

Tim was inspecting the door as he spoke.

"This looks like an ordinary Yale lock," he said. "I should be able to break the door down if I can find something to ram it with. It's probably alarmed, but we'll just have to put up with the din until we can stop it."

There was a wood shelter some yards away from the office. Tim went hunting. The shelter was piled to the ceiling with neatly-cut pieces of wood that had been stacked like an interlocking Chinese puzzle. Tim viewed them critically. Each was of uniform length and rather too short for his purposes. He'd picked one up, thinking he'd have to make do with it, when he spotted an iron crowbar propped against the side of the stack.

"Perfect!" he said to himself. He ran back to the door. "Stand back!"

The crowbar had a flattened end which, after some exer-

tion, he was able to insert close to the lock, between the door and the frame. He pushed against it as hard as he could, using the crowbar as a lever, and was gratified to hear the sound of wood splintering.

Sweat was pouring from Tim's forehead and his hands were hurting, but he felt triumphant.

"We're really beginning to get somewhere now," he said to Juliet through gritted teeth. "I'm going to break it down."

He took a run at the door and barged at it with his shoulder. He'd almost forced the lock now. One more assault and it yielded, hanging askew on damaged hinges. There was no answering cacophony from an alarm.

He entered the office cautiously, Juliet following, and found the light switch. It was a very ordinary room, similar in most respects to the study in the house, but more utilitarian. Situated to the left of the door, the desk was also bare except for a desk tidy containing several biros inscribed with the words 'Start Construction' and the company logo. There were more pristine hanging files and a single bookshelf. It contained a row of building regulation manuals and directories, all lined up with military precision, and just two other books: *The Greek Myths*, Volumes I and II, by Robert Graves. To the right of the door was a large steel table bearing a workstation, a model in the process of construction and various cutting and measuring implements arranged in a row at a precisely ninety degrees to the edge of the desk.

Tim pulled at the single desk drawer. He'd half expected it to be locked, but it opened easily. It contained only more pens and other small items of stationery. His disappointment was palpable. He gestured at the files.

"Someone's going to have to go through those and the ones at the house," he said. "They may give us some clues. But there's nothing obvious to help us find those girls. Come on.

We need to get Ricky and a WPC over here so we can meet the famous Mr Dixon. Perhaps I was wrong and it's Frederick Start who's behind it all."

He turned to go, his shoulder aching where he'd bust the door. He felt very tired.

"What was that?" said Juliet, cocking her head.

"What?" said Tim. He was halfway out of the door.

"There it is again. It's very faint. It sounds like a dog barking."

Tim lost interest. "It probably *is* a dog barking. Everyone round here has dogs and noise travels for miles."

"I don't think it's coming from outside. It seems to be deep under the floor."

Tim turned round.

"Tell me when you hear it again."

They both stood stock still and silent.

"Now! Can you hear it?"

"My hearing's not as acute as yours, but I think I did catch something." He knelt on the floor, which was covered in thick carpet tiles, and put his ear to the ground. They waited again.

"I can hear it now," said Tim. "It sounds like a dog whimpering. More than one dog, probably. We didn't find out what Start did with his dogs, did we? But it seems inconceivable they're somehow trapped below ground."

"He specialised in underground building work."

Tim was tapping the floor. He took a knife from the row on the steel table and slid it under one of the carpet tiles.

"As I thought, the floor's solid concrete."

"What does that mean?"

"I'm not a building expert, but I think it means that if there is an underground complex, the entrance is via a door – as opposed to a trapdoor," he added, seeing too late that he'd

made Juliet blench. "Help me search the walls. Look for any strange markings or panels. Start behind the desk. I'll move that hanging file rail out from the wall."

Tim was still struggling with the rail when Juliet gave a cry.

"What's wrong?"

She didn't answer, but emerged carrying something and silently handed it to him. It was a red patent handbag from which the shoulder strap had been removed.

"The bag that Marianne Burrell described! Is there anything in it?"

"No. But it proves that either Matthew Start brought the woman called Helen here or he stole her handbag. And the strap is missing. Did you get a look at the ligature when you took Councillor Start to the morgue?"

"No. Start was with me all the time. They'd covered the neck in deference to his feelings."

"What's the betting it's made of red plastic?"

Tim nodded grimly.

"Help me with this, will you? It's not heavy, but the wheels are hard to budge."

Juliet grabbed the end of the frame nearest to her and pushed. Tim yanked at it at the same time. It curved away from the wall at his side. Tim peered behind it. A small box had been set into the wall at waist level. Closer inspection showed it was a touch keypad.

"Come and look at this! It's a keypad. It must open something. This has to be a false wall."

Juliet squeezed between the desk and the frame of files to reach him.

"Could there be a door hidden there?"

"My guess is there is. It's been very well done: I can't see any irregular gaps in these painted bricks. But we need the code to that pad. Veronica Start won't be any help. We'll either

have to crack it or get a crew in here to dismantle the thing and hope it's not booby-trapped."

"Veronica Start may already have helped. She said that Start was fixated with the date of his birthday. The work that Katrin and I have been doing confirms that. Try it first. 9th July 1970."

"I wonder if he used six digits or eight. I'll try both."

Tim keyed in 09071970 and 090770. Neither produced any result.

"Try it in American."

"What?"

"Reverse the month and date. I'll do it if you like."

Juliet keyed in 070970. Nothing happened. Then she tried 07091970. A small light at the top of the keypad began to flash green. Almost soundlessly, a panel slid back in the wall, revealing a massive door behind it and another keypad.

"Surely he can't have used the same code twice?" said Tim. "There would be no point."

"No, but he was an obsessive," said Juliet. She tried the two 'American' numbers again, followed by 090770. A green light showed on the second keypad. The huge door didn't open, but there was the distinctive clicking sound of a lock being released. Tim gave the door a push; it yielded a few inches. He pushed again; it opened very slowly.

He could just make out a steep flight of steps descending into blackness. He scratched around for a light switch but couldn't find one. He turned to Juliet, who was standing behind him.

"Just help me to . . ." He got no further. A mammoth shape came springing out of the gloom and lunged at him. He saw a flash of eyes and frenzied teeth before he was knocked to the ground and almost pitched headlong down the seemingly endless stairs. The dog towered over him, snarling low growls from the depths of its throat, yellow teeth bared.

Chapter Seventy-Two

THERE IS ONLY a little water left and Philippa has it all. This morning she took the bottle and refused to give it back to me. Yesterday I shared it between us, but now I want to give the last of it to the girls. They must be here when The Lover comes back. I can die now; I have seen them, I am fulfilled. I expected too much when I hoped they would be able to love me. It is a small sadness: I care only that they survive. They must not die.

I look across at them. They are still together, as far across the room from me as they can get, but very far apart. There is no spark between them, no interest, no compassion even of the most impersonal kind. Would Ariadne have been kinder?

Cassandra is ill. She is taller and stronger than Philippa; her hair is glossier; she is better spoken, but she's not a street fighter and she can't cope. She will not speak or look at either of us. She is slumped on the floor with her legs splayed, toes turned inwards, like a rag doll. She won't assert her right to the water and certainly won't fight for it. I see the spirit ebbing out of her.

Philippa is crouched in the corner beside her. I placed the water bottle in the middle of the floor this morning as we agreed, and she snatched it. Cassandra barely showed she'd noticed. Philippa is hunched like a wild dog guarding its food. If we all die in here, she will be the last.

Thinking of dogs cheers me. The Lover adores his dogs. He's left them on guard outside. I know he won't abandon them.

I hear a retching noise. It is Cassandra, vomiting into the waste bucket. It's the stench that's made her ill.

"Rest on the bed," I say. "Please. I won't come any closer to you."

She doesn't reply. They're both avoiding the bed today. Perhaps they notice more than I do that it stinks of death.

Chapter Seventy-Three

DON'T STARE AT a savage dog, Tim told himself, struggling to remember what he'd been taught about dog attacks. He willed himself to turn his head away but was too scared he'd miss the animal's next move. Its yellow eyes bored into his, its lip curled back to expose huge canines. The beast was slobbering, its early low muttering now building alarmingly to a crescendo.

Juliet was shouting.

"Tim! Roll to the side!"

Not understanding why, but trusting her, he flicked his body sharply to face the wall. Dimly, he was aware that the dog had switched its position. A second gigantic shape brushed past Tim. He remained lying where he was, inert, his face pressed against the cold concrete. The darkness evaporated.

"Are you OK?"

Light footsteps approached. Juliet's voice again. She tapped his shoulder gently.

"Tim, the dogs have gone."

He turned over, sat up.

"Christ!" he said. "I was bloody scared out of my wits. Did they set for you?"

"No. I opened the outside door and they ran out. They were scared, too."

"Did you shut the door after them?"

She nodded.

"I found the light. It's on the other side of the wall." She peered down the staircase. "There's another door down there. God knows what we'll find behind it."

"I'm going to look but I don't want you to come with me. If we're both trapped in here, we'll never get out. Prop that door open, go into the office and call for back-up and an ambulance."

"Shouldn't you wait for them to arrive?"

"No. Whoever's down there could be in a bad way. A few minutes might make all the difference."

"I don't think you should go in alone and unarmed. You don't know . . ."

"The sooner you get help, the safer we'll both be. Give me back that crowbar."

Chapter Seventy-Four

No. Please God, no.

Chapter Seventy-Five

TIM WAS AT the foot of the staircase fiddling with another keypad. He was methodically trying the combinations Juliet had come up with for the other two locks. The third of these worked. Still dazed from the encounter with the dog, he wasn't sure which order of digits had succeeded.

The door creaked open haltingly: it didn't run as smoothly as its counterparts. Stepping beyond it, he found himself in a dimly-lit cavernous area with a low ceiling. Chairs and a television stand rose like squat statues from the shadows. He could make out a sink set into a kitchen unit, a ghostly fridge and a cupboard with shelves above it. There was an intense smell of fungus. The place was clammy, airless and ice cold. He shuddered, less from the cold than from a gnawing sense of dread.

He moved forward cautiously, gripping tight the crowbar. One area of wall was concealed by a plastic curtain. He flicked the curtain back with the crowbar, dislodging a copious scattering of black mould. His scalp crawled. While trying to wipe the muck from his face with the back of his hand, he uncovered a vile toilet and a handbasin overhung by a contraption that he guessed was a makeshift shower.

Deeper in this cavern two more doors stood side by side. A light was showing under the nearest one. Suspecting that the room in darkness might conceal an assailant, he plunged towards the further door first, kicking it open as he turned the handle. Inside was the outline of a made-up double bed. He tore back the covers to check that no one was hiding beneath them, raising a plume of stench, and briefly dropped to his knees to search beneath the bed. Nobody. There was nowhere else in the room to harbour an attacker. Tim turned his attention to the other room.

He stood with his ear close to the second door, marshalling all his senses. He thought he heard a small sound – not a voice speaking, more a cry or mewling noise – but it was so faint he could have been mistaken. He adopted the same surprise tactic as before, leaning on the handle as he kicked vigorously with his foot, but this time the door didn't yield.

"Fuck!" he thought. "If there's anyone in there, they'll know I'm coming now." He had to act swiftly. He jammed the crowbar between the door and its frame and leant on it with his full weight. The wood was sturdier than he'd expected, but he'd caused some damage. He repeated the action, and then again. No reaction came from the room beyond, no attempt either to repel or assist him. He had another go, this time breaking the lock into pieces.

Tim pushed the door, fearful of what he might find, yet in a strange way relieved. One way or another, the search was almost over.

Chapter Seventy-Six

The policeman is too late. He should have come sooner.

Chapter Seventy-Seven

TIM HAD STEELED himself to find three corpses. In his mind he'd played out the following sequence of events: Ariadne Helen had died; Helena Nurmi, Cassandra Knipes and Philippa Grummett were murdered by Matthew Start; Matthew Start had killed himself.

What he actually discovered shocked him to the core.

Two of the women in the room were alive and unharmed. They sat in opposite corners, as far away from each other as possible, separated by a narrow child's bed. One of them was weeping silently. The other rocked to and fro, murmuring under her breath. She didn't pause when Tim entered or indicate she'd registered his presence. Her rhythmic rocking was obsessive, vacant.

The weeping woman looked up at him, staunching her tears so she could speak.

"I had to do it," she said imploringly. "Please understand. She was her father's daughter. She was selfish and cruel. She killed Diana. And I had to save Cassandra. After I failed with Ariadne, I had to save her."

The woman looked past Tim at a spot concealed by the open door, eyes wide with fear. Tim edged round it. The corpse he saw lying crumpled there turned sightless eyes to the ceiling. Its face was purple; its tongue bulged from the mouth. The legs were wide apart and pointing in opposite directions, unnaturally immodest.

Tim dropped to his knees to feel for a pulse in her wrist, in her neck, but he knew it was hopeless. Philippa Grummett's body was already growing cold.

Chapter Seventy-Eight

THE EGREGIOUS MR Dixon had departed, saying that he could wait no longer and would return on the Monday. Superintendent Thornton had let him go, but was adamant that Start should be detained. The Councillor would be spending the night in the cells.

Weary and shocked, Tim was thankful that he wouldn't have to contend with the slippery Councillor and his likely even slipperier lawyer that evening. However, he now had an unexpected visitor whom he'd agreed to see as soon as he found out who it was.

"Mr Cushing." Tim greeted the sombre little man, who had stood to attention when he and Juliet appeared. "Please sit down. Before you say any more, Mr Cushing, I should warn you that, although you have come here of your own free will, I am about to file charges for some very serious crimes. It's my belief that you may be mixed up in some of them. We therefore have to caution you and advise you of your right to have a lawyer present."

"I still want to tell you what I know. Caution me if you like."

Tim glanced at Juliet.

She cleared her throat and said in a distinct voice, "Mr Cushing, you do not have to say anything. But it may harm your defence if you do not mention, when questioned, something which you later rely on in court. Anything you do say may be given in evidence." She paused for a short time. "I'm going to tape the interview. For the purposes of the tape, it is now 23.08 on Sunday 8th February 2015. Present in the room are DI Yates, DC Armstrong and Mr Peter Cushing."

"Ask me any questions you like. But I'd like to tell you what I know first."

"Go ahead," said Tim. He settled in his chair, his fatigue evaporating. Juliet, too, felt the adrenalin kicking in.

"Nearly twenty-five years ago, I was employed by Start Construction. I was a draughtsman. I got on well with the boss and he asked me to teach his son how to draw plans, so we spent some time together."

"You mean Matthew Start?"

"Yes. The Starts were quite an odd family. Fred's wife left him just after I joined Start's and he and Matthew both took it hard. Carol Start had custody of the daughter – she was much younger than Matthew – but she came to stay with them quite often. That's why they had the au pair the year that Matthew started working for the firm. Helena, her name was. Helena Nurmi."

"What was she like?"

"To be honest, she was a bit odd as well. To me, she didn't seem well-suited to looking after a kid. She was quite gloomy and a bit alternative, like, and she didn't say much. Seemed to me to have something to hide."

"Did Elizabeth like her?"

"Who? Oh, I'd forgotten that the girl's name was Elizabeth. I've no idea. I don't remember seeing her much. What I do remember is that Matthew and Helena spent a lot of time together. There were weeks and weeks when the girl didn't come, so I guess she was at a loose end. I'd put them down as an item before the winter was out."

"What makes you say that? Matthew denied she was his girlfriend after she disappeared."

"I saw them out once or twice. I wasn't that much older than them, remember. We went to the same places. I don't know how she felt about him, but he was keen as mustard on her. Then she disappeared. Or so we were told later. At the time, Matthew and Fred said she'd gone home, back to Finland. There was no reason not to believe them. It was quite a long time after she left that the police started to enquire about her. Everyone at Start's was questioned. We knew Matthew was under suspicion for a while. Then it all seemed to blow over."

"Then what happened?"

"Nothing, for a while. I set up my own business, but I kept friendly with Fred. He often put work my way. He'd started a kind of club, a group of local businessmen who supported each other, and he asked me to join it. It was a bit like the Masons. Sailed close to the law, sometimes, but nothing major – back pocket jobs, the odd scratch my back and I'll scratch yours type of thing. Funnily enough, a lot of us were chapel – that's how Fred met most of the others."

"He called the group The Bricklayers?"

"Yes. I was flattered to be asked to join. I'm no saint. And we didn't do anything that worried me particularly. Not then." Cushing's mouth set in a grim line. "Four or five years after Helena Nurmi left, Fred asked some of us round for a meeting at his house. He'd moved: he'd given Matthew the house in Blue Gowt Lane. Matthew was there, too. He was in a funny mood."

"What do you mean by that?"

"He was kind of wound up. Like a cat on hot bricks. But hyper with it, if you know what I mean. He was married by then, to one of the teachers at the High School."

"Veronica. Was she there?"

"God, no. Fred wouldn't have asked a woman to the meetings."

"Who *was* there?"

"Only a few of us. Fred didn't ask everyone. There was the Methodist minister, Victor Hames – he's since passed away. Frank Shields, who ran a haulage company that Start's often used. David Grummett, a businessman in Boston who was one of Fred's old school buddies. And me."

"So six of you altogether?"

"At the time, yes. Matthew started to tell us what it was about. He said that he and his dad had helped Helena Nurmi to escape from the police because they were trying to get her deported back to Finland on a murder charge. All that stuff about her disappearing had been a trick. Matthew didn't believe she was guilty of the murder. He said she'd been in an abusive relationship and someone had tried to frame her, so they couldn't risk letting her go back. Fred had found her a job in another part of the country and set her up with a flat and a new identity."

"You believed all of this?"

"Yes, it sounded a bit far-fetched, but stranger things have happened. And Fred sat there nodding and agreeing with everything. What they said fitted with what I knew of the girl. As I've said, she was strange, as if she was hiding something. Anyway, Matthew carried on by saying that she'd gone off the rails a bit, got in with a bad lot and had a baby. She was panicking now because the false identity they'd given her wouldn't stand up if she had to register the birth. He said she wasn't up to looking after the kid. He didn't say why, but he gave the impression that she was on something."

"And you believed this, too?"

"I'm not sure I believed all of it. I thought he was broadly telling the truth, but that he'd probably got her into trouble himself. Judging from how he used to be with her."

"So you went along with it. What about the others?"

"Well, Victor never saw any harm in anyone. He thought the sun shone out of Fred's arse, so he was onside straight away. Frank Shields would do anything that Fred said: most of his business was built on deals Fred had helped him to set up."

"Like yours, in fact?"

"Yes, if you want to put it like that."

"What about David Grummett? He's related to Bob and Ivan Grummett, I think."

"Yes. They're all brothers. He's an oddball, but he's not like the others. He spent quite a lot of his childhood having treatment for a bone disease. He lived in a residential hospital where he got his schooling. He turned out quite different from the rest of the Grummetts. It was something that interested him. That was what Fred capitalised on."

"What do you mean?"

"David was obsessed with the nature / nurture argument. He was always talking about it. Still is. He doesn't have kids himself – something to do with whatever was wrong with him – and he's a rich man. Richer even than Fred, probably. So when Fred said we should help Helena by putting the baby out for adoption and share the costs of it, he jumped at the chance. He had a friend whose wife was desperate for a child and suggested that he might be a good bet. He wanted the kid to be brought up carefully by well-off parents, see if she turned out well."

"She?"

"The baby was a girl."

"You're talking about Cassandra Knipes?"

"Yes."

"When you say 'share the costs', what costs were they,

exactly? Arthur and Susannah Knipes surely had enough money to bring up a child."

"Yes. But they were very chary of the idea at first. They only went along with it because they had no alternative. The adoption societies thought they were too old, and Arthur was already disabled. Actually he was a lot less keen than Susannah. She was the one who talked him round. The Bricklayers helped by paying for a false birth certificate and various other things that put the girl on the map – we got a health visitor on board, that kind of thing. Fred organised all of this. The rest of us just paid a contribution."

"How much?"

"It was more than you'd think. David paid most of it. But Cassandra was just a drop in the ocean compared to the next ones."

"You say next *ones*? How many were there?"

Peter Cushing's face contorted.

"Two. Twins. A couple of years later, Matthew came back to us with the same story. He said Helena was pregnant again and needed our help again. None of us were interested this time except David – not even Victor. I think we all felt we'd gone too far first time round. But Fred said we were in it up to our necks now and we had no option but to do the same thing again. I wish I'd stopped there, even so. The second lot turned into a nightmare."

"The second girl was Philippa Grummett? You're saying she had a twin?"

"Yes. Diana. David was really chuffed when we found out it was twins. He'd been reading up on something called the Minnesota Study, where twins are separated as babies and brought up by very different kinds of family. He was dead keen on trying this out. He wanted one of them to go to a poor family, the other to one that was much better off. His brother

Bob and his wife agreed to take one of them. They'd got a girl just a bit older – Kayleigh, you've met her – and it was unlikely they'd have any more kids. There was no chance of them paying for her, though. They said they'd need us to provide for her. David and Fred agreed to pay most of it: the rest of us would just chip in a bit. The Grummetts were supposed to be taking Diana, but David and Fred couldn't find anyone who'd have Philippa – in fact, Fred almost came to grief after he approached someone and they threatened to report him. So they decided to leave the twins together for a few months, wait until it died down, and try again. Apparently this suited David – he had some notion about giving them what he called a 'folk memory' of each other when they grew up, a vague recollection that they'd been together without actually being able to put their finger on it. I can tell you, I was shitting bricks by this time. David's ideas struck me as diabolical."

"What happened to Diana?"

"She died. It was a cot death, the Grummetts said. That's all I can tell you. Fred told them to get rid of the body. He said the rest of us didn't want to know what they did with it."

"Did you find out how they got rid of it?"

"No. God knows. The Grummetts kept Philippa and David's little experiment was spoilt – except that he could still compare Cassandra with Philippa. That's what The Bricklayers' meetings turned into – comparisons between the two. And Ivan Grummett joined us. David's idea. The Knipes avoided us as much as they could, so he'd use Ivan to spy on Cassandra. The original Bricklayers – the group set up for business purposes – no longer existed. We were all about David's experiment now. I know that Victor was as horrified as I was. He was supposed to have died of natural causes, but I've always wondered if he topped himself. He and Frank and I knew we were trapped, locked into it, especially after Diana died."

"Presumably it wasn't a coincidence that you moved to a house just up the road from the Grummetts?"

"No. I wanted to keep an eye on her, as much as I could. It was criminal, really, putting that girl with Bob and Ruby. Bob's OK, but as you'll have seen, he's only half sharp. And Ivan's a really nasty piece of work. I've got more than an inkling that he was blackmailing the Knipes, taking money from them in return for keeping quiet about where they got Cassandra. Bob was probably in on it: He'd do anything Ivan told him to."

"And Ariadne?" Tim shot the question out before Cushing could ponder.

"Who?" Tim observed Cushing closely. He didn't think he was pretending.

"We'll come back to her. Did Frederick Start get rid of Alex Cooper because he was unco-operative about using the school for meetings?"

"Yes. He brought in Richard Lennard – or persuaded the other governors to appoint Lennard, anyway. He's got something on Lennard. Paid off his gambling debts, or something."

"But why was Start so keen on holding the meetings at the school?"

"Respectability. Fred's all about respectability and his place in the community. He had to make his weird son fit in."

Chapter Seventy-Nine

IT WAS EARLY on Monday morning. Tim and Juliet had been summoned to Superintendent Thornton's office before they began interrogating Frederick Start.

"Do you think you've got to the bottom of this now that Cushing's confessed?" said the Superintendent, no doubt, Tim thought, with one eye on his budget.

"I think it'll be many months before we find out the exact truth, sir, especially exactly who was responsible for what. We think we know who most of the perpetrators are, but there may be others, and several have yet to be apprehended. We do have a rough idea of the sequence of events, unbelievable though some of them seem."

"Do you think we should charge Helena Nurmi with murder?"

"The crown prosecution service will probably push for it. If she's charged, she's almost bound to get off with a plea of temporary insanity. But she may be wanted by the Finnish police for a cold case murder."

"Ironical, isn't it?" mused the Superintendent. "Talking of the CPS, Ms Trotter's asked for a meeting this week to talk about whether Ruby Grummett should be charged with criminal negligence."

"Another irony. Ruby Grummett and her family have a lot more to worry about than that now."

"Quite so, Yates. We'll have solved a good number of crimes by the time we've finished, won't we? A good thing I put Armstrong onto that cold case. Well done, Armstrong," he added belatedly.

Juliet wasn't listening. She was still reeling from a call she'd had that morning from Louise Butler.

"You really are married to your job, aren't you?" Louise was venomous. "Didn't it even occur to you to call me to say you'd been rescued?"

"I didn't know you knew about it," Juliet said weakly.

"It wasn't important enough to you to find out," said Louise, and finished the call abruptly.

Andy Carstairs had just arrived for work. He was sitting outside the police station in his car, gazing vacantly out of the window. He'd have to pull himself together now and get into gear for the day, but he'd been flattened. He'd called Jocelyn Greaves several times since she'd been expelled from the school grounds almost forty-eight hours before. Each time the phone had gone to message. Finally, he received a text from her: Please stop.

Acknowledgements

FIRST OF ALL, I'd like to thank Chris and Jen Hamilton-Emery for all the wonderful support that they continue to give the DI Yates novels. Your unfailing enthusiasm, encouragement, good humour and sheer kindness, not to mention the faith you put in my work, is something that I know most authors can only dream about; you have also discovered and enlisted the help of Tabitha Pelly, a genius of a publicist. And I'd like to thank all my readers, both those I know and those I have never met. Your interest in the books, and the lively comments that you send to me direct and 'virtually', are a constant source of inspiration. It's impossible to thank everyone individually, much as I wish I could, but I feel I must single out especially the four friends who have supported me right from the start: Pamela, Robert, Madelaine and Sally, and also Alison Cassels at Wakefield One and her vibrant and sympathetic reading groups. My family continues to give me its own very distinctive brand of support, without which the books would certainly be the poorer: as well as James and Annika, Chris and Emma have made their own inimitable contributions and Clive has helped with memories of long ago. Finally, I'd like to thank Michele Anderson, Headmistress of Spalding High School and Adrian Isted, Head of the English Department there, for their hospitality and for 'lending' me their building. I hasten to add that all the SHS characters in the novel are entirely fictitious!

NEW FICTION FROM SALT

KERRY HADLEY-PRYCE
The Black Country (978-1-78463-034-8)

PAUL MCVEIGH
The Good Son (978-1-78463-023-2)

IAN PARKINSON
The Beginning of the End (978-1-78463-026-3)

JONATHAN TAYLOR
Melissa (978-1-78463-035-5)

GUY WARE
The Fat of Fed Beasts (978-1-78463-024-9)

MEIKE ZIERVOGEL
Kauther (978-1-78463-029-4)